TO PANAMA

POPAYAN

Quito

Ambato

Manta
Puerto Viejo

Guayaquil

Puna
Island

Tumbes

Motape

Cajamarca

Guamachuco

Truxillo

Jumin

Chancay

Juaja

Callao

Lima

Sacsahuaman
Cuzco

Abancay

AMAZONIA

PERU

Lake Titicaca

Puno

Huarina

Huyoayo

Arequipa
Molendo

CHARCAS

La Plata
Potosí

CHILE

SOUTHERN OCEAN

BRIDE OF THE CONQUEROR

BOOKS BY HARTZELL SPENCE

The Big Top
(WITH FRED BRADNA)

Happily Ever After

Vain Shadow

Get Thee Behind Me

Radio City

One Foot in Heaven

BRIDE

OF † THE

CONQUEROR

A NOVEL

BY

HARTZELL SPENCE

RANDOM HOUSE : New York

To Lampert and Laurie

AUTHOR'S NOTE

Some of the letters and documents directly quoted in this book, and some conversations, are from the Huntington Library collection of Pedro de la Gasca manuscripts entitled *From Panama to Peru,* as translated into English by the Maggs Brothers, debt to which is hereby acknowledged. The Espinosa letter quoted by Father Gasca in Chapter 32 is the translation of Sir Clements Markham from the Hakluyt Society publication, *The War of Las Salinas.*

To Dr. Hugh S. Rice of the Hayden Planetarium, my gratitude for accurate meteorological data and a correlation of movable feast days to calendar dates during the years 1546–1548.

For much hitherto unknown documentation of Francisco Carbajal, including his real name and origin, here published for the first time, I concede great debt to the contemporary Peruvian-Spanish scholar, His Excellency Don Rafael Loredo of Seville.

HARTZELL SPENCE

PANAMA

I

✝

I came to the New World to marry a man to whom I had been betrothed as a child, only to discover on my arrival that he was dead.

He was not much of a loss, as men go, though probably would have been no worse husband than any other. To him, may God give him gentle rest, I really owe a great deal. For his death, inconvenient as it appeared at the time, permitted me to participate in an adventure only men hazard, and even then only the hardiest.

My name, requiring much ink, is Doña Eloisa Marta María del Cristofora Leóvigilda Canillejas, of a family well-known in the Estremaduran town of Cáceres. My intended husband was the heir of the family Rioseco, three times a marquis and five times a count. He was poor but noble; my father rich but a knight only. So we were betrothed when I was three years old, and my father supported the entire Rioseco connection during all the years of my upbringing. As a Rioseco bride, I was given careful education for the life at court, taught to read, write and think, to converse, to be suspicious of everyone, to flirt and seek favor, and other virtues most Spanish girls never learn.

The marriage was to have been celebrated on the seventeenth anniversary of my saint's day. But within a few months of this event, my fiancé suddenly journeyed to the New World. In far-off Peru, richest of all the king's possessions, the conqueror-governor had been murdered in a civil war. A priest sent to restore order had failed. Now a Rioseco cousin, Don Blasco Nuñez Vela, was given the awesome powers of a viceroy and a set of new laws designed to destroy the conquistadors and their possessions. Here, naturally, was the family's chance to make a fortune, for when great wealth is broken up, someone must be the gainer, and why not my betrothed? He was appointed equerry to the viceroy, and departed in November of 1543.

I was to follow by the first safe convoy, and marry Fernando in Lima, the capital of Peru, since he might be some years consolidating his new possessions. After two years, Nuñez was installed in Lima. But the settlers had resisted him with such force that the king decided to send a strong judge to replace him. This was luck, for the new official was a Dominican friar named Pedro de la Gasca, well-born and above betraying me, and he agreed to take me with him. I was much pleased. The postponement of marriage was irksome to me, for I was almost nineteen and still unwed, an awkward position difficult to explain to my friends, and contrary to God's will, as I had reason to know from my own temptations.

God gave us one of the swiftest passages ever made to the new colonies. Sixty-one days after leaving San Lúcar de Barremeda, on the eve of Saint Martha's Day, Tuesday 27 July, 1546, we anchored off Nombre de Dios, the gateway to Panama, raised the banner of the Emperor Charles, and signaled for lighterage ashore.

This should have caused great commotion in the town, a primitive settlement of a few score thatched huts. You would have thought that the whole populace would rush upon us, avid for news from Spain and zealous to dispatch the king's business. Instead, four steam-hot hours sizzled

4

away, until Lota, my maid, complained that my gold-bodiced brocade from Grandmama, which I had donned for this momentous landing, was ruined by sweat.

Not until the cool of sundown did a longboat, rowed by eight men in full armor, put out from shore. At the tiller was a crimson-vested, stringy-bearded swordsman, stocky, powerful and arrogant.

Father Gasca awaited him at the gunwale of our little caravel as serenely as though no insult had been paid him. The friar was quite unattractive physically: his mouth turned down, he had the nose of a goshawk, his dark eyes bulged, his mustache was cropped too much and his beard not enough. His arms were too long and his legs too short. Yet, as I had discovered on the long voyage, love shone from him as a single white rose beautifies an ugly pot. Always he had been as he was now, gentle, patient, tender, tolerant. Beside him stood a tall, fiercely proud young Castilian who had wooed me the entire trip, but whom I knew only as Valentin; and a sour, lank, aged lay brother of the Dominican order named Don Pedro Hernandez Paniagua, who had been monkishly aloof from me even at our common meals.

The swart leader of the boat crew came aboard, his right hand alert to his sword hilt. Contemptuously he surveyed the unimpressive, ill-proportioned figure who stood as humbly as a beggar in his sandaled feet, white robe and black hood of the Dominican order, tonsured head slightly bowed, apelike arms folded into his sleeves.

"Priests again!" he said.

"God be with you," Gasca replied, and introduced himself.

The warrior was Hernán Mexía, captain of the port. He made clear at once that he was not in the service either of the viceroy of New Spain at Panama, or of the colony's governor. He served another master of even greater power, to whom he referred as "his lordship." Casually, Gasca inquired who this great lord might be.

"Gonzalo Pizarro," Mexía answered pompously, naming a bastard half brother of the late marquis. "We have proclaimed him Governor of Peru, and every man has sworn to uphold him. Already Pizarro's fleet controls the seas from California to Chile. He is invincible."

"So?" Gasca said meekly.

"Quite so," Mexía continued, "as you yourself must learn if you dare to affront me. I am charged to intercept all communications from Spain. I open them all, even those bearing the king's seal. And I am commanded to kill anyone who steps foot on these shores without Pizarro's permission, including your reverend self."

"He must receive me," Gasca answered sternly. "I represent the king, and I come to restore the peace."

"There is peace," Mexía retorted. "For the first time there is peace, and His Lordship means to preserve it, even against the further bunglings of the king's representatives who would rob us of all we have fought for. I cannot permit you to land."

"So?" said Gasca. "It was my understanding that I was to succeed His Excellency Nuñez Vela, who at last report ruled in Lima. What of him?"

"The murderous villain is dead," Mexía answered, explaining that the viceroy in arrogantly enforcing the new laws had been ousted. But instead of returning to Spain, Nuñez had landed in the north and raised an army. At a bloody battle he had been killed.

"What of his followers?" I heard myself cry out.

Mexía saw me for the first time. But he was not surprised. He did me the courtesy of bowing.

"You must be," he said, "you could be none other than the rich and beautiful lady for whom every bachelor in

6

Peru is waiting, Doña Eloisa Canillejas of Cáceres, betrothed of the Marquis of Rioseco."

"And my fiancé?"

"He is your betrothed no longer," Mexía said brutally.
"He also was killed in the battle."

He gave me little time to recover from this.

"I paid 500 gold castellanos to Pizarro for the privilege
of guarding this port and being the first to offer you my
service and protection."

I could not face such candor. I turned toward Valentin.
He looked queerly at me, smiling acquisitively. I sought
Gasca. He was squinting reflectively at Mexía as though
wondering just how much Pizarro's captain would pay
for me.

In confusion I ran to my cabin.

II

✝

That night, which I had hoped to spend ashore for the first time in two months, I roasted in my tiny cabin. I, from the highlands of Cáceres, was unaccustomed to such damp heat. Captain Mexía resolutely insisted that Friar Gasca could not go ashore.

But the morning brought him back again. After an hour closeted with Gasca, he surprisingly changed his position. To be sure, he promised nothing beyond the hospitality of his miserable town; but at least we felt land again under our feet.

I went immediately to Mass at a thatch-roofed chapel. I did not feel like going anywhere, for although I had not once been seasick, I now rolled up and down on the hard land as on an ocean swell, not yet accustomed to the immovable earth. I felt very much like the time my Aunt Sortella satisfied my curiosity about manzanilla, and let me drink all I could of it. The windows had turned askew and the landscape had played tag with me, and when I had put my foot down, it was such a long way to the floor. But to the church I went, all the same, staggering like an innkeeper's tipsy daughter. Since God and Our Lady had given us safe passage, the least I could do was to thank them properly. Besides, it was my saint's day, and if I did not stay on the good side of my patroness Martha, who knew what might happen to me?

While I was gone, Lota moved all my trunks into the hut assigned to us by Captain Mexía. She stacked the fifteen of them around the reed walls, a clever precaution against interlopers. These country women instinctively know how to do everything. Who would have thought of that but she? She took one look at the fragile shelter, little better than four poles with a few husks for roof and dry reed sheathing, and the idea came to her of protecting us in this manner. Now we could be quite comfortable, and this curious rabble that attended Hernán Mexía would have difficulty with their very apparent designs. Their commander certainly set them no decent example.

We were not even installed when he came to talk to me. He looked over my luggage and my person with equal frankness, and asked if I was comfortable.

"Yes, thank you," I said, dismissing him. He sat down, indicating that he was the master of Nombre de Dios, choosing for a seat the trunk next to the one I had opened. He felt the brocade of one of the gowns, commenting that it was of material better than any found in Peru. I asked him to leave, since I was weary.

"But we must become better acquainted," he said. "After all, I have an investment in you. Does it not flatter you that I have paid heavily for the privilege of being first?"

"It proves your grossness," I retorted.

He did not like that.

"In Peru, we have learned to be rough," he explained, rising and moving a step toward me. "We have learned to seize what we want, before someone else gets it. And then to defend it with the sword. When I heard your marquis describe you in Lima, and the dowry you were bringing with you, I decided that he was not worthy of you, but I was. So I am here."

He came toward me, arms poised to embrace me.

"On your peril," interrupted a quiet voice behind us. Mexía spun, flashing his sword. Before him stood Valentin, his blade bare in his hand.

Mexía was about to strike, for though Valentin towered over him, I felt that this captain would fear no man because of size, when suddenly he stared into Valentin's face, slowly cast his eyes up and down the Castilian's big-boned torso, then deliberately sheathed his weapon.

"Your pardon," he said bitterly.

Valentin did not move. "Get out," he said.

Mexía nodded assent, but he had the last word.

"You had better speak to the friar before you oppose me," he said, and left.

Valentin could not explain the meaning of this, but cautioned me to sleep with my eyes open. I thanked him for helping me.

For the landing, Valentin had candle-waxed his boots and brown suede stockings and burnished his chain mail with ashes. On his head was an old-fashioned Flemish helmet, as flat on top as a tortilla and as little protection. He had very nice legs and the mail hung boldly from his lusty shoulders. His head sat well, too, in a bushy brown beard, something I had not noticed until he had donned his armor. He had deep brown eyes, high Castilian cheekbones and a really fine Roman nose which, in a fighting man, ought long since to have been broken if he was actually the warrior he looked. Unless, of course, that bold broadsword protected him. In Estremadura we had long ago abandoned the Damascus blade for the shorter Toledo, and perhaps I was not used to the awkward look of the older weapon. Valentin could not afford new arms, that was certain.

"I will remain near you, unless you send me away," he said.

This was my opportunity, and since he was a very excellent card player, I led a low four, as in Calabrasella.

"You must guard me or I have no one," I murmured. He leaped on the trick, but with too high a card for our little game.

"It is all I wish in life," he burst out, reminding me of his extravagant romanticisms of shipboard. "To be near you, to breathe the attar of your presence, quaff the wine of your commands, work for you, and rest at last in your arms."

"Steady, my brave Valentin," I said. "We are ashore now."

"I mean it," he said. "Nothing any longer stands between us."

This Valentin was a very spirited young man, as I had discovered. He had much amused me. For like most girls, I wanted to be loved, but not with the finality a man means by the word. Across the table or across the room I loved to feel the vibrations a man gave off when he wanted me. On our tight little ship, the only woman amid eighty men, these pulsations had daily grown more intense. Everyone, except Gasca and the uncommunicative Paniagua, had throbbed in my direction, and none more so than Valentin.

Hot-headed and hot of breath, he had protected me from everyone but himself. I owed him too much and, like every man, he ended by begging favor for favor. But I was of other mind. The sturdy land had thrown back not alone the surf but also the romantic inclinations of shipboard. It did not seem possible that only yesterday I had been so conscious of love, and as panting after it as any bawd. The confines of shipboard, which permitted all too clear observation of what was in every man's mind

11

and daily grew more boldly imaged there, had affected me, without doubt. Only Gasca's influence, I was sure, had saved me from mortal sin on so moonlit a voyage.

Valentin must have felt Gasca's spirit, too, or he had taken me, cat-clawing and scratching, on one of those many evenings when we sat on the high poop deck watching the moon play on the phosphorescent sea. For just when I had hoped he might try to seduce me, and by force so that no sin would be on me, he had withdrawn as though His Excellency had touched him on the shoulder.

And now I did not want him at all. It was one thing to flirt with a handsome giant when within a few months I was to marry a man I did not love. But now I had my future to consider, and I had been too well-trained to let changing fortune obscure my identity. There were 10,000 men in Peru from whom to choose, if half of what Captain Mexía said was true.

If this be crass, my education was to blame. The court of Charles the Fifth was no arena for amateurs, and my mother, a country woman whose chief virtue was a capacity for being caught constantly in childbed, was hardly the proper mentor for the bride of a marquis high in royal favor and physically close to the throne.

I was placed early, therefore, under the tutelage of my widowed Aunt Sortella, who reared me. She was a Santillana of Old Castile, closely related to the illustrious house of Mendoza. She was fat and twinkly, and inclined to perspiration, but famous for her love affairs and therefore one of the most influential ladies of the court. She had read Petrarch's Latin version of *The Decameron,* and the saucy Boccaccio's love poems in Italian, and Pilatus' Latin transcript of *The Iliad* and *The Odyssey,* and much else, sacred and profane. By the time I was twelve, she could no longer risk wrinkles about her eyes, and so had a secretary read to her. And I, sitting with her, was much

12

amused when irritably she adjured her scrivener to skip the dull prayers and history and get on to the bedchamber scenes, which she had repeated twice over. Whatever practical knowledge I own is the product of her dear instruction.

So I knew how to handle Valentin. I told him bluntly that I was indisposed to concentrate my affections until I had surveyed the field.

He laughed. "You will look them all over," he responded, "and then you will return to me. Meanwhile, more than ever, you need someone to guard you, and by your leave, my arm is reliable."

"I need protection, yes," I replied, "and would accept it gladly, alone as I am in a land of barbarians. But nothing more."

"Your servant," he said, and bowed mockingly.

"It must be clearly understood," I insisted.

"I understand," he agreed, "but a sleeping dog sees everything that passes, and I am content for a moment to sleep."

"Hardly a likely manner in which to guard me and my possessions."

"For that I shall be wide awake."

"Others also are wide awake," I suggested. "Gossip cannot be killed with a sword. You must give no one cause for bad whispers which will precede me to Peru. We both follow the entourage of His Excellency Father Gasca. You will do him, as well as me, great disservice by any rashness. Protection is one thing, idolatry another, and I cannot accept the one if it breeds the other."

"You could not stop my loving you."

"Oh yes I could," I rejoined. "I could hurt your pride and make you hate me. But I will not, so long as you give me no cause."

He flushed brightly, but moved not a muscle.

"I am your servant," he repeated, this time tensely.

"See that you remain so," I replied, and dismissed him.

Lota, too, had difficulties, but of a cruder sort. If ever lesson was needed that men are but upright-walking dogs where woman is concerned, Lota learned it that day. She was not pretty, my diligent little Lota. She was flat-footed and flat-busted and had almost no neck between her thin shoulders and her brown-haired head. Her hands and bare feet were calloused trademarks, her face was menial and had two unhappy moles on the bridge of a bulking nose. But she was as precious to me as my dowry, and loyal besides, and her dullness of wits was an advantage, for she did not think to question. If I had told her to kill, she would have done so calmly.

I gave her a jeweled poniard which Fernando's father had given me. It was small enough to carry in the bosom— cold at first but not uncomfortable—and Lota had stabbed enough pigs in her lifetime to know its use. On shipboard she had lusted for the New World as much as I, and had romanced a helmsman whose curls caught even my eye. I was confident that she would find a husband in this new land, if only because of the scarcity of women, of far greater pretensions than she could aspire to in Cáceres. How she had begged to come with me! I wondered how she felt now, with bold ruffians all about and no other Spanish woman on this side of the peninsula? There were ladies in Panama; quite a society, I was told. But until we reached that Arcadia, we must wall ourselves behind my trunks, and Lota would sleep on a pallet at my feet. My iron dowry chest had been taken for safekeeping to Father Gasca's shelter.

Late in the afternoon, the friar called on me. He looked about my barricade with much amusement, before remarking that he was pleased to see me writing a letter rather than in tears for my fiancé. He offered prayers for poor Fernando's soul, then invoked God's mercy and the Holy Mother's protection against all the dangers which now threatened me. When we had kissed his crucifix and risen from our knees, he sat down with me as gently as a grandfather, to discuss with me my future. He did not treat me either like a baby or a silly young woman. The time for all that was past. I was now an adult burden which he carried on his back, and we must both make the load as light as possible.

We wasted no sentimentality on Fernando. No condolences, no tears. Such hypocrisies were as foreign to his direct, practical nature as to mine. God's will was done, and that was that. Lamentations disturb only the living; the dead cannot hear them.

I asked him point-blank the meaning of Hernán Mexía's insinuation to Valentin.

"That is what I would discuss with you, little sister," he answered gravely, and told me that Mexía still refused to let him cross the isthmus to Panama City. Until he reached that seat of government, however, he could not begin his work.

"Therefore we must not offend Mexía," he concluded. "He is our only link between the present and the future."

"So you propose to insert me, like so much tarnished brass, into that chain between himself and you?" I demanded angrily.

Gasca's serene eyes opened wide at this outburst.

"You must realize, little sister," he said, "that I cannot return you to Spain. You would be ship captain's property before you reached Cubagua. Therefore, from now on you are, like myself, a member of this enterprise. Now that Nuñez Vela has been murdered, the king is no longer represented in Peru. Nothing, least of all your life or mine,

15

is as important as restoring his majesty's authority. Further, I promised your father that I would see you safely married, and that I mean to do."

"And to whom, may I ask?"

The friar considered this silently, crushing the knuckles of his hands.

"It is already evident," he said at last, "that you are a rich prize in this country, to secure which many able men would labor valiantly in our cause. So I tell you what I have already told Captain Mexía, that he wins you who most helps us overthrow Gonzalo Pizarro and return Peru into the hands of God and His Majesty. I think such a one would be worthy of you."

"And I have nothing to say in the matter?"

"When has any girl had anything to say in the matter?" he responded. "It is in the hands of God."

III

✝

Next morning Father Gasca returned early, a smile on his hawkish face. The embargo which prevented the friar from crossing the isthmus did not apply to me. Therefore I was asked to go to Panama City and persuade one Admiral Hinojosa, commander of Pizarro's fleet in the Southern Ocean and Mexía's superior, to receive the king's emissary. Gasca believed that Spanish authority in the capital of New Spain, in the person of Viceroy Mendoza, would be strong enough to prevent Gasca's ejection from the country, once he reached that city.

Of course I consented. I had no mind to face my friends in Cáceres, too old to wed and fit only to become the maiden aunt who, full of piety and noble works, attended her parents in their old age. I must go on.

At once the friar warned me of the difficulties of my position. For a priest he was remarkably acute to reality. I could have kissed him for speaking frankly, not suggesting indelicacies by courtly phrases or Latin mottoes, but facing up to them like my dear Aunt Sortella in roundly descriptive Castilian. Fortunately, I did not blush, and for the first time since we sailed from San Lúcar we conversed as colleagues rather than as busy man to inconsequential woman.

As he spoke, I wondered what Mama would think of

17

this! I could see her blanch and stare, grow red, perspire, cast her eyes down in tears, kneel in the first light and beseech Heaven with her orisons that I be restored to the loom, the household keys and the nursery, which are woman's destiny.

First, Gasca considered the problem of my dowry, which many men would covet and some try to steal. There was my person, equally vulnerable to theft. Gasca even mentioned matters which my own mother had never discussed with me, such as provision for my illnesses, for in this unnatural and unfriendly country, nothing must be overlooked or left to chance. Fortunately my chest contained maravedi and ducats as well as plate, so I could pay my way. But the inconveniences to his excellency were enormous, and for me there was danger.

He agreed with me that I should go into mourning for Fernando. Black became my mountain fairness, there was variety of it in my boxes for Mass and holy days, and it would be a constant reminder that I was not yet free, or of the mood for dalliance. I decided also to wear constantly the big gold Cross and chain Mama had given me as a talisman. It would protect me, and enhance my bosom, especially on the tight-bodiced black lace gowns I would be wearing for a while. If this conceit amused the friar, his face did not reflect it.

"You will be accompanied to Panama," he said, proving that everything had already been planned even without my consent, "by both Captain Mexía and our own Valentin. I think—" his eyes sharpened with mischief—"that the two of them will be so busy parrying each other that they will have little time to molest you."

We set out that evening up a sluggish river in a rough-hewn canoe, heavily netted against mosquitoes. I was permitted only one trunk, containing my prettiest black

18

clothes, and Lota a hamper. The rest of my luggage remained with Gasca.

In the friar's final words to Captain Mexía, which I was sure were directed at the admiral in Panama, his excellency's scheme for the subjugation of Peru emerged. He, the frocked priest, without retinue or men-at-arms, bore royal and ecclesiastical authority in one person, to forgive past sins both religious and temporal, and bring Peru to a fresh start. His lack of army or bluster proved his peaceful intent. His only desire, he told Mexía, was to make Peru safe for her colonists, and then return quickly to Spain where a bishopric awaited him. He wanted nothing for himself. This was a new anthem among the voices of conquistadors, one dissonant to the captain's ears but oddly pleasing. Mexía listened as though it were sung in Latin which it behooved him to translate for his mortal and immortal well-being. He was wary, this Mexía, a typical Andalusian.

We journeyed up the River Chagres and across a lake called Gatun to a miserable village named Cruces. There we spent the night. Captain Mexía, away from his duties, was fascinating. Stroking upriver, he sat beside me—which made Valentin sulky—and, after an hour devoted to the exotic landscape, was amused to answer my questions about his adventures.

Truly, men have all the fun. Mexía was the only person who had ever really told me what men do when they are away at the wars. Now I understood why they preferred their campaigns to the dull life of praying and sitting, gaming and love-making, that occupied gentlemen at home. War, the captain made clear, is man's big chance to flee domestic drudgery and home responsibilities, to see the world and to make a great fortune. The risk of death is nothing to the rewards of survival.

19

Mexía was as familiar with this road across Panama as I the route from Cáceres to Badajóz. He had lived with those parrots, macaws and herons never seen at home, hunted the jaguar, and the tiny deer about the size of rabbits which flipped across our vision. He could name the snakes and lizards on the river bank and decide with one squint which were poisonous and which harmless. With him I felt no fear.

Next day we followed a handsome stone road, better than any in Spain, from Cruces forty miles across the Cordillero del Bando into Panama. Here there was no jungle such as faced the Ocean Sea, but most fragrant valleys of the type found after crossing the Sierra Moreno from the north and riding down upon Seville. We had no difficulty picking up porters. I was comfortably swung in a litter, while Captain Mexía and Valentin rode, one on either side of me, on thin but steady horses, pushing the pace to encompass two days' ride in one.

The captain worked hard to entertain me, while Valentin, little more than an armed escort, rode sulkily alongside, listening to every word but saying nothing himself. Of all Mexía's talk, one description so took hold of me that I could not forget it. Valentin also was impressed when Mexía mentioned a terrible fellow who commanded Pizarro's army. His name was Francisco Carbajal.

Even allowing for Spanish exaggeration, this Carbajal was a fantastic monster. Mexía said he was eighty years old, yet as robust after women as a man Valentin's age. Everyone in Peru referred to him as "The Demon of the Andes." Men crossed themselves when his name was mentioned, as though he was the very devil. Even Mexía feared him, and predicted that ultimately he, rather than Pizarro, would be Gasca's deepest thorn and possibly his murderer.

If he be half so bold as pictured, I thought, a bloody task confronted our mild believer in the force of love.

How Gasca could possibly overcome such violence of spirit and such a monument of vicious deeds as Francisco Carbajal, God in His wisdom alone knew. But attempt it he would, even though it cost his life.

On this grim speculation we broke from the mountain suddenly upon Panama. Hard beyond lay the vast blueness of the Southern Ocean, a flashing sunset mirror, across which, though it was difficult to believe, lay Cathay.

I was delighted to see a city with trees and plaza, and hear the toll of church bells for the first time in sixty-five days. Sticky-hot as it was, I welcomed it, for I saw at once that the women, despite the climate, dressed exactly as at home. And I had the wardrobe to impress them.

I was lodged most comfortably in the best house in town, no less than the residence of the viceroy, Don Antonio de Mendoza, Count of Tendilla. For this I had wily Gasca to thank. My late fiancé had been a distant cousin of the Mendoza house, and for me the friar had pleaded kinship.

I allowed myself to be pampered in a soft bed all the next day before I arose to confront the admiral.

IV

†

Lota paid as much attention to my toilet as though Hino-josa was to be my bridegroom, instead of my adversary.

First she must wash my hair. Already she had learned the tricks of the household, and knew that in this wet heat my hair, shorter than most but thick, would never dry, even in direct sun. A ground stone called talc, as fine as Toledo's red dust but mined in Mexico, was worked into my scalp to draw off both damp and grime. It brushed out easily, though with such mess that the ablution was performed in the walled garden behind the house.

Then in a Bavarian porcelain tub I was scrubbed and rubbed, my first full bathe since leaving Cáceres three months ago. After this, Lota carefully smothered me in a freshly distilled unguent of musk, cinnamon and violet. My dress, a Segovian watered silk of such severe cut that I looked more fourteen than nineteen, and if white would have served for a first communion, was steamed of all its travel wrinkles, and some black felt slippers and silk stockings were drawn from my wardrobe. I wore no jewelry except the gold crucifix necklaced at my throat.

Safflower with lemon juice gave my cheeks a girlish glow, and French chalk covered the rouge to make it look natural. My hair was drawn up as high as it would tug, and secured with a tortoise comb. After all this, I really felt my best for the first time since leaving home. If the admiral did not find me attractive and sweet-smelling, I told Lota, it certainly would not be her fault.

When I descended from my bedroom, the viceroy, his wife Doña Angela, and their son Francisco, were drinking wine in the patio. The men jumped up, and Doña Angela frowned.

"I don't think, dear cousin," she greeted me, "that you should show yourself so boldly."

"But I must impress the admiral!" I exclaimed. "That's why I did it."

She shook her head. "It is dangerous to be pretty in this country," she insisted. "Beauty in Panama or Peru is like water on a desert. The men are starved for it."

But the men had no such reaction, so I knew I was right. Women never want another—and younger—to outshine them. The viceroy stepped forward to take my hand and lead me to a chair, and his son, who is middle-aged and fat and the father of eight children, poured my wine himself, instead of clapping his hands for a servant.

"My beloved wife is a wise woman," Don Antonio told me, gazing at me reflectively and, for an old man, strangely, over his Bohemian wineglass. "I agree with her that you must be careful, for you will excite this town more than would a visit from His Holiness. But I am glad you favor us. As Doña Angela says, we are starved men."

His wife rustled her shoulders and stared at me.

"No wonder," said the son, "that Captain Mexía paid to guard Nombre de Dios."

"Is it such common knowledge?" I asked.

"Unfortunately," Doña Angela retorted, "it is. It is not seemly that any woman be so vulgarly bandied, especially one who enjoys the favor of my own house. It will reflect on me."

"Now, now, Angela," said her husband, "you women certainly discuss each other frankly. Why spoil our pleasure?" Then to me, he explained that the Marquis Rioseco had stupidly lauded me so highly that now every tongue was out. Since no other unmarried girl of wealth and family had ever come to the colony, I was a curiosity. "You are not quite so beautiful," the viceroy continued, "as we were led to expect. You are not as long-legged, for one thing . . ."

"Antonio!" his wife injected sharply.

"Forgive me," the viceroy said, toasting me with his glass. "And your nose is impish, my dear, rather than patrician. That nose alone will get you in trouble here."

He inquired of my father, whom he knew by reputation, and finally of Aunt Sortella.

"You know her?" I exclaimed in delight.

"Who does not?" he said, and shrugged, sidling a quick glance at his stern spouse, "and besides, we are distant cousins. But one does not remain distant long from such a one. She was the favorite of the Marquis of Sotomayor, I believe, when I last visited Spain."

"His Excellency, the Minister of State, has since perceived her many charms," I said, demurely for the sake of the vicereine's propriety.

Don Antonio's white eyebrows lifted quickly.

"A remarkable woman," he said, as we smiled together. "If you need favors at court from this far land, you are certainly in a position to obtain them."

Captain Mexía was announced. He had arrived promptly at a quarter to the midday turning of the glass. I hardly recognized him, for a barber had cropped his hair and trimmed his reddish beard to a rakish point at the chin. A scrawny mustache, dropped like that of a Manchu, gave him a fierce look. He was dressed as for court, in a white satin doublet embroidered in gold, brown hose and matching suede slippers. His cloak flashed at the throat with a large gold clasp into which were set two square emeralds

24

the size of shoe buckles. Gold darted from his sword harness. He was a rich and not unhandsome escort, though no taller than I.

He, meanwhile, stared at me so rudely as to ignore the vicereine.

"Mother of God!" he said. "What has happened to Doña Eloisa?"

Recovering, he bowed low to Doña Angela, kissed her hand, and gave her all his attention. But not for long, because Valentin entered. He too gleamed clean. His clothes could not compete against Mexía's splendor, but his deeply tanned face, strong and loving, spoke more for him than any finery. His eyes, too, opened when he saw me.

"Doña Eloisa," he bowed, "has flowered. You are beautiful, my lady."

Mexía had not expected Valentin, and demanded his mission.

"Why, I accompany the lady to the admiral's house," Valentin answered blandly.

"I understood I was to do that," Mexía said.

"And by your leave I also," Valentin replied. "My orders were to see that Doña Eloisa was not left alone in the company of any man."

Mexía flashed a glint of anger, but only for a moment.

"All we need now," said he jovially to the viceroy, "is Pizarro himself."

"He will not be far behind," Mendoza responded. "The lady's journeys will all be well-escorted."

En route to the interview, which included the noonday meal, we walked across the plaza to the cathedral, ugly outside and overdecorated within. There I gave thanks again to God, the Blessed Mother, and my patroness Saint Martha, for safe journeys. I feared, however, that I must perform an act of contrition on account of this, for during my prayers to Martha, the beloved sister of Lazarus and

25

Mary, I was impishly overcome with mirth that the intercessor for good housewives whose patronage I begged, should have for daughter as errant and undomestic a girl as I. Did she, the perfect housekeeper, frown that I remained unwed and unfulfilled this long, and now was steeped in masculine enterprises so far removed from keys and loom? Anyway, she probably had never before had so difficult a creature under her protection, and perhaps I would get special grace, just as the ugly child gets the most milk. I knew this flippancy was untoward, and resolved to confess it to Father Gasca and ask for penance.

Then on we went. What I could see of the city was robust and flourishing, the knights elegant in brocaded satins with Córdoban or Florentine leather harness and boots. I saw schools, both Franciscan and Dominican, a hospital of the Mercedarians, and shops the equal of those in Toledo and Seville.

Admiral Hinojosa, oddly, was housed with the governor of Panama, Don Pascual de Andagoya, who met us at his own gateway. Andagoya was a geographer whose explorations of Panama had won him nobility but at great cost, for though he could not have been more than fifty he was white-haired, gnarled, and death walked with him. That he lodged the admiral, and that my host the viceroy permitted it, indeed proved the power of Gonzalo Pizarro, though of course both the viceroy and the governor had been friends of the Pizarros for years, and in a new country men in authority must sustain each other lest all perish. Significantly, perhaps, Andagoya soon excused himself and did not spill salt with us.

The admiral awaited us in the patio, where dinner had been set. Don Pedro Alonso de Hinojosa was a knight of near seventy years whose character buckled upon him, shining like a silver breastplate. I recognized him at once for an Estremaduran and said, as he bent to my hand, that

I knew well his city of Badajóz, a mark to which he responded by admitting knowledge of my father, a good beginning. Captain Mexía he saluted as an old friend, with the bravura of camp companionship and shared adventures.

When Valentin was introduced, the admiral appeared startled and cautiously gave the newcomer opportunity to boast his origins. He was not satisfied with the evasive word that Valentin was a Castilian. He shook his head, then looked intently toward Mexía for a moment as though awaiting explanation; but getting none, he merely exclaimed, "Remarkable!" and handed me to dinner.

Hinojosa pushed Valentin and me for news of Spain; but this yielded, as the bean soup gave way to a bubbly and remarkable fish called pompano and thence to a joint of deer, well-washed in glasses of Spanish wine, to reminiscences with Mexía of days in Peru. So I discovered that Mexía and Hinojosa had paralleled adventures. They had sailed to Peru in the same expedition, joined Pizarro at the same time, and both had been seized upon by the marquis for those characteristics of fearlessness and clear mind which were the nature of both.

They much discussed, as serenely as though it was last Sunday's bullfight, an incident of the first civil war, during which Mexía and the Marquis Pizarro's half brother Gonzalo were jailed by the rebels in the Temple of the Sun in Cuzco. Admiral Hinojosa and a fellow townsman of mine, Don Lorenzo de Aldana, had smuggled them candles with which to burn away their wooden window bars. Gonzalo and Mexía loosed the bars but did not escape, unarmed as they were, fearing a trap. So Aldana, overpowering the night watch, took his lamp and made the rounds. As he reached the temple, he changed his song from "The midnight glass is turned, another flows; it too shall flow its course if God so wills," to an old Estremadurian ballad which Gonzalo would surely recognize: "Time it is, O cavalier, time it is to flee from here." At this, the prisoners scrambled through the window and followed the crier, who led them to a spot where Hinojosa had assembled horses. The four men fled in safety from the most strongly fortified town in Peru to join the marquis in Lima.

"I remember you well at Chupas, too," Mexía said next, and then, turning to me, he went on, "The admiral wore a suit of red velvet with gold buttons over his armor, so that every one of the rebels would know who he was. Only a very brave man would do a thing like that."

Like all old men whose deeds are in the past, Hinojosa warmed more to the recollection than to the wine. I ventured the comment that in all the wars of Peru, the admiral had been on the king's side, as of course a gentleman from Badajóz would be. He acknowledged the compliment in a way which proved him clever.

"Yes, my dear Doña Eloisa," he said emphatically, "I have always aligned myself with the just cause, as I do today."

That brought us to the matter we had all been avoiding, and the stage cue was for me.

"I know nothing of politics," I said, "but I am sure that a Hinojosa of Badajóz would never espouse a wrongful cause."

"Thank you," he said, and raised his wineglass to me. Over mine, I flirted back at him.

"To Estremadura," I said, "land of just and valiant men."

"I, too, will drink to that," said Mexía, the Sevillian. So we toasted Andalusia, too, and then Valentin, who up to now had been able to contribute nothing, proposed a glass to Castile. Again I saw Hinojosa's eyebrows lift and his quick dart for enlightenment toward Mexía, which was returned by the slightest shrug of the shoulder. What did

Hinojosa know—or think he knew—about Valentin?

"Since you are a man of honor and I could not think ill of you," I recalled Hinojosa to my own eyes, "and an Estremaduran neighbor besides, I know you will be kind enough to assist a helpless maid of your own hill country."

He expressed his sympathy, so long as it did not impeach his honor. So I explained how I had been widowed before ever I had married, and asked whether, from his knowledge of contemporary Peru, he thought I might safely journey there to begin a new life.

Silently he examined this innocent question as though inspecting it for a trap, his eyes amused but his face as stern as an inquisitor's. He caressed the stem of his glass with deliberate fingers, then smiled.

"There are many illustrious knights in Peru," he said, "any of whom would murder his own wife to possess you."

"I would love to be fought for," I laughed, "but murder is another thing."

"Murder is the life force of conquest," he went on, "and no hands are clean. In Peru you will find the best families of Spain represented in the worst atrocities. Men who were taught at home to slaughter Moors and rob Jews find no sin to confess in rape and murder of Indian savages, or in assassination of fellow countrymen who try to take from them what they have suffered many hardships to gain. I tell you this so that you will consider whether any man of the New World is worthy of you—or of any decent woman. Peru is a lawless country, and no place for a gentlewoman."

"Or a gentleman?" I asked him.

"His Lordship Don Gonzalo Pizarro is doing his best to calm the country and restore its peace."

Quickly I said that such matters were no concern of mine. Only my own future worried me, about which I must reach a decision. I hinted that Father Gasca might help me.

29

The admiral did not so much as flick his white beard.

"He is my confessor and my friend," I continued, "and I beg you to let him come to me."

Negatively he shook his head.

"He is a harmless priest. Surely you would not deny a child her confessor."

No answer.

"The day after tomorrow is the birth date of Saint Dominic, which Father Gasca must observe with special devotions. Let him say those prayers here, among brothers of his order, for the good of his soul. Then if you decide to send us home, we can both go from here as easily as from Nombre de Dios."

No answer.

"I desperately require my confessor, Don Pedro," I said. "Even at Mass today my thoughts were wayward and require penance. Do not, I beg you, stand between God and me."

He offered me his own confessor.

"But Father Gasca is my guardian also," I persisted. "My entire future is involved. You, an honorable knight from my own province, my one protector in this strange land, will help me. You cannot deny me this."

Hinojosa shrugged.

"I am more versed in the ways of war than of God," he said, "and in the sword thrust of men than the rapier touch of women. I also am an old man, conscious of my sins and the nearness of death. I shall send for your priest."

I arose, went to him, and kissed his cheek.

"But let this priest beware," he said, drawing back, "for my duty is to guard this port for my brothers, the men of Peru, and that I shall do even if I must spill priestly blood."

"You are the master here," I said. "What could you fear from a friar and a woman?"

30

V

†

On leaving Admiral Hinojosa, I begged Captain Mexía to speed a messenger quickly to Father Gasca, telling him to come at once. I suggested that Valentin could hand me across the plaza to the viceroy's door. Mexía would not comply.

"First," he said pointedly, "let me see you safely home."

So I had two escorts, neither of whom said a word. If they had been guards walking me to jail, they could not have been more uncommunicative. Evidently, Mexía had planned to send Valentin across the isthmus in the night while he himself walked me home, so he was furious. And Valentin must have surmised that he would have me to himself. Now, angry at each other, they had nothing to say to me.

At my door, both kissed my hand and neither would leave before the other.

I was scarce in my room, after telling Viceroy Mendoza of Hinojosa's decision, when Lota appeared, all teeth, and whispered that Valentin was in the garden. It is a wonder all girls are not raped in this country, when one's own maid can be bribed to unlock a gate.

"Well done," I complimented him. "How much did it cost you?"

He laughed. "Lota likes me," he said. He came forward

as though he would kiss me. For a moment, remembering the evenings at sea, I almost let him. Instead, I pushed him away.

"Remember what I told you, Valentin," I said. "All that is past."

"You came down to the garden."

"From curiosity, not from love."

"Love is what gardens were planted for," he replied, turning me and crushing me into his strong arms, trying to pull my body into his.

"Lisa! Lisa!" he whispered.

There was nothing for it but to stand quiet, for the least resistance, I knew, would madden him into indiscretion. I must calm him, even with falsehood.

"It is hard for me, too," I whispered, feeling his lips on my cheek and ear, "but this is not the time."

"It is never the time," he said angrily. "You need a spur put to you."

This angered me. "Are you man enough?" I taunted him, and again pushed him away.

He came forward again instantly, but I was ready for him.

"Who are you?" I said.

"A man, as you are a woman."

"No, no, Valentin," I prodded him. "The admiral—he recognized you, or saw some resemblance in you. Do you hide a terrible secret that you could not be polite and enlighten him when he questioned you? What did he find so remarkable in you, for that was his very word?"

"I don't know."

"How can we be friends if you tell me lies?"

"I honestly do not know," he insisted.

"Still evasive," I said petulantly. "You ask me to love you. How can I love a man I do not know?"

"Love is not a matter of heraldry, and you do not identify a lover by armorial bearings."

"Oh, don't you?" I scoffed. "Do you not suppose that the scullery and stable show up on a man's cloak as boldly as the Golden Fleece? Hinojosa, now—when he wore red velvet in that battle—do you not think he would as well have been known a gentleman from his conduct, had he been buskined?"

"You see the scullery and stable in me, then."

"In this dark I see nothing. That's why I ask."

Valentin slammed a fist into his other hand. Then he said, "I am Valentin Guerrero de Selva."

"Guerrero," I said. "The warrior. A goodly name. Of the family of Ávila?"

"My mother was of Ávila, though my father was of Arévalo, and I will not tell you more. If you cannot love me without a recital of pedigrees, then you are not worth loving."

"That spirit I like," I said, but the remark was a dire mistake. He bubbled a low laugh, and at once was upon me.

"Yes," he gasped. "You are a wench at heart, and love to tweak a man with your body. But like the braggart whose hand goes quickly to his sword, you are a coward in performance. It is time you learned that when you light a fire in a man, it can scorch."

I did not wish to cry out, for the vicereine would never live down such a scandal as covert lovemaking in her garden, and no man hence would look at me except wantonly. Silently I fought Valentin with my fists, but on his armored shoulders I only bruised my hands. He was clumsy but powerful, and had bent me to a bench when Lota rushed quickly to us with a hiss of warning.

"Someone comes, someone comes!" she said frantically.

Valentin at once released me and without a word disap-

33

peared the way he had arrived. Lota sped after him, to lock the gate, while I, furiously angry at myself for my own stupidity, ascended the stairs to a porch overlooking the garden, and repaired my disarray. A hot moon, well-matching my temper, began to climb the low branches of the cacao trees espaliered along the wall as I waited to give Lota the razor of my tongue for unlocking the gate to Valentin. But the moon was such a glowing charcoal and so increased my heat, that I soon fled indoors.

In a moment Lota appeared. Before I could say a word she grinned broadly and pointed below. Someone else was in the garden.

Curious, I returned to the porch. But I did not descend to the garden. For there, in the first light of the rising moon, stood Hernán Mexía, stocky feet planted on the paving stones before the fountain. A lute was in his hand.

He sang three serenades of Andalusia in a rich high tenor, though he played the accompaniment indifferently. Doña Angela joined me on the porch, and the viceroy, too. When Mexía saw that I would not come down, he blew me a kiss, bowed to the viceroy and vicereine, and climbed the garden wall.

"Pursuers! Pursuers!" Doña Angela complained testily. "They will keep us awake all night, and be the death of you."

The entire brotherhood of the monastery of Saint Thomas Aquinas went out, robed, hooded and chanting, to greet Gasca on his arrival in Panama.

The friar well deserved this honor, of course. He was a Master of Theology from the seminary of Alcalá de Henares. Further, he had headed the council of the Inquisition at Valencia, and had been inspector of courts and finances for the entire province of Valencia. Now he was His Majesty's personal investigator of conditions in the

New World. Few Dominicans had risen so high in the Franciscan-dominated court of Prince Philip, and his arrival gave the Order of Saint Dominic a fine opportunity to parade its prestige before its rivals. The coincidence that this was Saint Dominic's birthday permitted the spectacle to be staged with all the somber brilliance of which the Dominicans are capable.

Naturally this processional, led by cross and torches, attracted spectators, particularly from the 600 sailors who manned Admiral Hinojosa's twenty-two warships and were rotting with nothing to do, apparently, except make assaults upon my Lota every time she went to Mass or market.

I had not spoken to Valentin since his brutality in the garden, but I very much wanted to witness Gasca's arrival, so forgave him that he might accompany me. Swaggering, he led me from the viceroy's house, but wilted when we encountered Mexía at the gate. The captain was in light mail under a scarlet cape, his head was defended by a morion, and he carried both sword and dagger.

"My lady," he greeted me, "should not venture out among the sailors without the strongest escort. Permit me to accompany you."

He was very gay, and deferential to Valentin, which proved his wisdom. Occasionally, relating some droll and not quite proper anecdote about Peruvian life, he incensed Valentin, but my younger escort did not remonstrate. The truth was that Valentin never spoke much, except when making love. So I was pleased to have a loquacious and interesting companion.

There was great curiosity about Gasca's mission, Mexía said as we strolled to the outskirts of the city. Since every man had a slow charcoal fire for a conscience because of his own dubious deeds, there had been furious speculation and much rumor that His Excellency meant to hang them all. Of course they wanted to see this monster personally.

Gasca disappointed them. He was accompanied only by Don Pedro Hernandez Paniagua, the solemn Loaysan who had come with us from Spain. He had been a colleague of Gasca's in Valencia, and had been brought along, I thought, because he had proved a henchman worthy of absolute trust. But he made no impressive appearance, was solemn and uncommunicative.

This humble entourage, so different from the bannered panoply which Spaniards associate with power, quite winded everyone, including the monks. But Gasca, though a poor and halting speaker, greeted the welcoming party with a simple speech. He had come, he said, in peace, as all could see, and would do nothing to marshal the arms of any man.

"My fiat from His Majesty," he said meekly, "is one of inquiry and rectitude. I have royal powers to grant a free pardon for past rebellion against the Crown to all, without exception, who at once submit to His Majesty's government. If the new laws have unjustly injured you, I have power to revoke them."

He looked over at the rabble of sailors. "You men of Peru," he said, "say you have taken arms against your king only because the new laws are not in His Majesty's best interest and would ruin the country. I say to you, therefore, lay down your arms, for the laws are as of this moment revoked."

"Jesu!" exclaimed Captain Mexía in awe, as a mighty stir from the onlookers cut the stagnant tropical air. I could feel the shock that assailed every man, and then the reaction as the sailors began to laugh. How could this friar, they cackled, without army or even a retinue, enforce such words?

We were surrounded by a crowd. When they jeered, I asked angrily why they were so uncivil.

"Promises, my lady," one responded, "we have heard

before. Did not Judge Vaca de Castro, another priest, say the same? He set aside the laws, so the king removed him and sent us Nuñez Vela. What happened to him? He is white bones in a rocky grave at Añaquito. Nobody can defeat Pizarro, and certainly not—" he pointed toward Gasca, "—a mendicant friar."

Gasca felt the scorn. He looked directly at the crowds of Peruvian sailors.

"I know I must prove myself an honest man," he said blandly. "It is a sort you are not used to."

They laughed again, and a few cheered.

"But I say also this!" He now was stern, and there was the power of sharp steel in his words. He argued that, having revoked the laws, he had removed the only cause for rebellion. He would accept as truth their claim that they had acted for the king up to now, and pardon them; but if they persisted in mutiny, then they were rebels, and would be so judged.

"Let us," he concluded, "together discover the truth of this disturbance, and together set it right, that you may all live to enjoy the fruits of your labors in Peru. I come not to fight, but to inquire, and how may I inquire without the help of your answers—you who know, where I do not, what is best for you. So I say to you, *fiat lux*—let there be light—and in that light let us go forward in peace and love."

With that he shrugged, kissed both cheeks of the abbot who had led the procession of his brothers in Christ, and joined them singing as they chanted their way back to the monastery, which swallowed him up.

As the gates received him, and we walked homeward, I turned to Mexía, who had seemed fascinated with the friar's back. "What do you think of him now?" I said.

Nervously he curled the wisps of his straggly mustache, and rolled his eyes. "Is that all?" he demanded. "No deaths, no arrests, no hangings? No spoil?"

37

"That is all," I said.

He shook his head. "The men will say," he decided, "that if this is the sort of governor His Majesty sends to us, Pizarro need not trouble his head much about him."

"Is that what you think, too?" Valentin inquired.

"I don't know what to think," Mexía answered. "My eyes have been blinded by our beautiful companion. I'm afraid I have been ambushed. You do not realize what fear Pizarro casts at every man's back. Only a stronger fear can overcome him. Your friar speaks of peace and love. Peace never enforced promises."

"What has Gasca promised you?" I asked abruptly, hoping to surprise him into an admission. "Me?"

"He promised me first place in line," he responded frankly. "But I am afraid it will be a long line."

"And therefore a long wait," Valentin inserted. "I was in line before you."

"Lines," said Mexía grimly, "can be broken down." His fingers twitched toward his sword.

VI

†

For a week Gasca kept us all waiting. He did not even appear for the Feast of the Transfiguration. In all those seven days the city, the waterfront and the ships scarcely stirred. If Gasca ran to Dominican form, he would use the methods of Inquisition—the quick arrest by night, the secret trial, then the gibbet or the stake. But no hangman's noose dangled in the square before the wooden cathedral, and no faggots were assembled for an auto-da-fé.

Valentin, in a good doublet, but with a steel cuirass beneath it to protect his broad chest and back, his Flemish helmet on his head, visited all the inns and bodegas to make the acquaintance of Hinojosa's ship captains, and even dined and shared a cup of wine with several of them aboard their vessels.

Meanwhile I had nothing to do. I had made possible Gasca's reception in Panama. After such a whetting, I felt sharp for other duties, the more so because women are customarily excluded from masculine affairs. But Father Gasca now ignored me. Being under his guardianship, I could do nothing for myself. Like everyone else, I, too, waited.

With much time for reflection, I made the only possible decision concerning myself. Since I could not return to Spain, I must perforce continue to Peru with Father Gasca.

I was even excited to be made a prize for the valiant captains. The man who served Gasca best would win rich rewards and become a great personage in the New World. Therefore, if the priest wished me to marry well, he could assure my future no better than by his present method.

I had no conflict concerning my own loyalty. God had not sent me to the New World in the company of Gasca, and rid me of my intended husband, without design. I was to serve some purpose, unclear as it might be at the moment. Therefore I would give the friar my fealty. Indeed, being a Canillejas, whose family for sixteen generations had fought to unite Iberia under a strong monarchy, I must support the king against a rebel. Whatever Gasca required of me I would undertake with all my heart, even if it pitted me against Pizarro himself.

But if Pizarro refused to yield? There would be a long and monstrous war. Against Pizarro and Carabajal, how could Gasca hope to prevail? If he were defeated, I in common with all his train would become Pizarro's spoil to dispose as he wished.

Therefore, I made careful inquiry from the vicereine, Doña Angela, and discovered that Gonzalo Pizarro was a bachelor, though like most of the conquerors he was several times a father. Further, this Pizarro, for all his bastard swineherd background, was the foremost man in the colonies. Whether Gasca won or lost, it behooved me to make myself as attractive as possible to this man, if there was opportunity.

As for love in marriage, I was not illusioned. My wise Tía Sortella taught me that love is a delightful plaything, and like most toys educational, but that the playroom and the marriage bed are separated by a long and draughty corridor. Since this is so in every house, it must be truth. I had only to reflect on my own mother, and my rakish aunt, to realize that a wise woman requires only two things of a husband: longevity and a demanding mistress. The first she must have to preserve her home; the second to save her beauty, for nothing so ages a woman as too many children, except widowhood. Particularly in a new country, to be partnered well was everything. The best, if Gasca won, would surely be my lot. In Gasca's defeat, the best would be Pizarro.

On the eighth day after Gasca's arrival in Panama, the viceroy himself brought to me a strange creature who begged audience. He had followed me home from Mass. He was wizened and small, with razor eyes in a head more Indian than Spanish, hair to the shoulder and bound at the sweatband with a beaded thong. He was clean-shaven, as by a razor. A shirt once white covered his chest, and knee-length pantaloons his meager thighs and buttocks, below which brown bare legs ended in moccasins. I should have refused to see him, but the viceroy evidently esteemed him and, indeed, called for a glass to honor this guest, then pointedly left us, desiring no privy to our talk.

"I am Pedro Gallego," he affirmed proudly.

"Should I know the name?" I asked.

"I am also called *El Huésped*. Does that signify?"

"Nothing, Señor, except that you have been much a guest."

"Truly spoken," said he, and explained that the odd appellation of "The Guest" came from the proverb, "Guests and fish both smell on the third day." He was the mailman for all Peru, and sought audience with Father Gasca, yet dared not approach the friar boldly, since most of his traffic was for Pizarro. All the New World mails, he asserted, were the private charter of a single cousin of the king's, and Gallego held the exclusive subcontract for all the west coast south of Panama. Thus if Gasca desired letters delivered anywhere in Pizarro's realm, Gallego must be the carrier.

I promised to take him that night secretly to the monastery. Then I sent a messenger to find Captain Mexía. He came to me after the siesta.

"Forgive me for neglecting you, beautiful lady," he greeted me, turning my hand to kiss the palm. "Only most strenuous activity has prevented me from helping you relieve the tedium of this brick-oven city."

I told him about Pedro Gallego.

His eyes saddened. "You called me—for this?"

Then he laughed. "It was presumptuous of me, I suppose," he said, "to fancy I was summoned to entertain a lady."

"Why, Captain Mexía!" I exclaimed playfully, "what boldness you speak."

"You are not displeased?"

"Of course not. But what can come of it?"

"God giveth, and God taketh," he replied. "At the moment He seems to favor me."

He laughed again and became businesslike. He knew Gallego well and vouched for his profession. But when I asked if he was to be trusted, Mexía looked at me as though I had no sense whatever. "Who is ever to be trusted?" he shot back. "One makes use of everyone, and turns treachery to advantage if he can."

That night, covered by a cape and black hood so that I looked almost Dominican, and escorted by two of the viceroy's household guards, I took the mailman to Gasca. We were led to a vaulted refectory that smelled of kale and onions. There Father Gasca awaited us. The dinner stench was so heavy in that unwindowed hall that I asked his excellency to call for a brazier of burning olive pits, which soon cleared the air of both the repast and the pungent scent of the candles.

Gallego went directly to the point, a mark in his favor with the straightforward Gasca. He explained that the Incas long ago had organized swift runners called Chasqui

42

who sped in relays across the coast and the mountains on the Inca's royal business. Gallego utilized their system, their rest camps and trails, but with lesser speed, to make regular trips between the important towns. He produced a list of his routes, the starting days of every month, and a map on which was marked every town in Peru, and the tambo of every Indian chief.

Gasca's eyes gleamed through the candlelight.

"Forgive me," he said, "but do your letters by chance ever fall into the wrong hands?"

Gallego twinkled. "I am a merchant," he said. "If the price was right, I might let someone look. But not destroy, Your Excellency—I have my reputation to remember."

Gasca smiled, and asked whether letters, written in Peru for delivery in that country, might be deflected through Panama for his scrutiny.

Gallego admitted that, for a price, this might be done. "Even the wind," he commented blandly, "follows gold. And hear this, Excellency. As God is my witness and Saint Anthony my patron, I have ever been the king's man. Behold also, my business can prosper only in a peaceful realm. Therefore I have much reason to see Pizarro overthrown. Like Saint Anthony, I can be tempted of the Devil, and thirst in the deserts, and yet be loyal." He said he sailed next for Peru five days hence. Gasca requested him to return to the monastery on the evening of the fourth, when he would have many letters for the pouch, and gold of equal weight.

"You are magnanimous," Gallego said, bowing. "I only charge that much of the ignorant."

"Then hold me ignorant, as I hold you loyal, and we shall prosper together," Gasca replied. He turned to me. "Tomorrow morning, my little ward, sharpen well your quills and come to me here. We have much writing, you and I."

Evidently Father Gasca wished to make known his presence and his motives to every man in New Spain. With Paniagua's help, we wrote to the Archbishop of Lima, to the mayors and captains of every town, to such loyal outlaws as one Diego Centeño who hid with scores of followers in caves near Arequipa in the south, rather than bend the knee to Pizarro and the demon Carbajal; and to every priest, merchant, factor, alcalde, licentiate and many more I could not even enumerate, but several hundred in all. These letters conveyed, in different words, the same message: that the disputed laws had been revoked; everyone who promptly joined the king's banner would be pardoned for every sin both against God and Crown, and protected in what he owned.

Father Gasca spent many hours over a letter to Pizarro himself, in which he enclosed a missive from His Majesty.

When Gallego had sailed, happily burdened under such a great double weight of letters and gold, Gasca sought me out privately.

"You are a splendid scrivener," he complimented me. "I was not aware that such learning, both in Castilian and Latin, was the endowment of young ladies."

I explained quickly how my ambitious father, knowing that the fusion of our house with that of my fiancé would enhance the name of Canillejas if I, as the Marquesa Rioseco, were influential at court, had from my earliest days pruned me, like a fig tree on a garden wall, to yield choice fruit. Thus had I learned some French and history from the Sisters of Saint Clare, and Latin from the Franciscan brotherhood of Santa María la Major, as well as practical political matters and etiquette from my Aunt Sortella.

"Ah, yes," he smiled. "The viceroy has told me of your celebrated aunt. Before this adventure ends, we may well require her illustrious patronage to circumvent the lies that will be spread of us."

It is difficult to convince a priest that a woman is good for anything. Denying her as flesh, he must also deny her as an intellectual companion. Baser men, interested only in the former, often discover the latter—at least, so Aunt Sortella instructed me. Now I must convince this friar that I, a mere woman, was valuable to him in this great enterprise on which he was embarked. I sought to impress him that even as Tía Sortella might be witful for him in Spain, I was of her mold with the further advantage of proximity.

"Not too much of her mold, I pray," he cut in, twinkling, and then conceded that against his judgment he must include me in his work. The letters we had written, he pointed out, had bared all his strategy for the conquest of Peru, and he must assure himself of my loyalty. So I told him of my decision during the long days of inactivity. He laughed lightly at my determination to beguile Gonzalo Pizarro against the possibility of Gasca's defeat.

"Do not molest yourself with such anxiety," he responded. "If fight we must, you will remain safely here in the vicereine's house until the issue is decided."

"You mean I shall not accompany you to Peru?"

"Not in the event of war. I could not undertake such a responsibility."

I was very upset. To forestall my saying words I might regret, Father Gasca quickly distracted my attention by asking how I progressed with Captain Mexía.

"I have not exactly lain in straw before him," I pouted.

"For my sake, little sister," he went on, "invite him to dine. I want him to remain attracted to you."

"And I?"

"You could do worse than Captain Mexía," the friar said.

45

VII

✝

As soon as the Feast of the Assumption of the Beloved Virgin was past, I invited Captain Mexía to luncheon. Lest my gesture appear too obvious, and because I thought it would be amusing to keep both my men together, I had Valentin also.

Being hostess to two gentlemen, even in another woman's house, was quite exciting. Doña Angela was pleased, too. For the first time in nearly three weeks she could dine alone with her family; though, lest public decorum be outraged, her table was set within sight of my own.

It being mid-August, the repast was spread in the patio. Lota served us, and very well, too, had she worn her shoes; but that was expecting too much, since she even begrudged donning them for Mass. She had developed the annoying habit of listening, even eavesdropping, on my conversations, for which I could not chastise her, since I should certainly have done the same with all this excitement afoot.

We had a turtle soup with okra; boiled needlefish with onions and turnips; a poorly aged goat cheese; a mushy thick native fruit with the amusing name of avocado, so called because like a lawsuit it is hard to stomach; another pulpy staple called the banana which can be skinned and eaten raw, as we did, or sliced and fried; and the season's first white grapes from the viceroy's quinta in the hills.

There was also a solid Córdoban wine, too sweet for my taste but pleasing to our Andalusian guest.

Mexía was of Seville and like all of them provincial. He also was sometimes vulgar, and twice, though Valentin was present, suggested that I entertain him further during the siesta. I was accustomed to such talk in whispers, for almost every man will say it, given opportunity; but I hardly expected it across a table. I was amused, but Valentin was offended. He should not have been, for Sevillians fancy themselves the world's greatest lovers and irresistible, even though most of them are bow-legged and ride mules, and smell of ship's tar and onions. Seville's famous Don Juan was mostly a legend and, as everyone knows, legends are the daydreams of eunuchs, poets and other nonperformers; yet these Andalusians talk as though they were the legend reincarnate for whom all maidens are privileged to swoon away their virtue. Give me a stout Castilian, or a peasant Aragonese, or even an impetuous Catalan. For I am sure that the eely Andalusian, for all his talk, is a poor performer. At least Aunt Sortella says so, and I guess she has tried them all, including the melancholy Galician who was her husband and, I gather, not the worst of the lot.

Having lived his entire life in sunny country, Mexía was amused by a recital of my life in Cáceres. He could hardly believe that we must put a brazier of charcoals under the dining table four months a year to warm our feet, and that in winter we sleep in beds set close to the chimney stones. He had never slept in a bed, only on a couch in the Arab fashion. When I told him of Aunt Sortella's bed, which is high off the drafty floor, enclosed in a damask tent, and wide enough for one to roll over twice, his eyes grew piggy and I knew he found me wanton.

But he was impressed when I described our house, which was begun in the Tenth Century by a Saracen, on the foundations of an old Roman bath. Both hot and cold artesian wells rise there, and these Arabs knew the value of water. The clever infidel built his palace directly over the baths and piped the water throughout the house. When my ancestors, at that time of Oviedo and Asturian Valdesota, drove the Arabs from the west, they enclosed the palace in Gothic walls and added a second story, but otherwise changed it little. Thus in the wars of León, my family withstood a seven-month siege and, since their water supply could not be cut off, they survived. Even today the basement stands four feet deep in water, which runs out continually through the wash troughs and stables into the gardens, and as a child I liked to go below with a torch and examine the sixteen marble columns the Romans left, which now support the house.

Evidently the droopy-mustached captain thought I was trying to impress him, and therefore favored him. He preened himself. But he also asked many questions about Gasca until finally, over the brandy, I thought I had discovered why Mexía had been sent to me. He seemed to be wavering, as though he wished to join the friar, and sought reassurance that our priest had the iron in him to best Pizarro.

Here I could not initiate him. Nor did Valentin, which confused me. I had never been told, since a mere woman is never enlightened to man's affairs, just where Valentin stood in Gasca's entourage. He knew much, yet did not seem to have the friar's confidence, a most contradictory situation.

"I can tell you this much," Valentin volunteered finally. "I happen to know that His Excellency has such power conferred on him as the king himself would have if he were here. I also know that when the friar was summoned by Prince Philip to undertake the journey, Gasca was bold enough to decline unless everything was done his way. The prince was aghast, and sent His Excellency to Charles himself, who was at Venlo in the Low Countries. 'I want this power and I want that; otherwise you can go hang,' Gasca told the king. His Majesty was impressed. Here was no spineless self-seeker, no greedy relative of a great lord. He gave Gasca everything he asked for. And hear this. The king even gave him four sheets of parchment signed in blank with the imperial signature, which Gasca can fill in with any order he pleases."

"Mother of God!" Mexía exclaimed. But he soon recovered. "Parchments are not swords," he reflected.

"Or even shields," Valentin agreed.

Mexía squinted sharply.

"You have so little confidence in him, yet accompany him?"

"I travel with him," Valentin responded. "There is a difference."

One thing I had learned in Panama. This was that blunt inquiry was never made into the families or motives of New World adventurers. So many heroes of the conquest, and later arrivals, had fled jail, gibbet or Inquisition, that even their identities were carefully concealed. Mexía therefore did not press the matter. Instead, he asked, "What will the friar do about our lands and Indians?"

"He is empowered," Valentin answered promptly, "to confirm them or take them away, enlarge or diminish them, or bestow new ones on loyal men who now have none."

"Santa María!" Mexía exclaimed. "If there is war, and Gasca wins, the pack will be shuffled!"

"It is something to decide—which hand to play," Valentin said.

"And death to him who loses," Mexía added.

"Yes," Valentin agreed gloomily.

I injected that there was a very simple solution, namely that every man choose for the king against the rebel, as it seemed to me every honest knight should. I told Mexía that

Gasca had already sent south, by the mailman Gallego, a written offer to Pizarro to pardon his rebellion and confirm him in all his wealth. Mexía leaped to his feet at once.

"This I must communicate to Admiral Hinojosa," he said.

Despite his haste, however, he had something else on his mind. As he thanked me for my hospitality, he touched my bosom. I ignored the gesture, but Valentin's hand went to his clumsy broadsword, his face flamed, and he reached for his cape in anger.

"Control yourself," I whispered. "Will you undo everything?"

But he would not hear me. He rushed to the street, overtaking Mexía before the captain had gone twenty steps.

"Mexía will kill him," I screamed to the viceroy, who immediately left his own dining table and joined me at the window. "Your Lordship, you must help him!"

The viceroy did not answer, so ridiculous was my appeal. Thus ignored, I did the unpardonable—I ran to separate the antagonists.

Mexía met Valentin's rush cautiously, testing the swordsmanship of his taller and heavier foe. But as his Toledo blade began to parry Valentin's sweeping cuts, a cold smile enveloped the captain's face. Giving ground, he unbuckled his cape to free his arms. Hotly Valentin beat him back, having the advantage of a longer and heavier weapon and angry aggressiveness. Mexía, white teeth showing his pleasure, parried the attack with panther quickness, not thrusting at all. He reminded me of a grayhound playing with a rabbit. Valentin's charge could not last. When, out of breath, he hesitated an instant, he suddenly saw his sword fly across the stony street. Mexía's grinning teeth were at the pommel end of death, and a Toledo tip was at Valentin's helpless throat.

Mexía saw me running toward him. He flicked a dagger

from his belt and brought its weighted handle across Valentin's jaw. My self-appointed hero went down, and he did not arise.

Mexía, well-satisfied with his pleasant exercise against a much larger man, recovered Valentin's sword, handed it to me with a bow, and walked happily away. I could not let Valentin see me there, so I put his weapon beside him and ran indoors to the window. In a moment Valentin arose, shook his head, felt his face and departed.

That same evening Gasca was summoned in audience by Admiral Hinojosa. Naturally, I accompanied him, for had I not begged the commander of Pizarro's fleet to permit my confessor to come to Panama City? Logically, then, any discussion between the two men must be to settle my future.

Of course, my destiny was the least concern of both. I was a convenient excuse for bringing together two adversaries who otherwise, Spanish courtesy and legalistics being what they were, could not meet at all. For Gasca I also served another purpose, as witness to the interview. Notarized testimony of eye and ear observers to all official acts is more necessary to the Spaniard than bread and wine. Gasca could not take Paniagua with him, or Valentin, without giving his informal call the trappings of formal negotiation. Men are silly about such things. A woman, now, defending her home against another woman, would go to her and scratch her eyes out, leaving no doubt as to her purpose. But a man, defending the king against a rebel, must wrap the whole affair in ambiguity and punctilio.

Mexía was present to make the introductions. The courtly admiral paid me the usual compliments, and I thanked Mexía for his afternoon's mercy.

"He is your special ward, then, this lad?" Mexía asked.

"No, no," I replied promptly, "he is a foolish boy who

51

has much to learn, and I thank you for the patience of your instruction."

Meanwhile Gasca, who had craftily donned a robe the sleeves of which were frayed, thus emphasizing his meniality among the assembled resplendent knights and ship's captains, had met the admiral. Neither Gasca nor I was invited to be seated, a pointed request for brevity.

"You have decided the lady's future?" Hinojosa asked, for I had to come first.

"She remains with me," Gasca said.

"Then you return immediately to Spain?" Hinojosa suggested.

"Immediately on completion of my mission," the friar replied, and that was the end of talk about me. Here was a direct challenge to Hinojosa's authority which must be met, thus permitting the admiral to inquire concerning Gasca's duties, so that he might make proper report to his superior, Gonzalo Pizarro, in Peru.

Gasca was brief, and more vague, it seemed to me, than need be about his purpose and his authority. He assumed that Mexía had already carried the ham bone home from my lunch, and that over dinner Hinojosa and his guests had all gnawed at it. So he merely skimmed his errand of its fat, exposing nothing of the lean meat underneath.

"Show me these powers you speak of," the admiral interrupted.

Gasca spread his awkward hands. "At the proper time," he responded. "They are many and would take half a day to examine."

"Do they give you the right to confirm Gonzalo Pizarro in his governorship of Peru, to which he is entitled both by his many services to His Majesty and by the general voice of the people?"

Gasca's hawk face twitched and a great sadness spread over him. Here was the one question he could not answer affirmatively, the one concession he could not make. To place a rebel in governance over his spoils would have been too humiliating to royal authority. He could promise Pizarro anything but that.

"I assure Your Excellency," he mumbled, "that I am empowered generously to reward every loyal servant of the king in Peru."

"You equivocate," Hinojosa scoffed.

"But I do not prevaricate," Gasca replied, "as you must in due time see."

Hinojosa held out his hand, and the interview ended.

His excellency walked me to the viceroy's door, and I tried to cheer him in his failure.

"Oh, this is splendid," Gasca said. "I have sown doubt, and will reap uncertainty. Then I shall sow the uncertainty and harvest conviction. Such husbandry may take two seasons, but it must eventually fill our bins."

I had been aware as soon as we left Hinojosa's presence that someone followed us. The night was starry but otherwise of little light. For the first time since our arrival, a cooling wind from the Southern Ocean blessed the city. We crossed the plaza under a grateful fan of trees. But Gasca noticed neither nature's solace nor the peril that walked behind us.

"So we stay in this fuming town indefinitely?" I pouted.

"No," Gasca rebutted solemnly, "we work. The admiral will now write a letter to Pizarro telling him that I have no power to make him governor, but only to forgive his many sins. That will cut off Pizarro at the knees."

I wondered, hearing the careful steps behind but not daring to look around, how much protection this friar would be in a scuffle.

"Either Pizarro must come out in open rebellion," Gasca went on, "in which case most of his followers will realize his ambition is at their expense, or he must surrender Peru to me. Let him ponder this decision well."

He smiled into the delicious night. I hurried him across the dusty street and slapped loudly on our door with my hand. Whoever trailed us had also crossed the road and become a wall shadow.

"Hinojosa will send his fastest ship with this letter," Gasca mused. "We must smuggle a spy aboard."

Lota opened the viceroy's gate and admitted me. We both received Christ's blessing from Gasca's hand, and an ungainly and lonely man shuffled on his sandals into a darkness scented of gardenia.

"One moment," I whispered to Lota. "Clang the gate, but remain outside with me."

Lota's serenest accomplishment was her ability to do as she was told without question. We were as invisible now as our pursuer.

After a long moment, part of the garden wall detached itself from the mass. Hernán Mexía gazed up at the viceroy's house. Lota gripped my arm tightly. The captain faded away.

"Why are you so excited?" I asked Lota when we were safely inside the patio.

"I think he was looking for me instead of you," Lota answered.

"What is he to you?" I asked, aghast.

"Whatever he wants to be," she said.

VIII

A formal suitor, hat in hand, called on me next evening and remained exactly the hour of courtship. I was shocked. The arrogance of the conquistadors is past belief. After telling me he had paid for the privilege of meeting me at Nombre de Dios, I should not have qualmed, I suppose, when Hernán Mexía thus vowed openly for my hand while pursuing my maid in secret. Truly, these New Worldlings were capable of anything!

He had greased his boots since yesterday and put a dagger point to his fingernails. Also, he was glitteringly dressed, from head to calf in Italian velvet the crimson of a cardinal's hat, smothered in exquisite embroidery, with Flemish lace at sleeve and shirt front. Around his neck and across his breast flashed a chain of gold from which dangled six curious medallions, once the Inca monarch's earrings. The only thing lacking in his distinguished caparison was an emblem of knighthood.

The grandchildren giggled as this suitor was ushered in by the vicereine, who masked her amusement behind a mien of Spanish dignity. Since one of the women must sit with me, Doña Angela served as duenna, greeting my caballero as though I was an overripe daughter of her own, then sitting behind her needlework in the prescribed manner. Having been betrothed so young, I never had been courted. So I was truly glad to see the little fellow.

The privilege to make suitors miserable is one of woman's few pleasures in this world, and an excellent school in which to learn the ridiculousness of husbands.

"You favor me, Don Hernán," I said when he had been seated circumspectly in a straight-backed chair, his plumed velvet hat across his knees, his back as erect as an imperial guardsman's, his heels tightly together. He looked up shyly at this knighthood I had bestowed upon him. Perhaps I should not have played with him thus, but merely addressed him as "captain."

"I have favored you since first I heard of you," he answered. "But the rough ways of Peru were a mistake. I apologize for my crudeness."

"You need not," I rejoined. "I like occasionally to hear what men say only to each other. I just do not like to be touched."

Doña Angela frowned over her needlework. At this, Mexía looked down at his plumed hat, speechless. He wanted so much to be a gentleman, but Peru had not taught him how. "You must teach me," he mumbled, "how to be worthy of you."

He had asked Father Gasca for permission to sit with me. When I suggested that his brother captains in the fleet might think him disloyal to Pizarro for paying court to Gasca's ward, his dauntless smile returned. They would all be calling with him, he assured me, had he not discouraged them. "Do not forget," he said, "that I paid for the honor of being first. Let me declare my intentions."

Doña Angela was so shocked at this that she pricked her finger with the needle. She sucked away the blood with a quick gesture and looked sternly at the captain.

"The rules for a first visit, sir, do not permit love talk," she scolded him sharply.

There was a suffocating pause. Mexía's eyes appealed to me to help him. To relieve his embarrassment—he was as awkward and self-conscious as a boy behind a stable—I suggested that he tell me of Peru, the one subject he knew thoroughly.

"Would anything in Peru make proper discourse?" he answered, completely discouraged.

Ever since Mexía had first mentioned him, I had been curious about Gonzalo Pizarro's army commander, the eighty-year-old Francisco Carbajal. If there was to be war between Pizarro and Gasca, then the more the friar knew about this so-called monster the better. So I asked Mexía if it were true, as I had heard, that during the Battle of Chupas this Carbajal, seeing his infantry waver before enemy cannon fire, had discarded his breastplate and helmet, thus exposing his body nude to the waist. Then shouting, "See, they cannot harm us," he had run downhill among the ordnance.

Mexía confirmed it. He himself had been captain of 160 pike in the battle, and was therefore under Carbajal's command.

"When we reached him," Mexía said, "he had overrun the artillery position single-handed, bodies lay like cut grain about him, and he was turning the falconets about to face the enemy."

I expressed doubt that one man could do so much; but Mexía was firm, and told me what he knew of this man whose deeds had built for him a reputation equal to those of El Cid and the Chevalier Bayard.

Mexía first saw Carbajal at Cuzco. He had arrived from Panama when the Marquis Pizarro let the very dregs of New Spain enter Peru to resist a year-long Indian uprising in 1536. The story was that Carbajal, as soon as he landed at Callao, had stolen a red mule and, with a dozen renegades, taken after the Indian besiegers. Acting more like highway bandits than soldiers, Carbajal's band in one week had opened a road to Juaja, a highland town thirty-

57

six leagues from Lima, important, like Madrid in Spain, as the junction of roads from all extremes of the country.

For this feat, the Marquis rewarded him with a small farm near Cuzco, where he went with his wife, a sharp-tongued Italian harpy of gentle birth named Catalina Leytón. Being unusually wise in the ways of war, Carbajal diligently cultivated his lands all during the conflict between the Marquis and his one-time partner Almagro, taking no side even though the great battle of the Salt Pits was fought within cannon sound of his house.

"That seems odd," I told Mexía. "I should think he would be in the thick of it, if only to enrich himself."

"Not Carbajal," Mexía said emphatically. "He said he had fought for forty years in Italy as a loyal king's man, and civil war was never in anyone's interest."

Once the strife was ended and the rebel Almagro slain, Carbajal began to ride his mule, which he called Bermeja (The Red One) into Cuzco almost every night to drink and gamble and wench Indian girls. Mexía then was captain of the Cuzco guard. Many a night he broke up Carbajal's brawling, hoisted him on his mule, and slapped The Red One's rump homeward.

No small farm could long finance the appetites of such a Hector. Shortly before the Marquis Pizarro's death, Carbajal wheedled from the governor the post of sheriff at Cuzco, an honorarium which included the use of an Inca palace.

Soon he became a legend throughout Peru. His brawls were no less historic than his feats of arms. One prisoner untactfully escaped jail without paying the sheriff's usual bribe. Carbajal, on his mule, pursued the culprit across the mountains and in two days found him in that vast Andean wilderness, and hanged him to a tree. With the same vigor he cleared the roads of *salteadores*, the armed bands of Spanish brigands who, having arrived too late to share legitimate spoil, roamed the country, torturing petty Indian chiefs into digging up their hidden gold, looting farms, and running off cattle. Attacking one such camp, Carbajal found himself surrounded by a dozen bandits. Jumping from his mount and shouting profanely, he had killed four and wounded three others before his troops arrived. His only wound was a cut fingernail.

After each of these triumphs he returned to Cuzco for a prodigious orgy. In his wine he told warlike stories too authentic to be lies. No battle of the peninsula had escaped him, for he and war found each other. In Peru, it was equally futile to oppose him as sheriff, card and drinking companion, or love rival. Yet men cultivated him for his wonderful stories of war, his advice in all manner of battle situations which always was cunning and ripe in experience, and his singing and lute playing, particularly of the Nativity carols, which reminded his friends of Spain.

After the murder of the Marquis Pizarro, Carbajal went with Gonzalo Pizarro to Potosí to explore for new silver mines. He had some luck. But true to his convictions, he tried to flee Peru with his wife and his wealth when Gonzalo rose to dispute the king's government. Pizarro sent a cavalry troop of eighty men, commanded by Admiral Hinojosa, to arrest him and return him to Cuzco.

"You must command my army," Pizarro told him, "or I will hang you as you have hanged so many swordsmen of Peru."

What could the man do? "I am not eager, Your Excellency," Carbajal told Pizarro, "to put my hands in the warp of this cloth, but with things as they are now, I promise to be the principal weaver."

A few nights later he entertained Pizarro in his own house. My little Hernán Mexía was there, and Admiral Hinojosa, and several others. Over the plentiful brandy, Carbajal proposed that Pizarro throw off Spanish dominion and become King of Peru. Then the country would have only one loyalty. A fleet in Panama could easily prevent Crown officers from traveling southward. The Emperor Charles, occupied in half of Europe, could not possibly finance an armada to crush rebellion in far-away new lands. With the wealth of the Inca empire, Pizarro would in a few years be master of New Spain from Colorado and the Rio Grande to the Straits of Magellan, an empire larger and richer than Spain itself.

Carbajal had worked out the plan in detail. Pizarro would marry the Coya, the ranking member of the royal Inca house, and restore the native customs under which millions of Indians had fashioned an absolute monarchy for their ruler. The conquerors, many already married to Inca women, would become dukes, marquises, counts and knights, as befit their services to His Majesty Don Gonzalo. Mexía himself would be created a count.

When Gonzalo objected that he could not take so violent a step, Carbajal pointed out that he had already ousted from the country the king's judge Vaca de Castro, and now openly defied an even higher authority, Viceroy Nuñez. Therefore neither Pizarro nor any man in Peru could hope for mercy from Charles the Fifth, and independence of Spanish rule was their only chance for survival.

At that moment Carbajal's wife, who had been in the next room, thrust her voice into the conversation.

"Such foolish talk," she snapped, "will cost the lot of you your heads."

Mexía, telling me this story, ended it with a hopeless shrug.

"What did Pizarro decide?" I asked.

"He did not say no," Mexía answered.

Accepting Pizarro's silence as a mandate, Carbajal cast off his hitherto unwavered loyalty to the throne of Castile and Aragon, and organized a mighty army. Then to show his strength, he rode boldly one night into Lima, dug from their beds three men who had deserted him, and hanged them. At this audacity, Nuñez Vela's bungling court fell apart. The citizens arrested the viceroy, packed him and his suite on ships for Spain, and opened Lima's gates to Pizarro. Nuñez, refusing disgrace, landed in northern Peru. He was tracked down by Carbajal, then defeated by Pizarro in battle just north of Quito, where my fiancé died. Nuñez, wounded, was murdered by a knight, one Benito Suárez, whose brother Nuñez had slain in Lima. Now Pizarro was in fact ruler of all Peru.

"With such turmoil," I asked Mexía, "how can Gasca bring peace to Peru?"

My suitor's hour had turned the glass, and he arose to leave me.

"It is what every man asks," he answered.

"But you have decided to join Gasca," I said, holding out my hand. He bent low over my fingers, kissing each one of them. "Yes," he replied, "I have. The price for victory has risen since you arrived."

A few minutes later I had another visitor. Valentin sought me, his face troubled.

"There is a rumor, my lady," he said, "that one of Pizarro's spies has decided to kidnap you and take you to Pizarro."

"How exciting!" I gasped.

But Valentin took the matter more seriously. He said that a ship sailed shortly, carrying an important letter from Hinojosa to Pizarro. The plan was to put me also aboard.

"With your permission, I will guard your house for a few days," Valentin said.

"I will be grateful to you," I replied.

IX

✝

My knowledge of this hateful Panama climate now received a first-hand addition which I had hoped to avoid.

I saw hell. For weeks thereafter, the reflection of my mirror, a death mask, reminded me of an ordeal which mercifully was much of the time fogged in delirium. My complaint, so everyone said, was common to almost everyone who remained long in Panama. It was an agony unimaginable.

What ailed me had no proper name, though the physician knew how to treat it; it was never encountered until the exploration of Guatemala and the pestilential swan's neck of land called Panama. The soldiers called it convulsions, and that indeed it was. There were two varieties: God's, visited on man for his sins and from which you usually recovered; and the devil's, in which the depths of hell opened, and prayer alone might save you. Mine was the devil plague. With dear Father Gasca kneeling at my couch and his Dominican brothers in the monastery keeping vigil, I survived.

I was walking home from Mass, on the day of the Feast of the Nativity of the Beloved Virgin, when suddenly I became weak and dizzy. Fortunately, Valentin was with me. The heat had been nauseating, so I was not alarmed. I clung to Valentin, and found his stout shoulder as comforting as he, from the delight in his eyes, found my arm exciting. Before we had crossed the plaza my legs became paralyzed. I fell. Valentin carried me home.

Doña Angela thought me sunstruck and put me to bed. For a day nothing happened except that I was alternately hot and cold. One moment I would be in such fever that I swam in moisture, the next so chilled that my teeth rattled together in my jaws and all my muscles jumped, sending my arms pawing and my legs kicking. When this condition did not abate toward the second nightfall, the physician was summoned. He ordered the window shuttered, and a charcoal brazier lit in the room to make an oven and sweat the fever from me.

By morning, when he called again, the symptoms of my malady were pronounced, and my agony also. My throat had closed so I could neither eat nor drink, my jaws were locked, and the rigor which first had attacked my legs now bound every muscle. Toward noon, merciful heaven took my reason from me, so that in delirium I could withstand my suffering.

When my mind cleared—I do not rightly know when it was—the room was black and fiery hot, and I could not move. Somewhere close at hand I heard Father Gasca's voice in prayer. I was in the most peculiar position. My jaw was tight against my collarbone; yet my spine was drawn back as though I was on a torturer's rack. Had I been able, I should have screamed, but I had no voice.

When next the physician came, Doña Angela and Lota forced my lips open and a bitter brew was poured between my teeth. I later discovered that the medicine was made of the bark of a bush that grows in Peru, called by the Indians quinine, and by the Spaniards Peruvian bark. I could not swallow, for every muscle of my throat was as tight as a lute string. With my chin drawn down and my

63

neck stretched back, I could scarcely breathe and suffered the agonies of hell. My head thumped as though drums beat beside my pillow. I was on fire from fevers. My precious Lota somehow forced the fluid down me, and a purgative doubly bitter. Then she spent what may have been hours rubbing me with searingly hot unguents, to relax my contracting spine and keep the pressure from dislocating every bone in my back. Without her ministrations I should have become a hopeless cripple. She worked ceaselessly for days, at what effort to her I never knew but could guess. Often, in moments of mental clearness, I heard her praying God for strength of arm to continue the massage, and felt her tears drip on my body in the dark. Now and again scalding rum was administered, after which I was carried by a strange, silent woman to a porcelain tub and immersed in water so viciously hot that I could not have endured it, save that it was less frightful than the continuous backward bending pressure on my spine, and the downward viselike weight of my jaw. Of arms and legs I had no memory whatever.

This continued for a week. Hernán Mexía, who called every afternoon promptly at seven to inquire for me, ransacked all the ships of Hinojosa's fleet for the bark whose extract alone was specific for my malady. Valentin for days on end boiled water in a huge kettle. From the foot of the bed constantly came to my numbed ears a sound more unguent than any medication: the sure, confident voice of Friar Gasca in prayer. Oh, what debts of love I owed to all my friends!

Was it the eighth, the ninth, the fourteenth day that the devil relaxed his hold on me? I did not of my own mind know. The others said it was the eighth. I had been plunged, delirious and dying, into another boiling bath, which relaxed my spine and jaw. Whereas previously this easement had lasted only for moments, this time even in my stupor I felt the pressures decline, and tried by grunts and groans to tell my saviors. The viceroy's voice from the door suddenly cried out, far away, "That's it, that's it. Do you hear her? Merciful heaven be thanked, it is breaking at last." From that moment I improved.

Saint Matthew's Day passed before I was up again, utterly a hag, face drawn and old, hair thin, limbs weak and bony, and with twenty pounds to gain to fit my clothes.

As usual, there was the wise will of God in this.

When, just before I was stricken, Valentin had warned me that I might be kidnapped, I had half-hoped that I might be. If Father Gasca intended to leave me to wither in Panama's heat while he had all the fun of conquest, here perhaps was my chance to journey—and ahead of him—to Peru. But in the agony of illness, I promised God and the Holy Mother unswerving loyalty to Gasca henceforth, if They saved me from death. Were this not enough, the friar's prayers, which I deemed to have been much responsible for my recovery, had put me forever in his debt, an obligation I could not disown while he lived. So I was committed to his cause not only by inclination but by the most sacred vows.

The kidnap scare passed while I was ill. The ship which bore Admiral Hinojosa's report to Pizarro had sailed. In spite of his occupation with me, Father Gasca had secreted a spy aboard, a Dominican friar named Francisco Barahona, who posed as a missionary priest. He was to organize the priesthood and the loyal elements in the population in advance of Gasca's coming.

God also favored me by inflicting the malady here, where there was a chance to save me. Had I been ill on shipboard or in a house less favored than the viceroy's, I should surely have died. But the disease strikes only once, so now if opportunity came for me to journey to Peru, I need have no fear of it.

My relations with Valentin and Mexía, however, were greatly complicated. They became accustomed to the viceroy's house as though it were their own, coming and going as they pleased, without anyone questioning them. I could not step from my room without finding one of them in the patio or the garden. In the tension caused by my sickness they almost came to blows, Doña Angela told me, in their zeal to serve me. Now that I was well again, I knew that I would be besieged by them. And Mexía, of course, would try to resume his nightly courtship.

Father Gasca was kind enough to say that my malady was heaven-sent to aid him. He was looking for an excuse to do nothing, waiting for his many strategies and letters to weaken Pizarro; so I provided him three weeks of excuses to see no one.

When I was most ill, Mexía told Gasca of a Negro slave named Béatriz, who was skilled in the tribal lore of my affliction. Gasca promptly bought her for 396 pesos and brought her to the vicereine's household to serve me. She it was who had lifted me to the water vat, and had alternated with Lota in rubbing my back. She remained permanently thereafter in my suite. Béatriz was an ample woman of soft voice and lovely black eyes, a calm sureness appealing after Lota's tempestuousness, an excellent seamstress and cook. I did not know how to treat a slave, and when I asked Gasca, he said she was as worthy of God's love as any other creature.

So I treated her exactly as I did Lota, and found myself in trouble for it. For example, seeing my hair fall out alarmingly, Béatriz massaged my scalp with an evil-smelling oil twice a day, and brushed my hair until my head tingled. Lota did not conceal her anger. Every time Béatriz touched me, Lota's eyes flamed up.

Just how deeply Lota was injured, I did not learn until I was well-mended. I awoke from my siesta one day to a frightful racket in the patio. Since I heard Lota's voice, I hurried to investigate.

What a tumult I discovered in the lower court. Valentin was thrashing his sword at Captain Mexía, and Lota had her dagger at Béatriz's throat.

I separated the women, figuring the men could look after themselves. Such screams and dramatics my Lota indulged, that I felt sure she was the guilty party. Béatriz, calm and silent, merely pointed to Lota's bosom from which, of course, the poniard had come. But when I told Béatriz I understood, she continued to point and Lota to protest, until I shouted to Valentin to assist me. The swordsmanship stopped at once, and both men gathered about us.

In high anger, Lota tried to rush away, but Béatriz again seized her and the fight, without the dagger now since I had taken it, began all over again. I was most embarrassed. Seeing this, Mexía bowed and withdrew, while Valentin separated the adversaries once again. I dismissed Lota and demanded an explanation of the other two.

Béatriz nodded toward the gate, through which Mexía had departed, then to the door through which Lota had disappeared, and touched her own bosom. She knew very little Spanish, and in her agitation was quite speechless. Neither Valentin nor I made sense of it. But I had in my hand a paper of Gasca's which I did not wish to leave upstairs. This Béatriz took from me, folded twice over, inserted in her bodice, withdrew again, and pointed to the door. Obviously she accused Lota of giving a note to the captain.

"Why were you fighting?" I asked Valentin tartly. I was now too weak to stand, and Béatriz helped me to a bench.

"I am ordered by Gasca to make friends of all the ship's captains, including Mexía, and win them to our cause," he said.

"You certainly were friendly," I retorted.

"Oh, that," Valentin laughed. "The captain is teaching me how to use the sword, a matter in which I would seem to require instruction."

With this reminder of the encounter with Mexía in which Valentin had been so humiliated before my eyes, I could only applaud him.

"But what is Béatriz trying to tell me, and why were you having your lesson here, disturbing the viceroy's house?"

He explained that he had called to see me and was told that I had not yet risen. As he waited, Mexía crossed the patio in company of Lota. He had been with her in the garden. Valentin thought nothing of this; the captain had met her there for short periods while I was ill, and they were often together in the town. Seeing Valentin, Mexía had suggested a lesson while Valentin waited. If nothing else, this indicated how demoralized was the vicereine's household on my account. They had hardly begun their duel when Béatriz entered, seized Lota from behind, and with one hand reached inside Lota's bodice. Out came not a letter but the poniard, over which the women were struggling when I arrived.

I could not believe that Lota would steal one of my papers or Mexía take it, since Lota could not read and would not know one manuscript from another, nor, probably would Mexía. I went upstairs and demanded of her an explanation.

Lota began to cry.

"You have stopped loving me," she wept. "Béatriz has taken my place."

I told her this was nonsense.

"No, it is not," she insisted. "Ever since you returned to your senses you have preferred her to me. But that's all right, my lady. I can get along without you. Captain Mexía will look after me."

This did not seem the time to accuse her of theft, or to inquire of her how Mexía could woo us both at once. I placated her, vowed I could not exist a day without her help, and begged her to resume her place at my side. She calmed quickly, after which I sent her on an errand.

Then indeed I searched my room. That morning, feeling strong enough to help Gasca with his correspondence, I had sent Béatriz to the monastery. She had returned with some roughly drawn letters which I was to put in proper form.

I distinctly remembered the one on top, not for its addressee, which I did not recall, but because it was written on the back of a note Gasca had received from someone else. Now in all the pile there was no such parchment. It had disappeared.

X

†

The Feast of Our Lady of Mercy was celebrated in Panama
that year in a manner which must have saddened the
Mother of Christ. In Spain it is a harvest festival, with
jousting, bullfights and family outings. In Panama City
it was a debauchery by Admiral Hinojosa's sailors, all of
whom were lonely, far from their women, and frightened
by the impending collision between Father Gasca and
Gonzalo Pizarro. After the Mass, they stormed and stripped
the taverns, for they had not been paid in two months,
and so could not buy their wine. Drunk with mob spirit
and brandy, they looted the town. By noon the respectable
population had been driven into strongly defended houses.
Such was the power of Pizarro that neither the viceroy
nor Governor Andagoya sent troops against the rioters.

In the midst of this anarchy, the mailman Pedro Gallego's galleon was blown into port by a rain-drenched
breeze stirred up by the solstice. He took his pouches
immediately to Father Gasca at the monastery, and I was
summoned from my siesta to assist the friar.

Béatriz and I set out at once, Lota having disappeared.
Rain, beginning before we set out, poured down on us as
from a milldam. Fortunately I wore a wool cloak which
shed most of the damp, though the perspiration caused by

such a garment so thoroughly doused me that I could not have been wetter in the rain.

The monastery of Thomas Aquinas lay on a gentle slope near the harbor. By now the sailors, surfeited with spoil, had fled the wet to gaming tables indoors, or soused along garden walls. We were not molested in the shabbier district, through which we walked. As we passed a small Mercedarian church, a man stepped from its porch and seized me by both arms.

"Captain Mexía!" I cried out.

I bit him until he freed my hands, then scratched his face, and kicked him. Béatriz pounded him with a stick she had picked up from the street, but he was protected by a casque and mail and did not feel her blows. Realizing her impotence, she fled.

Mexía twisted one of my arms behind my back, so that if I moved, my elbow would break. "Now we will walk down the street," he said amiably, "like two lovebirds celebrating the feast day. If you resist me, I will break your arm."

"What do you want with me?" I was angry enough to bite his fingers off, but could touch him nowhere.

"I am taking you to Pizarro," he said.

I was helpless, my wrenched arm needles of agony. We stumbled together down the hill. Only one man encountered us and he laughed. To him I was just another wench in altercation with her lover. Such women always scream for help, and never get it.

Thus we reached the waterfront, where a skiff and two sailors waited. I was thrown aboard at the bow, and Mexía, shoving off as his men seized the oars, warned me that if I jumped into the harbor he would salvage me with a boat hook.

Still the rain fell. It, the Feast and the siesta had driven everyone from the wharves.

71

"If you look behind you," Mexía said calmly when we were well offshore, " you will see a large galleon at anchor. She is my ship. We will clean her up for you, and you will be comfortable."

I was not going to show any fear. Indeed, I felt none. The anger which had boiled in me had subsided, and my wits returned. I was just provoked at my stupidity. Warned against this very event, I had forgotten it completely after my illness, thinking the danger past, and I would not have suspected Mexía, anyway. Looking about, I saw no possible weapon except a small iron anchor at my feet. The rowers were far away, even though their backs were toward me, and Mexía in the stern, untouchable. I could not jump, and the captain knew it. My clothes were too heavy, and besides, I could not swim.

"I thought," I said as we pushed into the bay, "that you wanted me for yourself."

"I do," the captain replied jauntily, "but I do not like to stand in line, and your elegant courtship is not for me. Now I will try Peruvian methods."

"And what if Pizarro keeps me for himself?"

"He will keep you, but not for long. Then he will give you back to me."

Of such monstrosity I could speak no more. I was also angered that, with such avowals of courtship and loyalty to Gasca, he had so deceived me. My Aunt Sortella had schooled me better than to be undone by such devices.

"I thought," I said unhappily, "that you were genuinely won to Gasca. You are both a good and a bad actor, Captain Mexía."

Gaily he agreed. "We have all mutually used each other in this little game, my lady," he said. "You, your stupid friar, your clumsy young lover, your foolish maid and I. Each has contributed according to his means. Never before

72

as a spy have I had opportunity for so much sport at so little peril."

"You may yet be in peril," I warned him. "When Lota discovers she has been deceived, she will kill you for your sins."

"It is one of the hazards of my profession," he answered blithely. "Mine is a recognized subterfuge, and therefore no sin, for a spy has only one loyalty, and God surely will forgive me, even if Lota does not. Did He not permit spies in Canaan? Whatever a spy does in his employer's interest is meritorious, even when it concerns gaining the intimate confidences of a lady's servant girl."

"You are a swineherd," I said.

"Call me rather a practical man," Mexía said proudly.

We were now perhaps halfway to the galleon. While we conversed, a small sloop had put out from shore, one of the harbor fishing craft, many of which seine the bay. I prayed to the Virgin that the fisherman would pass closely enough to hail, for the wind favored him. He pulled off on a long reach quartering our course. No chance.

Mexía, his back to the land, did not observe the sail, and the oarsmen were unconcerned. I dared not stare at the sloop, but even through the rain I saw that it was oddly rigged, with a long bowsprit, though the little boat carried only a mainsail. So swiftly the wind shoved her that soon she was ahead of us. Mexía saw her now, but did not heed her, since she was well away.

She tacked, and sped to intercept us.

"Row faster," said Mexía.

Only one man was aboard the sailboat. He was nude to the waist, bareheaded, and had a reddish beard. I saw him tighten the sheet as he pointed closer to the wind.

"Stop rowing," said Mexía.

As we lost way, the sloop eased her helm. There was no

doubt now that the fisherman wanted to overtake us. Mexía drew his sword and set it across his knees.

"Row," he ordered. Then louder, "Bend your backs!"

He stood up in the skiff.

Now I saw the reason for his anxiety. Only a crossbow shot across the water separated us from the sloop. Distinctly I could see an intent face at the tiller. The man was Valentin.

"Holy Mother be thanked," I prayed, "for Thy intercession and for hearing my supplication. God give him courage."

The sloop hove down on us, her mast tilted from the wind, sail tight. No matter how fast or slow we rowed now, the wind was with Valentin. He came on, securing the sheet, eyeing the angle of approach.

"He's going to ram," Mexía said coldly. "Get those oars in the boat."

Valentin stood up. Two cat steps took him to the bow of the fishing boat. He lifted the odd bowsprit in his hands. It was a harpoon such as spear fishermen use, as long and stout as a lance.

Like a knight on horseback, he charged down on us.

He had lashed the tiller and could not alter course. Observing this, Mexía commanded the oars back into the water and turned his stern toward the sloop. I bent low, held tightly with both hands, and wondered what I should do if the skiff capsized.

The harpoonist drove toward us, holding his weapon like a lance. Mexía fell on his face to avoid its point. The barb struck one of the oarsmen in the shoulder and catapulted him into the water. Valentin cruised by our stern. He was too busy even to shout at me. Dropping the harpoon, he resumed the tiller and came about. As he coursed down upon us again, he resumed his lancelike stance.

The maneuver confused Mexía. He could not fight a

harpoon with a sword, nor could he row with only one oarsman. We lay dead upon the water.

The doused sailor swam around the skiff and seized the painter close to my hand. I took up the anchor and brought it down on his fingers. He kicked aft, screaming.

Valentin was upon us again. This time he would strike us amidships. Shouting furiously, Mexía leaped to the abandoned oar. He turned the skiff so that the harpoon passed harmlessly over him as the sloop cruised almost closely enough to touch. The remaining oarsman, to escape being speared, sprawled forward toward me. With all my strength I hit him with the anchor. He dropped like a kedge in a mudbank.

Valentin flew across the wind, turned and approached. Mexía, at our stern, tried to haul his man aboard. Valentin threw his tiller hard to bear along the bow of our boat. He stood, one hand on the rudder, the other outstretched as though to catch me. He came in perfectly. Mexía, deciding he meant to board us, let the seaman fall again into the water and poised his sword.

The sloop came about. Her stern washed in a quick swish into collision with our bow. Ducking her swinging boom, I jumped. Valentin secured me in his strong, bare arm. We sheered off.

"Saint Jago!" Valentin's exultant shout leaped across the water. He let go the tiller, and kissed my rain-soaked lips. A moment later we both dived to the deck as the sloop jibed and the boom whipped about. We almost swamped.

Reminded thus of his responsibility, Valentin secured his course. The breeze would take us ashore in a few tacks to windward. The first of these brought us within hailing distance of Mexía. All three of the skiff's occupants now were in the boat and on their feet. One inspected a smashed hand, another rubbed his head. As we went by, Valentin waved boisterously. "Better luck, Captain," he called. There was no reply from the rowboat.

"It is like home," Valentin commented when we were well away. "I always used to joust on Our Lady's day, but never on a nag like this." Quickly he added, "Are you all right?"

"Wonderful," I said.

"Even in the rain you are beautiful."

"That's the test," I agreed.

"I think I should kiss you again."

"I think so, too."

He leaned forward and I aft, but the result was not very satisfactory. It reminded me of the time when I was a little girl, and a boy had tried to kiss me as we stood toe to toe on a swing; I had almost lost a tooth.

"That's no reward for a knight who has rescued you from the dragon," Valentin said.

I slid to him, put my arms around his nude shoulders, and kissed him hard. His beard was soft and moist. His lips parted.

"Ah, Lisa," he sighed. "You must let me rescue you every day in the week, and twice on Saints' days. Mind your head, we are coming about."

The sloop swung to her new course. "How did you know I needed help?" I asked. He said Béatriz had roused him from his siesta.

"You came out even without your sword!"

"There was no time, Lisa. Once you reached the galleon, I could do nothing."

He must love me very much, I thought, to rush out unarmed and half-naked to help me.

There seemed no doubt that Lota had told Mexía I was en route to the monastery accompanied only by Béatriz, and I grieved that she had been so far duped. However, she had herself given me plenty of warning.

Valentin landed us at the wharf, and carefully tied the sloop. Béatriz stood nearby under the shelter of a porch. She had a cloak for me.

I insisted on being taken directly to Father Gasca. We paused only long enough for Valentin to cover himself properly, and for Béatriz to reach the viceroy's gate. We found the friar, the sour Paniagua, and Pedro Gallego together. The latter sat jauntily in a window stripping a pineapple. The other two inspected a mass of mail; Gasca was dictating, Paniagua writing.

"Thank God you have come," Gasca said. "I was beginning to worry."

We told him of our adventure. I was a little angry that he was not more concerned. He chuckled at the description of the harpoon joust, but made plain that we had work to do, so not to prolong the tale. "Your escape is an omen," he said. "God protects us and wishes us to succeed." He put Valentin and me to work, he sorting and I copying letters.

The postman had indeed been blown off his course by Gasca's golden wind, and brought many letters destined for delivery in Peru. Taken together, they proved beyond doubt that, far from peaceful, the land of the Incas was an erupting volcano. Men complained of being searched, imprisoned and tortured, and mentioned dozens of hangings by Pizarro's Marshal Carbajal. There also was evidence that the first fruits of our many letters already delivered by Gallego were dropping from the trees. A score of missives addressed to Pizarro from the highlands warned him that a priest in Panama conspired against his lordship; and, said one, Gasca's letters "are crafty like hidden poison, designed to kill men." The friar smiled long over this.

The only evidence of the spy whom Gasca had dispatched south was contained in a communication from a captain in San Miguel, the northernmost port of Peru,

77

that Barahona had arrived there, had been arrested on suspicion, and released.

Two letters Gasca had me copy in full. One, from a merchant in Truxillo, a coastal town not far from Lima, to his brother in Spain, prophesied that Pizarro soon would be king of Peru, for he had minted new coins bearing his own likeness. "The country is intimidated from Cuzco to Charcas," he wrote. "Such cruelties does he perpetrate that throughout the country he is regarded as a fury from hell rather than a human being." The other, from a Pizarro spy, advised the governor precisely what to do, "if Your Lordship desires to be king of this land."

Pizarro had not replied directly to Gasca. Instead he had written Admiral Hinojosa a tirade in the calligraph of a scrivener, to which Pizarro had appended an ornate cipher, proving him illiterate. He said he had saved the country from ruin and would fight if Gasca entered Peru.

Long past the hour of compline, when the postman began to be impatient for the return of his mails, Gasca waved a paper. It was a petition to him from sixty-three men of Lima, demanding that he stay out of the country. They were, they said, sending an embassy to Spain to appeal for the appointment of Pizarro as permanent governor.

"See if any letter tells who these ambassadors will be," he asked us all. We searched a hundred parchments before Paniagua held aloft the answer. Pizarro advised Hinojosa to be on the lookout for the men, named as the Bishop of Lima and Lorenzo de Aldana.

"I know Aldana well," I exclaimed. "He is of Cáceres and often dined with my father in the old days. But I was small and he will not remember me."

He it was, I recalled, who had with Hinojosa helped Mexía and Gonzalo break jail at Cuzco during the civil war. Father Gasca was effusively pleased.

78

"I think, little sister," he said, "that when these gentlemen arrive, you should quit your mourning and entertain your fellow townsman in your most impressive manner. As for the bishop, God has already favored us." He did not explain this crypticism, though pointedly I waited for him to do so. As the postman secured his parcels, accepted his gold, and hurried away, Valentin stepped forward.

"Your Excellency," he addressed Gasca, "may I beg the favor of a word with you?"

The friar, absently humming a *Te Deum* to himself, was with Paniagua sorting the letters all of us had copied. His ill-featured face, favored only by its serenity and confidence, turned slowly toward Valentin as he contemplated this interruption.

"Yes, my son," he said, so quietly that his slow syllables scarcely rose above the rustle of the papers, "we are always ready to profit from your counsel."

"Sir," said Valentin, greatly encouraged, "I regret that Captain Mexía has made a fool of me. I should have suspected that he was a spy. I would redeem myself."

"Your humility is becoming," Gasca answered, "but your premise should be reversed, and therefore is no cause for regret. It is you who have made the fool of him."

Valentin lowered his head in embarrassment at this neat phrasing which restored the one asset he could not part with, his pride. Bluntly then he asked Gasca to appoint him my protector.

"Ah?" said Gasca.

Valentin proposed that he marry me, for there would be no temper in Pizarro's blade if he kidnapped a married woman.

Gasca sniffed his hawk-shaped nose, and reminded Valentin that, anywhere in the New World, to make a married woman into a widow was easily done, and he would have no burden of Valentin's death added to his sins, already onerous enough after all this stealing of letters. "No, no, Valentin," he said. "I appreciate your bravery, as I am sure our little sister does your gallantry, but it is not possible."

"I don't see why not!" Valentin flared. "I want her."

"Ah, yes," Gasca agreed placidly. "So do many others."

"Would you increase your sins by making her a cheap prize for your own ambitions, as I have heard said you will?" Valentin goaded him.

Flint struck in the friar. But he remained calm.

"My son," he said firmly, cutting Valentin as with a sword, "when you boarded our vessel unknown at San Lúcar and begged us to take you with us to the New World, we were reluctant to do so, for our design was to avoid any appearance of retinue. You appealed to God's mercy, to which every man must submit, and vowed to serve us. You have been reticent to tell us who you are, so we cannot fortify ourselves against any hazard you bring with you. You have breached our trust by tempting our little sister's emotions, which I forgive both because I can understand youth's temptations, and because our ward, protected by Christ and His Mother, has been stronger than you are. However, your very rashness, as in your encounters with Captain Mexía, has been most useful to us, and your conversations with men of the fleet have been exemplary and of great service. Yet you are young, and almost defenseless, and have much to learn. Grow up, young man. Grow up, and prove thyself. Meanwhile our little sister is my ward, and I hold myself able to protect her against Mexía, or Pizarro—or you."

He turned away, addressing his friend Paniagua.

"Brother," he said, "since this Gonzalo Pizarro says he will fight if I go to Peru, I must send an ambassador to convince him of his folly. Will you undertake the journey?"

Paniagua bowed.

"You understand the danger? Pizarro is a man of easy rages and may make you the victim of them."

"That is for God to decide," Paniagua said.

Gasca explained that he could now do nothing more until Pizarro either yielded or, formally and in writing, declared war against the king. Paniagua, clothed as the king's ambassador, would carry letters to the governor, and bring back a reply. The answer which Pizarro handed to Paniagua would be, in effect, his own death warrant or his reprieve. On his decision depended war or peace.

He then asked me to join him on the morrow for another bout of letter writing. "Meanwhile," he concluded, smiling, "continue your love of your servant Lota, who will suffer enough for her own sins, and return to her the poniard you took from her—she needs its protection on these iniquitous streets."

I was so shocked that he knew anything about the poniard that I gazed down at my bodice, although of course the weapon was not there or I should have used it against Mexía earlier in the day. Gasca was greatly amused.

Valentin escorted me home. He was withdrawn into himself and would not speak, though I thanked him again for rescuing me.

"It was gallant of you," I said finally, "to offer to marry me."

"But not of you," he retorted, "not to speak up for me."

"How could I?" I said. "I was not asked, either by him for advice, or by you for my hand. When men play games, the women are excluded."

"This was no game, Lisa," Valentin answered sadly. "I love you. I thought, from the way you kissed me today, that you loved me, too. You do not think me worthy of you. But by God I shall one day be."

"Don't swear, Valentin," I said, crossing myself. "Do not invoke God's wrath against you."

81

"You do care, then," he said. We had reached my door. I took his hand and pressed it.

"I like you very much, Valentin," I answered. "I love your loyalty and devotion. But, like Father Gasca, I wait to learn who you are and what you are made of. Prove thyself, Valentin, dear friend, and make me love you."

He smiled. "I shall remind you of your words," he said. He bowed most courteously. Here was a new accomplishment, this bow, and comely. Valentin was taking lessons in more than swordsmanship.

"Choose well your time, then," I warned him, before I retired to a much-needed rest.

XI

†

The next two months passed in the dullest boredom; every day there was rain, but little else. Captain Mexía had, of course, stopped his daily courtship, so I had not even that diversion.

Friar Gasca, however, was content. Reminding us all of the proverb, "Do not shoulder the sickle till the wheat is ripe," he waited serenely for his husbandry of letters to take root and grow in Peru, depending on the climate there to head them abundantly into long-strawed grains. But I, impetuous despite prayers for patience, was of a nature to act, not to sit. Only the vows I had made during my illness fortified me against the temptations of idleness.

I did not question Gasca's strategy. It was right as method, in a land easily inflamed to bloody arms. It was right also by God's law, as Gasca pointed out in a Michaelmas sermon he preached in the cathedral.

By the end of September, our friar and his mission to Peru were the only topics of debate in Panama. No one was neutral. Those who dared spoke Gasca's cause. They were the king's representatives, the merchants who had lost their southern trade, the new arrivals who feared Pizarro's realm since no one was secure there, the women who were not safe on streets crowded with impatient and fearful men. For each of these faithful there was a renegade whose only hope of gain lay in war and plunder. Even the fishermen stayed close to land, fearing seizure of their vessels by Pizarro's fleet. The few traders who risked the Peruvian journey either returned stripped of their goods, or disappeared into Pizarro's conspiracy. The peaceful exploration and colonization of even distant California and the River Colorado ceased. The governors and captains in all these places, and in San Miguel, San Domingo, Honduras, Nicaragua, Santa Marta and New Granada, had received letters from Gasca, in the king's name, calling on them to stand ready with arms and men. Throughout all this hot land nothing was done. Like me, everyone waited.

When Gasca appeared at the Feast of Saint Michael to preach the sermon, a great crowd of the curious responded. Most of them had never seen him. Aside from his entry into the city on Saint Dominic's day, he had been a shadow rather than a man of flesh. His ungainliness, his unattractive countenance as he ascended the pulpit in his black-hooded habit, his first stumbling words, caused everyone to wonder whether such a man could be responsible for so much ferment, which, like a closing vise, daily gripped with increasing pressure. The worshippers saw no Xíminez, no Savonarola, but rather a meek Francis of Assisi who, his clumsy hands buried in his sleeves, quietly turned to the words of Saint Paul: "Render to no man evil for evil. . . . If it be possible, be at peace with all men. . . . If thine enemy hunger, feed him; if he thirst, give him to drink; for by so doing thou shalt heap coals of fire upon his head. Be not overcome of evil, but overcome evil with good."

I, who had come to know him so well, understood that here was a summary of the man. My thoughts were paralyzed in the reality that soon this saint must collide with the master demon Carbajal, who to me, as report after report of his exploits reached us, had become the archetype of evil. Could Christ really defeat the anti-Christ? Oh, we had all heard so, in every sermon on every Michaelmas. But who of us really believed it? We so desperately wanted to think it that we held it true, ignoring beasts who daily in so many ways proved it wrong. I did not remember what Gasca said that day. I was praying for his success. There could be no peace, in Peru or elsewhere, unless Gasca proved that a monster like Carbajal and a cannon like Pizarro, who knew only force of arms, could indeed be defeated by love. Were such prayers ever answered? Not really; at least, not yet. The sword, not prayer, cut down the beasts who rose to torture the whole world with their ambitions. So I prayed for Gasca. "Oh, Holy Mother, intercede with Thy Son to give this man, His saint, a victory without bloodshed, and demonstrate to all men that evil is overcome by good. For if Gasca cannot prove it, who ever again will be saint enough to try?"

Following Michaelmas, the Feasts of Saint Luke and All Souls melted away the days. Our wait was further tensed by the departure of Paniagua. Admiral Hinojosa finally agreed to let Gasca send the ambassador as the quickest means of joining the issue of war or peace. The strain of waiting, conspiracy and tension had begun to affect him, too; for every day he saw renewed evidence that the king's men in Panama, Viceroy Mendoza and Governor Andagoya, were weary of Pizarro's arrogant domination over their authorities, and quietly were rallying the governors of Mexico, Guatemala and other colonies against him. To forestall this challenge, and gain time, he provided a ship and crew to convey Paniagua south.

But weeks passed and we heard no word of Paniagua's safe arrival. Peru or the sea had swallowed him. Such silence was ill-omened and I could scarcely bear it. Thus when, four days before the Feast of the Presentation, in late November, the brigantine bearing northward my fellow townsman Lorenzo de Aldana was sighted offshore, I threw aside my five-month mourning in ecstasy. At last I had something to do.

By now Panama was a boiling cataract of current-swept men. That very morning, as though the ship from Lima had provoked it, a gibbet had been erected in the square before the cathedral. From the haste of its construction, it was undoubtedly for prompt use. More incredible, it had been reared on order of the peaceful friar, Pedro de la Gasca.

I could not in my heart believe that Gasca would hang anyone, even though he had much cause. Yet there the gibbet stood. The men of Admiral Hinojosa's fleet trembled as every spike was driven into it, and ran expert seamen's hands over the splice in the hangman's noose. To the further peril of Pizarro's sailors, Viceroy Mendoza that day threw the prestige of his position openly to Gasca's side, a valiant defiance of Pizarro; for the first time in a year, Mendoza's troops patrolled the town against the sailors. A long line of seamen queued before the cathedral, as though ready to leap inside and claim sanctuary.

Before Aldana had even anchored, out had come all my boxes. With the help of Lota and Béatriz, I inspected and repaired my wardrobe. After months in black, how wonderful it was to run my fingers through brocades and cast my eyes on blues and azures, greens, crimsons and cloth of gold, and feel against my body again the cool of silk, the weight of damask, the sensuality of velvet!

I met Aldana at the wharf as he came ashore. It was indecent; but I approached him anyway, propriety or no, just for the sight of a new face. The men of Cáceres have always glinted their eyes at rich apparel. In my impetuosity I perhaps overdid it. Anyway, I wore a red robe made for the visit to our house in Cáceres of the great Duke of Medinaceli, with whom my father shared some cork forests in the south. It had a standing collar from which the velvet swept to the ground in a short train. Lota got me into my wooden corset by putting her knee to my back, while Béatriz laced the thongs over the tight bust. Since the robe was lined in brown, I selected a sleeved over-shawl that matched the lining, and a Lugo lace skirt with a double row of brown pearls from belt to hem. I wore my hair up, and gold slippers with crimson heels.

I remembered Don Lorenzo even before he stepped ashore. His closely cropped upper lip prompted me. His beard was as robust as any, but he affected a shaven lip because his teeth were so even-white, and he wanted to show them off. When he had dined with my father, I, peeping through the grille, had thought him all teeth. Well, he still was, for his legs were indifferent and stout, and his soldierly shoulders sagged fleshily. He had been eating and drinking too much of late, I feared, for that leanness our Cáceres menfolk favor was no longer on him. His eyes, brown, were tired and dissipated.

He received me handsomely, even pretending to remember me. When I asked him to dine at the viceroy's table that night, he acted as though he had never received such a compliment. His eyes valued my pearls—I was wearing a doublestrand necklace, too—more than my person, and he was quite surprised at what he saw. Father Gasca, who was with me at the jetty, shortly after departed with the bishop, a Franciscan named Geronimo de Loaysa, brother to the archbishop of Seville. The moment I saw him I recalled the taciturn Paniagua, who was as like his lordship as one brick matches another.

Promptly at ten o'clock Don Lorenzo appeared for dinner. I was impressed at once with Aldana's sincerity, and told him that if he were a partisan of Gonzalo Pizarro's, then the rebels in Peru indeed must have just cause for revolt.

The viceroy sensed, however, that Aldana was deeply

disturbed, and attempted to draw him out, inquiring into the rumors of Pizarro's kingship. Aldana confessed that the governor much fancied being called "his lordship," had set up a court in Lima, and dined nightly with as many as seventy followers, surrounded by servants in distinctive livery.

The zealousness of the military commander, Francisco Carbajal, had even more revolted him. "He is a devil," Aldana said, "and men who are much with him say that he is counseled by a familiar who sometimes takes the form of a wolf. No man in Peru is safe from him who does not uphold Pizarro's sovereignty, for he is determined to make Pizarro king."

He told us—Doña Angela and her fat son were also present—the facts on Carbajal's exploit which struck such fear into Lima that its citizens overthrew the viceroy Nuñez Vela. Impudently Carbajal had sent a note to Nuñez, stating that he was two leagues away and that he would enter the city that night to arrest three men who were "traitors." About midnight he rode to town on his mule, accompanied by six companions. The watch, fearful even of Carbajal's shadow in the moonlight, withdrew before him. At a lodging on the banks of the Rimac River he descended from his mule, put his shoulder to the gate, cuffed the doorkeeper spinning with a blow to the ears, and went alone into a dormitory where twenty men slept. Flashing his night lantern into every face, he found his victims, and carried them off.

The sun was just lighting the eastern mountains when the traitors—Aldana said they were men from Guamanga who had been forced into Pizarro's army but had fled— were hanged from a single tree. Carbajal explained that he was executing them as an example of the fate awaiting all men who resisted Pizarro, then calmly sat down beneath the leafless winter tree. As the bodies soared aloft, Carbajal called to the executioner, "That's high enough, now. I want them to shade me from the sun. They kept me up all night, let them give some service while I sleep."

But this was nothing, Aldana went on, to a story he had heard at Puerto Viejo en route to Panama. Near Juaja a detachment led by Carbajal encountered a Dominican friar walking alone on the great Inca highway. Suspicious of everyone, Carbajal stopped the priest and had him searched. In his garments were a dozen seditious letters to notorious rebels, including some to Diego Centeño, who alone offered organized rebellion to Gonzalo from the Arequipa caves. "He hanged the priest!"

"Was his name Fray Barahona?" I cried, thinking immediately of our own spy.

"No, that was not the name," Aldana said. He had known the friar slightly as a pious missionary of Ambato. Carbajal had hanged him over a native burial vault, then sent word to Pizarro, who was hunting in that neighborhood with a goshawk, telling him, "Come here, My Lord, and let me show you a friar who guards a sepulchre." Pizarro, arriving, ordered the priest cut down and buried. "The devil take you, Carbajal," he said; "how could you do this?" Carbajal answered, "I had to, Sire. He was a postman who carried letters from the devil Gasca."

For a moment Aldana could not eat his fish. Suddenly I thought of the rescue of Captain Mexía and Pizarro from the Cuzco jail, and of Aldana's part in it.

"Time it is, O cavalier," I sang, "time it is to flee from here."

Aldana was startled. He, too, must have remembered the days when he fought on the king's side.

"Perhaps it is time," he said. "Who is Carbajal to kill a servant of Christ? No good end can come to any man who defies God in this way."

The viceroy pushed his mood by telling him of the saintliness of Gasca, a contrast which deeply moved Pizarro's ambassador. "You must see His Excellency," the viceroy concluded, "and know these things for yourself. Then you will know also where your own loyalty lies, both to God and king."

"I must see him," Aldana said. "I have 50,000 pesos in gold to give him if he will return to Spain."

The viceroy and I both laughed aloud at this.

"He cannot be bribed, then?" Aldana asked.

"Not even with a cardinal's hat," I said.

Though the fruit had not yet been served, the viceroy rose and suggested he take Aldana to the friar at once. The vicereine likewise stood up, so Aldana could do nothing but follow Mendoza. At the door, however, Aldana held my hand longer than he needed.

"You were most gracious to receive me on my first evening," he said warmly. "I shall call again. We of Cáceres are not easily separated, are we?"

I assured him that we were not.

The two had scarcely left the house when Lota appeared, gesticulating silently toward the garden. Expecting Valentin, I followed her, and in a moment confronted Captain Mexía. I would have called the house guard, but he silenced me with the remark, "My lady mistakes my motive." Then, seeing Lota had withdrawn, he added in a whisper, "Unless by chance I might interest you in myself."

At this affront I turned to leave, but he arrested me. "I have word for your ear alone," he said. I told him to speak quickly and go. I was very angry.

"Hear this, then," he said in low tones. "Fifteen of the twenty-two captains of the admiral's fleet would surrender to Gasca."

Surely he did not expect me to believe him.

"If Gasca says the word, we will board the ships this night, kill Hinojosa and the seven resisting captains, and deliver the fleet. Then His Excellency can easily prevent Aldana and the bishop from reaching Spain."

"What new viper's sting is this?" I spat at him. "You are bold indeed to think you can fool me twice."

Again I turned away, but he spread his hands eloquently to stay me. "This time, my lady, I serve His Excellency, Father Gasca. I swear it on my hope of heaven."

"Pig and son of a pig," I hurled at him, using this epithet no lady, and few men, ever employed, to prove bluntly my contempt of him.

But he could not be insulted. Calmly he said that if the viceroy and Governor Mendoza now openly espoused Gasca, they must have good reason. Therefore the time had come for himself, and the captains, to save their own necks and wealth by begging that clemency the friar promised.

Still I did not believe him, though military adventurers have always been quick to shift allegiance to the winning side. Gasca should know of this development, however, that was sure. Perhaps he had raised the gibbet for the very purpose of frightening the commanders of the fleet into submission.

Lota appeared from the shadow and impudently draped her arm through Mexía's. This outraged me.

"Why do you come to me?" I asked the captain. "Are you so afraid of Gasca you cannot tell him yourself?"

"You are a realist; he is a dreamer. You can persuade him to accept us."

Again I scoffed, and Lota said, "Tell her about Paniagua, Captain; that will convince her."

He refused to do so, however, until I threatened to have Lota flogged until she told me herself. Then he enlightened me of intelligence sped that evening overland by swiftest Indian runner, that Paniagua's ship, running short of provision, had dropped the ambassador at Manta, in northern Quito province, far from his destination. From there he had taken canoe to Tumbez, where he had secured horses for himself and a Negro servant by stating falsely that he was in Pizarro's service. The lie had caught up with him before he had gone ten leagues. He had been arrested and jailed at Motape, after surrendering all his documents and letters.

"Something must be done," I cried. "If you are loyal as you say you are, you will help Paniagua."

"How do you suggest it be done?"

Of course I had no proposal. I told him I would haste to Gasca with the offer to seize the fleet and return with an answer; meanwhile he should think about the problem of Paniagua.

If his purpose had been to lure me from the viceroy's house at night, I forestalled it by taking with me to the monastery six members of Mendoza's household guard, and Béatriz also. Father Gasca was again in the refectory, but he was not alone. With much ceremony he introduced me to His Lordship the Bishop of Lima, Geronimo de Loaysa. Also present were the viceroy, Governor Andagoya, and Aldana. I almost showed my surprise that the spidery friar had already drawn into his web both of Pizarro's emissaries on their very day of arrival. Truly, he worked miracles. He was smiling and confident, as always, but there was a vigorous and decisive aura about him that told me his negotiations with the Peruvians were highly satisfactory.

I told them of Mexía's offer to seize the fleet. Gasca, oddly, did not doubt he told the truth. But he would not accept the offer. "Tell him," he said, "my thanks; but the fleet must surrender without bloodshed, else I do not want it." He turned back to his guests.

So I blurted out my news of Paniagua. Surprisingly, it was the bishop who rose in shocked surprise.

"You are sure of it?" he said.

I told him exactly how I had secured the information, and of Lota's prompting which had uncovered it.

"I knew my cousin had reached Tumbez, and was grieved not to see him there," his lordship said.

Gasca saw my puzzled countenance, and bowed to the bishop. "My ward does not know, Your Lordship," he said, "that Don Pedro is not only our brother in Christ, but your cousin in flesh, and for that reason he accompanied me on this undertaking."

I should have known, of course. Paniagua was of Loaysa. I should at once have identified him with the famous family which had produced two bishops from the same womb, particularly since the Loaysas, like myself, were Estremadurans and had a house at Truxillo, home of the Pizarros, not twenty leagues from Cáceres. No wonder Paniagua was so bitter-stomached, when one of his cousins was the second-ranking Church authority in Peru and the other the cardinal primate of Andalusia, archbishop of Seville, and president of the king's Council of the Indies! No wonder, too, that Gasca had brought with him the one man whose good name could not be defamed on either side of the Ocean Sea, with two such churchmen to champion him!

"If my cousin, the king's own ambassador, is imprisoned, then you have truly convinced me," the bishop told Gasca. The friar gave me a beatific glance of triumph. "But we must have verification."

Viceroy Mendoza said he would go at once to Hinojosa, who would know if the story were true. En route to the waterfront, he escorted me home.

"Gasca makes progress," he exulted. "Pizarro made a great mistake in his petitioners to the king. He should not have sent such honest men. If this word you bring is indisputable, it may nudge both Aldana and His Lordship into the king's camp. You have done well this night, my cousin."

Mexía, this time without Lota, awaited me in the patio. I gave him Gasca's answer. He shrugged and turned to leave. I had to remind him of his end of the bargain. Straightway he looked me in the eyes, and said there was only one way to secure Paniagua's release, and that was for me to go and plead with Pizarro. He said he would take me in his ship. When I laughed he swore by every holy image that he was a changed man, and that he urged me only because he was sure my action would be a great contribution to Gasca's cause, and the ship's captain who took me would therefore gain an edge on all the rivals for my hand.

"I thought," I said, "from the way you have pursued Lota, that you were no longer in line."

He shook his head in puzzlement. "I do not understand this myself," he said, ignoring the barb about Lota. "I failed to buy you, though I paid 500 gold castellanos. I sat in your sala as a suitor and won only a backache. I could not kidnap you. Now I must try the last extremity—I must become an honest man, and win you. At least the spoils of war are something I can understand."

When I said Gasca would not permit such a rash venture, he countered that the friar need not know. This quite took my breath. To reach Peru as a captive was one thing; to journey there of my own accord, another. Here, perhaps, was my chance to become an active partner again in Gasca's enterprise, and also to escape miserable Panama. Yet how foolish to trust this man, even though Gasca himself seemed assured of Mexía's new loyalty.

Mexía said he had been ordered to leave in a few days for the south. Viceroy Mendoza had a policy of dumping on Peru all the highway bandits he rounded up, to save the trouble and expense of hanging them. There were forty of them now in jail, and even Admiral Hinojosa wanted them out of the way in such an anxious time. Mexía would carry them to Guayaquil, but would gladly take me all the way to Lima.

I said I would think about it, a lame and miserable deferment which utterly unmasked to Mexía my excited desire.

XII

Lorenzo de Aldana promptly repaid my courtesy to him. He called on me next morning at eleven. He came, he said, for the good of his soul; but it was of the flesh he spoke. He told me all about himself. He was even more veteran in the New World than Captain Mexía, and younger besides, though certainly not as handsome as Valentin, my other suitor. Aldana also was, I suspected, mightily ambitious despite his wealth.

He had journeyed to New Spain during the last days of the Mexican adventure, and had joined Pedro de Alvarado y Contreras in the conquest of Guatemala. He then was persuaded, because of his courage and iron physique, to associate with Francisco Pizarro in the invasion of Peru. He shared the original Inca spoil and, to hear him talk, had greatly multiplied it. Successively he was governor of the province of Popayán which later became New Granada, was overlord of Quito, and corregidor of Lima. I gathered from his talk that he had been a stern administrator, mediaeval in his barbarity, contemptuous of the Indian populace he was supposed to protect from the rapacious settlers. If Marshal Carbajal succeeded in enthroning Pizarro, Don Lorenzo would be created Duke of Arequipa, a rich land in the far south of Peru, and the chance to found a noble dynasty appealed to his proud nature. However, he was canny enough to realize that if Gasca prevailed, he would be better off a living Croesus, vassal to the king, than a dead duke.

Anyway, he said, he needed a wife. Being of Cáceres, he was understandably fastidious. Nothing would suit him, he told me, but a girl of his own hill country who understood Estremaduran habits and spoke our tongue with the proper Castilian roll. If he joined Gasca, he asked, would he find favor with me?

I replied that I was flattered to receive the proposal of so distinguished a gentleman, but that in the absence of my father, Friar Gasca was my guardian, and he had already announced rather publicly that he would award me to whoever most helped him in the subjugation of Peru.

"So?" Aldana mused. "And you submit to that?"

"Peru is not yet subjugated, my lord," I replied, "nor am I."

He laughed. "Hear me, then," he said. "I have known you since you were in ribbons. If I should turn from Pizarro's ambassador to Gasca's general, who would have better claim to you than I?"

"I would not know, sir," I said. "Would you trade Duke of Arequipa for a king's generalship?"

"For you, why not?" he countered. "Especially since I might also be trading death for life. . . . And now, if you will excuse me, I must settle the matter with Gasca."

Had Gasca, like Joshua, commanded the sun to stand still, the rest of the day could not have been longer. As the tended glass never runs its sand, nor the watched pot boils, so a day of waiting never ends. The temperature of the public, after the arrival of his lordship the bishop, and Aldana, matched the sun over this shadeless town. On the blistered streets men hugged the walls, both for shade and protection. The air was so charged with tension that sober

97

members of the colony guarded their backs from possible attack as they screened their faces from the sun.

Shortly after noon, by Viceroy Mendoza's order, all the sailors were rounded up, counted, and sent to their berths in the harbor, lest anxiety cede to violence and brawling.

Admiral Hinojosa, however, spent the afternoon ashore. He was busy in a perspired round of calls, from the archbishop of Panama's palace in which Bishop Loaysa stopped, to Governor Andagoya's mansion which sheltered Aldana, to the monastery which housed Gasca, and to the cathedral, where God dwelt. Each time he passed my windows I saw him, weighted with age and heavy-hearted with responsibility.

His was a decision which few men, fortunately, were born to face. He entered the revolt in Peru in the honest conviction that the king's laws would ruin the country. Having committed his loyalty to Pizarro, he found the reason for that allegiance swept away by Gasca's proclamations. His dilemma was deadly. Should he remain true to Pizarro and his friends in Peru and risk the wrath of God and king, or ally with Gasca, turn back Pizarro's envoys, and invite certain death from Pizarro if Gasca failed? His instincts, I was sure, as well as his inbred knightly loyalty, were with the crown. But the king was far away, Pizarro close to hand. Who best could govern Peru: Pizarro who knew conditions at first hand, or a Hapsburg king who could not even separate good from bad advice, or truth from lies? Whatever Hinojosa's decision, I felt, watching him pass, that ultimately he would do that which he felt would benefit Peru rather than himself. He was un-Spanish in that respect.

Next morning when he sought Viceroy Mendoza's council chamber as a neutral ground for meeting Gasca, I knew that he had not yet composed his tortured mind. But he was ready to do so, that was sure.

I was not going to be excluded from this historic meeting. Since it took place in this house in which I had lived for four months, and in which I had nearly died, I greeted the guests one by one as they arrived and ushered them to the chamber as though I had every right. Such tactics always work. No man will take issue with the presence of a woman, lest she make a fool of him. Far better to ignore her, which is precisely what they did.

Viceroy Mendoza attended in the role of mediator. He was flanked at his right hand by Governor Andagoya, who had lost most of his remaining life in the anxiety of these past days. For Pizarro appeared Aldana, though more deference was paid, I fear, to the overwhelming bishop, who was not a man to yield second place in any council. At the foot of the table, in a new black taffeta cloak Béatriz and Lota had spent two nights sewing, was Fray Gasca; on his right, in the absence of Paniagua, sat Valentin. I was by the door to challenge intruders.

"The time has come," Admiral Hinojosa told Gasca after much talk had accomplished nothing, "to see these powers you possess. You have argued much, implied much, shown nothing. We would see all you have."

Gasca rose, bowed toward his lordship the bishop, and stretched a hand to Valentin, who drew from under his cape a red morocco packet bearing the crown seal in gold, opened it, and laid one of its contents on the table before our gangling friar.

"First, my commission," Gasca said, and passed it down the table for the men to see, each in turn. His manner was that of a lawyer who would disclose no second document until the first was safely back in his hand. The commission was impressively adorned with royal ribbons, and the signatures of members of the Council of the Indies, Prince Philip and the emperor.

Even Viceroy Mendoza stared frowning when he saw it,

an expression of which Gasca took quick advantage. "I see you have observed, Excellency," he said drily, "that I even have the power to send *you* home to Spain."

"I did not realize that your authority extended so far," the viceroy commented weakly.

Gasca said his power was absolute throughout the new world, not only in Peru but in all other Spanish possessions, even Hispaniola and other islands of the Carib Sea. There was nothing belonging to the crown on this side of the ocean which Gasca could not commandeer, preëmpt and use, including the royal treasury and the king's borrowing power.

"*Mirabile dictu!*" exclaimed the bishop. "But this—" he patted the document with his hand, "—gives you jurisdiction even over priests!"

"Precisely, Your Lordship," Gasca said, bowing. "Your own reverend personality is not exempt. Even priests have been known to conspire against kings and their ministers, and that event we would avoid. I have the right to banish any priest from Peru."

When the commission reached Aldana's hand, Gasca sensed at once that this arrogant conqueror could not read, so quickly spared his pride by suggesting that he summarize its contents. He was named president of the Royal Audience, or high court, and therefore was supreme judge of Peru. He was placed at the head of every department in the colony, civil, judicial and military, and was therefore, he said, a supreme autocrat. He was empowered to declare war, levy troops, appoint and remove from all crown and ecclesiastic offices.

"It is the power of the king himself," Hinojosa observed, staring shakily at the friar.

"I seem to need it, Excellency," Gasca remarked drily. But having caught Hinojosa's attention, he did not let go of it. Looking straight at the admiral, he asked Hinojosa to mark well that he had the power to confirm every man in all his wealth, both in land and Indians, or to remove such assets at his pleasure. "But there is an even more important authority," he went on, "which I hold separately."

Valentin handed him a parchment which Gasca spread on the table. "Read this well, Your Excellencies," he said forcefully, "for here lies my heart as well as my power."

It was a proclamation, conferring on Gasca a royal prerogative to pardon all offenses, and grant general or individual amnesties for crimes, without any exceptions; therefore it included Pizarro as well as all his henchmen.

Aldana threw up his hands in a gesture of surrender. He looked about, stared straight at me, and muttered the old ballad: "Time it is, O cavalier, time it is to flee from here." Then he turned back to the smiling Gasca.

"If the king reposes such confidence in you, Excellency, who am I to resist you? Permit me to be the first to beg your amnesty and accept your pardon, and I will work for you. In these authorities lies the future of Peru—and my future also." Again he gazed at me.

Gasca bowed.

His lordship the Bishop then spoke. "To resist would be treason," he said. "It would also be morally wrong. All we have ever sought is justice. That, I am now convinced, we have obtained. God has led you to us, Excellency, and to His will we humbly submit."

Again Gasca bowed. "I have prayed that Your Lordship would be moved to understand me," he replied. "There can be no doubt that our cause is undebatable and our method reasonable. I shall rely on Your Lordship's wisdom and counsel."

But Admiral Hinojosa was not so impressed. Again he asked his original question: did or did not Gasca have power to appoint Pizarro as governor of Peru?

Gasca gestured, and Valentin placed on the table four

papers utterly blank except for the crown seal and silk and the king's signature. He said these *cartas blancas* were to cover any unanticipated eventualities; therefore he did have such authority as Hinojosa bespoke. The admiral appeared gratified and would have commented, but Gasca silenced him.

"But it is not a step I would ever take," he said sharply. "Pizarro must not be governor of Peru. I am prepared to confirm him in all his wealth, and restore him as an honorable vassal in the king's sight. Beyond that anything he might ask is mere ambition for power—at the expense of all his friends and all Peru."

"It is true," Aldana admitted unhappily. "Here on this table is everything the colony ever demanded, and more. We revolted against the new laws, not against the king. I am devoted to my leader, who left his estates to defend us. But what we asked is won. I cannot be bound in honor to support Pizarro's kingship in bloody contest with the crown, that must end in the ruin of us all. I declare, my lord admiral, that honor lies in submission. Your loyalty to Pizarro ends if you receive for yourself and for him a pardon with honor."

"Why pardon?" Hinojosa insisted doggedly. "I have done no wrong."

"Not yet," Gasca injected significantly. But he said Pizarro had done grave wrong, in ousting Vaca de Castro, in dogging and killing the viceroy Nuñez, in condoning Carbajal's many hangings. "He has done much that defies forgiveness."

"Would you hang or imprison him?" Hinojosa inquired.

"Not if he yields the country to me, and promptly."

"You will write all this down?"

Gasca explained that he had already done so, in letters borne to Pizarro by Paniagua.

102

Hinojosa sighed. He looked about the table. "You are all of one mind?"

The bishop and Aldana nodded firmly, grimly.

"Then I, too, submit," the admiral said.

Gasca went to his knees, the bishop also. The other heads bowed, while the friar thanked God for the wisdom and courage of Pizarro's representatives. He then rose briskly, and turned at once to the admiral, commanding him to appear with all his sailors and captains, in the cathedral square at five o'clock. He did not mention the gibbet that stood in that very place, nor did he need to, for questions were in every eye. So the conference ended.

Lorenzo de Aldana remained behind.

"We are now partners, little cousin of Cáceres," he said.

"You spoke to the friar?"

"I did, indeed. It seems there are other aspirants, but I anticipated that, for neither Panama nor Peru has seen your like before."

I curtsied. "You honor me."

"I honor myself," he replied pompously. "You will consider me your suitor."

"I shall indeed, and proudly."

"For the present, Doña Eloisa, that is all I ask. As the friar says, and truly, let us see which of us renders greatest service in this adventure. I am confident the honor will be mine."

He kissed my hand as though I was already bargained and exchanged.

XIII

Long before five o'clock I was at my window in the viceroy's house, watching the crowd assemble. Word of the
surrender had penetrated to the far hills. Even the hus-
bandmen had deserted their harvest to see what use was
made of the ominous scaffold. The buzzards, which usually
soared over the more squalid lodgings, circled the plaza as
though they might find food there before the day ended.
The 15,000 residents of the city swarmed unanimously to
the fateful scene.

Admiral Hinojosa led his ragged sailors to the cathedral
steps and drew them up in anxious complements, then
placed his captains in a single line, with himself at their
head.

I noted carefully the actions of Captain Mexía. Like
everyone else—with the possible exception of Valentin,
since no one yet knew his motive for journeying to Peru—
I too had a decision to make that day, and Captain Mexía
was involved in it.

When first I had thought of meeting Pizarro, I considered Gasca's position hopeless against the mighty governor.
Now my feeling was precisely reversed. After the morning's
surrender by Admiral Hinojosa and Lorenzo de Aldana, I
held Gasca in much greater respect.

But I could abide no longer the inactivity of the past two

months, or the thought of being left chastely in the vice-reine's house. My only chance of honorable escape, without breaking my vows of loyalty, lay in striking out boldly for myself. If my rashness helped the friar, so much the better. In imagination I even fancied myself as persuading Pizarro to yield! At the least, I could plead for the release of Paniagua. And if Gasca lost? Then there were worse prospects than being empress of Peru.

The viceroy had ordered the plaza decorated as for the Feast of Saint Jago. The flags of Castille and León, the haughty royal standard, the viceroy's emblem, the banners of the knights of Santiago and Calatrava, and even of Montesa proving the presence of Valencians, waved on lances facing the cathedral, while broken all along the church front were the pennants of Christ, Our Lady, and the Archbishops of both Panama and Peru.

Promptly on the hour the cathedral bells struck; the wooden doors opened. A great procession of priests and friars preceded the archbishop of Panama and the bishop of Lima to the steps. Behind this splendid parade walked Gasca, alone. Slowly he ascended the scaffold and stood motionless, his head an inch from the deadly noose.

From the east came a mounted guard heralding the viceroy, who ranked his hundred men at arms in full steel and lances, fronting his own house, their backs toward my window. From the south emerged Governor Andagoya on a black stallion, his escort and pages in yellow satin and white ostrich plumes. Following from the north, threescore gentlemen of New Spain walked in pairs, exhibiting their best doublets. They ranged in two long rows before houses jammed with sightseers at every window and across the rooftops. Then the rabble, temporarily pushed aside, fought for what space remained, until from my window there was a forest of faces and nowhere could the ground be seen.

105

A brother from the Monastery of Thomas Aquinas summoned silence. Gasca stepped forward. He told the populace that the fleet had decided to uphold the king against the oppression of Pizarro. A congress of shouts scattered the buzzards.

He announced that every man of Peru who came forward this day would be pardoned of all offenses against the crown, without fear of punishment. There was another great roar, and several girls began a fandango which the viceroy's guards smothered.

Gasca nodded his head. Admiral Hinojosa, bearing in weary dignity his seventy years, slowly climbed the scaffold and presented his sword in surrender. Gasca accepted it. The admiral retired. One by one the fleet captains followed their commander, giving up their arms, then returning to ranks. Mexía, I noticed carefully, was among them, neat, shining of sword, serious and impressive.

Viceroy Mendoza paced ceremoniously to the base of the gibbet, shaded from the sun by a crimson velvet canopy held aloft at the four corners by mounted lancers. He asked all the men of the fleet who desired amnesty to step one pace forward. Without hesitation the entire line moved up, Mexía among them.

Valentin, dressed in the king's colors and white stockings, recited the oath of allegiance to Castile. The viceroy asked all the sailors to swear it. They did so loudly. Then Valentin, in stately dignity, scaled the steps to Gasca's side. He unrolled a parchment and, since he could not read, from memory intoned a proclamation from the king. It conferred free pardon for all past offenses on every man of the fleet.

Gasca placed his hand on the wind-swinging noose, and the plaza tensed.

"As ye may not enter the Kingdom of Heaven unless ye be born again," he said quietly, "so ye men of Peru who have conspired and taken arms against your king are dead by this noose. Now rise ye all again, and enter into the kingdom of your lawful lord."

He summoned to him the admiral, and each captain in turn, and handed them back their swords!

Oh, it was a dramatic moment. Everyone wept and shouted. I have never seen so many tears, even at a Requiem. The significance was overwhelming. The effect had been attained in so few words. The captains had been commissioned to command their own ships, and thus lost nothing. What greater proof of Gasca's belief in their honor than that here in the plaza, in the sight of all, he restored to the men their rights and dignities? If any pledge was needed that Gasca was a man of his word, here it was. Everyone sensed it.

The fandango started again, and this time was not halted. Street dancing and songs turned the plaza into a fiesta, through which the religious filed chanting into the cathedral, Father Gasca at the very last. Once again, as on his arrival in Panama, the townspeople saw this odd friar swallowed up by doors on which were marked the Cross of Christ.

Captain Mexía appeared beneath my window and signaled that he would dance with me, for now lutes and singers had taken over the plaza. I went down to the door to thank him and congratulate him, but did not invite him in.

"I am proud of you all," I said. "It is a glorious day for Castile."

"And for me, my lady," he answered. "I never did have much stomach for Pizarro's kingship. I am a man who prefers to serve Spain."

"Now I am willing to believe that," I said, "even though before you were a spy."

"One must live," he said, "and after all, until this day

my loyalty rightly lay with Pizarro. Do not forget that."

"I do not," I replied.

"Have you made up your mind about our little enterprise?" he asked.

Carried completely away by the impact of this momentous day, I did not hesitate.

"Come for me at the hour of the first watch," I said, "and I will be ready. Lota and Béatriz will both accompany me."

PERU

XIV

✝

Before dawn I was en route to Peru.

Such was the confusion of the vicereine's house, which had not recovered its discipline after my illness, that no one challenged us even when my trunk was carried through the garden gate with myself, Lota and Béatriz after it. Had I realized that the escape might be managed so easily, I should have brought more luggage. I hated especially to leave behind my comfortable clothes, and take only my most glittering apparel.

Our vessel was a galleon of 260 tons with the amusing name of *Santa Suzana*. I thought it quite fitting that I be borne to the land of rapine that was Peru in a ship named for the protector of chastity. The sailors had another epithet for their vessel, however. They called her *La Apurada* (The Exhausted One) because so often, belaboring this uncertain coast, she had been ransacked by winds and currents. They were superstitious of every creak of her rigging, and of course followed the tradition that a warship that harbored women would come to no good end.

Quickly we stood well out into the Gulf of San Michel, the wind freshening as we beat beyond the lee of mountainous Cape Mála. Here we picked up a peculiar wind of the Southern Ocean which blows almost steadily out of the northwest from before the Feast of Saint Nicholas until

111

after Epiphany. At this same season there also is a current, called the *Nina,* which flows south, contrary to the normal and much stronger north-north-westward sea. We had set out under the most navigable conditions of the entire year. God willing, we should hail Callao, the harbor of Pizarro's City of the Kings, in a month, about the time of the Feast of the Nativity.

I could only pray that my rash conduct did not mortally embarrass Father Gasca's enterprise. I had calculated the risks, I fancied, as would a man. I was not the least afraid for my life. Spaniards were too practical to murder a young woman in a land where the feminine commodity was scarcer than gold. My dowry was safely lodged in the monastery with Father Gasca; to possess it, anyone must gain me also. Command of my person would be easy, demanding only force and cruelty; but I was not as worried over this great weakness in my armor as I might have been three months before. Father Gasca had convinced me that there was good in every man, and a way to recruit man's nobler impulses against his baseness.

My Aunt Sortella would not have shared the friar's belief. She taught me that all men are base, but that a woman can harness any man to her cart by dangling a bag of oats before his eyes but feeding him sparingly. Between the worldly wisdom of my aunt, and Father Gasca's example, I felt armed with both sword and shield against any male adversary. The bag of oats I would dangle before this Pizarro was a trunk of my best clothes, and the contents of my jewel case.

After I consented to go with Captain Mexía, I naturally had a fit of misgiving, and almost changed my mind. Despite Mexía's oath of loyalty to the king, and Gasca's own faith in his sincerity, I still could not trust him, remembering the kidnapping. But his position really made little difference, for at least he would take me to Pizarro, and from that moment I was in his lordship's power in any case, and I relied on Lota to protect me from Mexía on the voyage. My uncertainty welled from fear that Pizarro might use me as a hostage, and force some concession from Gasca, thus embarrassing rather than helping the friar.

What jelled my resolution was the arrival of a desperate message from Paniagua. The commander who had arrested, robbed and jailed the lay brother at Motape had concluded from the letters he bore that he worked against Pizarro. So Paniagua was taken a day's journey inland from the coast to Máricavilica, where there was an Inca-built granite prison. Gasca's ambassador would be hanged unless Pizarro interceded. Someone, therefore, must plead with him, and at once. This news hardened my spirit, for an appeal to Pizarro on Paniagua's behalf seemed an employment for which I was as well fit as any other, and better than a man. Thus I forgot caution once again, and boarded the ship with great determination and excitement.

My only guilt was that I had not told Valentin of my plans. After all his befriending—and how tedious most of it must have been to him—I had left him without so much as a word. I had been tempted even at the last midnight to summon him and pay him the courtesy of trust in him, but did not do so lest he dissuade me.

But I knew that I would miss him. I loved his romantic talk; it was ornate and florid, as the wooing of young men always is, but it quickened me. When I had thought I loved Valentin, we had been at sea, en route to the New World. Now, with crackling sailcloth and chaffing timbers singing to me, I kept listening for his voice. Why was I not romantic about him ashore? Perhaps because any lad of near my own age, however clever, contrasted poorly with the older men of my Panama acquaintance: Gasca, the viceroy, Hinojosa, even Mexía. Woman is happy only with a man wiser than she, and one who could beat her if he chose. Or, as Aunt Sortella would say, there is much to be said for an old bull; he does not champ and hoof the ground, but he rules the herd. Devotion is not enough; mastery must be implicit in the relation. I think if Valentin, instead of begging, had beaten me, I would have loved him very much, as I did the day in the boat when, like a knight in armor, he rescued me from kidnapping.

On arrival aboard the galleon, I was lodged in a forward cabin reachable only by a companionway from above, thus giving me as much privacy as one ever found aboard a ship. Béatriz spread her bedding under the porthole, so that if anyone dared climb down the anchor chains and approach us, he would step on her. Such an episode was not likely, for the port was so small that only a grommet could have squeezed through it, and he with difficulty. Lota did not join us.

I saw a few of the ruffian prisoners come aboard. They were a cutthroat lot, and were taken below and chained for safekeeping. Each of them carried with him all his worldly belongings, in sea chest or duffel, for to loose even such villains in wild Peru without sword and armor would be to condemn them to quick death. These possessions were carefully locked in a storeroom, to be returned to each man on landing.

By midday we coursed well out to sea. From the deck I could see that all chance of pursuit was gone. In the harbor the wind had died and the tide turned contrary. Captain Mexía, after the watch had changed, set his course and retired to his cabin. Béatriz and I went below again, for the sun was bitter, and we had not slept during the night.

Before I had even unlaced my dress, there was a frightful pounding at the door. When I opened it, Lota fell through. She certainly had not entered of her own accord. Her face, browned under Panama's sun, was fixed and dazed. She opened her mouth several times pitifully. When

114

she would not rise, Béatriz carried her gently to her own pallet, straightened her bare legs, and caressed the back of her neck with soothing hands.

At first Lota merely shook her head back and forth. When she tried to speak she choked, as though the words she must say were better dead in her than uttered. Béatriz crooned several throaty noises, like a mother animal, and Lota, turning with a scream, threw her arms around Béatriz's great shoulders and, burying her face in the slave's comfortable breasts, wept out her agony. I went to her finally and took her hand, asking her what had hurt her.

She looked up at an oil lamp which swayed over her head, following its course with her eyes. I stroked her wild hair to neatness, and rubbed her forehead. She closed her eyes.

"God and the Holy Mother forgive me," she mumbled, "for I am the worst of sinners and hell is too easy for me. Captain Mexía has discarded me."

I put my arm around her and supported her head on my shoulder. Poor thin Lota! Her body was nothing but a faggot of bones. She told me that she had placed her belongings in the captain's cabin. Mexía, on entering his quarters, discovered her bedding. He summoned a grommet to remove the gear and throw it down my companionway. When Lota protested, Mexía slapped her face and ordered two seamen to drag her to my cabin.

The captain's action was a greater shock than this sort of treatment would usually be to a servant girl, since Lota must acquire a husband soon, and confidently expected to marry Mexía, for had he not stopped courting me about the time Lota had discovered her condition?

At the dinner hour, two boys brought in salted pork, boiled onions and fresh grapes. Lota was calm enough to eat her share. I sent the captain my compliments and asked to speak to him.

115

About eleven o'clock I was invited to his cabin. It was handsomely paneled in Mexican mahogany, had a fine Italian chest, and a Moorish fruitwood table inlaid with ivory and mother-of-pearl. The captain seated me with great courtesy and offered me a glass of manzanilla. He was comfortably clad in a loose leather jacket which he had not bothered to lace over his ruffled shirt. His legs were strong and shapely, and well set off in tight cotton hose. At ease on his own ship, alert even when relaxed, his ears cocked for alien creaks in the planking and portentous surges of wind and sea, he was an exciting individual, confident of his strength, accustomed to command.

"You wished to see me?" he said.

I asked for explanation of his treatment of Lota.

He was not perturbed. "When I swore to uphold Gasca, a vow which incidentally I believe it is opportune to obey, Lota ceased to be useful. If you mean that I should marry her, I need hardly remind you that I aspire higher. Further, I have forty ruffians below decks who, if I know the breed, will try to break out, capture my ship, and turn to piracy. Until I have landed them at Tumbez, the first good port in Peru, I must not be diverted for a moment, and indeed will scarce close my eyes. If Lota must sleep at someone's feet, let them be yours. If she bothers me, I will throw her overboard, so keep her locked up."

I told him I thought this shabby treatment of one who, from the condition of her body, had meant much to him.

"She encouraged me," he replied calmly. "And list you further, one does not inquire, arriving late at the inn, whether the bed be occupied."

"You mean," I gasped, "that you disclaim the child?"

He shrugged. "The pilot who brought you from Spain passed her on to me. Let us see when this bastard is born before we debate who should claim it. And now, by your leave, I must see to my duties."

116

On the day of the Feast of Saint Nicholas, the seventh from Panama, we passed Buenaventura, the first port of the southern mainland and chief sea outlet of Don Sebastian Benalcázar's territory of New Granada. We did not land. Still favored of wind and current, we surged smartly toward the equator along a brown, mountainous coast, standing well seaward to take greatest advantage of the wind.

In all this time, Mexía had remained close to his helm. Though often I was near by, he paid me only the courtesy of a nod. Our fifth day at sea, with the air so stifling that Béatriz and I fled our cabin for the less choking bread oven of the high poop, locking Lota below with great reluctance since we feared she might attack Captain Mexía, the brigands raised monstrous clatter in the hold below. They screamed of smothering, and rioted so loudly for water that I feared for our lives. Mexía armed his sailors with swords and pistols and stood his quarter-deck unmoved. The grommet turned the glass many times and sang his pipe-voiced call to God. The crew assembled aft for evening prayers and dispersed again. The din continued below decks.

Lota chose this time of outcry and tension to make an attempt on her life. She tried to squeeze her poor body through the porthole and so escape us. But she succeeded only in hurting herself. For two days she groaned on her bed as though her child cried within her. Béatriz huddled over her for many hours, her dark eyes whitely outlined with trouble. Of such things I knew nothing, for there even my frank Aunt Sortella had been remiss. I could only pray for Lota, and leave the ministration to Béatriz, who was wise in all of woman's afflictions.

Lota wanted very much to die. Ignored by her lover, locked in a torrid cabin, she had brooded too long and wept for herself. She felt that she had wronged me, though

I vowed tediously that she had been of great value to both Gasca and me. Her destroyed pride, which was Castilian more than Estremaduran and therefore formidable, overrode even her anger, and left her depressed and silent, an unusual condition for fiery Lota. If a priest had been aboard, I think she might have responded to confession. I tried to reason with her as a confessor might, for her sins were nothing compared to self-destruction. I pointed out that while she lived there was hope, but if she killed both herself and the child, she would be doubly damned. This made no impact on her. I did calm her, however, by reminding her that if she took her life while she was in my charge, her sin would be on me, too. She rallied at once and swore she would do me no harm.

Again the tedious days, becoming ever warmer, flamed away. Captain Mexía expected to raise Guayaquil on the first of Advent. The day preceding this season of the birth of Our Lord, we sailed well inshore on a course more easterly than south, near the Island of Puna which marked the mouth of the Guayas River and our prisoners' destination. A choppy swell and a land breeze whipped our galleon to violent pitching, until Béatriz, white-lipped and seasick, staggered to our companionway and disappeared.

Almost instantly, Lota was beside me. Béatriz, too ill for caution, had left the cabin door unlocked. In that nauseating stifle of the equator, I could not send Lota below. She was much calmer now, and needed an airing. Together we watched the sun go down, until it was only an orange eyebrow above the water.

Behind me I heard a snake-hiss in a hatchway. I swung about. Flat against the wall, rat-dirty and waist bare, crouched Valentin, a finger to his lips, one hand gripping his broadsword. As casually as I could, I strolled toward him.

"The prisoners!" he whispered. "They have loosed their chains and secured their weapons. Warn Mexía."

I raced to the quarter-deck, Lota close behind me. The captain observed our odd conduct. I shouted his peril.

He had time only to alarm all hands before the first desperado was upon him, squirming up an open hatch behind his back.

Lota saw the assassin and threw herself upon him as he raised an axe to split Mexía's skull. The attacker fell, Lota's jewel-handled poniard in his throat.

Mexía had no chance to acknowledge the debt. From below swarmed ragged men, brigands and loyal sailors together. Evidently the prisoners had broken open the arsenal, for they were well-armed.

Lota and I found perilous refuge against the pilot's bittacle as the melee became general. Mexía, his helmsman, the pilot and the deck watch defended the quarterdeck. But the sharpest fight was astern where the prisoners, enraged at Valentin's betrayal of them, screamed for his life. Their shouting attracted many sailors who, seeing tall, broad-torsoed Valentin flailing his heavy sword, joined him. Quickly Valentin organized them, reminding them they would surely die if the prisoners won the ship, thus no risk now was too great. Forty men, however desperate, were no match for twice their number of sailors under such leadership as Valentin aft and Mexía forward displayed. Systematically the ruffian leaders were isolated and cut down, and the galleon's cat-quick crew drove the others through the hatches and secured them once more.

Even before the fight ended, Mexía had turned his helm toward the adjacent island of Puna. In shallow water, by the last light of dusk, he threw overboard two spare spars. One by one the surviving bandits were heaved into the bay. All the belongings of the captives were stowed into a longboat which was set loose upon the water. Before this grisly task was finished, we had put about on a course due south by west, leaving thirty-one cursing men clinging to spars and longboat, which floated shoreward on the tide.

Mexía began to cleanse his decks and feed nine brigand dead to the sharks. Valentin for the first time put down his sword and looked about. He saw me, waved, and approached. I was still on the quarter-deck, sick at what I had seen.

Valentin's hair was matted with filth. He reeked of long confinement. His left shoulder was bloodily gashed. But he could smile.

"You did not think to leave me behind?" he asked. He was exhilarated by the fighting, with the confidence of a young man who had met his first test of arms and knew himself well-acquitted.

"You were magnificent," I said. "You fought like a veteran."

He dismissed this laughingly, reminding me that in Panama he had practiced diligently under the best of tutelage, that of Captain Mexía, a master. "I am still awkward," he said, glancing ruefully at his shoulder. "The lance and the arquebus are my weapons." Then suddenly he seized my shoulders. "Lisa, Lisa!" he cried out, "why did you not ask me to come with you? You could have trusted me."

At his touch my calm returned.

"I should have, Valentin," I said. "My conscience has troubled me about you ever since we sailed."

"And your heart?"

"I must not consult it at this moment. Excitement, and the fear that you might be killed, have done strange things to me."

All his old boyishness returned. He hugged me once quickly.

Mexía now resumed his quarter-deck, scaled his eyes across sails and sea, checked his helm, and then came forward. But it was to Lota behind me that he turned, humbly, and acknowledged himself forever in her debt. She missed her chance. Flaming, she said he owed her nothing, and that she counted on God to kill Mexía for her at a better time. Then archly, like a barefooted duchess, she stamped to our companionway and disappeared.

Valentin explained his remarkable presence. Father Gasca had known all about my flight, and had put Valentin aboard!

There was only one way to accomplish this, since Captain Mexía would never have accepted him. With Viceroy Mendoza's co-operation, Valentin had joined the prisoners. By the time Gasca summoned Valentin, the plan had already been made. He told Valentin that in view of Paniagua's peril he had, after prayerful meditation, decided that my impetuosity might serve him well. If I thought I might successfully make the first contact with Pizarro, he was inclined toward agreement.

"I am beginning to learn," he told Valentin, "that women can be of constructive use in great affairs, a lesson I should long since have met in the example of our sainted Queen Isabella."

Gasca had also admitted that no amount of study would teach him woman's method. Therefore he would not presume to advise me, but let me sail my own course, he piloting me only with prayers. But he would feel easier in conscience if Valentin, after vowing on his knees to protect me even from himself, accompanied me to the City of the Kings. He had planned to reveal himself when the prisoners were discharged, unless he learned before then that Mexía had broken his vow and was kidnapping me; in that case he hoped to head a mutiny, since all the sailors had taken Gasca's oath.

Mexía presented his thanks, but coldly. His frosty mien proved him reluctant even now to accept Valentin. He said he thought his actions had proved him loyal. "I must be even more zealous," he grinned, "having been a spy as well as a Pizarro man. But I know when the time has come for a snake to change his skin. A spy is nothing if not clairvoyant; all the stars reveal Gasca ascendant, and I do not wish to die. Therefore I have joined him. But what of you, young man? How do we know we can trust you?"

"I am as anxious as yourself to reach Peru," Valentin replied sharply.

"That I do not for a moment doubt," Mexía said, his teeth gleaming. "You give yourself away at last, proud young man of Arévalo."

Valentin flushed. Mexía attacked again. "No one," he said tautly, "could look so much like the Demon of the Andes as you do, without being his son. Come, admit it."

Weak as I was from the excitements of the day, Mexía's words quite winded me. I stumbled to a hatch cover and sat down. Mexía roared to a grommet to bring me brandy, then mercilessly resumed his offensive against Valentin.

"Our mission to Peru is perilous enough, young sir," he said, "without the presence of one untrustworthy. It is time you explained yourself."

Valentin was more ashamed than unhappy.

"I cannot," he muttered, "for I do not know, myself."

Mexía was not so easily mollified. Either he had witful answer, he said, or Valentin would be chained in the hold.

Reluctantly, every word hacking at his pride, Valentin told us why he had joined Father Gasca's ship at San Lúcar. Even as a boy playing games he had been taunted that he was not rightfully a Guerrero son, and he could not discover the truth, for the man presumably his father had been killed in the Italian wars before Valentin's age of remembrance. With his mother he lived in the Guerrero house in Arévalo and, when he became old enough, he assumed his father's knighthood among the gentlemen who owed allegiance to the town. But though he was big and strong, jousted well, and showed more than ordinary handiness with the new firearms, he was passed over, without explanation, for his father's captaincy, which had been hereditary for five generations.

When his mother died, the stories of his bastardy had circulated again, with a viciousness of which only one's boyhood friends are capable. His mother had left him nothing, any ambition he might have was blocked by the challenge to his paternity, no well-born girl would look at him. Shamed, he could stay no longer in Arévalo.

He determined to find this Carbajal and learn the truth, for everyone in Spain had heard of the fantastic exploits of Carbajal in the new world. If Carbajal, who from reports was a great personage, would acknowledge him, Valentin would throw in his lot with his father. If denied, he was at least better off than at home, for across the seas the measure of a man was his deeds, not his escutcheon.

Then, horrified, he had learned in Panama of Carbajal's true measure. Instead of seeking out a hero, Valentin discovered he sought a notorious rebel and quite possibly a demon. Now he did not know what to do. He was as illy futured in the new world as he had been in Arévalo; for which was more despicable, a black escutcheon at home, or kinship in Peru to a man hated and feared by everyone?

He did not ask us to answer his question, for he had already done so in his own mind. He had sworn at San Lúcar to serve Gasca. This he would do, for rebellion against the crown was not in him. Since deeds were the only guarantee either of the present or future in the New World, he would prove himself worthy of respect and perhaps, on Gasca's battlefields, win that knighthood which was so obscured.

And further, Valentin concluded, his spirits rising, he and Mexía seemed to have exactly the same stake in Father Gasca's enterprise. They both wanted to prove themselves worthy of me.

Mexía had no answer to this. His sword hand relaxed.

"If Carbajal is my father," Valentin added doggedly, "who better than I might persuade him to abandon rebellion and return to the king, who ever commanded his loyalty before Pizarro forced him into conspiracy in Peru?"

Mexía smiled under his odd mustache.

"Well, then," he said, begrudgingly accepting the inevitable, "we are allies because we must be. But we are also rivals, and I will kill you if you take unfair advantage on my ship."

"You forget," Valentin replied, "that I swore on my knees to protect Doña Eloisa even from myself. I will be equally zealous in protecting her from you. You taught me too much of swordplay for your own good, Captain. I could best you now."

He stared at Mexía, who answered his gaze for a long moment and then turned away, a clear admission that Valentin spoke the truth.

"And another thing," Valentin added, seeing his hand was now on top, "you have still to prove to me that you are loyal."

Again they stared at each other, and again Mexía broke the contact. Much relieved, Valentin turned to me.

"In my sea chest there is a letter for you," he said, and went immediately to get it. It was from Father Gasca.

Ever of direct mind, the friar did not reproach me. Instead, he gave me all the information which might be helpful when I confronted Pizarro. The documents Paniagua carried, he revealed, were two: one from His Majesty, commanding Pizarro's obedience to Gasca; the other, from

Gasca, inviting co-operation. Gasca begged me to be conciliatory and provoke no war.

This off his mind, he got around to me.

"Be not disturbed by false assumptions," he wrote, "that the bearer of this message carries my special patronage where your own person is concerned. Being unknown in Peru, he may be singularly advantageous to you. Perhaps God put him aboard our vessel at San Lúcar for this very purpose.

"As for yourself, make no absolute promises, for no one will help you keep them. Trust no one but God; hence never be deceived. If in danger retire, for to flee and to run are not the same, and it is better that people should say that there you ran away, than that there you died. If in doubt, recall that against God's wrath no house is strong.

"May Our Heavenly Father attend you, as will the prayers of all who love you. Return to us pure in heart, and in good season. Now go with God."

XV

✝

I had not expected to find Lima such a city. For a town which would not celebrate the eleventh year of its founding until Epiphany, it was quite remarkable and a credit to our Spanish nation. Callao, the port, was also extensive, though at our arrival the merchants wrung their hands before idle warehouses, and the dozen ships in the harbor gathered worms.

We had planned our arrival carefully, after much discussion. Captain Mexía would pretend to Pizarro that he remained a loyal spy who had prevailed on me to give his lordship a first-hand view of Father Gasca and the friar's mission. Valentin would say he had used the voyage of the *Santa Suzana* as a convenient means to reach Peru for his own designs.

Valentin proposed the interesting notion that no risk whatever was involved to any of us in such a course. No one could possibly know for many months—if our own crew remained silent—that Pizarro had lost both his fleet and his ambassadors to Father Gasca. Captain Mexía agreed, but vouched that five minutes after the sailors from the ship went ashore, there would be no further secrecy.

Here was a real peril which we could not allay, until Valentin decided that our first days in Lima would be so precarious that we might be required to run for our lives, a course impossible if the sailors were scattered through the brothels of two towns; therefore the sailors would not be permitted ashore. The *Santa Suzana* would be anchored in the harbor after discharging us, turned seaward and ready for instant flight. If we did not require such transport, the vessel would be sent north to Truxillo, where Mexía's cousin was captain of the port, and where the sailors could go ashore under oaths of secrecy. Since all the crew had taken Gasca's knife and vowed to serve him, they were all now eligible for Carbajal's noose, and thus could be relied on to keep silent.

To be sure this was clearly understood, all hands were piped on deck. Valentin, in a speech which frightened even me, warned the men of their peril if knowledge of their new loyalty became known. When he told them they would not even be allowed ashore at Callao, they were relieved rather than angry.

This disposed of all our immediate problems except that of Lota. Since she had saved Captain Mexía's life, she had become arrogant and difficult. She carried her child on a sour stomach, and was of no use to anyone.

Naturally, her spleen centered on the captain. With his desperado cargo disposed of, and under obligation to her for saving his life, he tried to rally her from her odd humor. At first she would not speak to him. But finally, only a day from our destination, the captain eased her bitter heart.

He asked me if I could part with a pretty dress. I gave him an old taffeta and Florentine gold silk, which I had brought with me only because, after my illness, it fit me better than any other. I had quite recovered my weight, so it hardly became me, and besides, the silk was drying out.

Mexía gave the dress to Lota. She put it on—it was baggy on her poor bones—and we found a gold chaplet for her hair which quite altered her appearance. She refused, however, to wear sandals, though I offered her a pair of mine.

In this attire, she giggled over Mexía's extravagant compliments like a virgin rather than a woman burdened with child. Now the captain asked me for mascarilla to daub on her cheeks, thus whitening her dark skin and covering the moons of sadness beneath her eyes. With safflower on her cheeks, and rose and cinnamon water under her arms and down her neck, she became quite gay, a mood Mexía encouraged. He told her that she could continue to occupy my cabin aboard the galleon at Callao (indeed, we could not let her out!) and that he would find an Indian to wait on her. He would, he added, also reside aboard the vessel. The implications, of course, were obvious. At this renewed interest in her, Lota rallied, putting on such airs as though she were already a captain's wife.

This incident cost me my coral beads, too. When the time came to pack, Béatriz sulked, her eyes sullen. Now and again she stared at Lota's finery, hissed jealous noises, then raised her puffy eyelids for my reaction. I did not blame her for wanting some recognition for her own miracles of diligence. I took from my jewel case the coral that wraps three times around my neck, and asked Lota to give it to Béatriz as a gratitude. Béatriz was so proud of her new possession that I suspected she would sleep with it. On her great frame, the coral did not look so large as on me, and it was not her color. But it was jewelry, for which every woman hungers.

On our final evening at sea, with San Lorenzo island a distant beacon for the port of Callao, Captain Mexía invited Valentin and me to his cabin. Sheepishly he handed me a familiar parchment. It was the document written by Gasca on the back of a letter, which had been stolen from me by Lota in Panama. It was addressed most respectfully to one Don Diego Cepeda, president of the *Audiencia*, or high court of Peru. In it, Gasca appealed to Cepeda, as a crown official, to persuade Pizarro to surrender.

Mexía told us that Cepeda had gone to Peru with Nuñez Vela to establish the first royal court in the colony, and thus to enforce the new laws. But far from being the man of integrity demanded of this position, he had conspired to overthrow Nuñez, deposed his three fellow judges, and then had written the document proclaiming Gonzalo Pizarro the governor of Peru. Now he was sole judge, and also a lieutenant general, second in command of the army under Carbajal.

Valentin proposed that he, in secret, deliver the letter. If it did nothing else, it would seem to confirm that Gasca remained virtually a prisoner of Admiral Hinojosa's in Panama, thus supporting our story of our reasons for journeying to Peru. Mexía consented. As he told me privately, such a gesture by Valentin would commit him to Gasca's cause.

We sped boldly into Callao. From the deck I saw a long rock jetty, and spacious docks well-built and as sturdy as any in Spain, behind which were so many whitewashed warehouses that I lost count at eighty. On the south shore, flying the crimson and gold banner of Castile, was a white frame customs house where cargoes must be registered and crown duties paid. Beyond, on low ground, lifted the roofs of many houses, some quite pretentious, indicating that the merchants here lived well and were numerous.

The City of Los Reyes, called Lima by everyone in a corruption of Rimac, a river from which it drew its water, was a league inland, marked from our ship only by a flat, spireless cathedral in a green valley; beyond, not far away, reared purplish, snow-purified mountains. The climate was agreeable, kind to the flowers which, as in Seville and Córdoba, flourished on every wall and in every window of Callao.

An incoming vessel now was a curiosity, due to Admiral Hinojosa's vigilance in Panama. So a sail from New Spain brought the entire male colony alongside as we put in at the customs dock. So great was this press that Valentin, in alarm lest our secret be discovered, withdrew immediately to an anchorage in the harbor, then went ashore with Mexía to report our presence and business to the officials. Soon the children on the quay remarked my presence on deck. That brought Callao's housewives running. When I say running, I mean just that. There seemed to be little feminine dignity here. When Valentin returned and escorted me ashore in a longboat to meet the captain of the port, the women crowded about so enthusiastically as to impede me. They even reached out and touched my clothes, commenting on the texture and material.

Naturally, I had dressed to impress everyone. I wanted Pizarro's first report of me to arouse his curiosity. I wore the velvet robe, the brown pearls and gold slippers which had dazzled my fellow townsman Lorenzo de Aldana when he arrived in Panama. Before me the port captain bowed handsomely as he offered me the hospitality of his own house. His wife, my first sight of a native woman, very small, with tight black hair and one simple garment that you might call a chemise, invited some ladies to meet me.

One of these I determined to cultivate. She was an aristocrat, the widow of Illan Suárez, late of Talavera de la Reina, a distinguished gentleman who reached Peru as factor for His Majesty after the conquest. He had married this woman, an Inca princess—there seemed to have been dozens of them—who on espousing Christianity took the name of Matilde. She was fair of skin, in fact as pale as the English, tall and graceful, and very rich from the fruits of an estate worked by 5,000 native slaves. She had moved from Lima to Callao after the murder of her husband, and was acid about the political confusion. I thought that a

130

little sympathy for her might reward me. She was not the least cordial to me, just curious.

Everyone was avid for news; nobody knew anything but rumor. Their tongues skipped when they mentioned Pizarro as though his very name was terrifying.

I did nothing to dispel their serenity that Hinojosa still dominated Panama. Indeed, I told the port captain that my visit was for the purpose of pleading with Pizarro to permit Gasca entry into the country. This was not a falsehood, though it implied many lies. Dozens of women, whose husbands were in the fleet, swamped Mexía for word of their men. For two turns of the glass he was busy answering questions.

During this interval I sat with the women, who wanted for nothing, from their talk, except olive oil, wine and drugs, the import of which, along with everything else, had been disrupted. One of the ladies told of a curious incident that had occurred the preceding Sunday in the cathedral in Lima. It being the last Sunday before Nativity, the High Mass was populous. Doña Hipólita Cepeda, wife of the judge to whom Valentin bore Gasca's letter, arriving at the last moment, found her usual place occupied. She moved, with her daughter and two servants, to an empty bench across the aisle. Scarcely was she on her knees when Catalina Leytón, the wife of Marshal Carbajal, descended the aisle, preceded by a cushion bearer. Seeing her wonted place preëmpted, Doña Catalina pulled Cepeda's spouse from her prayers with a tug that ripped her bodice from neck to girdle. As she rose, her breasts exposed like those of a martyred saint, Doña Catalina spat in her face and screamed for her to get out. The injured lady declined, wrapped her garment about her, and returned to her knees. Doña Catalina moved on to oust a less sturdy victim. That afternoon, the warrior Carbajal forced his way into Cepeda's house. Not finding the family at home, he shaved

131

the heads of the two servants who had accompanied Doña Hipólita to Mass. "This," said he, "warns what will happen to Doña Hipólita and her daughter Doña Andrea if they insult my wife again." Carbajal returned to his own house, expecting Cepeda to avenge the outrage. Cepeda, however, took no notice of it.

The narrator of this tale was quite unconcerned, as though this sort of barbarity occurred often. Indeed, she and others present defended Doña Catalina on grounds that her husband, as marshal of the army, outranked a man who was a lieutenant general and president of the high court.

The story prompted recollections of other scandalous brawls between women, until I was led to inquire, for my own safety, what precedence prevailed in Peru. No wonder there were fights, for I could not understand the half of their explanations. There was social distinction between appointees of His Majesty and those given office by Pizarro; between Spanish aristocrats and commoners; between knights and merchants; between veterans of the conquest and new arrivals; between the Spanish-born *chapitones* and the native Spanish *criollos,* even though their blood might be equally pure, and of course between those of pure blood and the part-Indian *mestizos.* Somewhere in all this there was rank for the Inca royalty. But who came first, second or third, I had no idea.

This female gossip was interrupted by Hernán Mexía. He had orders to bring me straight away to Gonzalo Pizarro. I had not intended to let Pizarro order me about, but there was no help for it. So important was the least wish of the governor's that I was not even given time to change my clothes. This was just as well, since I had nothing better.

A fine coach of red and black lacquer, upholstered in yellow satin, marked by the crest of the late Marquis Francisco Pizarro and drawn by four gelded blacks, conducted Mexía and me to the capital. Both driver and lackey were sumptuous in French blue uniforms ornamented in burnt orange.

"Did you ask for this interview?" I inquired of Mexía.

"No, no, but he knows everything," the captain answered. "At least we are not under arrest, or we should not be driving in this state. In all Peru there are only two coaches, the other being in Cuzco. What do you want me to do?"

"You will introduce me and say that I come of my own accord and that you are sure His Excellency—"

"His Lordship," Mexía prompted me emphatically.

"Yes, yes, I must not forget that. You are sure His Lordship would wish to know of this Gasca at first hand."

Mexía warned me, solemnly and fearfully, speaking slowly, to beware of the governor, concluding, "His Lordship is irresistible to women, whether young, old, white, red or black. He has badly treated his mistresses, and married off the mother of his son to an ugly old man, and yet she loves him."

"Of course she would," I said. "Women are fascinated by ill treatment. But no more talk. I must think before I see him."

Thus we arrived in Lima. The city was constructed like every other colonial town, around a central square as required by law. The cathedral occupied the east side of this plaza. Feeling the need for guidance, I entered it for a moment. The interior was rich enough to impress Toledo, with ornate wood carving in the choir and altar, the walls aglitter with sheets of Inca gold and silver. The tabernacle was of gold encrusted with emeralds.

Breathing a quick prayer, I went out and walked the few steps to an adjacent palace which the marquis had built, now the home of his half brother. It was lovely, of white

133

stone interrupted by two first-story oriels of carved black walnut. Two guards in chain mail and morions, their overvests of the same French blue and burnt orange which had adorned the coachmen, haunched before the gate. They arose and crossed halberds as we sought entrance.

Inside the door, there was a guardroom stocked like an arsenal with swords, spears, pikes, lances, pistols and muskets, arquebuses and crossbows enough to supply 200 men. Fifteen halberdiers in chain mail scrutinized us. Their sergeant addressed Captain Mexía cautiously, as one who did not know whether today this one-time confidant of Pizarro was friend or enemy. Mexía told him we had been summoned. We were seated on a bench. One of the guards disappeared through a door which, I observed, was defended on the inside.

After a moment a friar in mendicant orders entered. Mexía addressed him as Fray Diego Martín; he was Pizarro's chaplain. The friar asked news of Panama which Mexía supplied. They were soon joined by a squirrel-faced creature as peaked as a moulting hen, whom likewise Mexía called by name: Pedro Guillen, secretary to his lordship.

Both these men, like the sergeant-at-arms, blew both amicable and indifferent, taking no chances. My escort held himself easily, with just the proper condescension, as befitted a favorite of the governor's in the presence of his lordship's menials. I was introduced to neither, and they pretended not to notice me.

We waited a half-hour before the inner door opened again. A page boy, again in Pizarro's colors and brazening a double-curved, Moorish yataghan in a silver-studded belt, flourished a bow before me and warmly saluted Mexía.

Everyone relaxed.

"Burgos, my lad," Mexía said, "I hope I shall find my brother the governor in good health."

"His Lordship salutes you," the page responded, "and

134

bids you welcome, Captain Mexía. The lady also. You will be pleased to come this way."

We followed him through a square court, bare except for a fish pond; down a low-ceilinged hall pungent with olive oil and onions, to a rose garden, and beyond it through a sentineled aperture to a lawn where a small field tent was set up on pikes. Two men were playing at bowls, admired by six others.

Then I saw him. He was just casting the mark, his back toward me, but there was no mistaking him. He was stripped to the waist, a willow trunk a head taller than the usual Spaniard, with muscle-rippling arms and shoulders, more man than I had ever seen before on one frame. There was a surety and economy of motion in his exertion, a confidence of manner, a co-ordination of physique, a vibrant power, that quite weakened my knees and watered all my resolution. If he had turned at that moment and tried to kiss me, I should not only have let him, but enjoyed it. Such a one was he.

Like all Estremadurans he was dark of skin; unlike them he was handsome and set up like a godling. He had long brown hair and a wonderful beard neatly trimmed; stout neck and legs; durable feet on which, in casting the mark, he danced surely. His hands, like everything else about him, were big and strong.

His opponent at bowls was a thin-faced, slightly stooped skeleton with the forked beard of a lawyer and the alert eyes of an intriguer. Like Pizarro, he had removed his shirt and doublet, and played in black hose and shoes.

Pizarro watched the mark fall. He stepped back to where a thin Toledo blade was spiked in the sod, rested his hand on the pommel and addressed his adversary. Now I could see his profile, high-foreheaded, Roman-nosed. "That will hurt you," he exulted, in a virile voice.

"Your Lordship nullifies my strength and exploits my

weakness," said the other, picking up his bowl and poising on the Persian prayer rug they used as a mat.

Pizarro enjoyed this answer. "Ten castillanos in gold that I catch you on this end," he said. "You do not favor a mark so near the ditch."

"You need two points, Your Lordship. It is a rash wager."

"Good, then make it twenty castillanos," said Gonzalo. "Luck and Our Beloved Lady favor me when I need them most."

"Very well," said the skeleton. He was not happy. I knew before he bowled that he intended to let Pizarro win. He was clever about it, however—a subtle bowler. The ball obeyed his long fingers. His first cast, thrown entirely from the shoulder without visible hip movement, spun precisely. It stopped two inches from the mark, directly in front of it. None of the spectators complimented this superb shot.

Pizarro keened his eyes toward the distant target. He threw with a poetic sweep. His ball was too hard, however, glanced off the mark, and bounced into the ditch.

"A toucher! A toucher!" Pizarro cried. One of the watchers ran down the green, picked up the ditched ball, spat on it, and put it back in its position.

Forked-beard nodded gravely. His second ball was short.

"You've lost your touch," Pizarro goaded him. "You don't like a long mark." His cast curled behind the mark and lay still.

"Splendid, Your Lordship," his opponent observed. Pizarro paid no attention. He was acknowledging the plaudits of the onlookers.

The next bowl was overthrown and ditched. The man who had spat on Pizarro's ball tossed forked-beard's bowl aside. His lordship's third try was well off the mark. He swaggered resolutely, however, as though this had been his intent.

An unhappy adversary examined the green. His best shot now was to protect the bowl which was closest to the mark; but he did not make it. I was sure the action was deliberate. He shot far short. Pizarro gloated and couched his last ball in his palm. Taking a giant step, he sped his bowl with all the force of his exciting body, straight toward forked-beard's first cast. The impact brushed the defending bowl aside, struck the mark, and carried both mark and Pizarro's bowl into the ditch.

"Another toucher," said Pizarro, "and it lies in the ditch alongside the other, with the mark. Pay me."

"It is useless to oppose you," the other said.

"In all things," Pizarro answered. He pulled his sword from the ground with a flourish, strode the length of the green and jabbed his weapon again into the grass. From the encouraging shouts of the courtiers I understood that only one end remained to be played. On it, Pizarro scored a point and won the match.

Now the governor of Peru, sword again in hand, approached us. I made a low curtsy; but I could not help looking up, to see the color of his eyes, and caught him gazing down my bodice. The eyes were the blue of Italian steel.

The governor embraced Mexía on both cheeks and pounded on the back. Then I was presented. While Mexía explained my mission, the page Burgos helped His Lordship into a silk shirt with ruffled sleeves. Pizarro did not put down his sword, but passed it from one hand to the other.

"Our capital is honored by your presence," he told me. "We have too few pretty pictures here. Where are you lodged?"

I had to find a definite answer quickly, lest he select a house for me. Almost without thinking, I replied that Doña Matilde, the widow of Don Illan Suárez, had been gracious enough to offer me her hospitality, an outright lie.

His eyes pigged a bit, he squinted petulantly, and demanded, "Why she?"

"I know no other, Your Lordship."

"Where did you meet her?"

"In Callao, Your Lordship, only this morning."

Pizarro turned to his opponent at bowls, who had resumed his shirt and a black velvet doublet and stood with the other gentlemen, an ear turned in our direction.

"Diego!" he called curtly.

The sidling skeleton almost ran to us.

"We have been sent an Epiphany gift by the Magi in Panama," he said, flirting with me. "Doña Eloisa Canillejas, she who was betrothed to the late clumsy Marquis of Rioseco. Young lady, this cadaver is called many names, among them His Excellency, General Don Diego Cepeda."

Cepeda bowed, and said he had been a ship companion of my betrothed on the journey from Spain.

"You brought a big dowry, I hear," Pizarro cut in. By now he had uncovered every inch of me with his glances. I told him it remained in Panama.

Pizarro put his left hand—the right still held his sword —on Hernán Mexía's shoulder.

"So you brought only half my Nativity gift, did you, my brother?" he inquired amiably. "Are you saving the rest for yourself, as repayment for your 500 castillanos?"

Mexía said he would gladly halve the windfall, Pizarro taking the dowry, Mexía getting me. Pizarro laughed, accepted a glass of wine from his page, handed it to me, and took up another.

"To your fortunate arrival, and our better acquaintance," he said, and asked what Mexía had done on the long trip southward that he dared speak so boldly for me. I retorted that the captain had kept me isolated, but not with himself.

Pizarro was pleased. "You are a fiery devil," he said. Deliberately he touched the end of his sword to his spur. "We like to break colts, do we not, Cepeda? Fillies, especially?"

"I know Your Lordship would be gentle with any colt you sought to train," I murmured.

"A purebred Arab we have here," Pizarro riposted. He put his arm about my shoulders and said he knew that we would get along well together. Then he invited me to dine with him that evening, and directed Mexía to bring me. Mexía bowed.

The lord of Peru raised his glass to me, drained it, tossed it on the grass at his page's feet, and strode indoors.

XVI

I hurried immediately to the widow of Illan Suárez, Doña Matilde. At her gates Hernán Mexía left me, to prepare his wardrobe for the evening's banquet, so I faced the Inca noblewoman alone.

Her house was compact, small and airy, inundated with roses, poppies and flowering cacti in every possible resting place: in wrought-iron ornaments on the walls, in window boxes and floor pots, in flower beds and on stands. Even the stairway, curved and balustraded in iron, which ascended from her patio to an inner balcony, was every step adorned with blooms in an ingenious wood trough which, when filled at the top with water, was irrigated to the bottom, the excess water flowing into a lily pool.

At the foot of these stairs Doña Matilde received me. Her eyes had an inexpressive quality quite un-Spanish, derived no doubt from her Indian ancestors; they were brown and looked right through me, saying nothing. Except for this disconcerting peculiarity and the fairness of her skin, she might have been a Galician: proud, straight, tall and graceful.

She did not make the interview easy for me. Motioning me to an iron bench, she stood before me like one accused.

Greatly risking the spread of gossip, I told her bluntly that his lordship had inquired of my dwelling, and that to protect myself I had presumed on the hospitality of her house.

"Why mine?" she asked sternly, in a rich, low voice.

"Because, Your Highness, this morning you impressed me as being trustworthy."

She was pleased at this, though still arch, and she had not been surprised that I addressed her by a title reserved only for the greatest personages. She was contemptuous of all Spaniards and their ways, however, as was plain in the regal carriage of her entire body, the arch of her painted brows, the hauteur of her high-piled hair, all arrogantly Indian and in defiance of Spanish custom. Conquered or no, her spirit was Inca, unadulterated and unassailable.

"I am a sister of the Inca Manco. Does that mean anything to you?" she asked. I regretted that it did not, and quickly she said, "I thought not, or you would not have come to me. Yet I do not blame you for lacking faith in your own people. We at least are honorable."

I bowed my head to escape her unblinking eyes.

She accepted this as a sign of humility, and seated herself on another bench, as straight-backed as though she was supported by a lance.

"I will tell you a story of death," she continued, "that you may judge the impudence of an appeal to me." Her voice was expressionless and slightly singsong, yet her words, pronounced in excellent Castilian, proved that she had exerted all her Indian discipline to master thoroughly the language of her oppressors.

She told me of her nation before the coming of the Spaniard, a highly organized, industrious 16,000,000 peasants who had only one excuse for life: to serve their lord the Inca, a direct descendant of the Sun, their god. The Inca was so great that no wife was good enough for him except his own sister. So the number of his wives was limited by the number of his sisters.

141

At the arrival of Francisco Pizarro, Doña Matilde's half brother, the Inca Atahualpa, ruled the mountain empire which stretched almost from Panama south for more than 3,000 miles, and inland halfway across the continent. Atahualpa had been garrotted foully by Pizarro, though he had piled the kingdom's national treasures in Cajamarca on the promise that if he did so, he would be freed.

Doña Matilde's full brother Manco was then recognized as the Inca, and Pizarro himself put on Manco's head the llautu, which was the fillet of kingship. Manco organized a rebellion and tried to drive out the Spaniards. In this war a half million nobles and warriors were slain, before the Inca was driven beyond the eastern mountains. In his last refuge he had been murdered, only a few months before my arrival, stabbed in the back by a Spaniard with whom he played an innocent game of quoits.

I sat, hands in my lap. I could not look at her.

Then she told me of her sister. During the days of Manco's revolt, Pizarro had sent him a pony by a servant, begging his favor. To demonstrate the treachery of Spanish friendship, Manco had killed the servant and sent back his head upon the pony. Manco was at Yucay, on a swift, beautiful mountain river named the Urubamba. By this time Pizarro had already taken into his house not only the Inca Atahualpa's chief wife, Azarpay, but her younger sister Inez, who became the mother of Pizarro's daughter Francisca. Azarpay and Inez were both full sisters to Doña Matilde. When Pizarro received the head of his servant, he took Azarpay, whom he had loved, stripped off her clothes, and tied her to a stake with rushes. She was beaten. When she would not cry out, she was shot with arrows until she died. Her bloody body was floated in a basket down the Urubamba to Manco's camp.

I shuddered.

"Do not sicken, my lady," said Doña Matilde, a bitter

142

edge in her voice for the first time. "I must yet tell you about my husband."

When the Spaniards reached the capital of the Inca empire, the rich city of Cuzco in the highlands, Atahualpa was already dead. Doña Matilde resided there in the house of her late father, the last Inca before the coming of the Spaniards. When the Spaniards rushed into her palace, they saw at first only gold and silver. When that was looted, they looked at the women. Like beasts, the female members of the royal household were goaded to the plaza. In other houses, the same had happened, so that in the great square were assembled two hundred women, and all the virgins of the House of the Sacred Fire.

Gonzalo Pizarro and his friends stood beneath a tree as the women were stripped naked and paraded. He and his men made their own selections; the rest were turned over to the army. Doña Matilde was chosen by Illan Suárez, a comrade of the Pizarro brothers. After a time Don Illan, to secure legally Doña Matilde's lands and vassals, caused her to be instructed in the Christian faith, and married her.

"Unfortunately for him," the princess said, "he was a good man. By the time the viceroy Nuñez Vela arrived, Don Illan was the foremost citizen of Lima. He was appointed to welcome the king's representative, a great honor. Because he opposed the new laws, he refused. Nuñez had him dragged from bed, and brought to his presence. 'I am as good a servant of the king as yourself, perhaps better,' my brave husband said. Nuñez stabbed him with his own dagger, and would not give me the body for burial. I had to dig it up in the night from a pit behind the cathedral."

She paused, and still I could say nothing.

"Such is my personal experience of Spaniards," she went on. "Let Pizarro take you into his house. When he has tired of you, he will give you to his guardroom. It has happened to many of my people. Why should it not happen to you?"

143

I told her quickly that such brutalities soon would end. I described Father Gasca and his ambition: a new, secure future for Peru; an Inca nation to be free vassals of the king rather than slaves of the conquerors; new and just laws firmly enforced; Pizarro overthrown.

"It is too much to believe," she said.

"No woman is safe in Peru," I impressed on her. "We must make it safe."

"The women?" she scoffed.

"Lawlessness thrives only in lands where women have no force," I said passionately. "There are enough Castilian women here now to compel stability, if you Indian wives will help us."

"We would do anything," she replied. "But it seems to me that we have already experienced everything. No new bestiality can be thought of to degrade us."

"It is not of degradation I speak," I said, "but of respectability. There must be a secure society in Peru, in which families can live without fear, in which womanhood is honored, as it is in Spain."

"It is easy to say."

I thought of my Aunt Sortella. *A woman can harness any man to her cart by dangling the bag of oats before his eyes, but feeding him sparingly.*

I smiled.

"Together, Your Highness, I promise you we can find a way."

Doña Matilde arose.

"You must be very weary, child," she said. "I will send for your luggage from the ship."

XVII

✝

I had expected Valentin to inquire for me, at least; but when Hernán Mexía and the coach returned to take me to Pizarro's dinner, I still awaited my proud young man of Arévelo.

"Where is Valentin?" I asked Mexía as soon as we had set out for Lima.

"He delivered the letter from Father Gasca to Judge Cepeda," Mexía said. "I have not seen him since, except when he returned to the ship, dressed in his best, and took away his things."

"He took his sea chest?"

"He did, my lady. Without a word of explanation."

I did not wish to communicate my anxiety to Mexía, so I complimented him on his appearance. He was turned out like a gentleman, and wore a stiff dignity also, like a high wired collar. His doublet of brown brocade with red threads had red and white striped puff sleeves which matched similar stripes on his knee-length breeches. His hose were of white silk, his feet were shod in soft Córdoban galoshes polished with lampblack. On his head was a brown velvet cap, at his belt a dirk in a black leather case. Under his doublet I heard the metallic clink of a corselet; otherwise he was unarmored. Around his neck was his chain of Inca gold; on his shoulders a black velvet cloak.

"No sword?" I asked, amazed.

"The guests of Pizarro leave their weapons in the armory," Mexía explained. "The dirk is to cut the meat."

"Meat!" I exclaimed. "On the Vigil of the Nativity?"

"Oh, there will be meat," Mexía said breezily, "probably young llama. Pizarro has a dispensation from the archbishop of Lima for all the holy days except Fridays and the Lenten fasts. He must keep up his strength to defend Peru."

I was shocked.

"Do not bother your head with these things," Mexía went on. "Many of the refinements of civilization and religion have not come to Peru, and we will delay them as long as possible."

"Why?"

His sharp teeth showed through his stringy beard. "Because men are strong only in a wild country. Refinement is the creation of women; men can stand only so much of it. That's why we welcome wars, which provide excuse to throw off effeminacy, and why we are so reluctant to end war and go home."

"What an odd notion!"

"Ask any man," Mexía said doggedly. "Wars are not fought to glorify nations, but to gratify man's dreams. During wars, big men become even more bloated, and we little ones can do exactly as we please. We become men. We shake off our responsibilities, kill, rob, plunder, rape, grow rich, taste glory. All these we can only imagine while lying beside a dull wife at home, or while tilling dusty fields by day. At the wars there is neither wife nor priest to say, 'You cannot,' or 'You must.' So, until women and priests rule the world, there will be wars, and men will rush to fight them."

"You admit, then, that priests and women can civilize men?"

146

"Unfortunately, yes," Mexía sighed. "In the end, we must go back to them."

I laughed, remembering my afternoon's conversation with Doña Matilde. What a shock awaited the men of Peru!

There was no relaxation of the guard at Gonzalo Pizarro's door. The halberdiers scrutinized all who entered before passing them through the armory and up a stairs. The banquet chamber was on the story above the street. It was a long hall with a ceramic-hooded fireplace at one end. The two carved oriels which I had admired from the street both vented on this room, their shutters open to admit a splendid breeze. From these windows one could see the low roofs of Lima southward.

Pizarro had not yet entered. There were perhaps two dozen persons present, hush-voiced, expectant and uneasy. Not a man wore a sword. I looked over the three women present and felt easy in my own clothes. In the evening, one should be cool and comfortable, and thus able to concentrate on being amusing. So I had put on a white silk paletot, almost Roman in cut, embroidered at hem and neckline by silver-threaded rosettes. Under this I was protected only by an ankle-length tunic reinforced across the bust. I chose this coarse cotton garment because it concealed the little poniard, which I had recovered from Lota.

The table was laid for thirty-one. The chairs were stiff-backed of some dark wood, and had leather seats. Backing the hearth was an extravagantly carved armchair. On the table was a prostrate blanket of roses. At each place was a wooden cup designed in mastic.

Mexía and I were seated in one of the oriels when I looked up and saw Valentin. He was brilliant in a maroon velvet doublet with hose to match, and pantaloons of yellow satin. Hanging on his arm and flirting with him over a long handkerchief, was a well-developed child of about fifteen years, in rich brocade.

147

"Who's that?" I asked Mexía.

"Why, that's Valentin. Don't you recognize him in his new feathers?"

"No, no, the child."

Hernán Mexía chuckled. "You dislike competition, do you not?" he said. "Don't look so surly."

I stamped on his foot. "Tell me who she is."

"She is the daughter of His Excellency, General Judge Cepeda."

"That fat, red-faced thing behind her in the gold robe— is that her mother?"

"The fat, red-faced thing is her mother, and don't call her that to her face. She is a sensitive woman and might stiletto you."

I saw Cepeda now, in black velvet and a white ruff. He escorted Valentin and his daughter around the room, introducing them to everyone. Doña Hipólita followed behind.

Doña Andrea was fresh-skinned, ripe and pretty. She had that dark Old Castile simplicity, a combination of humility and innocence which is the product of the nun-like upbringing of Castilian women. She was excited, her face flushed, her eyes acrackle with the contained excitement of a child at her first party. Valentin was amused by her naïveté, before which he could play the hero. She turned much to him, lightly touching him each time; at this, like all men, Valentin was extravagantly gallant.

Finally they came around to us. Cepeda presented his daughter and wife to me in that order. Both of them bowed.

"Señor Guerrero favors us," Cepeda muttered in his queer, low voice. "He has consented to be our guest while in Lima. The public hostels are quite impossible."

Valentin looked uncomfortable, but met my eyes firmly. Then the door opened. Two pages entered, followed by

148

two halberdiers who took stations just inside the entrance.

"His Lordship, the Governor of Peru!" cried the page named Burgos. Everyone who was seated jumped up at once. Pizarro bent his head under the door, paused, nodded, and walked directly to me.

"Our little guest of honor is most welcome," he said, "and most beautiful."

Valentin made a sour face. His lordship at once stepped back.

"Who is this?" he demanded sharply.

Cepeda sidled between them. "He is Señor Guerrero, Your Lordship, who arrived with Captain Mexía."

"So this is he."

Pizarro looked him over cautiously. His brows pursed. "Name of God, what did you say he is called?"

"Guerrero, Sire," from Cepeda.

"Where from?"

"Arévalo, Lordship."

"I knew it, and so did you, didn't you, old fox?"

Cepeda almost imperceptibly inclined his head. "I thought it as well to offer him the hospitality of my own house."

Pizarro's eyes caught fire. "So quickly, Diego? Both ends against the middle, again?"

"I live only in Your Lordship's interest."

Pizarro shook off his ugliness, and seized my hand in both of his.

"We neglect our Nativity gift," he said. "Forgive me, Doña Eloisa. Five hours is too long away from you."

Putting his arm around my waist, he took me to the dining chair at his right hand. Before he sat down, he unsheathed his sword and spiked it lightly in the floor. The remainder of the company fell into accustomed places. Hernán Mexía, as a ship's captain, was almost at the foot of the table, his back to one of the oriels. Valentin, as escort

to the daughter of the ranking dignitary, was across from
me, only three chairs from the head of the table. Flanking
him were Doña Hipólita and her daughter. Cepeda was at
my right.

I tried to catch Valentin's eye as Fray Martín called
prayerful attention to the solemn day it was—one on
which, I thought to myself, in Spain not even the king
would give a dinner. Valentin would not look at me. He
was too busy with Andrea Cepeda.

Often during the banquet, Pizarro stretched out his
hand to cup mine, and, after the wine was on him, began
to kiss it. Then he would look over at Valentin with a speculative smile.

"Why do you look at him like that?" I asked finally. The
spiced figs, the anchovies, the crayfish, and the tuna in wine
sauce had all been carried away by servants in the same
French blue and burnt orange which Gonzalo himself
wore. We were, indeed, settled down to a roast of a strange
meat somewhat gamier and drier than veal.

"Have you ever seen my commander in chief, Francisco
Carbajal?"

"From all reports, I have no such desire," I said.

"I will tell him that," he laughed. "If this Guerrero was
sixty years older and his beard was white, he would be very
like him."

"So Valentin has been told in Panama," I said. "Could
it not be a coincidence?"

"He also is of Arévalo."

"Of a prominent family," I said.

"Carbajal has climbed in the windows of many prominent houses," Pizarro rejoined, with a spice of envy. "But
let us talk about you."

So we talked about me, and about Estremadura and
Cáceres and Truxillo; and about love, and how lonely his
lordship was, and how he needed a wife to run his impor-

tant household. All the time both of us kept half an eye on Valentin who knew we were watching him and therefore became even more gallant to the quiet girl beside him. Doña Andrea constantly smiled. She was very happy.

During the coffee, the secretary Guillen appeared in the door and lifted an eyebrow. At once Pizarro's hand went to his sword hilt.

"Diego!" he jerked. Cepeda, who had not spoken a word to me, or to anyone else, during the dinner, arose at once, bowed, and went out. In a few minutes he returned, his face serene but his long-shanked body tense.

Pizarro leaned far back in his chair, lest I overhear what Cepeda whispered to him. He nodded, and Cepeda resumed his place.

"Why is Marshal Carbajal not here?" I asked to cover this awkward moment.

"I sent him to my estate in Potosí to bring back a shipment of gold and silver from my mines. I did not want him brawling here during the Nativity season—and besides, I need the money. My expenses have increased lately."

"Are the mines rich?" I said, anything to continue the conversation, since Pizarro was no longer relaxed, and I felt a hard anger was rising in him.

"The richest in Peru," he answered. "And that is enough even for a king."

Suddenly he held out his wooden cup to the page Burgos to be refilled, drained a beaker of brandy so fast that it dripped down his brown beard, and flung the cup from him.

"How shall we amuse our guest?" he asked me, his eyes embers.

"You amuse me exceeding well, Your Lordship."

"Would you like to see our favorite pastime, little filly?"

"And that is, my lord?"

"Arresting a traitor!"

He arose, tipping over his chair. All the guests were rigid.

"Hernán Mexía!" he spat.

The little captain arose at once, white-faced.

"Sire?" he said.

For a moment Pizarro breathed heavily. Then he smiled.

"Brother of my youth, brother of the conquest," he said. "I have a letter sent overland from Tumbez, brought to that port by a ship from Panama. Would you know what it says?"

Mexía, wary and fearful, said nothing. But he must have been thinking, as was I, that it could only be the ship that had taken Paniagua south, and therefore could not possibly bring the intelligence that Hinojosa had surrendered.

Pizarro leaned both hands across the table.

"It says that you conspired to kill my admiral, with intent to place the fleet in the hands of this friar, Gasca."

Mexía crouched, looking about for escape. The halberdiers at the door rolled their eyes alertly toward the lord of Peru.

Mexía was not the only one on his feet.

Valentin, too, jumped up. In a stride he whipped the halberd from one of the guards, and in a running leap pinned the weapon against Pizarro's throat, his back to the fireplace. Pizarro fumbled for his sword. I slapped it to the floor.

Mexía spun to the oriel at his back, and jumped from sight to the street below. Immediately Valentin relaxed, and threw down the halberd, though the two guards were now on him, and the armed one was ready to axe him.

Pizarro intervened. "Back," he shouted. "That pleasure will be mine!" He ran out the door and down the stairs, alarming the guard to pursue Mexía. The halberdiers seized Valentin and held him, one on either arm.

Pizarro returned in a moment, much calmer. The street

152

outside the oriels was a confusion of shouts and hoofbeats.

"Perhaps, my lady," Pizarro told me, bowing formally, "you will do us the honor of seeing how we conduct a hanging."

"You've caught him?"

"He cannot escape Pizarro," he said, and turned to the halberdiers.

"Release Señor Guerrero," he said. "We must not treat a son of our distinguished campmaster in this unruly fashion."

Nonplused, Valentin bowed his thanks.

"I want no feud with Carbajal," Pizarro told him coldly. "Besides, you did not kill me when you had the chance; therefore you are more worthy of trust than—" he looked about the room scornfully, "—my friends who did not defend me."

He surveyed Valentin with favor. "You think quickly and are brave, young man of Arévalo," he said. "You have no fear of death. I must make better acquaintance of you."

The heart now was gone from the party. No one knew what to do or say, nor how to cater to his lordship's erratic mood. Not even Cepeda met the governor's eyes.

"I must interrupt our dinner," Pizarro said. "I like the chase, and best when my hounds pursue a traitor. Excuse me."

Everyone bowed.

"And you, young man called Guerrero, will see the lady Canillejas safely to the widow Suárez's door."

Valentin bowed. Doña Andrea's face puckered momentarily, in a broad pout.

His lordship bolted in great strides from the hall.

I followed immediately, touching Valentin's arm as Doña Andrea had done, at the same time giving the girl an uplifted eyebrow of triumph. It was ridiculous of me to show my feelings thus to a child, but I could not help it.

153

As I was about to enter my carriage, Pizarro rushed out, mounted a black stallion, and rode away, accompanied by a dozen knights and two hounds. In the confusion, the stout wife of Cepeda tugged my cloak.

"I would favor a visit from you," she murmured, and walked away quickly.

I could have kissed Valentin for saving Hernán Mexía, at the price of what must have seemed to him certain death. But even in the dark, rocking coach he did not touch me or say a word.

Finally I spoke. "Why so silent, my hero?"

"I am suddenly frightened to death," he said.

I laughed.

"Brave fear never killed anyone," I said. "You were wonderful, Valentin."

"Thank you, my lady."

"Is that all you have to say?"

"You once reminded me," he said, "to choose my time with care."

There was no answer to that. If he could not see the time when it was practically breathing down his neck, he was a booby. Or was he thinking of Andrea Cepeda?

I asked if he had delivered the letter to Cepeda. He had, and it was well-received; but Cepeda was not one who could be figured out, nor one to talk, either. He thought the judge was perhaps receptive, but cautious.

"So you moved into his house."

"Where is there a better, since Carbajal will be away for two months? I could not refuse Cepeda's offer, lest I antagonize him."

"Of course," I said. "But it has danger. I am at Callao, an hour away from you, and Mexía is gone. Our forces are already divided. We must be very careful to keep track of each other."

He did not answer.

154

"What is the matter with you?" I inquired petulantly.

"I remember how pleased you were that Pizarro kissed your hand in front of all the company. And how your eyes teased him."

"That is ridiculous."

"Did you mention Paniagua to Pizarro?"

"When was there opportunity?"

"Every moment is urgent," he said. "How do we know Paniagua is not dead already—or that the news of the fleet's loss will not arrive tomorrow?"

"You are right, Valentin," I agreed, and sought his hand. He would not take it.

"Valentin . . ."

"Yes, my lady?"

"We must not make the mistake of suspecting each other."

No answer.

"Tonight I wondered, watching you and Doña Andrea, whether perhaps you had already gone over to the enemy."

"You need not worry about me," he retorted quickly.

"Nor you about me, Valentin. We each have our method, and we must trust each other."

Silence. We rattled into Callao strangers to each other. Then I saw that the galleon was gone.

"Valentin!" I cried. "Mexía has taken our ship."

"So I see," he responded. "How else would he get away?"

"Where can he go?"

"To Truxillo, undoubtedly, where he had planned to send the galleon. At least Lota is with him, and she does not hold Pizarro's hand."

"But now you and I have no escape."

"True, my lady," Valentin said. "Do you really want one?"

With that he descended from the coach, swept his velvet hat in a bow, handed me out, returned to his seat, and rolled away.

155

XVIII

✝

I did not see Pizarro again for a week.

Among his odd contradictions was a pious fealty to the Beloved Virgin. He carried a silver image of her wherever he went, or at least so I was told. In his own way, therefore, he celebrated the holy days: first the Nativity, the day after my arrival; then Saint Stephen's and the Day of the Innocents. Perhaps also, he did not want my presence to remind him that he had failed to capture Hernán Mexía. His only bow in my direction was to send his coach to Callao for my use. I suspected that this was not exactly an act of generosity. The footman was a powerful fighting man who, I felt, was as much to guard as to serve me. How easier for Pizarro to track my movements than to convey me about, or to save me for himself than to endow me with the patronage of his equipage?

Whatever the motive, I made good use of the gift. Accompanied by the widow of Suárez, I made many holiday calls, both in Callao and in Lima. With his lordship's coach before their houses, none of the women declined to see me.

Lima was an agreeable city at that season, and easy to encompass. The avenues were unusually broad, extending from the plaza at right angles. The architect had been more ingenious than most; he had taken advantage of the straight course of the Rimac, and low ground on its south bank, to put the town in a natural depression. Where each street met the river, a stone conduit tapped the current providing an aqueduct from which the townspeople dipped an unfailing water supply at their own gates. As a result, every home had a garden, and the city was a congregation of flowers, as in Córdoba, even though here, as in Andalusia, there was no rain during summer months.

I thought at first that the agreeable temperance of the climate was merely my imagination after the furnace of the equatorial sea. Now I learned that the same fortunate wind which raced me here brought this vicinity a change in weather. All winter—the season was the reverse of that at home, so that Easter was just before the Harvest Festival—an ugly haze constantly mildewed Lima, swamping the streets and muddying everything. For the first days after its onset, everyone had violent headaches. About the first of December a southerly wind blew the clouds away, and Lima emerged as from under a cape to rejoice in flower-blooming sun and cool breezes. This change of season made doubly bright the feasts of the Nativity, which were observed here with more gaiety and less contemplation of one's sins than at home.

Doña Matilde knew everyone and was greatly respected, so I was perfectly sponsored. She still did not like me, finding my frivolous giddiness alien to her Indian impassivity. We were like a Gaul and a Moor transiently allied to resist an invader, tacitly agreed to separate once our mutual peril was allayed. We never dined together except with guests, nor spoke except to further our cabal at the expense of Peru's caballeros.

This now had taken active form. Since first I had heard the epic of the ancient Greek heroine Lysistrata, from my Aunt Sortella, who was a storehouse of saucy tales, I had admired her passionately. In Spain, where no woman thought of defying any man, Lysistrata's action was past belief and therefore glorious. The more I pondered conditions in Peru, the more I became convinced that the Greek example was worthy of emulation.

So one evening I approached Doña Matilde. I told her how the women of Athens, weary of twenty-one years of constant strife with Sparta, had been persuaded by Lysistrata to deny themselves to their husbands until the war ended. In five days the men had capitulated—and the women had dictated the terms of peace. In Peru, I told the princess, where there were so few Spanish women, and where the Indians had been disciplined for centuries to obey unquestionably the orders of their prince, Lysistrata's feminine embargo might more effectively undermine Pizarro than bloody civil war.

Doña Matilde was intrigued. Amusement flecked her wondrous black eyes, and the parting of her lips was almost, but not quite, a smile. She agreed to help, and suggested that the scheme should not be confined to Lima, but organized also in Cuzco.

To load our guns in the former capital of the Inca empire, where six thousand native women were married to Spaniards, we called on two of Doña Matilde's sisters who now were wed to important Spaniards. These ladies were about to set out together for Cuzco to visit the Princess Tocto Ussica, baptized Catalina, wife of Prince Paullu Tupac Yupanqui, the richest and most prominent lord surviving from the Inca nation. Both women consented to abet the conspiracy. They conceded Doña Matilde's argument that every Indian woman of Peru would follow us, if ordered to do so by Prince Paullu, he being the grandson of the most respected of all Incas, Huana Capac. But they reminded us that the reason for this almost unimaginable conduct must be explained carefully to the participants, and the appeal made to them that their effort might be a

158

more important weapon against Spanish atrocity than the year-long military rebellion by the Inca men against the Spaniards.

The Incas, so lately brought under the benefits of Christianity, did not appreciate the sanctity of person. The princesses told me that in former times the wives and daughters of the chiefs and tribal leaders accompanied the men to war to do the housekeeping. If the battle was lost, the women belonged to the conquerors. They accepted this gracefully. Their tradition was that on the night of defeat the vanquished women arranged themselves in a circle about the fire. One sang, the others providing a chorus. Finally the victors came, joined hands with the circle, and at a certain point in the song, each man took the female closest to him and carried her off. The Spaniards had exploited this custom.

The princesses promised to speak of their plan to Prince Paullu, and send back his decision by swift runner. Thus quite by accident I discovered that in each noble Indian household, fast foot runners still were employed, as in imperial times, to carry messages throughout Peru. They made the journey from Lima to Cuzco, a week's effort on horseback, in three days. Through this system the Indians still knew, much more quickly than the Spaniards, all that passed in Peru. In Doña Matilde's own house there were three of these Chasqui, employed not only to race messages, but also to bring fish from the sea, meat and corn from the highlands.

After the Day of the Innocents, I felt enough time had passed to accept Doña Hipólita Cepeda's invitation to call on her. I was anxious of news from Valentin, for though I had seen him several times—and heard of him in every house—he had not come to me, or sent a message. This was easily explained: he feared interception of a note; and, if he was play-acting that he and I were estranged, he dared not see me. Yet I knew that despite this logic, he would have found method had he so desired.

To this interview I did not take her highness, Doña Matilde. I wanted to be alone with Cepeda's wife, and sent her advance notice of my coming.

She was an astute woman. She had accurately construed my gesture, and received me privately in a small drawing room hung with tapestries and ornamented by scrolled plaster moldings and door frame. Excellent French chairs, a marquetry table and one of the new Aubusson carpets so popular with Charles the Fifth, and thus the height of fashion, gave the salon a boudoir air, inviting intimacy.

I recognized at once that she suffered spiritually from humiliation, and hated both her husband and her position. The traditions of Old Castile were full upon her. She had been reared to dignity and honor, courtesy and piety, security and gentility, none of which she had encountered in Peru.

"You must find here, Excellency, a most difficult life," was my opening gambit, for I thought that sympathy was the attack to overcome her.

"Why, my lady?" she responded meekly.

"Peru is no place for a lady, as I have found," I said.

She interrogated my face.

"You are a Canillejas, descended from the family of Oviedo and Valdesoto. I knew when I saw you at His Lordship's dinner that you had not forgotten the tradition of your motherland."

"It is not a thing one forgets," I said, raising my head proudly. "When all of Spain but our little corner was in infidel hands, in Old Castile and Galicia my ancestors—and yours, Excellency—preserved the gentility which alone saved them from anarchy. My blood is red with it."

"Then why did you come here?"

"To help bring Castile to Peru, madame."

Searching my eyes for hidden meanings, she wiped her perspired forehead with a white lawn kerchief. "Yes," she mused, "yes, it is as I thought, and that is why I begged you to come to me. God sent you for a noble purpose, I am sure of it; but all the devils in hell will be working against you."

"I have no fear of supernatural devils," I said, "for Father Gasca is praying for me, and as I learned in Panama when I fell ill of the convulsions, his prayers can exorcise devils, else I would not be alive today."

She believed me, and became more calm. Then she said I must realize what demoralizing degradation a woman could reach in Peru when she must warn me against her own husband. With hatred of him in every syllable, she said he was the blackest devil of them all. He had already discerned that Valentin and I had not come to Lima as innocently as we pretended, he had already begun to embroil Valentin in his designs, and would as brutally use me, given any opportunity.

Her frankness shocked me. She was no fool, for all her obesity, and therefore there might be danger in words. Was she trying to draw me into a fatal admission, or probing for information useful to her husband? No woman, surely, so damned her mate without devious design. So I sparred cautiously with her, attempting to discover her motive.

Finally it came out. Over our confidences she began to weep, gently, deep inside herself. She had not been able to cry with a woman for so long that she had forgotten how. I went to her and knelt at her feet, as a daughter of Old Castile should, and took her hands in my own. Her fingernails were deeply bitten.

161

"I could stand my own lot," she sobbed, breaking down as I touched her, "but I cannot endure what my husband is doing to Andrea. How can I raise a daughter in this awful country, when even my daughter's father conspires against me?"

She anguished out all her maternal anxiety. When Andrea was not yet fifteen, Pizarro had arrived in Lima to be governor—some said king—of Peru. At once Cepeda had cast off his royal allegiance and joined Pizarro. Doña Hipólita might have reconciled this treason, had not her husband immediately cast his daughter at Pizarro's bed.

"Only His Lordship's awe of the Holy Virgin's wrath kept him from taking my daughter, with my husband's connivance," the poor mother wept. "At least Pizarro was the more honorable."

Cepeda, however, squirmed himself high into the governor's council without the sacrifice of his daughter. The father then schemed to marry her to his lordship, for Cepeda's position was tenuous. All the gentlemen of Peru hated him for the scoundrel he was, and piled on him and his wife every indignity. His station would be secure, the insults ended, if he were father-in-law to Pizarro.

Cepeda had not abandoned this dream, but now had incubated even more complex exercises, his wife told me. He feared the arrival of Gasca. If all the men in Peru who hated Pizarro's new arrogance and Carbajal's hangings leagued with Gasca, Doña Hipólita said, Pizarro would fall. Not one to be struck, whichever way the amputated limb fell, Cepeda now hoped to make of Andrea a venery for Valentin's sport, thus insuring for himself a brother, and perhaps at the proper time a son-in-law, in case Gasca triumphed.

"And Valentin—does he go along with this?" I asked.

"A mother never knows anything," Doña Hipólita replied, still tearful. "But there are dreams in my daughter's eyes that have never been there before, and she will be terribly, terribly hurt."

This precipitated another siege of weeping.

"Andrea could do worse than Valentin," I said ruefully.

"He has bad blood," Doña Hipólita protested. "How can he be anything but a beast with such a father?"

She believed the tale, which was the talk of Lima, that Valentin was the son of Carbajal. Since the old warrior was Cepeda's greatest rival and chief abaser, she had made diligent study of him, and credited him with no virtue of any kind. She had even inquired into his antecedents through a friend in Arévalo.

To test her, knowing she would never show me so dangerous a document if she were merely shamming hatred of her spouse, I asked her point-blank to let me see her friend's reply, since a thorough knowledge of Carbajal would be of great value to Gasca. To my surprise she rose at once, went upstairs, and returned with a parchment.

"Carbajal," I read, "is not of our great house of that name, having taken the title expediently during the Italian wars to claim patronage from Cardinal Carbajal. He was born about 1463 as Francisco Lopez Gascón, the oldest son of Bartolomé Gascón and Catalina López of Rágama, near here in the diocese of Ávila. He had two brothers, both of whom married locally.

"Gascón is an honored family, with a two-story house which even has its own oven to bake bread. It is on the Calle de los Cassos. There is another and smaller family house in the Calle de Solanco, which goes up to the church and is adjacent to the market. The Gascóns own much land outside the town, and must be rich, for the church of San Salvador has a marble Gascón burial vault.

"Francisco had a good education, first from the priests, then at the University of Salamanca. In six years there he wenched every girl and was in every tavern brawl. He became known as the "Sorcerer's Apprentice," for there was nothing he could not do with the dance, the lute, the saber and the bed. He finally fled to Italy, leaving his family to pay enormous debts, but shortly returned home with a wife, a monkey and a manservant. He lived so extravagantly that when his father died, his brothers proved in court that he had already spent his inheritance. So in 1524 he returned to Italy, where he immediately gained a reputation as a warrior and a favorite of the Cardinal's. There is much talk of his exploits, but of them I know nothing at first hand."

"I should like to copy this," I said.

"Keep it," Doña Hipólita replied. "Send it to Father Gasca with my prayers that he haste here and kill the monster."

Since she was thus committed, and her loyalty, in my mind at least, beyond challenge, I told her that I had not called on her without a design of my own. I described the cabal that Doña Matilde and I were organizing, and urged her to help further it in Lima. She knew intimately every woman of station, and thus could exert influence upon the wives of the men closest to Pizarro and most likely to affect his judgment.

Her face beatified as though I had conjured a miracle. Here was a blow which she herself could strike. Instantly she said that there were 123 ladies in Lima, and she knew them all. The exact number was on a tax roll recently prepared by her husband. In addition, of course, there were hundreds of lesser women scattered throughout the colony, and of these she spoke with real pity. They, she said, were the tragedies of Peru. All had been widowed at least once in the civil wars; but since their first husbands had looted the Inca empire, they were wealthy. Now they were bought and sold like real estate for their possessions, or given as favors by Pizarro to his henchmen as often as they were widowed, a condition that encouraged murder. They, indeed, could be counted on to help.

"They pray for the day, as do I," Doña Hipólita said, "when God establishes the law in this land. Ask anything of me that will make this country safe for my daughter, and I will do it."

I told her to await a signal from me, for the plan must be timed precisely, a finesse she readily understood. We were still discussing this enterprise when into the patio within our sight came Doña Andrea and Valentin. They had been strolling together—without a chaperone—and the girl's quickening love lay on her face like an April rose on a trellis.

Possessively, Andrea brought Valentin in to greet her mother. He, I noticed, was more reserved, but greatly enjoyed this attention, and he did not drop shutters over his ardor when he saw me.

"Doña Eloisa," he said cordially, bowing. Doña Hipólita squirmed away from him by taking both her daughter's hands. "Did you have a nice walk?" she inquired.

Andrea glowed, and Valentin grinned.

"We fed the doves along the river, and I showed Valentin all the treasures of the cathedral, and twice women spoke to me and said we looked such a nice couple."

Not even this drew a blush from Valentin. When I made my excuses and departed, he followed me to the gate, and demanded whether I had interceded with Pizarro for Paniagua. When I told him I had not even seen the governor since the Eve of the Nativity, he reproached me sharply, and said that he would undertake the task himself. He had dined with Pizarro the previous evening, and was to return to the palace again, so, with my leave, he would relieve me of our most urgent obligation.

I pleaded for time, saying I believed myself better fitted for the task. He did not like this, but yielded.

"I am your servant," he said, searching my face boldly, as though he wanted me to remember when last he had said those words.

"We are both servants of Gasca," I reminded him.

He closed his eyes for a moment, then returned to the house.

My coachmen, to escape the sun, had gone to a wineshop around the corner, but came running when they discovered me. I hurried, however, to climb unattended inside and close the door, for I was sure, while speaking to Valentin, that someone lay concealed on the floor of the vehicle.

Not until we were out of town did the figure uncoil and identify himself. He was Fray Barahona, Gasca's spy, but in a queer garb for a friar. He was dressed in the leather apron of a blacksmith. He motioned me to maintain silence, and scrambled to the seat beside me.

"This evening at compline," he whispered, "I will knock at the Suárez door. I shall say you summoned a confessor."

"Good," I agreed. "That will permit us privacy without causing any gossip."

"Now no more," he said. "Kick me awake before you leave the coach, get out quickly and slam the door without help from the footman."

I did as bidden. Promptly at the hour he rang the widow's gate bell. He had resumed his Dominican habit. Since Fray Barahona had departed Panama during my illness, I knew him only by sight. He was a Madrileño, hence a practical man. Further, he was young and strong and gifted in the crafts of his people. He had learned metalwork at the forges of Escorial. As a blacksmith he could wander at will about the country, for a skilled metalworker and horseshoer found board at any inn and lodging in any house, in return for his services.

He had already traveled a prodigious area. All the letters entrusted to him by Father Gasca, inciting the towns in the north, he had now delivered. From Tumbez he had gone to Quito, in both places being detained briefly because of his Dominican robes. Thereafter, in the leather of an ironworker, he had been unchallenged. Moving south along the great Inca stone road, he had carried his "missionary" message to Lataconga, Ambato, Mocha, Riobamba, Guancavilcas, Loja, La Zarza, Caxamarca, and Guamachuco, before turning coastward to penetrate the important town of Truxillo. In each place he enlisted the priesthood to organize a cell of loyal men against the day of uprising. Now he was enroute south to Arequipa, from whence he would work eastward to the mountainous mining regions of Charcas, thence back to Cuzco.

"It is amazing," he told me, "how avidly men embrace our cause. The farther removed they are from Pizarro's justice, the bolder they are, naturally. But even in Truxillo the men are ripe for deliverance."

I told him of Mexía's experience, and inquired for the captain. Fray Barahona had heard nothing of him.

"I came to you," the friar said at last, "in anxiety, but I am now convinced that my fears are nothing."

"Fears—for me?"

"Yes, my lady. Last night I had secret discourse with Valentin in the palace of the archbishop, who was kind enough to invite the lad to his house after both had dined with Pizarro."

Perhaps I tensed unnecessarily.

"Be not disturbed. Valentin is a loyal man."

"You are sure? He has not taken you in?"

"I helped him plot a few details. His work is greatly handicapped by worry over you."

"He mistrusts me!"

"He cannot understand what you are doing. And he is jealous, a blinding emotion. I betray a confidence when I tell you that I sought you out at his request."

"This child of Cepeda's—is he making love to her?"

The friar shrugged.

"It is in the hands of God," he said. "I am in no position to speak of such things, hearing only rumors. But he is loyal to the king, and it is of that activity that I would speak."

He told me then precisely what Valentin was doing. At Cepeda's house he met everyone of importance. This gave him opportunity to call on every man privately and test his sympathies. He already knew everyone on whom Gasca could rely in the capital of Peru.

To cover this activity and withdraw suspicion, he posed as an adventurer who had seized the occasion of my departure to reach Peru himself. Now, having seen Pizarro, he claimed to doubt the ability of a meek friar to oppose so strongly armed a lord as the governor of Peru, thus confirming his lordship's circle in its own security. Pizarro admired Valentin for his courage in attacking the governor to save Hernán Mexía. Impudent boldness, said Barahona, was the language of Pizarro and Carbajal. His lordship now sought to convince Valentin of the justice of his cause, and recruit the lad into his own service. Valentin was playing a delicate game very ably, Barahona said.

"And Cepeda?"

"He is a supple reed," the friar answered. "He can blow any way at all, even in breezes so slight that you and I would not feel them. Valentin thinks he would be less dangerous to Gasca as an enemy than as an ally, for the man can touch nothing without polluting it with his own intrigue. Valentin works hard, therefore, to convince Cepeda that His Excellency, Friar Gasca, cannot win Peru."

"It is all too devious for me," I said.

"Valentin demonstrates an excellent talent for deviousness," Barahona went on. "His very ingenuousness works for him. So far he has fooled everyone; including yourself, I fear. So be on guard against your own doubts, lest you betray your colleague and he lose his life. It is a thin yarn that binds head to shoulders in this country. Do not break it."

I promised to give Valentin my blind loyalty, if he would do the same for me.

"I will so report," Barahona said. "Now I must be on my way. It is a long walk to Charcas."

"One more question," I stayed him. "Have you heard from Gasca?"

He had. The friar was organizing an army, and planned to leave Panama on Easter Day. His destination was Manta. From that northern port he hoped to move inland and then south, liberating the towns and recruiting the faithful. Barahona was to spread this definite word, but he warned me to be prudent in my use of the information, lest inquiry be made where I had heard it.

"He is coming!" I exclaimed. Now I had the one gun heretofore lacking for my salvo against Lima and Cuzco: incentive.

"Tell him not to be alarmed if I do not return to Panama. A way may be found to deliver Lima into his hands much sooner than he could expect. And perhaps Cuzco, also."

"I am sending him tonight a list of the men Valentin thinks are loyal. I shall deliver your message, and pray for your success."

I was so excited by the news that Gasca had at last emerged from his web, that I hurried at once to Doña Matilde. With this proof of Gasca's determination in hand, Prince Paullu, I was sure, would help us.

She was in the patio with a stranger.

"Doña Eloisa Canillejas?" he inquired.

I nodded.

"I have a note for you from His Lordship."

The handwriting was Scrivener Guillen's, but the ornate signature was that of Pizarro himself.

"The octave of the Nativity," the letter said, "would seem an excellent occasion to test the filly among my Epiphany gifts, along with a new merlin hawk sent me by Carbajal. We propose, therefore, to go hunting on that date, and you will join us. We leave at dawn."

XIX

†

Never having been included in such masculine sport as hawking, I had nothing to wear. By some extemporizing and the assistance of my hostess, I managed a patchwork and hoped his lordship would not know any more than I whether it was proper.

To begin with, I had a blue velvet Genoan hat with a pale blue ostrich feather. Doña Matilde loaned me a vicuña skin jacket with matching skirt fringed full around with bright beads. My high-heeled black dancing shoes were just right to finish off. Now, with leather gauntlets on my hands, and my poniard handy, I was ready to set out.

The dagger caused no end of trouble. I could not secrete it in its usual place, for if I fell from a horse, I might be impaled on it. After much thought, I had Béatriz secure it by a strap to my right thigh, just above the knee.

To prove that I could keep the lord of Peru waiting, I arrived in the carriage a half-hour late. Pizarro was seated on his black stallion which, as restive as its rider, dressaged about before the palace as I drove up. With him was a detachment of twenty guardsmen. I was instantly mounted on a bit-fighting gray Arab gelding of ancient age and bad habits, named *El Galgo* (the grayhound) and we were off at a canter.

I was annoyed that Pizarro had given me so little attention. He raced ahead of me, carrying lightly on his left fist a little falcon no taller than a candlestick. We traveled north, forded the Rimac River at a shallows and turned west upstream. Within a few minutes the topography completely changed. From green valley we swept out into a brown plain, bare except for intermittent willow clumps along the river and infrequent outcrops of gray stone which harbored wind-beaten shrubs. Pizarro reined up before one of these boulders and at last recognized my presence.

"Hawks work best in the first light," he said petulantly. "You have probably ruined our sport."

"I'm sorry, Your Lordship," I said. "I am not accustomed to rising before the dawn."

He inspected my person, particularly the beaded fringe at the edge of my skirt, and smiled.

"I have always wondered what a lady wore ahunting," he said. "Now I know. She wears Indian beads."

"I was at some care to dress for you, Your Lordship."

"Then I forgive you for being late," he answered. "I'd rather catch you today than a bird, anyway. And so would you, wouldn't you, my beauty?" Here he addressed the hawk gently, and slowly stroked its head with a finger of his right hand. "Her name is *Navajada* (the knife). Isn't she pretty?"

The hawk, ugly and unblinking, her wings folded to within two inches of her tail, and her long slender toes spiked into Pizarro's gauntleted thumb, seemed to enjoy the caress.

"I thought hawks were fisted with a hood over their eyes," I said.

"Goshawks, tarfells, sparrow hawks, gyrs and peregrines, yes; a really good merlin doesn't need it. She flies poorly out of a hood."

"What does she catch?"

"Out here, we'll be lucky to stir up a nest of crows. The

test will be her first lark. There are some around here somewhere."

We rode on. The sun, and a dusty drift of wind, were both unpleasant.

Soon Pizarro began to sulk. I wondered what he had told his companions while he awaited me, when he was even annoyed that the birds refused to heed him. Evidently his escorts had their orders, for they remained behind us, out of earshot.

We approached a scrawny field of newly planted ground.

"That's maize," said Pizarro. "If no crows come in to eat the fresh seed, we'll go home."

We took shelter behind a cluster of great rocks large enough to conceal the entire party. Pizarro did not even look at me. For long minutes he squinted down the wind toward the river. Finally he tensed and showed his teeth.

"The crow is cunning," he hissed at me, "but he who catches her is more so. Here they come."

Lazily flapping toward the cultivated ground, moving upwind, a group of eleven crows approached. The falcon restlessly lifted a claw several times.

Pizarro raised his arm and cast the hunter. She shot away, wings outspread, measured the quarry, and turned straight toward her victims. The crows swerved downwindward for greater speed, grouped together. Like a puff of cannon smoke, the hawk vaulted high above them, by arching threats forcing them to turn back into the wind. This accomplished, she stretched, turned over, and dived. Through the center of the flight of crows she bolted, raking one of them fiercely with her claws.

"A beauty!" Pizarro cried exultantly. He galloped away for better vantage.

The wounded bird swiftly lost height. Heartlessly its companions raced away.

Up swooped the falcon again, high above her victim.

The crow did not fall. It hobbled along after its fellows, far behind them and at much lower altitude. The falcon struck again. A few feathers splashed from the forlorn crow before it pitched into the haven of a tree along the river bank.

Pizarro was close by, shouting to his companions. One of them dismounted and began to climb the tree, while the falcon fanned the sky in zooming circles. Surrendering to this double attack, the crow toppled from its branch. Instantly the hawk was upon it with her talons.

"Good, good, my beauty," Pizarro exclaimed, as he retrieved the hunter. "Carbajal trained you well."

He fed the pet from his hand a vile-looking pigeon's wing, which the hawk ripped apart viciously.

We flushed no further game in an hour, which was as long as Pizarro could tolerate inactivity. We returned to the river bank, dismounted, and watered the horses.

Then with great ceremony Pizarro seated me on the grassy bank, surrendered the hawk to a page's fist, doused his entire head in the river, and reclined beside me, his hair and beard dripping.

"Well," he said. "How do you like our sport?"

"I find it most brutal, Your Lordship. What sport is it when the victim has no chance to get away?"

"The crow eats our food and does not deserve to live," he rejoined. "The lark, now—that's a battle!"

"But the result inevitable," I persisted. "How would you like to be attacked by someone twice your size?"

"Many times I have fought two men at once," Pizarro laughed. "And—as you see—I am still alive. It is always a thrill when the lark, by speed and cleverness, gets away."

"So the next day you come out with a cleverer hawk, and destroy the lark, which has done nothing to hurt you, which is not good to eat, whose only sin is that he was valiant enough to oppose you."

174

"That is true, my beauty. Perfectly true. I cannot rest until an escaped lark has been brought to earth."

"Why?"

"Why, for the sport!"

"That's what I'm trying to understand," I pressed him. "I fail to see the sport of killing a defenseless creature."

"Hear me," his lordship replied intently. "God did not give me wings to fight larks in the air. I triumph over natural law when I find the lark's natural enemy, another winged creature, train her to my will, and make her win for me. There is a tremendous thrill in it. The same applies to the hound against the boar, and the ferret against the hare."

"And the gun against a fellow man," I said.

"Well, yes, I suppose so. Carbajal, now. I could never best him with a sword, but I could shoot him."

"And since God did not intend you to do that, either, I suppose that, too, would be sport?"

"It is always exciting to win against the odds, whether in war, or with a hawk, or a fishing line, or at bowls, dice or cards.

"For that matter," he swung closer to me, "breaking a colt and training her to obey, is the greatest sport of all."

"Again the hawk against the lark," I murmured.

He laughed aloud, and took my hand. He lay on his stomach, looking up at me.

"I could love you, Eloisa," he said.

"What makes you think so, my lord?"

"You talk up to me. No woman before has ever challenged me in any thing. You are exciting."

"I might scratch your eyes out, Your Highness."

"That also would be exciting." He began to play with the beaded fringe of my skirt.

I stood up.

"I am not a lark, my lord."

He rose to his knees and seized me. I did, indeed, scratch his eyes. Suddenly his face flamed with rage as I backed away from him, for my poniard was in his hand.

"Wretch!" he flung at me. "You come armed, against Pizarro?"

"I did not touch the weapon, Your Highness," I said, quivering with anger, "and you are vile for discovering it. You know very little, sir, about gentling a colt."

I retreated toward my tethered horse. At this signal, the rest of the party leaped to join us. Pizarro mounted in a fury, fisted his hawk, and galloped away.

I could not leave this mood on him, for I had not yet mentioned the subject of Ambassador Paniagua. So I pursued him. When he realized that it was I who spurred behind him, he slowed to a walk and waited for me. My poniard was in his belt.

"I must teach Your Lordship better manners," I said, forcing a smile.

"How would you begin?" He was still angry, but pleased that I had followed him.

"My first lesson would be on kindness," I answered, "and gentleness. Spain has come to Peru, my lord, whether you like it or not. I am not an Indian."

"Forgive me," he said. "I have never known anyone like you."

"Then learn from me, sir."

He brightened, sensing a new amusement.

"Very well, I am your pupil. What do I do first?"

"You return my dagger."

He looked surprised.

"Oh, no," he laughed. "This is a memorial I will not part with. It also is a lesson of sorts."

"You will return me my dagger."

"No."

"You are a stubborn scholar," I said. "For the moment we will go on to lesson two."

"What does that require of me?"

"A gesture, my lord."

Again he was surprised.

"A gesture?"

"At Máricavilica, near Motape, one of your captains has imprisoned a crown ambassador named Don Pedro Hernandez Paniagua."

"I know all about that," Pizarro cut in irritably.

"I'm sure you do, Highness. You greatly lack courtesy in making him suffer thus. He has done nothing to you."

"This game of going to school does not include such matters. They are for grownups, not for schoolboys. Get on with your instruction."

"The lesson was to be on courtesy, my lord," I said, "and Paniagua is as good an example as any. But if you are a coward as well as a clumsy love-maker, find someone else to teach you."

I really slapped him across the face with those words. He reared in his saddle, disturbing the hawk, and causing the stallion to stumble.

"If a man called me a coward, he would die for it," he spat at me.

"You will not receive Paniagua. Therefore you are afraid of Father Gasca. For a man of your strength, with an army at your back, to fear a frocked priest is cowardly, is it not?"

"I will not listen to you."

He spurred viciously, and galloped far across the plain. I needed all my strength to keep Galgo from following. At last I mastered the brute, and proceeded across the brown earth at a serene walk.

When Pizarro saw that I would not again pursue him, he returned to me at a canter.

"You are a devil and need to be beaten," he said.

I glanced at him, almost daring him to try it, but said nothing.

"Besides, this Paniagua does not need to come here. I have his documents."

"I was sure you had, Your Lordship. Otherwise you would not be so afraid."

"What would be accomplished by his coming?"

"Nothing, perhaps, except to prove that the hawk does not need to fear the crow."

"Who are you working for, him or me?" Pizarro said with renewed interest.

"In this case, sir, for you. I should hate to let Gasca think you are not strong enough even to receive his ambassador. Deeming you so weak, he might come here without your consent. He is a fine man, and I should not like to see him die."

Pizarro, whose mood could change faster than a juggler's tricks, was immediately gay again.

"What if I receive him and send him packing?"

"It is precisely what I should do if I were you. You are the master here. How can you better prove it than by receiving Paniagua, surrounded by your captains, in your own palace, with a loyal city at your back? Let him see what you are, and what folly it would be to oppose you."

He was intrigued.

"If I send for him, what about you?"

"What about me, my lord?"

"Would you return to Panama with him?"

I pretended to think long about this. Then I answered, "No, Your Highness. I have made my bed in Peru. Now I intend to lie in it."

"With a good husband?"

"It is every girl's desire, and I am not getting younger."

"Promise me you will not go away when I dismiss Paniagua?"

"I will indeed, my lord."

He slapped his rein hand briskly.

"Then I will do it. It is one way to keep you here."

"I very much want to stay."

"We will see more of each other. A student should see his instructor regularly."

"As you wish, Your Highness. I think you might profit by my lessons."

He surveyed me drolly, winked at me, and smiled.

"And you, too, rash young filly, will learn from the instruction. What is the proverb? 'The teacher learns more than the pupil.'"

"It is often so, my lord," I said, and smiled boldly at him.

We rode on, following the river. Pizarro was silent. From time to time his eyes squinted into the sky. Now and then he glanced speculatively at me. Then he became galvanic. Before us a bird took wing from a gorse-covered rock.

Instantly Pizarro cast his falcon. The hawk raced after her prey.

"Now we shall see what my beauty can do!" Pizarro shouted. "Come on. We must be fast to follow this flight."

Already the adversaries were almost out of sight, climbing recklessly. As the lark rose, the hawk scaled higher, striving to get on top. But this was no cumbersome crow, rather a bird as fleet as herself, though without quite the rising power. Each time the hawk threw her body up to dive, the lark broke away in a circle, ever climbing, straightening upwind long enough to measure the pursuit, then dartfully out again in a wide arc.

Twenty times the birds circled. Now they were so high

that only the larger hawk was plainly visible from the ground; the flitting, twisting, turning, looping lark a faint meteor only.

"She's been fed too much and exercised too little," Pizarro called. "She should be on top by now."

The hawk gained altitude, and began to drive the lark down.

I prayed to God and the Virgin to let the lark escape. But at each attack the lark lost height. It would race downwind to gain speed, wheel into the wind to rise, to be met instantly by its cruel oppressor.

"She's sluggish," Pizarro complained. "The lark eludes her."

Again the hawk climbed above, lay to her side and plunged. Again the lark, seeming to stop in mid-air, avoided the deadly rush.

But this time the hawk did not soar back to the attack. She kept coming down, in a sprawling spiral, like a leaf thrown from a tower. She struck the earth, bounced, and lay still. The triumphant lark vanished down the wind.

Pizarro reined up.

"It sometimes happens," he explained ruefully. "Not enough heart for the work. Under the exertion, the heart broke, killing her. I must tell Carbajal his gift comes from a weak strain."

I raised my eyes to the sky into which the lark had disappeared.

"Thank you, Father; thank you, Mother," I whispered.

And then to Pizarro, I added, "Lesson number three, Your Lordship, might be that occasionally the lark is stronger than the falcon."

Pizarro surveyed me impudently, appreciating my meaning.

"There will be another day," he said. "As I told you, I will not rest until the lark is brought to earth."

XX

✝

The twelfth night of the Nativity and next day's feast of
Epiphany were observed much differently in Lima than
at home. In Cáceres, professional mummers performed
before the altar in all the churches, after which families,
even down to unkissable cousins, assembled in the best
house of each connection to exchange gifts. Next morning
we all went to Mass again, to hear the priest announce the
date of Easter, which was calculated by His Holiness'
astronomers in Rome.

Just a year ago I was a part of all that. Since then I
had traveled from Cáceres to Seville to Cádiz to San Lúcar
de Barrameda to Panama to Peru, an odyssey unimaginable
when I was born, for Panama City was then only nine years
old, and the existence of Peru was unknown. I left Spain
an intended bride, and now had not even a lover, though
several suitors, none of whom I knew a year ago.

In the widow Suárez' house in Callao there was no
observance of the twelfth night. Indeed, I had the best
sleep in some time. I was up early, to attend the Epiphany
Mass at the cathedral in Lima. Everyone was to be there,
so why not I? I wished to be thought important in this
country. Besides, the date of Easter in this year of 1547
had unusual significance, and I must know whether it
was late or early. If Gasca planned to sail for Peru that

day, thus endowing his venture with all the significance of the Resurrection, I must calculate my own plans to coincide with it. At least it would be an easy date for all to remember.

I drove to Lima in a peculiar silence. I should have been accompanied by church bells all the way. But not even the cathedral tolled welcome to Epiphany. From all over town, gentlemen walked with their ladies and servants to the house of God. I alighted from the coach amid a press of people, some of whom made way for me as though they had heard I belonged to Pizarro and therefore enjoyed a special favor.

"Why are there no bells?" I demanded of the almoner at the door.

"They have all been melted for Pizarro's cannon," he replied, careful to let his voice imply nothing.

Inside, I did not know where to sit. Remembering tales of the mayhem which had overtaken those who were presumptuous enough to preëmpt favored places. I chose a bench less than halfway down the aisle, close enough to hear the sermon, but beyond the range of feminine jealousy.

Soon I saw Valentin. He entered with the Cepeda family, and sat beside Andrea. He was dressed in a brilliant military uniform of French blue, trimmed in burnt orange, the Pizarro colors!

The archbishop of Lima, accompanied by a splendid procession, entered and assumed his chair. The Mass began.

I was on my knees when I felt a tap on my shoulder. Looking up, I saw Pizarro. He beckoned to me. Clearly, I was to follow him. With him was a gentleman I had met once briefly at Doña Matilde's house: Judge Benito Suárez, brother of Doña Matilde's late husband. He was a veteran of the conquest, one-time confidant of Marquis Pizarro, now high in Gonzalo's esteem. His hands were bloody, for he, to avenge his brother's murder, had caused the viceroy Nuñez to be beheaded on the battlefield of Añaquito, and thus invited the wrath of the king. He had as much reason as any man in Peru to fear the coming of Friar Gasca.

In this traitorous company, I was handed down the main aisle, through the rail, and seated in a loge to the left of the altar, facing the archbishop's chair. This box, crimson-canopied and marked with the armorial bearings of the late marquis, conferred churchly distinction on the ruler of Peru. If any of the 2,000 worshippers had doubted that I enjoyed Pizarro's patronage, they were now convinced. I wondered what Valentin must think, and dared not look toward him.

I also wondered, as the archbishop himself proclaimed April 10th as Easter Day during his sermon, whether Pizarro and Suárez who sat beside me, and Marshal Carbajal, far in the mountains of Potosí, sensed that the date had more than religious significance for them. But Pizarro was not listening, and Suárez did not stir.

After the Mass, Valentin sought me out as I waited for my coach.

"Your new uniform is radiant," I greeted him.

"Thank you, my lady," he replied with calm reserve. "It is the equipage of the commander of Pizarro's household troops."

Before I could recover from this surprise, he added, "I should like to pay an Epiphany call upon you this evening, if you would not be disturbed. I have a friend I want you to meet."

"I would love to see you, Valentin," I said warmly. He bowed and moved away, hurriedly to overtake the Cepeda family.

Back at the widow's house, a party awaited me. Doña Matilde for the first time demonstrating any friendship, had laid in the patio a dinner for herself and me. On my chair was a large package tied with a yellow ribbon.

I hurried to my room and brought down the gift I had wrapped for her, and also one for Béatriz.

As is always the case when giving to a woman who lacks nothing, I had long pondered what to present to my hostess; it must be handsome, to reward her long hospitality, an extravagant gesture which would prove my fondness for her. I had selected my largest manta. It was of the most exquisite Brussels lace, a family treasure so soft that it crumpled in the hand like cotton, yet sprang back without harm to its original shape. Doña Matilde, of a race whose women were artists of needlework, had several times exclaimed upon its superiority to any handicraft she had ever seen. There was nothing to equal it in Peru, and she knew I prized it. To an Indian, a gift is an expression of love, and sacrifice must flavor it.

When Doña Matilde saw this offering and ran loving hands through it in possession, she looked at me for the first time smiling. At last we were friends. She said not a word, but bowed her head. For an Inca princess to bow was the highest patronage.

I then opened my gift from her, thus discovering that her highness harbored a sense of humor. Before me was a provocative costume unique to Peru, of which I had noticed many examples, even in church. The skirt, of native cotton into which were woven broad red wool bands and beaten gold and silver threads, was very narrow at the bottom, requiring tiny steps. It was pleated in small folds from the waist downward, to be tight and form-revealing. The hem was trimmed with lace and tiny silver bells to call attention to the feet; since mine were small, all the better. I could imagine how I would look in it, with silk-stockinged ankles revealed. Above the waist, the garment had a mantle, with a hood of light black silk. It was drawn tight at the beltline, and passed back over the head and across the face. When worn, as it always was, to cover one eye, recognition was difficult. In a land where women often visit houses they should not, it was a convenient ensemble.

I insisted on putting it on. Béatriz brought me some black satin slippers, and gold bracelets for my bare arms.

"Since you are now to be a conspirator and must frequent dark places, I thought you should have the proper wardrobe," Doña Matilde said.

I kissed her cheek.

"You are wonderful to me, Highness," I said. "If God permits, I hope to repay you."

She did not reply.

For Béatriz I had selected from my jewels a hair brooch in the shape of a gold star, in its center a cluster of five small diamonds. I wanted her, too, to feel my gratitude.

This done, Doña Matilde and I sat down to dinner. Over the fruit there was an interruption. A mounted courier in Pizarro's colors rang the gate bell with a violent racket. A moment later, Doña Matilde's porter brought me a package.

In it was my poniard! Tied to the pommel was a note.

"Your pupil salutes you on Epiphany Day. Know that as a special gift to you, I have summoned a certain friend of yours who should arrive in a fortnight. Why did you not tell me he is a cousin to the bishop of Lima?"

"If my teacher has her books in hand, let her come to me tomorrow at seven. At that time, let the instruction be on the subject of love."

Valentin arrived, in his splendid new accoutrement, shortly after seven. With him was a strong, well-set-up young man not much older than himself, with black curly hair, tanned and shaven of face, whom he introduced as Joge Griego. I liked him at once; he was gently spoken, and his black eyes were humorous and intelligent.

"We are business partners," Valentin explained casually, glancing at Doña Matilde, who was just leaving the room.

When my hostess had gone, he explained hurriedly, as though in fear of being overheard, that Griego had discovered a silver mine and knew where there was a fortune in gold, but Pizarro would not give him title to the lands because he had made firearms and powder for Nuñez Vela. But Pizarro had given the silver mine to Valentin, who took Griego as his partner.

"How splendid for you," I encouraged them. "Where are these properties which will enrich you both?"

The Levantine explained that the mine was near Jumin in the highlands, and that the ore was 50 percent pure silver. He had discovered the region while exploring for a farm, and was about to begin work at an inferior shaft when the cacique, or local chief of his Indian workers, had told him of a larger and richer vein twelve leagues away. The only difficulty was that the new mine, in Inca times, had belonged to the sun god, and the Indians were afraid to labor in it, or even show Griego where it was. After much persuasion, Griego and the cacique set out for Jumin. En route, an eclipse occurred, scattering the guides. After a month's coaxing, Griego reorganized his search. This time, approaching the town, an earthquake shivered the ground. Before two such omens of the sun's wrath, the native held his secret. But Griego had in time discovered the mine in a hillside, filled with water. Now he required both patronage and labor to pump the property dry and make it productive.

"And the gold?" I asked.

Here the Greek looked sheepish. He had not yet found it. It was at Chan Chan, an Indian graveyard near Truxillo.

Several years before, on his arrival in Peru, Griego had dug there, hunting for two solid gold fish, ornaments of a dead king. One was large, the other small. He had unearthed one, a goodly fortune. But when the local cacique saw it, he said, "Oh, that is the *peja chica*." Now Griego would go back for the *peja grande,* for he had spent the other in three years of subsistence.

"We will both be rich," said Valentin. He handed me a dish, hammered of pure silver, so soft as to be almost pliable. It was the first fruit of the mine at Jumin, actually only a sample of ores found above the waterline in the shaft.

Valentin knew that I awaited some explanation of his employment under Pizarro. To my consternation he began to speak freely before his new friend. Seeing my anxiety, he explained that Griego, being a Greek, had no legal right even to be in Peru, a colony restricted by law to Castilians; his only chance for survival lay, therefore, in winning recognition from the king's government by some worthy service to His Majesty. This he hoped to accomplish by providing gunpowder for Father Gasca, since he was noted, despite his youth, as a chemist of great skill, and an engineer of deep learning, as were so many of his countrymen. He had a new formula for gunpowder which was twice as effective as any powder previously known.

Griego informed me that there was much sulphur and saltpeter handy to Jumin, so that he and Valentin could make powder while extracting silver. No one would be the wiser, since the Indians under no circumstances would approach the mine after such dire omens. Thus when Father Gasca arrived, traveling as he must down the Inca highway, he would find ample stores of explosive awaiting him, a commodity otherwise exceedingly scarce. Valentin, in turn, would secure for Griego from Gasca the right to settle permanently, and own property, in Peru.

Now I turned my attention to Valentin, asking why he had changed his raiment. He told me that Pizarro now trusted him. But since Valentin must be positive, he had tested the governor. The opportunity arose when one of Carbajal's hanging squad, idle and unpaid with the marshal far away in Charcas, was caught stealing from the palace larder on a night Valentin dined with his lordship. The culprit was a half-breed named Ancón. Pizarro immediately ordered the man hanged. Valentin objected.

Oddly, Pizarro had listened to him. Valentin argued that death, for such a trivial offense, was brutal, and unworthy of a man of the governor's eminence.

"He looked at me strangely," Valentin said. "I do not understand it."

"Someone has been teaching him the art of kindness, perhaps," I suggested.

Whatever the cause, Pizarro argued that if Valentin knew so much about treating menials, he should take charge of the household as captain of the palace guard of eighty men. Valentin had accepted at once. It gave him an excuse to move from Cepeda's house, where his work was done, into the palace itself, where he might keep an ear bent to everything. It also gave him the military rank of captain, important to every man. And, as he pointed out, he would be on hand if I had trouble with Pizarro.

I noticed an ugly bruise under the hairline at his forehead, and hurried to examine it.

"Not so hard," he begged me, backing away, "it is tender."

"Where did you get it?" I demanded.

He grinned proudly, and told me that he was practicing for the annual Conquerors' Tournament, which would be held on the last day of January. As guards' captain, he was expected to tilt a few lances against Carbajal's best cavalry;

Pizarro himself, the best lance in Peru, was giving Valentin instruction on how to unseat the marshal.

"Carbajal!" I exclaimed.

"He always wins the tournaments, Lisa."

"And since there is no one left to fight him," I said indignantly, "Pizarro searches for a new victim."

"Indeed not, my lady. He is going to wager on me."

This development frightened me, but I could neither do nor say anything. Men are nowhere more foolish than when they are trying to kill each other in the name of sport; but it is not a condition any man ever understands.

As though this was not enough excitement for a fiesta, Doña Matilde approached me when my guests were gone.

"I heard this evening from Prince Paullu," she informed me. "He has given the word."

"Not yet, oh not yet!" I implored her. "We must await the proper time."

"It is already done, my dear," she replied serenely. "By now there are already angry men in Cuzco, and next week tempers will be short in Lima also."

She gave me the widest smile of our acquaintance, before wishing me good rest and lilting up the patio stairs.

XXI

†

The next afternoon, promptly at seven, I arrived at Pizarro's palace as he had commanded. Since he had reminded me of my books, I went armed with a missal in red morocco. His lordship was not amused by the gesture.

"If this is a joke," he said, "I am afraid my chaplain would find it in very bad taste."

"It is not a joke, Your Lordship," I replied. "Love is of many kinds, and a teacher must be prepared to answer any question. Would you discuss the love of God for man, or of man for God, of love abstract or specific, of man to man, of man to woman? First, we must determine what love is."

"I know what love is," Pizarro answered.

"Good. Then you teach me, for I am much in doubt."

He was better pleased with this. He took the missal from me, as though he did not trust it, and put it on a taboret of marble inlaid with ivory. He had planned his setting well, in a shaded arbor of his walled garden, behind a trellis of red roses. There, besides the table and two chairs, was a couch overthrown with a Tabriz carpet.

"I often take my siesta here," Pizarro explained away the litter. "When I am in the garden, I am not disturbed."

His sword, however, was impaled in the ground within easy reach.

He helped me to remove my cloak, and frowned again, for prominently at my throat was my big gold cross. Quickly I sat in one of the chairs. In a moment he sprawled upon the couch, his arms behind his head, his spurs over-hanging the edge of the rug.

With puzzled face he assessed me. I sat quietly, hands in my lap, wondering what gossip Lima would enjoy this night, now that the governor of Peru had taken me to the arbor in which he was never disturbed.

Pizarro, an impatient man, could not endure the silence. As though it reproached him, he sat up abruptly.

"Why so pensive, little filly?" he asked tenderly. "Do I offend you?"

"Not at all, my lord," I replied. "You are the most exciting man I have ever seen."

"Then why do you sit so demurely, like a nun at vespers?"

"I await your instruction. You were to teach me the meaning of love."

This was a dangerous lead, one I should never have dared make to most men, who would know how to capital-ize it into a conquest. Pizarro, however, was a heavy rogue who thought only of himself. After some speculation, he lay back on his couch.

"Well, then," he pronounced irritably. "Love is the attraction of a man to a woman."

"Is that all, Your Lordship?"

"Is it not enough?"

"Perhaps to Isabel de Vergara and Maria de Ulloa, but not to me."

He sat up again at this mention of two of his former mistresses, his face tortured. Then he looked very sad, and fell back again.

"It is ill of you to wrack me when my son has just died," he said.

"I did not know, my lord," I said. "I meant no offense."

"Gonzalochico, my crown prince."

"I am sorry, my lord. But you surely have other children?"

"Hernando took my other son to Spain. I have heard nothing from him, and Hernando is in jail."

"No daughters?"

"What good is a daughter? She was with my brother Francisco's daughter Francisca in Quito. But I am now moving the girls to Arequipa. They should arrive here any day en route south."

"Why do you move them, my lord?"

He reddened.

"If there is a war, I want them to be safe."

"Will there be war, my lord?"

He jumped up angrily.

"Questions! Questions!"

He glowered down on me, then sat once more, cooling out slowly, as does a blacksmith's iron.

"Is your daughter beautiful?" I asked.

"Francisco's is," he muttered. "Mine is too big of bone."

"How old are they, Your Lordship?" Any questions, any at all, to avoid our lesson.

"They have just been confirmed," he answered. He looked at me strangely, then laughed aloud.

"Suárez—the one who was with us at Mass yesterday—wants Francisca for himself. Imagine giving the daughter of a marquis to a judge with six concubines! Yet he crowds me."

He stared at me again.

"How about giving her to Valentin?" he burst out excitedly. "That would tweak two noses, Suárez' and Cepeda's. These foxes need their grapes poisoned. Both conspire against me."

192

"You are very good to Valentin," I said. "I hear you have given him a silver mine."

"Everybody in Peru has a silver mine," Pizarro replied. "It is easier to give him a mine to work than to pay him from my own purse."

"That is clever of you," I said.

He smiled hungrily.

"You are the only woman in Peru I want to think me clever."

"Oh, I do, my lord. You are handsome and strong and brave. If you had love, now, to go with it, you would be a very great man indeed."

Languidly he held up one hand.

"Yes," he said. "All I need is love. . . . Come here, little filly."

I laughed lightly.

"Are we that far along in the lessons?" I asked. "I was thinking of a different sort of love, my lord. A love that could make you great."

He jumped from the couch and took me roughly by the shoulders.

"You are the very devil," he cried out. "You turn all my meanings in another direction."

Now he was upon me, his tremendous arms about me, his fingers trembling vagabonds over my neck and shoulders as his lips bit into mine.

"Filly, filly," he whispered, "don't taunt me this way."

"For God's sake, my lord!"

"I love you. Before God and the Virgin I love you. I was the loneliest man in the world. Then you came, on the breeze that blew away the winter fog. Now the flowers bloom again in my heart, and spring is here inside me. It is a moment God has given us."

His kisses were like hot irons.

"Kiss me, too!" he insisted.

"My lord, you forget yourself."

"The contrary. I would give you something to remember. Something to smile over when you are old and see the birds nesting. Kiss me, little filly."

Again he explored my lips, but discovered nothing.

Bitterly the lord of Peru relaxed and, holding me at arms' length by the shoulders, stared down at me.

"You know I could make you love me," he said savagely.

"No, my lord. You could take me, but that is no way to make me love you."

"What do you want of me?" He pushed me back into my chair and flung himself with a crash onto his couch.

"I want you to learn what love is," I responded. "I did not bring my missal for nothing. In it you might read an instructive proverb: 'Better a dinner of herbs, where love is, than a roasted ox, and hatred within.' You ask me to hate you, my lord, not to love you."

He glowered.

"Shall we resume our lesson?" I asked quietly. "Another reading? You see, I was at some pains to prepare for this meeting, as an instructor should. May I read where I have marked the place?"

The governor of Peru was too angry to reply.

I picked up the missal. From one of the readings for special days, I quoted Jeremiah. "Though thou cover thyself with scarlet, though thou deck thee with ornaments of gold, in vain do thou make thyself fair; thy lovers despise thee; they seek thy life."

His big hands clenched and unclenched. He chewed a wisp of his beard.

"It is not enough to want love," I pursued him. "It is necessary also to be a good lover. Considerate, my lord, kind, understanding. He who would rule a woman—or an empire—must have these qualities. With them, the ruler would be passionately beloved by all his people, and by his woman also."

"You do love me, then," Pizarro said. He was much quieter now, but belligerent and tense.

" 'How canst thou say I love thee, when thy heart is not with thee? Thou hast mocked me, and hast not told me wherein thy great strength lies.' . . . That, my lord, is what Delilah said to Samson."

"Yes," he shot back, "and look what happened to him."

"True, my lord. He lusted, he did not love, and so brought his house down upon himself. I could not enter any man's house of sand."

He sat up. Clearly the lesson was ended, and I had made no impression on him.

"One moment, my lord," I said, going to him and touching his arm. "All men are good and you also. You just refuse to admit it."

At my touch he grasped me and flung me beside him on the couch, his body suffocating me. His eyes fierce and not two inches from my own, he retorted, "All men are good, but not for everything. Women are good for only one thing, as I will show you. I am the teacher now."

He was an anvil upon me, but he needed both his hands to do his will, and when he released my shoulders, I wrenched my body, tumbling us both to the ground. Up before him, I seized his sword from its sheath of earth, and drove it toward him. But he was a panther, anticipating the threat even as I thrust, so that I caught him only lightly in the soft muscle of the left arm. Blood covered his white satin sleeve through a long puncture of the cloth.

He struck the sword from my hand with a sweep of his good arm, seized me one-handed and hurled me down. I ripped the dagger from my bodice, and held it so that he could not fall upon me without impaling himself. Again he slapped, my poniard flying as his blow numbed my wrist. Now indeed was I helpless. He stood over me a moment, gloating, thrillingly powerful in his rage.

"The lark," he laughed as he rubbed his bloody arm, "has been brought to earth."

Calmly he began to expose me. I reached to my throat, ripped the gold Cross from its chain, and held it before his eyes.

"Holy Mother protect me!" I prayed aloud.

He reeled back, averting his eyes. I arose.

"My lord is a monstrously poor pupil," I said, quivering so that I almost dropped my Cross.

Then I ran through the garden gate.

XXII

✝

As my hostess Doña Matilde had predicted, masculine tempers grew short in Lima. Only on feminine faces were there any smiles. Gonzalo Pizarro's countenance was perhaps the blackest of all, but he covered his wounded arm behind a loose-sleeved blouse which well hid his secret.

I did not know precisely how our conspiracy circulated to all the Castilian females of the colony; but evidently none wanted to be excluded, and the Indians, of course, responded with their usual discipline. Doña Hipólita Cepeda had reached all the well-born Castilians, spreading the campaign over her sherry glass, and from them it expanded by contagion. The project had just enough humor and danger in it, and promised so much for the future that within a few days it was miraculously effective, from all accounts. The men went about like puzzled children, in aggrieved sulks. There were several duels, one death, and unfortunately a few cases in which women were abused. But these last humiliations only the more entrenched the resolution of their sisters.

Doña Matilde's own brother-in-law, Don Benito Suárez, who I later learned was known to the women of Lima as *La Mosca* (the fly) from his agility at entering bedroom windows, was the most puzzled man in all this land. The Indian girls in his household resolutely followed the orders

197

of their prince. Benito irritably used his dagger when persuasion failed. When he awoke next morning his house was empty. All six of his slaves had disappeared, and none returned. A few nights later he "fell" as he attempted to enter, by his usual route, the home of a gentleman who, as captain of one of Hinojosa's vessels, had been more than a year in Panama. Don Benito's arm was broken. His male companions made much sport of this, but there was a bitterness to their risibility suggestive of kinship to his predicament.

Incidents such as this spread the campaign without much impulsion from me. Spanish women have a wonderful sense of humor, and this was the first outlet they had ever found for it in Peru.

Pizarro, preparing for the tournament and greatly enlarging his army, spent little time in his palace for the next fortnight. He did not recognize my presence in any way.

On Saint Agnes' Day, the governor paraded before Lima the new army Carbajal had built for him. If this was a demonstration of his power, it was well-timed. Rumors of Gasca's activity, of the defection of important men in outlying districts, of entire towns threatening to throw off allegiance to Pizarro, and other wild stories, had everyone in fear.

Doña Matilde and I watched the parade from the balcony of a friend's house. Valentin did not march, nor Pizarro. His lordship, flanked by his personal guard, each of whom, on a black horse, was in full armor made of Peruvian copper and silver, each with a casque surmounted by brilliant toucan feathers, reviewed the troop in front of the cathedral. At his right hand was the Archbishop of Lima, at his left the Bishop of Cuzco. This honor to the clergy, I suspected, was to prove that no friar in Panama represented the Church in Peru, and that the local clergy stood with his lordship and would bless his defiance of Gasca and the king.

Pizarro displayed a thousand men, equipped as not even a king could surpass. No wonder he had ten thousand Indians working his mines in Potosí!

Carbajal, whom I had never before seen, led the parade on his famous red mule. He did somewhat resemble Valentin. Of course, in body armor and with lance at rest, I saw only his bare head. He was truly stupendous, an oaken stump hardened and impervious, leafed by a balding foliage of white hair, his face a Saint Peter mask of whisker through which projected two fierce eyes, a bold Roman nose and an almost toothless mouth that gaped like a tavern door. A giant of more than six feet, weighing all of three hundred pounds, his arms had the girth of ox joints, his neck was bovine, his legs tree trunks. He was a mounted castle, vast, impregnable, indestructible.

Behind him surged a strange array, unlike any army I had ever seen before, or heard of. I understood now why he moved so fast afield, for not a soldier walked, not even an artilleryman or pike. Instead of cumbering themselves with a slow supply train, Carbajal's men carried their own arms and munitions. Such a show of horses and mules alone was a fantastic fortune in a land where a single gelding cost 3,000 pesos of gold.

Carbajal had created this army by the unheard-of method of drafting all men of fighting age into service. If they deserted, he hunted them down and hanged them. But as they marched, I observed evidences of Carbajal's genius. Armies traditionally had been composed of illustrious captains whose own vassals rallied to their banners. Carbajal had abandoned this most knightly custom of chivalry. His soldiers were formed in companies, all under

199

Pizarro's own ensign, so the men had only one loyalty, to Pizarro himself.

If the governor staged this exercise in the hope that Ambassador Paniagua would see it, he was disappointed. The lay brother arrived next day aboard a vessel from Truxillo. He came at once to see me, and brought news of all my friends.

Mexía was in Truxillo, openly walking the streets, loudly organizing loyal king's men against the day when they might throw off Pizarro's oppression. Not even the governor's guards there molested him, for the entire town, if Paniagua was not deceived, eagerly awaited Gasca.

Lota lived like a queen aboard Mexía's galleon. Paniagua was not one to gossip, but he did say that Captain Mexía was most solicitous of my maid, and might take her with him to Panama, for his vessel would carry Paniagua northward.

Paniagua was not received in the palace of his cousin, the absent Bishop of Lima. He was rebuffed, and compelled to seek public lodging. He had heard at Truxillo, of course, in the greatest secrecy from Hernán Mexía, of Gasca's annexation of the fleet, and of Bishop Loaysa's and Aldana's defection to the king's side. But knowing that this news had not yet reached Lima, he promised me not to mention it, even in his negotiations with Pizarro.

The next day Pizarro received him. Paniagua took me with him, in gratitude for my negotiation which had secured his release from jail. Further, he needed a witness, and knew no reliable man except Valentin who, of course, could not be thus exposed. We were received in a low room hung with armor and tapestries interwoven with the red and gold banners of Castile. Pizarro sat at the head of a large table. He was in crimson and gold-embroidered velvet, a royal figure. At his right stood Carbajal in dirty leather; to his left Cepeda in black velvet. There were a half dozen others, of whom I recognized only Benito Suárez. None of them was seated.

My shock, of course, was the close appearance of Carbajal. The demon was indeed an old Valentin, bone for bone, from head to foot.

The formal trappings in which Paniagua was received proved the decisiveness of the occasion. On this negotiation depended war or peace; it might decide, indeed, whether I would become the wife of Gasca's most valuable captain, or empress of Peru! It also would decide my future conduct, for I knew that any day, suddenly and without warning, Pizarro would learn of the Panama disaster. On that day he might, in his rage, hang me for a traitor or a Gasca spy. But if he did not close the door to further negotiation, if he did not arrogantly defy Gasca, then I might well be able, by guile or pleading, to convince him that his best advantage lay in yielding Peru to Gasca without a fight; though, as I had discovered, I had precious little effect upon him except to arouse his lust.

If he decided for war, then the women's campaign must be intensified; though if it failed, it might easily cost me my life. If he sought peace, who then had done enough, at this date, to win my hand? The arrogant Aldana, surely.

So more rode on this meeting than the future of Peru. Much more important to me was the effect it must have upon my life!

Evidently the council had already discussed Paniagua's visit, for several documents were spread on the table which could only be the letters from His Majesty and Gasca which had been taken from Paniagua at Motape.

I took seat quickly by the guards at the door, Paniagua alone confronting his lordship. As he approached the governor, Paniagua suddenly developed a knee limp he had

201

not possessed before, and I thought to myself, "You old fox, seeing everyone standing, you know you are supposed to kneel to His Lordship, so you plead a sore leg!"

Pizarro was not deceived. He waited for the genuflection. Then calmly he took my jeweled dagger from his belt and imbedded it in the table. His sword already was implanted in the floor at his right hand.

"Old man with your gray hairs," he called scornfully, "what brings you here?"

"I was sent, sir, by the Judge Pedro de la Gasca in the name of His Majesty the king."

"I tell you," Pizarro replied abruptly, "that even if the king sends 50,000 such as you, I do not care a tomin." [1]

"Especially, sir," Paniagua rejoined bravely, "if they come on an errand of peace, as I do, and with no more desire to disserve you than I."

Gonzalo scoffed this away.

"Tell this priest that the sea and the land both fight for me, and I have the good will of the residents. Tell him I have 4,000 men, the best in the world, who would turn back 8,000 invaders."

Paniagua barely bent his head in assent.

Turning now for a square look at the ambassador, Pizarro shot out, "Are you a member of the war council?"

It was an adder's question, implying that Gasca plotted armed conflict. But Paniagua was no fool.

"Where there is no war, there can be no such council," he responded. "The judge is a priest. He has never seen war and does not wish to. If Your Lordship will not receive him, he will return to Spain."

"Ha!" Pizarro ejaculated triumphantly, and at once, as he did so often, shifted his mood from wrath to joviality. He asked for details of Paniagua's journey, smiled when the ambassador complained that he had slept on vermin-

[1] tomin: a coin of almost no value

202

lively mattresses as black with dirt as ink, and had been seasick en route from Truxillo.

"That's where you got your limping knee, no doubt— from the seasickness," Pizarro commented scornfully. "Proceed."

Paniagua explained in great detail the powers Gasca possessed, even to the letters signed in blank. During this exposition Carbajal, who had chiefly been fussing with a hangnail, began to stare intently at Paniagua, fascinated by the narration.

"To defy His Majesty's written request," Paniagua concluded, "would be the height of folly."

"I agree," Carbajal boomed out, the first of any of Pizarro's companions to come to life. "These powers are more dangerous than all the lances of Castile, for how can you kill them? Let us pave this chaplain's path with bars of silver and plates of gold."

Cepeda now intervened. "Softly, campmaster," he said quietly. "It is not that simple. We deal with a cunning man, who would know how to hang us once our necks were in the noose."

Cepeda moved deliberately to a window, and placed his leg upon the sill; he had been standing a long time, and this was the only way he could rest his muscles while in the presence. He looked at Paniagua.

"You say the friar will pardon us. For what, since we have not transgressed?"

"What do you want, then?" Paniagua asked.

"Approbation," said Cepeda promptly.

"Very well," Paniagua assented placidly.

Pizarro did not like the bargaining sound of this discourse.

"See here," he cut in testily. "I am to be governor, because we would not trust anyone else."

Paniagua straightened his weary and aged frame.

203

"Indeed, sir?" he gasped. "Governor? Against the king's will? Your Lordship should reflect that such a thing cannot be done. See the king's power—how he has prevailed against the Turk and France together. Reflect on your duty. And upon your present opportunity to become one of the richest and most honored uncrowned men in Christendom, mentioned in history as a benefactor, loved by all." (Here Pizarro shot an odd glance at me.) "Ponder these things, and you will see that the governorship is insignificant."

Pizarro inveighed long then on the king's mistakes in governing Peru, and the colony's vast richness and importance to his majesty.

"The king," he concluded, "could ill afford to lose Peru."

"In that case," said Paniagua evenly, "you contemplate freeing it from Spain?"

Pizarro rose. On his next answer everything depended. I gripped my hands tightly together and braced my breath. The governor was a long time silent. He looked out the window, distastefully I thought, as though what he must say curdled his stomach and shamed his heart. Slowly he returned my dagger to his belt, fumbling with the pommel clasp. He straightened his back and scowled.

"I cannot give up the enterprise," he said softly.

Paniagua appreciated his indecision, and also the courage a man had who would declare his freedom from the strongest king in Christendom. "You are young and strong, sir," the ambassador reminded him soothingly, "and might live in peace and dignity another forty years."

Pizarro stiffened.

"I had rather live ten years and be governor."

"If they let Your Lordship live so long," Paniagua ingratiated.

"Well then, six."

"Neither six nor even two."

Cepeda's clever mind revolted against the brilliance with which Paniagua enforced upon Pizarro's mind the brevity of the life of a traitor, and could not permit it to continue. This was obvious from his interjection. "God has saved him from other perils," he told Paniagua, feigning lightness of spirit.

But Pizarro did not even hear him.

"I must die governing," he insisted, this time with finality.

"Is that your answer?" Paniagua asked sadly.

"There is nothing more to be said. I will give you formal answer this day week."

Paniagua bowed, and my heart stopped beating altogether. It was to be war, and death. And from this moment, I was a traitor to Pizarro, a Gasca spy, marked at any time for whatever monstrous fate Pizarro decreed.

Pizarro turned, and gazed sadly at me, and yet challengingly as though now the throne of Peru would be his—and I also. He opened the door to indicate that the interview was ended, held it as I passed through. As we met he raised an arm. I paused.

"You promised me," he said, "that you would not leave Peru."

"I keep my promises, my lord," I said.

He heeled quickly about and returned to the conference room. Carbajal greeted him with booming words. "So be it," I heard him say to Pizarro. "I am eighty-four. At best only a few years remain to me. I guess I have just as long a neck for the hangman's noose as the rest of you gentlemen."

Softly Pizarro closed the door, and I heard no more.

I took Paniagua to his hostel in my coach. He had been on his feet for three hours. After his long journey and imprisonment he was weak, unwell, and had a toothache.

"It means a terrible war," I said, breaking an awful silence.

"It is just as well," Paniagua said dolefully. "Pizarro cannot live in peace. Only war can gratify his vanity and give his life meaning. . . . This Carbajal, though, is other flesh. I should feel better if he were on our side."

XXIII

The great tournament of the conquerors was held just south of Lima in an amphitheater almost surrounded by bold rocks and ancient terraces. In other times, the land had been an Inca parade ground; before that, a primitive temple. This ruin, with its many elevations, provided a vantage on which Pizarro had pitched his own pavilion.

Since so many warriors of Peru bore no escutcheon proud enough to post on tent or tree, the knightly exercises of this country were not tests of family arms. Rather, sides of sixteen lancers each were chosen by two challengers, the combatants rallying to the banner of their leader. Thus each waving device concealed a host of sins! The melee was conducted with muffled lances on which the finials had been replaced by pads the size of fists. The object was for one side completely to unseat the other, until a single pennant dominated the field. After this show, individual knights listed against each other, the winner of the previous year's tourney defending his title against all who dared dispute it. The victor then selected from among the spectators his "lady of the day," who was received by Pizarro in the governor's enclosure. She in turn bestowed the day's prize upon the champion. Wagering was heavy on all the events, and in past years men had been ruined during the afternoon. Pawnbrokers set up their stalls and were as busy as anyone in the lists.

I was invited to witness this gala from Pizarro's tent. Doña Matilde accompanied me. We attended Mass in the cathedral at Lima first. The service was so jammed for the blessing of the lances—all the combatant knights participated in this ceremony except Marshal Carbajal—that there was no place to sit and scarcely room to stand.

Then in my coach we set out for the parade ground. We passed thousands of persons: some walking, wine jugs slung over their shoulders, their ladies in Indian, traveling hammocks or in Spanish litters; some men ahorse, carrying their women behind their saddles; some even in oxcarts.

The arena glittered with tents and the standards of prominent gentlemen. Picnics were spread all over the great plain, except on the listing field, which was bare except for two great tents: one of French blue, burnt orange and the Pizarro device at the north end; the other of practical brown muslin bearing an escutcheon which impudently quartered the arms of Cardinal Carbajal of Arévalo and a black bear standing upright, obviously the ensign of the army commander.

Pizarro's enclosure for his guests was worthy of the Emperor Charles. It was large enough to shelter fifty persons, covered entirely over by a canopy of gold and crimson brocade held up by two center poles and a dozen lances. Here were set a thronelike armchair on a dais and eight lesser seats below, each protected from the dusty ground by a Persian rug. From the elevation could be seen the entire plain.

Since none of his lordship's party had yet arrived, Doña Matilde and I strolled to the north pavilion. I hoped to encounter Valentin and wish him well, for he was to lead the governor's champions. Perhaps, I thought, he might ask to wear my colors. I had anticipated this by tying one curl with silks of the Canillejas green and amber. Many grooms hurried about, harnessing horses. The governor's equipment was dazzling: knee-length blankets of blue with orange trim, orange hoods decorated with the arms of Pizarro's father, a knight of Truxillo. The saddles were padded with velvet, and from each hung a silver-plated shield. All the steeds were black, protected by chain mail and nose plates. As I watched, the mounts were decked with red neckbands on each of which was embroidered *"Ave Maria, gratia plena."* No guardsmen were about, however, and at last I returned to the enclosure.

By now all the guests had arrived there except Paniagua. Seated on his dais was his lordship, talking to two girls just budding. In another group stood wily Cepeda, his daughter Andrea, and Don Benito Suárez, his left arm in a sling. Andrea's hair was in pigtails, one of which was tied with a love ribbon of emerald and yellow; but from the other, her colors were conspicuously missing. Quickly, lest they be noticed, I stripped off my Canillejas silks and hid them.

The children, as I had suspected, were the marquis' daughter Francisca, dark-beautiful and fragile, and his lordship's own Inez, coarse-featured, flat-nosed and overdeveloped. Both girls were self-conscious, shy, and, I thought, miserable.

My hostess, Doña Matilde, went at once to Francisca, and was well received by the child, her niece. Indeed, Francisca clung to her aunt's hand and begged to be seated beside her, hungry as she was for any maternal affection and sympathy. I was seated at Pizarro's right, Cepeda beside me. On his lordship's left was Francisca, beyond her Doña Matilde. This left the least places to Pizarro's own Inez, to Benito Suárez and Andrea. The latter sat unhappily beyond the chair reserved for Paniagua.

His lordship was elated and arrogant. Having openly

broken with Gasca, he was now in public rebellion against the crown of Castile. At last he could display himself as the ruler of Peru, and he wanted to show everyone that he could be a king. But the empty chair was to remind him all afternoon of the one person whom he could not impress: the king. Pizarro, however, did not appear worried.

"I regret," he told me, leaning confidentially, "that old graybeard is not on hand to see how mighty a lord can be."

"Paniagua has a violent toothache," I said. "He could not come."

"He will ache where his neck meets his shoulders before many days," Pizarro laughed. He asked me to note well what I saw, and write a letter to Friar Gasca for Paniagua to bear north, describing Pizarro's armed might as revealed both at the tournament and at the Saint Agnes Day parade. "Let the priest understand," he explained, "that today Peru makes a new start in the world, and that neither he nor the king possesses strength enough to frustrate us."

"I shall so report, my lord," I said.

"When Gasca is beaten," he went on, "we shall have another tournament." He tapped me on the arm. "On that day," he whispered coquettishly, "how would you like to sit here beside me, Empress of Peru?"

"It is an exciting prospect, Your Lordship. But Peru, like me, must still be conquered."

He laughed, and was about to continue when two mounted pages trumpeted a parade, and the thirty-two contestants passed in excellent order before us, four abreast. The men in brown were led by Carbajal who, for once, rode a horse. The salute for the men in blue was made by Valentin.

Unusually boisterous, Pizarro confided to me that this matching of the palace guard against the army was a deliberate attempt to foment rivalry between them. His first principle of governance, he said, was to keep everyone who served him angry at everyone else, for men who fought each other would not unite to attack him. Further, he confessed, he used even this simple tournament to remind his leaders of his great power. For this reason he had set Suárez where he could not talk to Francisca.

He glanced toward Cepeda.

"And when a man aspires so high that he fancies his own daughter is greater than a marquesa, I remind him, by putting her in her place, what I can as easily do to him."

Cepeda did not even blink.

The knights lined up for the combat.

"Any wagers, my lord?" I asked Pizarro.

"Oh, the army will win the melee," he said categorically.

"Surely someone should uphold your guardsmen," I said. "Ten gold pieces on the men in blue."

"Done," said Pizarro, delighted.

Four horsemen lined up at each end of the field. With visors down, they were unidentifiable. But neither Carbajal nor Valentin, recognizable because they were the largest on each side, was in the first rush.

Pizarro raised his hand. The knights, lances down, charged each other. Four mighty collisions raised their din over the shouts of the vast crowd of witnesses. One man in blue went down.

Pizarro cast me a self-satisfied glance as the horses sped on to the opposite ends of the arena and reined up.

Two new quartets of lancers readied to the marks. Again Pizarro's signal trumpeted them away. All eight were unhorsed in a furious crash. One was dragged the length of the ground before his frantic horse could be stopped.

"Five ducats we catch up with you now," I screamed over the confusion.

"Prepare to pay," Pizarro accepted, his eyes aflame with the excitement, as he sent the next group battleward. Two men in brown fell; only one in blue.

I held out my hand for the wager. Pizarro paid promptly from a chamois purse.

He now sat forward, and I also, for the last adversaries were on the mark. Closest to our vision were the two largest figures. It was Valentin against Carbajal.

"It also amuses me," Pizarro commented as he made ready to hold up his signaling hand, "to see what a son can do against his father. Any wager?"

"None, my lord," I said tensely. I was angry at myself, for I trembled and could not control the spasms.

The lances met amid dust and thunder. Splinters soared high. The horses reared and snorted. Both armored giants galloped safely away, their lances broken.

"By God!" cried Pizarro. "That was a blow!"

The other three pairs were down.

Seven men remained ahorse on each side.

There was a long delay while the field was cleared of arms and rubbish, and the horses of the vanquished were led away. I turned to see how my companions were enjoying the sport. Dainty Francisca sat rigid, not knowing whether to be excited or horrified. Doña Matilde was puzzled, not understanding the competition. Beyond her, Andrea wiped tears from her eyes. To my right, Cepeda sat glumly in his own thoughts. Inez glowed and clapped her hands. Suárez alone had not watched the combat. His eyes burned, and they were focused on Francisca.

Pedro Guillen, the governor's secretary, slipped quickly alongside his master, fright white on his face.

"Excuse me, Sire," he said.

"Later, later," Pizarro dismissed him. "Name of God, can't I even have an afternoon of—"

"I would not dare interrupt you, Sire, except with gravest cause."

"Get it over, then."

Embarrassed, Guillen glanced toward me.

"Come, come, speak and go."

"A letter from Quito, Sire," the secretary said. He swallowed, bolstered his courage, and plunged. "Puelles, your vice-governor, has been murdered, and the province has declared for Gasca."

Pizarro struck his offending scribe across the face, half-rising.

"I swear it before God," Guillen screamed, lying on the carpet, his nose bleeding. "The news is from Bachicáo, brought by the mails. I did not even wait to open the other dispatches before I brought you this."

He handed over the offending letter. Pizarro, of course, could not read it. He looked at the signature before handing it back.

Guillen crawled a few yards, then rose and sped away.

The lancers were a long time on the line before Pizarro, almost without seeing them, held up his hand. Even the clash of iron, the shivering lances, the clang of grounding steel, the screams of horses and onlookers, did not rouse him. His jaws gritted rapidly, so that the muscles jumped in his jowls. All the contestants were unhorsed. On each side only three remained.

Carbajal and Valentin squared against each other once again, along with two other pairs.

"The signal, my lord," I said.

"What? Oh." Pizarro's hand went up.

"It is the father against the son," I reminded him.

Immediately he quickened, and concentrated on the fray. The familiar tumult, the pounding of hoofs, was the same. Momentarily, glancing at Pizarro, I saw beyond him the daughter of Cepeda, a handkerchief-wrapped thumb between her teeth.

Carbajal deliberately passed Valentin without a contest, and the other riders all went down.

213

"The old fool," Pizarro growled. "Always playing the hero. He wants all eyes upon himself."

Valentin and Carbajal reined up and rested their lances. They alone of all the field survived. The crowd shouted. A group pressed so closely around one of the pawnbroker's tents that it crashed down.

But Pizarro would not permit the solo combat. He arose and motioned that the melee be declared a draw, explaining that the challenge round would lose its zest if the champion were unseated in the melee.

Wine and cake now were served, while the heralds announced that Carbajal would defend his title against all challengers. All the way around the arena the herald rode, inviting contestants. As each knight in turn failed to plant his standard in the ground, the crowd groaned and scoffed. Valentin still sat his horse, at the far line of his own troop. When the herald reached him, Valentin spurred forward to the line.

Pizarro shook off his absent mood. "A wager now against the blue?" he asked me.

"Not from me, Your Lordship."

He tapped my knee with his gloved hand.

"You are wise, little filly. Carbajal has an Achilles' heel, and I have told Valentin about it."

He explained that Carbajal always rode a mule because he had a double hernia and could not stride a horse for long without tiring. Now, after so much exercise in the melee, Carbajal might be unseated if Valentin's lance struck his shoulder. He rubbed his hands.

"How I have waited for the time when someone would unseat that old devil," he growled. "And to have it be his own bastard!"

"Have Valentin and Carbajal met?" I asked.

"Indeed not," Pizarro said. "I have deliberately kept

them apart. I want to tell Carbajal myself who it is who puts dust in his mouth."

He raised his hand and brought it down triumphantly.

The horses charged. The lances raced toward each other with the speed of cannon balls. Valentin, deep in the saddle, shoulders forward, braced for the impact. Carbajal, confident and wise, measured his target well.

The lances struck. Andrea screamed. Valentin took the shock on his shield, Carbajal's lance shattering with a crack like breaking bones. At the same instant Valentin's lance bore home, high on the opposing shield. Carbajal's bulk looped back over his horse's rump to the ground, dragging with it a scramble of harness as the sudden shift of his enormous weight broke his cinch strap and carried the saddle away with him.

The champion of Peru went down.

Valentin, lance at rest, rode his black mount about the arena in a tumult of cheers by victorious bettors, and derisive catcalls by the losers. As he did so, there was an uproar at my back.

Pizarro whirled, whipping his sword, and faced the disturbance. Two of his own guards struggled, just off the carpet, with a ragged-haired, ill-clad soldier.

"Enough! Enough!" Pizarro commanded. "What is this?"

The guards explained that the ruffian demanded audience with Pizarro. He had news, he claimed, for which his lordship would pay well. Pizarro let him step forward.

I recognized him then. He was a leader of the brigands from Panama whom Captain Mexía had thrown into the bay at the Isle of Puna. He blurted the news I had dreaded Pizarro to hear, of Admiral Hinojosa's surrender of the fleet, and the defection of Pizarro's ambassadors.

"Lying dog!" Pizarro cried out.

215

"Ask anyone in the north provinces," the newcomer said, shrugging. "The news alone caused a revolt in Quito, of which surely you have heard."

Pizarro lowered his sword, and turned on me.

"You knew all the time," he said bitterly.

"Yes, my lord, I knew all the time."

His lower lip drew down, almost in convulsions. Beyond me suddenly he saw Cepeda.

"And you, you double-dealing eel, who throws your daughter like a stew bone to my captain, you knew, too."

"He did not, I swear it," I cried.

Pizarro stared at both of us.

"My lord," I implored him, "the champion is saluting you."

He turned to face the arena. Valentin sat his horse before the enclosure, his visor open.

For the first time that day I had a good look at him. On his left shoulder he wore two ribbons which matched the emerald and yellow pig-tail in Andrea's hair.

Pizarro saw the colors, too. He scowled, then laughed.

"Doña Andrea," he called, "you seem to be the champion's chosen lady."

"Yes, Your Highness."

She came forward radiantly to receive and present the prize.

Pizarro relaxed. He looked about, his eyes settling deliberately on me, then on Suárez, then on Cepeda, and ultimately on the Marquis Pizarro's daughter.

"Come here, Francisca, my dear niece," he said, enveloping her shoulder in his huge arm.

He led her to Andrea, whose face went white.

"Here, Doña Andrea," he said gaily. "Take Francisca to the champion. She needs a brave husband. Let her be the prize."

Both Andrea and Francisca drew back in horror.

"You refuse?" Pizarro asked Andrea.

"It is cruel, my lord," the child sobbed.

I stepped forward.

"You cannot do this monstrous thing, Your Lordship," I protested.

Contemptuously Pizarro turned away from me. "It seems," he said, "that I must make the presentation myself."

He took his niece, weeping, by the hand, and strode forward to the champion. Into Valentin's mailed fist he put the tiny fingers of the Marquis Pizarro's daughter.

The crowd dinned its appreciation. The spectators had expected to see a sack of gold, and roared their delight at this romantic gesture.

"You see . . ." Pizarro said as he returned to his companions of the afternoon. "The people approve me. I don't need any of you."

He called his bodyguard, mounted his stallion, and galloped away.

XXIV

Doña Matilde and I returned from the tournament to Lima on foot. To impress on me that I was no longer in his favor, Pizarro withdrew the patronage of his coach. We had already asked Andrea, who was near hysterics, to ride with us, for her father had disappeared; indeed, we were inside the vehicle when four guards ordered us to hand it over to his lordship's daughter and niece.

Francisca also was near collapse, and I was relieved that she, alone and motherless, was given some attention. Valentin, who had shed his heaviest armor and dismounted when he comprehended Pizarro's gift, handed the child into the coach, assisted by Doña Matilde, and ordered a strong detachment to accompany her to the governor's palace.

In stunned numbness we watched the carriage depart. Suárez, who had remained with us, gritted through his beard, "It is enough to make a man sharpen his sword." Hatred was in his voice, his eyes, and his heart.

Andrea would not leave without speaking to Valentin. He told us to go to the house of Cepeda, where he would join us. He remounted and galloped to his men, who were striking their gala tent and stowing their gear.

So we began a slow journey homeward. Fortunately Andrea rallied and went with us unprotesting and silent. The news brought by the brigands of Panama had spread to everyone, and was the only conversation of all who passed us. Many, recognizing Suárez, stopped him and asked if what the ruffians said was true. Suárez, a death mask, curtly confirmed the rumor. Up and down the road his words sped, enflaming the excitement. As we reached the plaza, we saw a crowd already gathered before Pizarro's palace, awaiting some reassurance from his lordship.

Doña Matilde put her hand to my arm, and told me to send Suárez for Paniagua. "We need mature advice," she said, "and besides, I can cure his toothache."

Suárez hurried off, glad to be rid of three disconsolate females. Flanking Andrea on each side, Doña Matilde and I took the girl to her own house.

Her mother met us at the gate. She had already heard, evidently from her husband, what had happened. Doña Hipólita took her daughter tenderly in her fat arms, nursed her into the shady patio, and gave her brandy.

"I knew," she wept, "that this would come to no good end." Her tears calmed her daughter, who now looked up and said, "I will kill Pizarro if he kills Valentin, or makes him marry that—that baby."

"Someone else is very apt to save you the trouble," I responded. "Now in God's name be quiet so we may think."

Suárez shortly arrived with Paniagua. The ambassador's cheek was swollen, but he bowed to all of us with dignity.

"This town burns with the news as though from flames," he said. "Pizarro could not hold Lima a day without his troops. Now, how may I help you?"

"First," said Doña Matilde, "let me help you."

On her arrival at the house she had sent one of the Cepeda Indians away on an errand, and now held in her hand a fishbone as long as her finger. Paniagua recoiled.

"It is nothing, Excellency," her highness said, gently touching his face. "It is an old remedy of my people."

She held out the bone, realizing that Paniagua was of

219

inquiring mind, and intelligent, and explained that the bone was from the spurfish, spongy on the inside. When the gum above an infected tooth was pierced, the bone quickly drew out the poison into its own spursack.

Paniagua was tortured enough to try anything. He tilted back his head and opened his mouth. With a skillful plunge, Doña Matilde poked the sharp end of the bone into the swelling in his upper jaw. He winced. The rest of us watched, fascinated, tolerant of another's suffering rather than be reminded of our own. Soon the porous sack from the protruberant end of the bone began to swell and fill with liquid.

"You see," said Doña Matilde, "soon all your devils will be in the bone, and not in your mouth."

I told Paniagua, who already knew all the day's news, that we needed wise counsel. He shrugged, muttering between his teeth that Pizarro would have too many major problems for a few days to think of us. He feared most for Valentin. If his disloyalty to Pizarro were discovered, he would hang. But even here, he thought, events worked in our favor. On the morrow, when Pizarro handed Paniagua a reply to Gasca, the governor would be formally in a state of war against the crown, and would be too involved in martial preparations to consider petty problems. However, he feared for me, and suggested that I return in his ship to Truxillo.

I declined, and the Inca princess gave me a proud, encouraging look.

Paniagua now turned to Suárez, demanding where his loyalty lay. Having personally murdered the king's viceroy Nuñez on the battlefield of Añaquito, his neck was as long for the royal noose as any in Peru. Suárez admitted the deed, but insisted that it was a private revenge for Nuñez' foul murder of his brother. "I would kill the blackguard

Pizarro, too," he concluded, "except for my broken arm."

Paniagua merely squinted his eyes to see the end of the fishbone, which bloated rapidly. It occurred to me that Suárez, in his hot anger over the treatment of Francisca, might be put to very excellent use. I asked Paniagua whether he thought Gasca would pardon Suárez' offense if the judge served us henceforth. Paniagua nodded emphatically, watching the fishbone. He was feeling much better, and the color was returning to his face. The fishbone was as big at the end as a chicken heart.

"If I could believe that!" Suárez ejaculated.

"You can, sir," Paniagua assured him. "I give my word."

I told Suárez that if he deserted Pizarro, many men of Lima would follow his example, arguing that if he, red as were his hands, was forgiven, no other man had anything to fear. So I suggested he make a dramatic escape, one that would be talked about throughout the colony. He promised to do so, joining Paniagua in Truxillo.

Valentin stormed in through the garden gate, lest he be seen entering Cepeda's house. He had removed his heavy armor but was still in chain mail. He rushed not to Andrea but to me, with news that the palace was in bedlam. A messenger had arrived from the south. Diego Centeño, who had never yielded to Pizarro and who had been hiding in a cave near Arequipa, had risen up and organized a new revolt in the southern province.

"God be praised," Paniagua said, in his elation dropping the fishbone from his mouth; but its work was done, and he did not try to recover it.

Valentin said he had avoided both Pizarro and Carbajal, but Ancón, the boy whose life he had saved, informed him that the marshal had taken his defeat in very good grace.

I told Valentin to pay some attention to Andrea, since he still wore her colors on his shoulder. He reddened, turned, and went down on his knee before Andrea and her mother. Quickly he convinced her to withdraw while we planned our escape.

"You will take me with you?" the girl pleaded.

"You, too, will escape, I promise you."

She did not notice how he had parried her question. Her child's heart accepted his words with all the implications she wished to hear in them. Obediently she rose, excused herself, and retired on her mother's ample arm.

Valentin was determined to remain in the Pizarro house, a course emphatically approved by Paniagua. So it was decided that he should return there at once, and convince his lordship of his loyalty. He must not communicate with me. He was to watch for a dramatic moment during which Suárez might escape, and help him safely away to Truxillo. Then, from his inside vantage, Valentin was to convince other men to follow Suárez' example, so that Pizarro's captains would dissolve into the night.

I did not tell him that some persuasion would also be exerted by the women of Lima. But en route home finally to Doña Matilde's house in Callao in a sedan chair provided by Madame Cepeda, I told her highness that the time had come to tighten our campaign, and make it militantly effective.

That night she dispatched swift Indian runners to Centeño in Arequipa and to Prince Paullu in Cuzco. To both we detailed all the significant news. To Centeño I wrote, in Gasca's name, that I had good reason to believe that if he marched to Cuzco he could take the city without a fight, and thus cut off Pizarro's strongest citadel. I suggested that his forces might also prevent any further gold and silver from reaching Pizarro from Potosí, thus undermining the governor fatally, for few men would be loyal to him once they were not paid.

To Prince Paullu, her highness said that the women of

Cuzco were to abandon their conspiracy once Cuzco had pulled down the Pizarro ensign and raised over the town the banner of Castile.

This done, I donned my provocative garment which conceals all but one eye, and visited several houses in Callao. The Spanish women in each instance promised to follow me, and to spread the word throughout Lima that the embargo would end there when the city was free.

This done, I went anxiously to bed.

Paniagua next day received from Pizarro a written defiance of Gasca which was, in effect, a declaration of war. The ancient took leave of Doña Matilde and me with real regret, arguing until his ship lifted anchor that we both join him in flight to Truxillo.

Diego Centeño occupied Cuzco in a fortnight.

The civilizing influence of the women worked there very well. As Centeño approached the city with 200 men he had rallied along the way, the most eminent knights of the town, among them Prince Paullu Upanqui, went to his camp at night and escorted him to the Inca capital. Not a sword flailed in Pizarro's defense. Centeño then sent a strong detachment into Charcas, on Prince Paullu's assurance of intelligence from the mining country that even the governor's commander there, the husband of a one-time Inca sun virgin, was ready to submit. And so it proved.

We, of course, did not learn of this development for some time. Pizarro's messengers, however, were even slower than ours. He did not confirm the disaster until the day of the harvest feast, the Monday following the second Sunday in Lent, though he suspected it when his flow of gold and silver stopped.

Meanwhile Lima was a razor's edge. Short of money, Pizarro broke open the king's treasury to pay the troops, and debased the coinage. On the day the first military payroll was not met, more than 100 men disappeared in the night, led by the most traitorous villain in all Peru after Pizarro, Carbajal and Cepeda—none other than Benito Suárez, the assassin of Viceroy Nuñez. Lima exploded with the news. That night a crowd of merchants and their families loaded all their possessions on a galleon in Callao harbor, and raced northward.

Marshal Carbajal sent fifty men to track down Suárez and his companions, for their horse prints were visible in the sandy soil north of the Rimac River. The fifty joined Suárez, and did not return. In a fury, Carbajal jumped on his mule and set out in pursuit. He caught up with eleven stragglers, and hanged them all.

At the same time Cepeda, whose duty was to calm the civilians, went to Callao and burned all five remaining ships in the harbor to prevent other desertions. Carbajal, returning from his massacre, learned of Cepeda's action. According to Valentin, the old warrior struck his head brutally with both his hands. "You arrant fool!" he screamed. "You have burned the guardian angels of Lima."

The ships gone, I enlisted one of Doña Matilde's runners to communicate with Hernán Mexía in Truxillo, hoping that he and Paniagua had not already departed northward. I pointed out to him that Callao was now deserted, and that a flotilla might easily capture the port.

The following day, a Sunday, Doña Matilde and I went in sedan chairs to Lima to Mass, as the best method of learning how Pizarro and the citizens had responded to all the shocks and rumors. The greatest surprise, however, occurred that day.

In the cathedral, banns were read for the forthcoming marriage of Valentin and Francisca. They were to wed on Easter Monday.

Valentin followed Doña Matilde and me to the street after the service. His face was anxious but unafraid.

"Pizarro now distrusts everyone, and tests my loyalty in this way," he explained hurriedly. "Besides, he thinks the marriage of the conqueror's daughter right now would take the people's minds from their troubles, and show everyone that he, at least, is not worried for the future. The wedding is to be a great spectacle. But don't worry. I will escape to Truxillo at the last moment." He smiled confidently.

I had time only to nod encouragement, but I could not resist asking him of an equally serious concern.

"What of Carbajal? Has he acknowledged you?"

Valentin shook his head.

"Pizarro forbids me to see him," he replied. "In this tumult there is nothing, for the moment, that I can do. I do not understand it, but it is dangerous. Otherwise, why should he keep us apart?"

XXV

Every day more men deserted Pizarro. Some fled to Centeño at Cuzco, others to Truxillo, and many more hid under beds and in closets in Lima and Callao. Even Carbajal, for all his energy and terror, could not prevent the exodus. By dozens and scores the night swallowed up the refugees; and only their women, who had given them cause to disappear, knew where they had gone. By the Day of Annunciation, the mighty army Pizarro had displayed on Saint Agnes' Day was cut almost in half. And those who remained were, like Pizarro and his commanders, edgy, ill-tempered and indecisive.

Even in this turmoil, Pizarro could not ignore Annunciation Day. On foot and unarmed, though accompanied by sixteen halberdiers, he followed the procession for the beloved Virgin about the plaza. But what began in adoration ended in rage.

Except for my one excursion to Lima for Sunday Mass, I had remained out of sight in Callao, fearing to tempt Pizarro's anger by public exhibition. With the city a fuse-lit cannon, none knew what he might do, or what small incident might explode the governor into a purge of all of us who had been against him at the tournament.

On the morning of Annunciation, however, I received a reply from Captain Mexía. He was still in Truxillo. He had not returned north with Paniagua because Lota had refused to accompany him. Heavy now, and expecting her child about the Feast of Mary Magdalene in July, she had persuaded herself that civilized Truxillo, with its comfort and servants, better suited her than the risk of a long and uncertain sea voyage.

So Mexía had remained behind. Luckily he did, he said, for Don Lorenzo de Aldana had arrived the previous day from Panama with five warships and 200 cavalry. Mexía at once raised the king's standard over the municipal building and led the populace, headed by Pizarro's own soldiery, to the jetty to greet the invader. Aldana had remained only long enough to take on water, before setting out for Callao with his flotilla.

"Aldana kisses your feet," Mexía concluded, "and bids you to caution until he can rescue you from the monster. As for me, I call you to bear witness to Friar Gasca that I, not he, delivered Truxillo, since he already claims the honor."

The imminence of Aldana might, I thought, so break Pizarro's spirit that he would depart Lima with his army. Already, I knew, a hundred spouses of important men goaded their husbands to persuade Pizarro of such a plan, if only that once again their beds might be warm at night. So I hurried to Lima, arriving during the Virgin's procession, and cautiously put the news of Truxillo's surrender and Aldana's invasion in the ears of Hipólita Cepeda, asking her to relay it to her husband.

I did not show myself, even to Valentin, for it was an unnecessary risk. Within a few minutes Cepeda, conspicuous in his black satin and white ruff, could be seen from Doña Hipólita's windows as he poured the disastrous word into Pizarro's head even as his lordship marched behind the Virgin. By the time the procession disappeared into the cathedral, everyone on the street knew.

Andrea, hearing I was in the house, approached me at the window. I had not seen her since the tournament. Whatever anguish she had experienced that day was now mastered, for she was more calm and mature than I had ever known her to be. She had a new suitor, in all the desperate excitement of the civil war far more important to her than anything except, perhaps, Valentin's forth-coming marriage. She still loved Valentin, without doubt; but not so much that she could not appreciate and encour-age another. He, she confided, was Valentin's partner in the mine, Joge Griego. Valentin had brought him to call one day, and now Griego pressed his suit as often as he came down from Jumin for mining supplies.

"I have never thanked you," she said at last, "for rescu-ing me on the day of the tournament."

"It was a very bad day for us all," I replied.

"The worst of my life," she laughed, "but it taught me something."

"Yes, Andrea?"

"It taught me that to love and to be loved are not the same."

"It is a hard lesson," I agreed, "but there is one even more difficult."

"More difficult, Doña Eloisa?"

"Not to wear your heart upon your face."

Again she laughed, then asked seriously what I thought would become of us all. Realizing that her thoughts were still on Valentin, I told her that Aldana should arrive be-fore Easter Monday, in which case either there would be a battle for the city or, as I thought more likely, Pizarro would temporarily abandon Lima to reorganize his forces. In either case, I doubted there would be time for weddings.

"These are days," I emphasized, "that we must all live one at a time, and the only importance is to remain alive."

Her eyes told me that she understood this, and also that her own chance of survival bested mine.

More to deploy my own attention away from this grim thought than to cheer her, I said, "Don't be discouraged, Andrea. When this is all over, Peru will need girls like you. It is you, and others your age, who will civilize this country. It is worth waiting for."

The crowd before the cathedral across the plaza had thinned now. Suddenly I saw Valentin. On impulse I left the Cepeda house and rushed to him as he strolled thoughtfully toward the governor's house. He caught me by the wrist.

"You crazy fool," he growled. "If Pizarro sees you he will have you into his garden, and this time you will not escape."

He wheeled and walked with me quickly into the sanctuary of the cathedral. It now was empty. Valentin relaxed. Not knowing what to say, he led me forward to the light of the votive candles newly placed in the side altar of the Virgin. Both of us knelt and said short prayers. Then hurriedly I whispered the news from Truxillo. He had not yet heard it, and gripped my hand tightly.

"Listen well," he replied. "His Lordship is a wild man, and this will make him worse. Something has come over everyone. Nobody seems able to think straight, and tempers are like triggers. Yesterday Cepeda called Carbajal a coward for not going after Centeño in Cuzco, and the old devil could have killed him. If this news of Aldana's coming is true, it will chase Pizarro out of town. Everyone urges him to go already. Promise me you will stay in Callao until the danger is past."

I gave my pledge, and inquired of his marriage to Francisca. He had not let go my hand. Now he gripped it tighter, as he told me that the governor was, if anything,

229

more determined to carry it through, since everyone, including Francisca, was so set against it. He must defy this rebellion against his power.

"And Andrea?" I asked.

"She has decided to live."

"I hope you have been attentive to her."

"I am sorry for her. This thing has been as hard on her as on anybody. I used her shamefully to get at her father, and now she is in love with me. It is a hard thing to overcome."

"She is lovely. Do you want it overcome, Valentin?"

He turned and crushed me, kissing me as though he would never have opportunity to touch a woman again. After that, he did not know what to do. Clumsily he let me go.

"Next time we kneel together before this altar, it will be for a different purpose," he flung at me, and almost ran away.

Not until after Passion Sunday did Pizarro break. By then his soldiery was under such tension and frustration that brawls and riots broke out every night. To prevent further mischief, and to occupy his men, Pizarro ordered the army out of town, to an encampment three leagues to the south. Carbajal was sent to defend Callao. Cepeda, throwing off his legal velvet for casque and mail, by decree became military governor of Lima. Of all the fighting forces, only Pizarro and his guard remained in town.

On the Wednesday before Palm Sunday, Aldana's five sails appeared off the port. Half the populace of Lima went to Callao to see them. Carbajal doubled his force.

Aldana did not land. Instead, he sent ashore a package under a white flag. Carbajal dispatched an aide on the fastest horse to carry Aldana's bundle to Pizarro, who had moved that morning from Lima to the main camp.

230

The waterfront returned to normal. Carbajal dispersed the idlers and forbade any trespass on the jetty. The mellow harvest sun went down.

Late in the night I was awakened by Béatriz. Silently she handed me a gown and motioned me to don it hurriedly and follow her. She ran away.

No one was in the patio as I descended the stairs, but there was an unusual light in the kitchen. There I saw Béatriz bending over a man in blue hose and knee-length cavalry boots. She was swabbing a brown curly forehead. I ran to take Valentin's head in my hands. A long, ugly saber cut crossed his temple and flared into his cheek, and his beautiful beard was a mat of blood.

He smiled at me, ignoring Béatriz' painful ministration. I knew she was far better versed to relieve his wound than I, so I did not try to help her. I sat down beside Valentin to give him what sympathy I could.

"I told you I would get away," he gasped, "but I had— some difficulty."

He told me that Aldana's communication, addressed to Pizarro, was a last demand from Gasca that the rebel surrender and accept the king's pardon. The scrivener, Pedro Guillen, read the message to his lordship in a voice of both fear and wonder, for none of Pizarro's followers except those who had attended the Paniagua meeting knew how disastrous were Gasca's authorities. Aldana reviewed them all again, as Guillen's voice became more and more hysterical.

In a rage at this cowardice, Pizarro seized the parchments, tore them to fragments, and threw them over his head, lest more of his followers discover the truth. Then he retired with Cepeda, to emerge in an hour with a proclamation, which Valentin and many others were summoned to hear. In it, in precise legal phrases, Cepeda, as supreme judge of Peru, declared Father Gasca, Lorenzo de Aldana, Hernán Mexía, Admiral Hinojosa, and Valentin traitors, and condemned them to death.

During the reading of the final paragraphs, Carbajal stamped in. He had been recalled from Callao with all his force. As the names were read out, Carbajal, still able to swagger and jest, spat out, "Excellency, what is the object of this process?"

"Its object," Cepeda replied calmly, "is to prevent delay that, if taken at any time, these guilty parties may be at once led to execution."

"I cry you mercy," Carbajal scoffed. "I thought there must be some virtue in the instrument that would kill them outright. Let one of the traitors fall into my hands, and I will march him off to execution without waiting for the sentence of any court, I promise you."

"Then you may start at once," Pizarro said coldly, and pointed to Valentin. But Valentin had expected some such maneuver, and was ready. He raced from the tent before any could stop him, receiving a single slash from Carbajal as he fled. He mounted Pizarro's own horse, the fleetest in Peru, and made off southward, soon outdistancing any pursuit and losing himself in the dark. By a devious circuit, bloody and weak, but knowing that all of Pizarro's army had left Callao, he rode to Doña Matilde's gate, slapped Pizarro's horse homeward, and knocked for admittance.

"At least," I consoled him, "if you are sentenced to death, you are in excellent company. But why were you included?"

Valentin shrugged. "Why not?" he said. "I have done him as much damage as anyone, but until now he did not choose to believe it."

Carbajal had been recalled from Callao, Valentin reported, because at dawn the army would march south to

Arequipa. Pizarro dared not face Aldana as long as Centeño was at his back, and he would dispose of one foe at a time.

"You mean Lima is free?" I shouted.

"Not a fighting man remained in it or near it as I passed through."

Joyously I rushed from the house to the jetty. No guard was there. I ran to the great iron circle which alarmed the town for fire, grasped the striker, and hammered violently. In a moment heads appeared in every window.

"Pizarro is gone," I shouted. "He is en route to Arequipa. Come build a beacon and summon Aldana in."

From pitchwood on the docks a fire soon blazed. Before long, on one of the ships, a cannon fired.

By noon next day the fleet had arrived. Aldana himself was the first ashore, and I the first to receive him. He swept me off my feet and held me high aloft. Even before he could set me down, I had babbled all the news. At once he ordered his cavalry to occupy Lima.

He then formed a guard. With punctilious ceremony he raised the king's standard at the customs house. The merchants shouted, and for the first time in many days found favor with their women.

I should hate to be a midwife in this town or Lima come next season of the Advent.

XXVI

Easter Day was jubilantly observed in Lima. To the usual greeting "He is risen," was added a new phrase, "Gasca is coming." Aldana had proclaimed, soon after his arrival, that the friar had chosen this supreme moment for his departure from Panama. So in all the churches a special prayer was read for his excellency's safe voyage. None who devoutly heard that supplication knew what another twelvemonth would harbor, except that it must bring either Gasca or death.

From every city except Arequipa, which Pizarro had entered without a fight since Centeño was not there to defend it, came reports, as Whitsuntide, Corpus Christi, Trinity and Rogation passed, that Gasca would be extravagantly received. From the highland towns, scores of men journeyed openly down the Inca road to join Centeño in Cuzco; along the coast, Hernán Mexía assembled large forces in Truxillo.

Only in Lima was there doubt. This uncertainty was of Aldana's own making. He ruled like a conqueror, not like the exponent of forgiveness and love that was Father Gasca.

We should have sensed earlier than we did that Aldana knew only the ways of the conquistadors, and could not change. On his first day ashore he moved into Pizarro's palace, thus declaring to everyone his mastery over the city. The next day he commanded Valentin to vacate the widow Suárez' house. Infirm as he was from his head wound, Valentin was moved bodily, with all his belongings, to the City of the Kings. Curtly Aldana told him that he would continue to serve as captain of the guard.

I protested Valentin's departure from Callao, for Doña Matilde had welcomed the presence of a man in her household in such uncertain times, and Valentin's nearness had given me comfort. Nobody knew when the grizzled Carbajal might make one of his spectacular raids on Callao and try to carry off both Valentin and me. I had no illusion about my own fate. Pizarro, I knew, would not rest until the lark had been brought to earth.

Aldana would not listen. "I heard," he answered me, "even in Truxillo, that this Captain Guerrero wants you for himself, and where better to deflower you than under your own roof? Do not forget that I have some claim on you myself. Did I not liberate Truxillo, Callao and Lima? Who has done more?"

Valentin would have resisted the order even then, had I not begged him to submit. This was no time, I reminded him, for Gasca's captains to fight each other.

But this was only the beginning. In Pizarro's palace were two cooks, Indians both. They had served the Marquis Pizarro, who had claimed them as part of his spoil from the household of the Inca, such artists were they with the native dishes. Gonzalo Pizarro had continued them in his service. They were old men now, and knew no loyalty except to their herbs and stew pots. About the Feast of Saint John in May, Aldana received a letter from Pizarro. It mentioned in detail the happenings in Aldana's household as proof that Pizarro knew everything that happened, and ordered Aldana to return to Panama before the governor sent Carbajal to drive him out. Somehow Aldana concluded that the spies in his house were the two cooks. He had them brought before him and accused them of villainy.

At the time, I was in Lima; lately, to have a hand in all that occurred, I often remained a few days with Doña Hipólita and her daughter Andrea. Cepeda had deserted his family when he fled south with Pizarro, and they lived by selling their valuables one by one to the merchants who now again had begun to flourish. So they needed both comfort and assurance, and welcomed me at any time.

A message from Valentin urgently summoned me to the palace. When I arrived, the cooks were being scourged to compel their confession. Both Valentin and I begged Aldana to cease this cruelty. Surely he must realize, we said, that Peru held no secrets. Did not Aldana know every move of Pizarro's? Were there not a hundred men ready to sell any information to either side?

Our interference only enraged him. Bitterly he turned on us. He knew much more than we realized, he shouted. He knew, for example, that I had secret ambitions to be empress of Peru. He knew that Valentin was the son of Carbajal.

"Perhaps," he threatened, scowling at Valentin, "it is you rather than these miserable Indians who have kept Pizarro informed. Are you the spy?"

Valentin hotly denied such a ridiculous insinuation.

"Then it must be the cooks," Aldana said. "Prove your own innocence, Captain Guerrero. Take these two out and hang them for their treachery."

Valentin demurred.

"I command you!" Aldana said.

Valentin shook his head. In recent days, recovered of his wound except for a manly scar on his left brow, he had resumed the old-fashioned accoutrements he had brought from Spain. Calmly he drew his great broadsword.

236

"You have no power to command me," he replied.

Aldana at that moment was in no position to defend himself, for he was unarmed except for a dagger, and he knew that if he ordered the men who flogged the Indians, all members of Valentin's household guard, to seize Valentin, he would again be disobeyed. His face livid, he left the room.

But that night he hanged the cooks.

The city was outraged. Nobody cared what happened to two lowly Indians; it was only that Aldana's high-handedness reminded everyone of Pizarro's methods, which Gasca, in hundreds of letters, had promised to end. Here once again were high promises and empty performance reminiscent of the two previous king's men, Vaca de Castro and Nuñez Vela. In both Lima and Callao, men began to act and speak as though they had been loyal to Pizarro all along.

Even before this incident occurred, another was in the making. Aldana's chief lieutenant and crony was one Carlos Váldes, the captain of one of the warships. He was an Asturian of agile mind and precocious ambition, ruthless and aggressive, an excellent officer. He had not achieved in the conquest either the fame or wealth to which he aspired, and now sought to repair his fortunes under Gasca. Of about Aldana's age but lacking in breeding, he began to call on Andrea Cepeda.

She and her mother were wary of this suit, fearing to provoke Aldana by discouraging a man three times Andrea's years and utterly unsuited to her tender innocence. When he became persistent, Doña Hipólita summoned Valentin and me, and asked for help. Andrea wrote Griego at the mine of it, too, for the Greek had showered her with affectionate correspondence. So Griego came to town and set himself up boldly as a love rival of the Captain Váldes, choosing the same daily hour to call at the Cepeda

237

house. Privately, Valentin attempted to chill Váldes' aspirations by telling him that Andrea had no prospects, her father was a traitor whose wealth would be confiscated, and that surely Váldes could set himself up to better advantage with a wealthy woman more his age.

This provoked Váldes to an angry demand on Aldana that Andrea, as the daughter of an arch-conspirator against the crown, was fair spoil of the conquest, which he claimed. Aldana at once agreed, and ordered Doña Hipólita to prepare her daughter for marriage to his lieutenant.

Griego was for killing the two men at once, but this was obviously impossible, not only because Aldana and Váldes had 200 men of the fleet at their backs, but because such overt dissension among Gasca's representatives would surely tempt Pizarro to recapture the city. Further, it was contrary to Father Gasca's methods, which we must uphold.

So Valentin, Griego and I called upon the Archbishop of Lima and begged him to intercede.

The archbishop was a warrior priest, a veteran of the entire conquest, and successor to Bishop Valverde who had absolved the Marquis Pizarro of sin in the cruel ambush of the Inca Atahualpa's army, which had been lured under truce inside a walled town and there slaughtered by cannon. Valverde also had insisted upon the murder of Atahualpa, because that Inca lord, unknowing what it was, had thrown a missal to the ground. Unlike Valverde, the archbishop was no bigot, but a missionary deeply concerned for the welfare of the Indian population. His position was delicate, for whoever ultimately mastered Peru, whether Pizarro or the king, he must still be in position to carry on the Church. He was aware of Bishop Loaysa's defection in Panama, which had his blessing, but he dared not defy openly the constituted political authority of Peru, whatever its changing fortunes.

On this issue, however, his duty was clear, for we charged

that Andrea's betrothal, against both her will and that
of her mother, made mockery of the sacrament of marriage. He summoned to him at once Andrea and her
mother, Aldana and Váldes, listened to each in turn, and
forbade the banns.

Aldana, however, had anticipated the result. He strode
to the window of the archbishop's residence and signaled.
Fifty men at arms seized the house.

He called his men to witness the conspiracy between
Valentin, Griego and, acting for her husband, Hipólita
Cepeda, with the archbishop to undermine Aldana's authority and provoke open issue to invite Pizarro's return
to power. He arrested the four of them, and sent Andrea
and me under armed escort to the Cepeda house with
orders to remain there.

Andrea reacted with all the emotional intensity common
to girls just flowering into womanhood. She wanted to kill
Aldana with her own hand, then to destroy herself. She
was desperate with fear for the safety of her mother, for
Valentin whom she loved, and for Griego who loved her,
and in tear-flooded depths of depression that she and her
mother had been wrapped by Aldana in the same black
cloth that covered her nefarious father. Her father was
right, she cried in my arms; even Pizarro was preferable
to the king's men.

The same reaction, I knew, would assail all of Lima.
Even Pizarro had not been arrogant enough to arrest his
grace, the primate of Peru. The incident might easily
throw the populace back to Pizarro. Then all was lost, for
the governor would not twice let the crown of Peru slip
from him. Aldana must be curbed, ruthlessly, and at once.

I sent an Indian to Doña Matilde, enclosing a letter
which I begged her to speed, by her swiftest runner, to
Hernán Mexía in Truxillo. He, smarting at Aldana's
claims to the liberation of Truxillo, would, I knew, come

at once. And he alone had men enough to make a show of force.

Mexía responded immediately. In ten days he entered the city with 200 men, a squadron equal to that of Aldana. I met him joyfully and together we confronted Aldana in Pizarro's palace, while the men of Truxillo grimly sat their mounts in the plaza, and every window of vantage was filled with frightened townspeople.

"What brings you here?" Aldana demanded of his old friend.

Mexía did not involve me. He said he had heard that Aldana had outraged the populace, and he had thus marched south to help Aldana restore order.

Aldana curtly ordered him to return to Truxillo, saying he needed no such help.

Mexía stood his ground, as well he might, with a powerful force outside the door, whereas Aldana's army was scattered on a dozen errands of forage for food and munitions. He said there was another matter which bothered him also, namely credit for the freedom of Truxillo, a record he desired to set straight.

"I realize," he said, glancing toward me, "that you and I, Captain Aldana, both vie for the same prize. My work in Truxillo is done. So I have come here, to see that I get my just dues, and at least an equal share in what may follow. If Carbajal raids you, you will need me."

Belligerently Aldana displayed written authority from Gasca, commanding him to govern Lima pending the friar's own arrival, and again ordered Mexía from the city. The little captain laughed. He said he doubted Aldana guided the city as Gasca would wish, and cited the hanging of the two cooks and the arrest of the archbishop and Valentin as examples of incidents that Gasca would never have condoned. Red-faced and angry, Aldana said he would report Mexía's insolence to Gasca, and seek new authorities. When these arrived, he would see Mexía hanged.

Mexía's only comment was to ask where Valentin was imprisoned, that he might release him. Aldana refused to tell. Then, indeed, Mexía lost his temper.

"Would you undo all the good that has been done?" he spat. "The day of arrests and hangings is past, Don Lorenzo de Aldana. You saw yourself in Panama how the friar forgave everyone. His representatives in Peru can do no less. You do not seem to understand the new order and must be taught."

As he spoke Valentin and Griego, dirty and uncombed, rushed into the room. Valentin enveloped Mexía in a bear hug. Mexía's men had discovered their prison and released them. Mexía ordered his men to drive Aldana's guards from the archbishop's house, thus restoring his liberty, and to find Doña Hipólita Cepeda and escort her to her home.

"I forbid it!" Aldana shouted. But the men obeyed Mexía.

For many minutes Aldana angrily stood his ground, until Griego suggested the simplest solution to the difficulty was to leave him alone in a room with Aldana, both having their swords. In the end, I drew up a parchment dictated by Valentin, in which Aldana agreed to share his authorities equally with Mexía and Valentin, until Gasca decided otherwise. But he signed it only when Mexía threatened to make him tenant of the prison which Valentin and Griego had vacated. To save his dignity, Aldana was permitted to remain in Pizarro's palace, with Valentin returning to his old quarters along the garden wall.

Mexía found lodgings in the house of Benito Suárez, who had returned with him. He needed larger accommodations than the palace offered, for Lota followed a day's journey behind him. To witness her arrival, I stayed in

Lima another night, and found Doña Hipólita no worse for her imprisonment. Indeed, she had lost considerable weight, which gratified her.

Lota made elegant entrance into the city, despite her heavy body. She was carried in a litter by Indian bearers. An Indian woman walked behind the palanquin as her servant. Lota was dressed in fine stuff and carried her head high. She turned to greet me, smiling as though we were equals. I saw that she had blossomed like a cactus after a shower of rain. Eating well, working not at all, waited on, dressed in finery, and blessed by that healthy blush all women seem to acquire at such a time, Lota had become presentable. The warts had been removed from her nose, and she even wore shoes, something she had never done for me. She bowed to me, suggested I dine with her one night, and then walked, on Mexía's arm, into her new home.

Valentin, who stood nearby, and whom Lota had ignored despite his salutation, joined me much puzzled.

"You have lost a maid and gained a rival," he said. "But I do not understand Mexía. How can he hope to win you when he so openly favors your servant?"

"It is not unusual, is it," I asked, "for a man to have a mistress? Many a bridegroom's bastards have watched him take the marriage vows, and not with their mother."

"Doesn't it disturb you?" he persisted.

"Not yet," I answered grimly. "I had rather be given to him than to Aldana, even though Lota and I were lodged in the same house."

He smiled brightly. "That I am glad to know," he said.

Mexía and Valentin had no further trouble with Aldana. He resented them both, but not openly, and he could not fight them so long as they stood together, which they did in every decision. They concentrated on strengthening and arming their forces to resist Pizarro, should he attack. Griego returned to Jumin.

So again the days passed in tension. The month of July covered Lima with its miserable cloud of fog, which seemed never to lift, though only a league away the sun shone as brilliantly as ever. And there was no word of Gasca. We had confirmed messages from Panama that he had sailed. Then nothing, although he should long since have reached Peru. Sailors recalled that Easter was the very worst season to navigate southward the coast of Peru, and feared that his excellency had foundered with all his vessels. This favored Pizarro's cause. Every week encouraged the governor to boldness. Convinced the Gasca threat would not materialize, he would resume the offensive swiftly. Everyone knew this. Rumors crept from Arequipa that Pizarro planned to attack, and that Carbajal had already set out for the City of the Kings.

My only diversion from this anxiety occurred on Saint Margaret's day, the twentieth of July. Lota delivered to the world a baby boy. I had not called on her, of course; somehow I could not accept her, as plainly she demanded, in friendship and near equality. But at news of her motherhood I threw off my pride and went to her with a gift of pomegranates and figs.

She was robust and clear of head, showing less fatigue than on occasions I recalled when she had spent the day at the Canillejas washtubs in Cáceres. She had the baby brought to me for inspection, and called him Hernán, to which, evidently, Mexía had not objected, for the date of her confinement clearly proved that her guilt had originated in Panama, and not on the voyage from Spain. Luckily, she did not ask me to stand as the child's godmother, for I should not have known what to say.

She was pleased with herself for producing her bastard on Saint Margaret's day, taking as an omen of God's forgiveness her bedding on a festival devoted to the patron of innocence and humility. She wore no shame at all. Indeed she was as brazen as any duchess who had produced an heir to a great house and thus expected special homage paid her. She prated, while nursing the child, that she, in her own way, had greatly furthered Father Gasca's enterprise. Had she not, she asked me boldly, by her sin won Mexía to Gasca's cause, without which Valentin and I would never have reached Peru? And was she not, therefore, entitled to great material reward when the spoils of Peru were divided among the faithful? Surely God thought so, or he would not have so blessed her on Saint Margaret's Day; and Gasca, if nothing else, was a keen interpreter of God's infallible ways.

I left her bedside in confusion, and went around to call on Andrea and her mother. The innocent freshness of Andrea would be an antidote to Lota's brashness. Andrea was happy again, she and her mother both confident that better days lay ahead. They were entertaining over a glass of sherry.

The guests were Valentin and Griego. At this rate, I thought, the Greek was spending more time in courtship than in mining; but that was not my burden, and I wished him every luck, though wondering what Valentin thought of it. As I entered, Andrea was fascinated by something the Levantine was saying, her eyes bright with admiration. I soon discovered what it was, for Andrea resumed the discourse as soon as I had spoken to everyone.

Griego was much improved by love. He was affluently dressed in brown satin doublet, was clean and well-tonsured. I wondered at his background, for he was confidently at home in the Cepeda salon, and I remembered that he was a man of substantial education. He had evolved a plan, he was saying, to restore the highland valley of Jumin to its ancient agriculture, once Gasca had settled the country. With much time on his hands, he had explored the land for two leagues up and down the plain, and had quietly begun to buy—in Valentin's name since he could not own land himself—a great tract from his share of the silver. At one time, he said, the land had been irrigated by the Inca. The old canals were still visible in many places. It was only a question of opening them and repairing them, and channeling a new source to the inexhaustible waters of the near mountains. This was all that the land required for great fertility. He, the engineer, knew just what to do.

"And I have means, my lady," he said, turning to me, "for I have at last found the *peja grande!*" On each visit to Lima, he had returned to Chan Chan for a day's exploration. On his last visit, following his stint of jail at Aldana's hands, his persistence had been rewarded. The big fish had been almost where he had first dug, and was of solid gold. Naturally he had hidden it away in a place only Valentin knew, until the war's end.

"There is an empire to be built in the highlands," he said dreamily. "An empire of fruit and olive groves and great fields of maize, and grass for sheep and cattle that will continue to be rich for generations after the silver is exhausted."

Here, in a permanent settlement with a future, was something a woman could understand, and both Andrea and I responded to it. It was a story of life and growth rather than of war and death. That very morning Valentin had agreed to be his partner in this venture also.

As the men arose to leave, I would have departed with them, had not Doña Hipólita insistently stayed me. She had heard from her husband. Following her abasement in prison, Cepeda had written swiftly to emphasize that no good was served by supporting Gasca, for at least Pizarro had not submitted her to the indignity of imprisonment.

245

He begged her, for her own protection, to remain aloof from further embarrassments against the day of Pizarro's inevitable return.

Even though Doña Hipólita loathed her husband, she respected his canny political sense, and knew that he would not have written her without cause, since he did nothing except after the coldest calculation. She said she would die before returning to him, except to insure her daughter's future; but she thought I should be warned that Pizarro must have resolved a plan for the recapture of the city, and for me to alert Aldana and Mexía. I promised to do so.

But still she stayed me, and in the end it was Andrea who blurted out that the letter had said still more. It inquired of me, and asked for specific information whether I still resided in Doña Matilde's house in Callao or had moved to Lima, and if so, where I now stopped.

"His Lordship cannot forget her," Cepeda wrote, "fool that he is, and means to have her for wife, since he cannot possess her else. We shall assure our future in the day of Pizarro's success if our family are the instrument by which the Doña Eloisa is delivered to the governor in a condition fit for marriage to him who will become emperor. Be guided by this thought, to your profit and perhaps to your life. For in this matter, as in no other, His Lordship is of constant mind."

"What shall I reply?" Doña Hipólita asked.

"Tell him I hold His Lordship no grudge, and he is ever in my prayers that he may yield to Gasca and thus save his life and dignity."

"Naught else?"

"Naught else is necessary," I replied. "Pizarro will in any case do what he likes, and if he is in truth to rule Peru, I had rather be his empress than headless bones."

XXVII

When the Feast of Saint Jago dawned and we had not
yet heard anything from Gasca, the three defenders of
Lima, Valentin, Mexía and Aldana, decided to relieve the
anxiety by a brave show of arms.

Four hundred men trooped their colors at the cathedral
in reverence to the patron of Castile who thirty times had
appeared to Spanish armies in moments of peril. Following
this service, almost the entire force, under both Aldana
and Mexía since neither trusted the other, sallied from
the city for a week of military exercises at Juaja, leaving
Valentin and Benito Suárez with a small guard at Lima.

That night, long after dark, galloping horses awoke the
household of Doña Matilde in Callao. Béatriz broke in on
me. Valentin was outside, shouting. Opening my shutters,
I saw Valentin below with two extra mounts.

"Bring Béatriz and come at once," he called. "Carbajal
has come for us."

I threw on my wool dress with the eye-concealing hood,
left my jewels and the rest of my wardrobe with Doña
Matilde, and rushed downstairs. Béatriz, for all her bulk,
refused to remain behind.

Doña Matilde kissed me, and pressed into my hand an
emerald ring in the shape of a condor which she always

wore. "Show this charm to any Indian," she said, "and he will help you."

We crossed the Rimac River, which in winter was so deep that the horses swam the ford, and headed northward, wet and miserable, under a cold-star sky. For half a league Valentin did not speak.

"You are sure this is not nonsense, Valentin?" I asked at last.

"Believe me, Lisa," he assured me, "it is death if we do not get away."

He told me that Ancón, the mestizo lad whose life he had saved in the incident which won for Valentin the captaincy of Pizarro's guard, had repaid the debt by warning of Carbajal's approach. The demon was camped a league to the south, hoping to find Lima drunk and unprotected after the Feast of Saint Jago. To prove that Pizarro was yet ruler of Peru, he proposed to enter the city at midnight, raid the governor's palace and hang Valentin, Aldana and Mexía, at the same time sending a detachment to Callao for me. It was the sort of boldness for which he was notorious.

"Where are we going?"

"To Truxillo, unless Carbajal catches us. We must go faster."

He kicked his mount, and I mine. At this accelerated motion, the silly silver bells at my skirt hem began to tinkle merrily. Valentin ordered me to rip them off instantly, lest their sound disclose us, and drop them in the first swift stream through which we passed. On we went. Béatriz, who was terrified of horses, followed my example in making no pretense of riding sidesaddle. Such a maneuver was impossible with high-pommeled, stiff-backed cavalry gear. Valentin had brought excellent stock, they being survivors from Pizarro's own guard stable. All were strong, sleek, and sure of foot.

The road, well packed so that even by starlight the horses followed it easily, began to wind up a rocky eminence into the brow of a biting wind. As we climbed, with much labor, Valentin admitted that he had wasted little time inquiring about the route of our journey. All he knew was that Truxillo was eighty leagues, more or less, to the north. His first objective was the Passamayo River and the town of Chancay on its farther bank.

"How far to the Passamayo?" I asked.

"If God favors us and we do not stop, we should arrive sometime tomorrow night. Getting over this cursed mountain will be the roughest. Fortunately we meet it first, when our mounts are fresh."

It seemed to me that a flight to Truxillo would be obvious, and that therefore we should seek other objective. When I suggested this to Valentin, he agreed at once. Unfortunately, he knew no other route. The plains were vast, and shifting sands often obliterated the road, so he dared not deviate from the coast. At first he had considered flight to Jumin, where his mine was, for Griego could hide us. But this was a trip through and over the cordillera, too rugged for women in winter.

Griego, he explained, reached the mine by traveling from the coast up the Guara River, across the mountains into the Mantera River valley, thence down onto the great high plain. But since we must in any case ford the Passamayo en route to Truxillo, and Carbajal would scarcely dare press us beyond that point, Valentin thought we might better remain along the coast, where seven towns would succor us, and the climate at least be merciful.

We rode on, at the rate of perhaps a league[1] an hour judging from our speed, Valentin in the van feeling out the road, which wound steeply upward, and often pitched sharply down over loose pebbles. I could understand why

[1] The Spanish league was about three miles

Carbajal, hernia or not, rode a sure-footed mule in Peru. Our mounts stumbled and occasionally slipped; but on we went. Twice during the night we stopped briefly at springs to water the horses and listen for possible pursuit. A mountain silence covered the land.

The first half-light of day, cold and ghastly, found us near the summit of the ridge. Béatriz, as strong of mind as she was big of body, had not once protested, and now drowsed in her saddle. Ahead of me Valentin, tensely concentrating, sang back the hazards of the road, that we avoid them. I could see the track now, wide enough for two horses abreast, bounded by flat stones, but rough and perilous. God's love alone must have guided our horses in the night, lest one of them had gone lame or fallen from a cliff. Valentin drew up wearily and squinted south. No pursuit was evident; but on the mountain that meant nothing. Carbajal, to whom the landscape was as familiar as his beard, might well have cut across to head us.

"We have made a good start," Valentin said, smiling cheerfully as Béatriz' eyes opened with a jerk. "Aldana's guards will run from Carbajal. But by the time he discovers us gone and has met the detachment he sent to Callao, we should have at least three hours start. God grant it may be enough."

He patted his horse on the neck, and we began the descent.

I welcomed the sun, which drove away our chill and dried our clothes. It did nothing to combat the wind, which continuously drove dust and sand into our faces. The northern face of the mountain, with its downward slope, was more rugged than the ascent. The horses were beginning to tire, and stumbled more frequently. We pushed on. The landscape was a scorched brownstone on which no life grew, crawled or flew except ourselves. For hours we were without water or any rest. Before us, northward, the

250

ground leveled out, an uninhabited waste as far as we could see.

Almost at the bottom of the ridge a thicket of trees marked a mountain stream. We dismounted and rested a half-hour, while the horses cropped feeble brown grasses at the water's edge. Both Béatriz and I were at once asleep. Only the urgency of our flight choked my protest when Valentin awoke us.

"Cheer up," he said. "We must be halfway to the Passamayo. From here it is all level going, and we will make better time."

I soon discovered that I, as well as Béatriz, could doze in the saddle, for the horses plodded gamely now across a desert. Often the highway was covered over by drifting sand, so that we followed upright stones set at intervals of a hundred paces to mark the way.

A cold chill throbbing in from the sea woke me. The sun was behind the wind; its day's work done, it closed its fiery eye and left us to the dusk. Behind, almost to the horizon, huddled the brown plain. No movement disturbed it.

"Sleep well?" Valentin asked, immediately alert to my waking. His eyes were deep-circled and weary, but his mouth was cheerful.

"Let me lead awhile, Valentin," I said, "while you rest."
He shook his head.

"We should be no more than four hours now from the Passamayo. If God permits us to ford it safely and gives our horses strength, we should be safe by midnight."

"There is a town there?" I asked. Oddly, I was not at all hungry, just dead weight.

"Chancay, but we dare not enter it. We will leave it on our left hand and go on to Guara. It is only a league farther, and has an Indian tambo where we can eat and rest. How do you feel?"

251

"If this cursed wind would die, I would be all right."

"Bless the wind," Valentin answered. "It drifts sand across our tracks."

I looked back at Béatriz. She was huddled unhappily, but by great effort organized a smile for me. I waved to her. "Soon, Béatriz," I encouraged her, "we will get rest and sleep." She nodded, hanging on to her pommel with both hands, for her horse limped on his right foreleg, and plugged along with his head low-slung. Béatriz was not even holding his rein.

With nightfall, the cold became intense. Valentin wrapped me in his cloak, and unslung a blanket from behind his saddle for Béatriz.

One step was as another for many hours. The horses had been rested, but had not tasted water since nightfall.

My mount raised his nose into the wind, threw up his ears, and moved forward more rapidly. In a few minutes his footing seemed firmer under me, as though the cruel sand had yielded to harder substance. Soon we passed a tree.

"Are you still there?" Valentin called. "The horses scent water. The Passamayo cannot be far away."

Now I smelled earth and growing plants. Under the dark, remotely starred sky I could not see the fields which must be there, dull in winter dress. In another half-league we came to a gentle river.

The horses plunged into it up to their knees.

"Don't let them drink too much," Valentin warned.

Warily he explored the stream, searching for a ford, and returned boisterous.

"Here's luck," he whispered. "There is a stone bridge. At least this time we will not get wet. Shall we rest awhile or try the other league?"

"On, on," said Béatriz.

The horses, smelling grass, balked at setting out again.

For a moment we lost our route. After the bridge, the road had turned west along the river bank toward the black, silent huts of Chancay. Cautiously Valentin sniffed his way until he discovered a northward track, and once more we were on our way.

Little more than an hour later we drew up at another river. This time the horses demanded a long drink. We crossed by an easy ford. At the far side was a hut of mud and rock. It was the Indian hostel of Inca times, still in use, but now under the ownership of a limping Spaniard. The host and his wife, wakened from sleep, received us well with goat milk, cheese and olives. A paddock behind the tambo, lively with the aroma of good hay, bedded the horses.

Valentin, placated by food and wine, fought sleep. He creaked to his feet.

"Rest well," he said to Béatriz and me. "Tomorrow, when you are ready, we will go on to Barranca."

He patted me on the shoulder, and Béatriz also, and staggered away to rest. Béatriz and I at once found our own quarters. They were a miserable lodging, with a dirt floor, no window, not even a hanging curtain across the aperture which served as a door. We fell on our litters without undressing.

The sun awoke me.

I raised to one elbow, wondering where I was.

Then I sat upright in a hurry.

His mighty bulk filling the doorway, calmly picking his teeth with a straw, stood Marshal Carbajal.

SIERRA

XXVIII

Seeing me wake, Carbajal took the straw from his mouth. He was truly an ancient Valentin in appearance, I could now see clearly.

"So this is the little lark the old hawk was sent to bring down," he grinned. "And in just the nest where I expected to find her."

I did not answer. Across the hovel, Béatriz eyed the brute as though matching her strength against his own. When Carbajal saw that he could not bait me, his eyes blooded.

"I like company with my coffee," he said. "It is boiling now. Before it cools, you will be in the patio, or I will drag you out by the hair."

I made myself as presentable as possible, which was not much. The garb I had worn from Lima was mud-stained and wrinkled, the skirt hem jagged where I had torn off the bells. I had no herbs for my face, or even a flask of scent.

"Stay with me, Béatriz," I whispered.

She fumbled in her bodice, took out her coral necklace and her star-shaped barret and slowly put them on. I could not but smile.

"We will make magic over him," Béatriz said solemnly.

We went outside. The door opened on a courtyard in

which stood one tree, below which a table was set with cups and wine. Carbajal sat astride a bench, chewing a tortilla. The innkeeper's wife came running with a half dozen hard-boiled eggs, her face taut with fear. Before the room Valentin occupied, two guards stood with unsheathed swords. In the paddock, many horses and Carbajal's red mule were eating hay.

"Come, my little lark," Carbajal called to me, his mouth full of food, a big hand crushing and shelling an egg.

I walked meekly to him and sat down. Béatriz stood behind me.

"The sultana and her slave," Carbajal jeered, eyeing us both. "What a pretty picture for a painter."

He broke a hard tortilla and handed me a crust of it with a dirty fist. Then he seized my chin and turned my head to one side, then the other.

"Overrated," he scoffed. "That's the trouble with a womanless country. When a female comes along who is well-born, she is immediately described as the Madonna."

He gorged another egg, roaring toward the kitchen, "Coffee, you bitch, coffee!"

The woman ran to him with a steaming pot, fumbling several cups in one hand.

"May I pour, my lord?" I asked, stepping forward.

"Well now, that's nice," said the marshal. "Nothing ever upsets a lady."

I drew three cups, handed one to him and one to Béatriz.

Carbajal sniffed the bouquet cautiously for scent of poison.

"Your health!" he said, laughed raucously, and drank the scalding brew.

Valentin stepped from his room. Obviously he had been taken asleep, for there was no mark on him. Guarded on either side, he walked to Carbajal. He glanced quickly at me, reproaching himself as though he had betrayed me, but showing no fear. I poured him coffee, but he did not take it.

Carbajal eyed him pleasantly.

"This is the first chance I have had," he said, "to see at close hand the mighty champion from Arévalo who unseated me at the tournament. . . . Good forelock, excellent poll, strong withers. Turn around and let me see your croup."

Obediently Valentin swung about face. Carbajal judged him over the coffee cup.

"H-m-m-m. Well shanked and fetlocked. In all, not bad. Turn around."

Valentin complied.

Carbajal set down his cup. He seemed puzzled by his close examination of this young model of himself, though the comparison was only physical. The same strength of limb, the same massive bone structure, the same bold virile high-cheekboned face and Roman nose and brow. But Valentin's eyes were clear and honest, the old man's bloodshot, crafty and squinty.

Carbajal, derisive through gum-gapped teeth, asked Valentin if he had any idea why Pizarro had so zealously kept them apart. The whining insinuation of his tone left no doubt that he had heard the rumors.

"I would not know, sir," Valentin said.

"You wouldn't know," Carbajal said, mocking him. "Nobody ever told you what all Peru speaks of."

For a long moment, breathing heavily, he continued to gaze at Valentin. Then deliberately he reached under the bench, brought up Valentin's broadsword and helmet, and began to examine them intently. He asked where Valentin had secured them.

"They were my father's, sir."

Carbajal cackled his amusement.

"Are you sure of that?"

"It is what I was told by my mother. I never knew my father; that is why I prize his arms so highly."

Carbajal softened.

"So," he said. "So."

Thoughtfully he refilled his cup. "How old are you, young champion?"

"Twenty-three, sir."

Carbajal drank speculatively.

"Yes," he said finally. "That would be right. Your mother's name was Teresa."

"True, Excellency."

"You were born in a pink stucco house on the Calle de Solanco where it turns past the market and rises to the church of San Salvador."

"That is true, my lord."

Carbajal slapped his knee with glee. He held out the sword and helmet.

"You should indeed prize these highly," he chortled, "for I left them under a bed in that house when your mother's husband returned suddenly on furlough from the Italian war. See the marks upon them: the initials F.L.G. Francisco Lopez Gascón! I had them made in Brussels. No ordinary arms were big enough for me."

Valentin closed his eyes for a moment as though in prayer. Softly he replied, "It is as I suspected, sir. I came to the New World in quest of you."

"Did you, now?" Carbajal breathed raspily, as though the wine was heavy on him. "But you did not like what you saw, and avoided your father."

"On the contrary," Valentin retorted, speaking up boldly. "You were away from Lima for two months after my arrival, and by the time you came, His Lordship had already directed me to avoid you. I was not permitted to visit your camp. I fought you in the tournament to gain your attention, thinking you would be proud of a son as strong as yourself. I hoped you would come to me then, that I might tell you who I was."

Carbajal blasphemed his saints and the Holy Mother. "I was under the same command, forbidden to see you." His eyes rimmed to an ugly slit. "Pizarro is no fool. He wanted no contact between a father and his son, for he knew that together we would be a match for him—or anybody. And now he sends me to you—to hang you."

Valentin's eyes closed again momentarily. "It is not too late for us to get together," he said then. "Come with me to Gasca, and together we will defeat this Pizarro who has wronged us both. I have a silver mine and much farm land in the mountains. After the war, they will support us both."

Again the ancient softened.

"You would offer this—to me?"

"Are you not my father?"

Carbajal stared at the helmet and broadsword. "Yes," he said, "I am your father." He admitted he had heard rumors even in Charcas that a son of his had reached Peru. At the tourney, he knew even from the way Valentin had sat in the saddle and had drawn his lance, that here was a spawn worthy of him. Eagerly he had waited for the lad to identify himself; but Valentin had not come. So he had convinced himself that here somewhere lay a dire Pizarro scheme, devious and deep, possibly spun by his enemy Cepeda. If he had fallen from the governor's favor, it would be like the governor to send an unwitting son to kill his own father. Now he knew that the situation was reversed. Pizarro had sent the father to kill the son.

"The more reason, then," Valentin injected, "that we should fight him together."

Carbajal flung the Flemish arms from him. "It is too late, young champion," he said bitterly. "Your chaplain

261

is not coming, and Pizarro is here. You forget my duty, which I have never shirked in fifty years of war. I am a military commander. I must hang you. Those are my orders." He paused, and some of his old irony returned. "But because you are my son," he went on, "I will let you select your own tree."

As though he dared not face Valentin longer, he motioned the guards to return Valentin to his room, chased Béatriz and me to our quarters, and stood, one spurred boot on the bench, watching us withdraw. As I passed my door, I saw him reach down, seize the great broadsword, and run his hand across the blade.

How I wished I could have been with Valentin at that moment! I wept for him; that was all I could do. The brutality of Carbajal crushed me; also the memory of Valentin's face as he confirmed what he had come all the way from Spain to discover.

With a shock I realized, too, for the first time, that I was about to die. A monster who would execute his own son, and frocked priests, would have no scruple over watching a woman hanged. I took my beads and prayed for a long time.

Toward noon, Carbajal reappeared at my door.

"You may wonder why you are still alive," he said briskly, "so I have come to tell you."

I thanked him. He said I owed him no gratitude; it was just that he could not find a priest. Ordinarily, he went on contemptuously, he would not hesitate to stretch the neck of a traitor and send him to hell with all his sins upon him, but in this case he owed his son decent burial.

"And what of me, sir?"

He cocked a speculative eye and puckered his mouth, as he replied that he had not decided whether to hang me or put me to some use.

"Hang me, my lord, when you are ready," I defied him.

He enjoyed that. Taunting me, he suggested that I, who he said had deprived his brothers in Lima and Callao of so much pleasure, ought to pay a little on account. So he knew. After the women's embargo, the word was sure to get out. No one can keep a secret forever. He said that if he returned me to Lima, a good many men might be found willing to settle my debt to them. "You do not fancy the prospect?" he inquired.

I could not speak to him.

"Good. Then I will take you back."

He showed his teeth again, and scratched his balding head. He had sent to Chancay for a priest, he informed me, but Valentín's hanging now must be postponed until morning, while Carbajal caught up on two nights of lost sleep.

"Until then," he dismissed me, "pleasant dreams."

Shortly after he had gone, Béatriz arose from her pallet, her finger on her lips, and left the room. The two sentries at my door paid no attention to her. The slave was not a prisoner.

After a long time she returned with a chicken broth and a bowl of pomegranates, and forced me to eat. As she crouched before me, she spoke softly.

"Captain Guerrero too has had broth."

"Thank you, Béatriz. You are a jewel."

"The captain has a friend who serves the monster. Do not give up hope."

"The man named Ancón!"

She nodded. "But the captain will not go without you."

"Tell him he must, if there is a chance."

"His friend says the monster has not sent for a priest at all. The monster does not want to see his son die. He has spent an hour with your captain, and it has shaken him."

263

So there was good in every man, after all. I said an Ave Maria.

"The monster would be happy for the boy to escape, if you are not included."

"Tell him to go!"

"He will not."

"Tell him if he loves me, he will go to Chancay and bring back help enough to free me."

Béatriz rolled her eyes hopefully.

"And if he cannot find any brave men there, he is to turn at the stone bridge over the Passamayo, riding in the river bed to ruin his tracks, and hide upstream. We will find some way to meet him and go to his silver mine at Jumin. There not even the devil could find us. But he must go first. In the confusion later, we will find a way."

Béatriz' big eyes lightened. She took my empty dishes and lumbered away.

When she returned, she nodded her head, then knelt beside me.

"In the twenty-third hour, if the monster sleeps, he will go."

She looked different, somehow. I realized that her baubles were gone.

"Béatriz!" I whispered. "What's become of your jewels?"

"There are two guards at the captain's door. They had to be bribed. Why do you suppose I wore my riches, except to make some man want them?"

She said this with dignity, but very sadly.

"I will clothe you in pearls, Béatriz," I said, and hugged her. She smiled hopelessly, as though this were a promise I would never keep, and resumed her couch.

I lay a long time on my bed, but no idea came to me for escaping Carbajal. I was terrified of him. I have believed all my life that worry is the most futile of all human occupations, arousing as it does only fear and self-pity, which are the sternest antagonists of decisive action. But now, ransacking the cluttered cupboard of my experience, I found nothing in it to combat Carbajal. All other men I had known were predictable; hit just right on the kneecap of their ambitions, they jumped. Carbajal, as Paniagua had truly said, was other flesh. He was too clever to be trapped by guile, too strong to be moved by force, too cynical to respond to tears; neither decency nor religion tempered him. How then to attack him? In his own way, he was as immovable as Father Gasca, as self-reliant and as forceful. He was a wall, over or under which there was no egress. Exhausted at last by futile thinking, I fell asleep.

Béatriz brought me a tasteless supper of cheese, bread and wine.

"The monster has wakened, upsetting all our plans," she said quietly, lest our guards overhear her. "He has hardened, and will hang Captain Guerrero at dawn."

"You mean it is impossible to get Valentin away?"

"The man responsible would hang."

"But the plan is ready to work."

"Yes, mistress, all is ready."

"This Ancón—how close is he to Carbajal?"

Béatriz told me the mestizo was master of the horse and mule train. Carbajal appeared to favor him, and played cards with him.

"Cards, you say?"

"It is what the others tell me."

If he was playing with Carbajal when Valentin escaped, no blame could be laid to him. From my finger I took the royal Inca ring of Doña Matilde's. If this Ancón was half-Indian, he might respond to it. I asked Béatriz to show him the gem, and tell him not to abandon the plan. Removing the remains of my supper, Béatriz went on her errand. She returned and handed me the ring. "It must have magic in it," he said. "He kisses your feet."

265

I asked Béatriz whether provision was made for our flight if opportunity arose. She said all three of our horses would be saddled after Carbajal's nightly inspection of his own stock, and would stand ready in the paddock. Now I must find a way to divert Carbajal so that Valentin, at least, might get away.

Carbajal ate his supper alone under the tree in the patio, to the light of a night lamp. Through my open door I saw him, restless, constantly in motion, as wakeful for alien sounds as a ship's captain on his quarter-deck. Valentin was on his mind, no doubt about it. The good that is in every man arose within him, revolting against filicide. He knew his duty and would perform it; but for once he had no taste for execution.

I made myself as attractive as possible under the conditions and went to him.

"Are you troubled, my lord?" I asked.

He was drinking chicha, an Indian corn brandy, from a *borracha,* that leathern bottle which topers have ever found convenient to disguise the amount of their consumption. His eyes were red, and his cheeks also.

"Troubled, my proud young lark? The hawk is never troubled, just wary."

He offered me wine from a bottle on the table, and invited me to sit down.

"That is the third time you have called me a lark," I said. "Is Pizarro really so angry with me?"

"He cannot rest, he told me, until you are brought to earth."

"So he sent a cleverer hawk than himself."

Carbajal was pleased.

"This old hawk brings down all Pizarro's birds who try to fly too high. I am the merlin on his fist, and I am always busy."

He scowled.

"The hawk is losing stomach for his sport," I said.

"I have no stomach for rebellion, and never had," the aged warrior retorted fiercely. "I stayed clear of the civil wars. I would now be in Spain if I had had my way. But—" he took a long pull on the *borracha*—"he who has bad luck ventures boldly, and a man driven by distress has the strength of thirty. Pizarro will again be master of Peru, and next time he will take my advice and let me crown him king."

"You do not really believe that, sir."

"A week ago I did not. Today I do. This chaplain of yours has not arrived. I have only to send word to the deserters naming a time and place for them to return, lest they all be hanged, and they will come."

"Even from the north?"

"From everywhere," Carbajal said contemptuously. "They threw off their allegiance easily enough; they will put it back on as handily. Look what happened in Lima the night before last. They groveled and called me 'friend.' . . . So you see."

He told me boastfully, for he was a great talker, that Pizarro would set out within a month up the southern road from Arequipa toward the highlands, to slip past Centeño into undefended Charcas. Having replenished his treasury there, and having subdued the province, he would descend on Centeño and destroy him. With nothing at his back, he could then deal easily with Lima. Carbajal had been sent to Lima as a diversion, so that Centeño would think Pizarro meant to deal with Aldana and Mexía first.

But I could not follow strategy when my mind was on Valentin.

"Why must you kill your son, my lord?" I inquired. "He has served Pizarro well."

"Has he, now?" scorned the ancient. "He circulated

through all the camp copies of your chaplain's clemency, persuading the men to desert."

"Did he!" I exclaimed proudly.

"That he did." Carbajal sounded proud himself. "Under the hawk's very beak."

"Such resourcefulness might be put to better use than the rope."

"Dead men never bite," Carbajal retorted. "Besides, as I have already reminded you, one does not scorn Pizarro and live. My bastard put the noose around his own neck when he spurned Gonzalo's niece."

"He spurned her?" I cried with delight.

"He did, the fool," Carbajal said with heavy disgust. "Many men told His Lordship that Valentin was a spy within his camp. He did not want to believe it, for he admired the lad's courage. So he put him to a test. The archbishop himself waived the banns and came to the camp, Holy Week though it was. 'Now,' said Pizarro, 'I give you my niece to wife, and then I will know your loyalty. You will be infantry commander of my army, and I will make you a duke in the new kingdom.' And the boy refused."

"He did not tell me!"

"From that moment," said Carbajal, drawing again at the *borracha*," he was a dead man."

He shook his head, ruffled his balding pate with a heavy paw, and began to sing a plaintive song.

"My little hairs, mother
One by one the wind has carried them off.
Alas, poor things!
My little hairs!"

"I have never heard that one before, my lord."

"It is an old gambling song of my student days, which one sings when he has lost everything, even his self-respect."

He was a sad old man, now. He had fought and brawled

through every war the world offered his generation. He was the military lord of Peru. And he had nothing. Now, too late, he had discovered a son worthy of his courage, and even this must be taken from him, by his own hand. Tonight, the Demon of the Andes hated even himself.

"You need amusement, my lord," I said, "to take your mind from your troubles."

His eyes, drunk and sullen, stared contemptuously at me.

"Women are all alike."

I bridled.

"You mistake my intent, my lord," I said sharply. "I, too, face an unpleasant future, as you well know. I would divert the thoughts of both of us with a little game of Calebrasella, perhaps."

He brightened.

"You play it? Well, I must tell His Lordship that I found a lark who played Calebrasella. This he will hardly believe."

"Where can we find a third?"

He fumbled over his empty bottle, and threw it down.

"Ancón," he roared, "Ancón."

A young man in his twenties, with the lithe Indian grace of Doña Matilde and fine brown features, ran to us from the paddock.

"Get the cards, Ancón. We are going to play Calebrasella with a lady. What do you think of that? And if you beat her, she will pay you in Lima."

He rolled toward the kitchen, where there were both table and light. I followed. Béatriz, true to my injunction, left a watchful post in the doorway of our own room, and shuffled after me.

"What's this?" Carbajal asked suspiciously. "Someone to signal over my shoulder?"

"I asked her to boil us some coffee."

"Coffee. Yes. That's good. . . . I need a slave. Since

you will not require her much longer, put her up as your wager."

"And yours, my lord?"

"I never lose."

"But I must know what I cannot win, all the same," I replied, as Ancón appeared with the cards and sat with us at the table. "My freedom, perhaps?"

He leered.

"After you have been to Lima you will beg me to hang you. . . . Cut, Ancón."

The mestizo alertly split the deck. Carbajal began to deal. In his enormous hand it was impossible to tell whether he juggled the forty cards or not. The last four he slapped to the center of the table.

Calebrasella is a deadly game. Each player receives twelve cards, the other four composing the widow. The trey is high card, the four low, the deck having no eights, nines or tens. Each player bids for the extra cards, called the widow. The winner then plays against the other two. Thirty-five points may be scored on a hand, but he who wins all the counters doubles his tally to seventy. Five hundred points are usual to the game, though much wagering may also take place during the hands, and one player always rises from the table with all the money.

"You have not made your stake, my lord," I reminded him. "Your mule, perhaps?"

"Ah, I could never part from old Bermeja."

"Nor I from Béatriz."

"Soon, my lady, you will be parted from your neck, so it can make little difference to you."

"The same might well be said of you," I retorted, "so in that respect the wager is even."

He flushed.

"Well, then, the mule, but precious little use you will

270

ever make of him. I assume we will forgive Ancón any stake, since he has nothing."

"As you choose, my lord."

Carbajal was as bold at cards as in speech, and easily bid and won the hand he had dealt, for nineteen points. Béatriz brought us coffee. Carbajal greedily seized his cup, drained it, and opened wide one eye.

"It is a bitter brew," he complained. "When you are my slave, fat one, you will do better."

Béatriz returned to the fireside, imperturbable. I was sure she had put some magic of her own in his drink, for my own cup was sweet and heavy.

Once, after a hundred points, Carbajal staggered to the door and called for more *chicha,* and told the guards before my door to get some sleep. When we resumed, I began to win. Either Carbajal was now too drunk to be clever, or Ancón was discarding decisive markers to me, for my luck had been bad. Carbajal became more belligerent, and oftener consulted his *borracha.* Once Béatriz raised her head, listening intently. I was just playing a card, and my hand faltered.

At once, Carbajal was on his feet and at the door. Neither sound nor motion disturbed the patio. He listened, breathing heavily, then returned to the table. The game resumed.

Soon I was a hundred points ahead. Not even a Carbajal could best two opponents in collusion. Following Ancón's lead, for he knew Carbajal better than I, we prevented the marshal from bidding any of a dozen hands. And he was now too drunk to notice the deception.

As he continued to lose, the old man became more boisterous and rowdy, screaming blasphemies of the crudest sort, damning Ancón and me to hellfire and his mother's soul to everlasting purgatory. Then Ancón stopped aiding me. As Carbajal bid at last and swept the counters for a seventy score, though on two plays Ancón might have thrown me a queen or jack for a point, I looked penetratingly at the mestizo. On his face was a half-smile, and I knew that Valentin was gone.

Béatriz knew, also. She put the coffeepot back on the fire hook. Carbajal looked at me drunkenly as Ancón dealt. He began to laugh, silently at first, then in profane spasms. Several times he tried to speak, but gasped only the word "you" before mirth overcame him again. Finally, wiping laughing tears from his bloody eyes, he pounded his great hands on the table so that even the cards jumped.

"You do not deceive me," he chortled. "I heard the boy go. Ancón, my lad, your debt to him is paid in full. Now let us resume our little game."

"How did you know?" I gasped.

"I know everything," he replied perfunctorily. He eyed me steadily, highly pleased with himself. He poked a vast forefinger across the table at my nose. "You are a brave young lady, so I will tell you something else. I am not going to kill you or even take you to Lima. I have orders to provide you an escort worthy of the bride of Pizarro, and bring you safe to Arequipa. I understand now what he sees in you."

Open-mouthed I stared at him.

"So you have nothing to worry about," he said. "Now let us see which of us plays the better with nothing on our minds." He picked up his hand and bid two.

When Carbajal's score reached four hundred, my advantage had melted away until only thirty-four points separated us. Carbajal was rapidly recovering his good humor, and halted a moment for another cup of coffee. This time he smelled it suspiciously before he drank, but satisfied himself that nothing was amiss.

Then luck, which had not favored me, laid in my fingers an almost perfect hand. If I could bring off a seventy, the game would end, and I would own The Red One. Only a deuce in spades which I must pick up with my trey, was uncertain. I led a low four. Ancón captured with a non-scoring seven, and led back the deuce. I took it with the trey, and the game was made.

Carbajal came to life.

"Conspiracy," he bellowed, seizing Ancón's wrist. "You fed her the deuce to let her win."

He started to his feet, fumbling for his sword.

Béatriz calmly wrapped her enormous arms about his head and shoulders, locked them tightly, and cried out, "Go, go."

There was no time to wait, for Ancón had already fled, and I could not fight Carbajal.

I ran to the corral. Ready were the two horses. Ancón was up on one of them. The other had been ridden from Lima by Béatriz, and I remembered that it had gone lame. Tied to a post, saddled and alert, was Carbajal's mule. I tightened his cinch strap, climbed into a well-padded cradle, and kicked him hard.

"I won him and he is mine," I shouted to Ancón, as we fled the tambo, leaving bedlam and cursing behind us. We made off due westward toward the mountains.

"Why this way?" I asked Ancón.

"Trust me, lady," he pleaded. "We will avoid pursuit."

"What about Béatriz? I feel like a dog, leaving her."

"She will be all right," Ancón said curtly. "Nobody ever hurt a valuable slave. She told me that if this happened, she would make for the house of the Princess Matilde in Callao. All my friends will help her."

We rushed away across the plain.

"What if Valentin returns?"

"He cannot, lady," Ancón replied. "No man in Chancay is brave enough to resist Carbajal. Now be quiet. Voices carry farther than hoofbeats in the night."

XXIX

As I had learned so recently, eluding Carbajal and escaping him were not the same. But I was confident that if anyone could outwit the marshal, Ancón's long experience of the demon's habits gave him the best odds. All night he rode as though a lariat pursued him.

We traveled in the beds of streams, and over shale and boulders, to obliterate our tracks. This punished us, me perhaps less than my guide, for The Red One was sure of foot and gentle even in the most treacherous going. In Carbajal's fleece-padded cradle, rigged to ease his ruptures, I was less uncomfortable than on the flight from Lima. By dawn we had outsped the plain and climbed, through thick underbrush, the bed of a small watercourse between two rocky summits. I had been forewarned, and now proved by test, the incredible surge of Peru's mountains to vast heights almost from the coast. I could go no farther and begged for a rest.

Ancón drew up at a vantage from which his eyes searched the horizon. Satisfied, he watered and tethered the beasts and urged me to sleep. He doubted, he said, that Carbajal would pursue us. For one thing, he no longer had his mule. For another, his usual tactic was to figure out where his prey logically would rest, and there by hard riding overtake and capture by surprise. For the moment, therefore,

Ancón thought us safe. But Carbajal would be dogged, enjoying the chase when momentarily outwitted, and in a rage for the return of his mule. With Indian stoicism, Ancón lay down on the grassy bank and was soon asleep.

I admired his discipline but could not emulate it. I was too fatigued to sleep, and torpid of mind. For a long time I sat watching the horse and mule graze, or squinting across the blue-canopied desert, listening to the squeaks and chirps of unseen forest creatures. I was filthy, possessed not even of a comb or change of clothing, my stomach a fire-wood knot of tension. I did not know where I was, or where Valentin might be. Constantly before my mind was the vision of Béatriz opposing the giant Carbajal. I was not worried for her life; in Peru a strong female black is worth 3,000 pesos of gold, or near 5,000 escudos of silver or copper. Not even Carbajal could overlook such a fortune. Further, I doubted he would punish her. Like Pizarro, he admired boldness and courage, especially in his enemies. Yet I castigated myself for abandoning her. Such a sensation was oddly new to me, and most disturbing. Until then, it had never occurred to me to consider the welfare of a servant beyond my own need of her. Like a booby, I began to cry, in silent, engulfing spasms of reproach, futility and self-pity.

Toward dusk Ancón awoke. At once he inspected every inch of the horse and mule, particularly scrutinizing the feet and shoes. He then unrolled a blanket from behind his saddle, extracted a hard Indian maize cake, broke off two bits of it, and offered me one. I ate it greedily, though it was unpalatable. He next produced a pouch full of dried corns, offered me a hand full, and sat down to crunch his own.

He doubted, he said, that we should attempt to find Valentin that night. Carbajal would expect such a maneuver. The marshal was more apt, Ancón reasoned, to

275

predict our flight northward toward Truxillo, the closest point of absolute safety, than into the merciless mountains. After ascertaining that we had not gone south through Chancay, he would ride to Barranca, eight leagues north on the coast road. Finding no trace there, he would soon figure out that our only escape was up the Passamayo River by an Indian trail to Pasco, thence down the Inca sierra highway to Juaja to join Aldana, who was known to be in that vicinity. But the old fox was cunning, and so intuitive that his enemies swore Satan helped him. He might even now be lying at the stone bridge over the Passamayo awaiting us. Our best chance, therefore, lay in securing a full night's rest, then tomorrow descending to the plain. With luck, we might get behind Carbajal as he returned from Barranca, dog him through Chancay and up the Passamayo valley. Ancón surmised that the hoary marshal, for all his cleverness, would not dream that he might be himself closely pursued.

I tried to thank Ancón for arranging Valentin's escape, for making possible my own flight, and particularly for accompanying me. Obviously, had I been alone, Carbajal would have recaptured me simply. Valentin, unencumbered of my presence, also was more mobile and therefore more secure. Ancón would permit no gratitude.

"On the contrary, lady," he insisted, "you favor me. For a long time I have wanted to run away. I am sick to death of hangings, and would see only one more—Carbajal's own. At that one I would gladly splice the noose."

He asked me many questions about Gasca's mission, wistfully as though it were a fantasy conjured to palliate the existing suffering. He fortified my own confidence by his avidity for Gasca's success. Also, he emphasized that once his excellency actually reached Peru, every decent human being, Spanish, Indian and half-breed, would scuttle to him.

None prayed harder, or were willing to contribute more to Gasca's success, Ancón told me, than the mestizos like himself. Many now were growing up, though most were still almost babes. For them there was no hope except a stable colonial government. Maltreated by both conquerors and Incas, the mestizos were, he said, for the most part foundlings of the conquest. Only gentlemen who had actually married native aristocrats dignified such offspring.

Ancón was born in Mexico, his father naming him in a jest, due to the bay color of his skin. He did not know who had been his mother. His father had taken him to Guatemala, more as a hostler and servant than as a son. He journeyed to Peru in one of the many caravans of adventurers who lusted upon the Inca empire before the conquest had been consolidated, his father enrolling under Almagro for the exploration of Chile. At the Battle of Chupas, where Almagro was defeated by the Pizarros, Ancón's father had lost his life. Since then, Ancón had been almost a slave to Carbajal.

He also gave me a geography lesson on the mountains of Peru, which he knew well from his sorties with the marshal. Beyond the coastal range, he said, there lay a vast plain a day's journey wide, high, cold, windswept, fertile, and rich in many ores. Punctuated by ridges, lakes and gorges, it extended from Potosí, where it was two-thirds of a league above the sea, all the way north to Popayán, a distance of 1200 leagues. On this route the Inca nation had built its highway, eight marching men wide, with bridges spanning the chasms, and hostels a day's journey apart. East of the plain jutted an even higher mountain range, before a descent into the humid jungles of Amazonia.

Our destination, if ever we discovered Valentin, was thirty-six leagues across a mountain summit to the mighty plain. There lay Jumin, and Valentin's mine. From Jumin south to Juaja, where roads branched in all directions, was twenty-one leagues farther. From Juaja south to Cuzco was another twenty-one leagues, and west to Lima only thirty-six. Thus the town had been a military base both for the Incas and the later Spaniards.

"He who controls Juaja," said Ancón thoughtfully, "controls Peru. From there Father Gasca must organize his fight against Pizarro."

Night swiftly blankets the sierra, bringing with it monstrous chill. Since we could not light a fire, we huddled under a cliff. Now, indeed, I slept.

By high sunlight, after dried cake and corn kernels, we returned to the coastal plain. Among the foothills we advanced delicately toward the River Passamayo. Westward and far away, I soon saw the church spire of Chancay; much later, the stone bridge. In a clump of shrubs we waited the day away. A farmer, goading his oxen across the bridge at sundown, alone utilized the road during our vigil.

At dusk, Ancón slithered on foot to the river. For a long time he read the marks of travelers in the stream and on the bridge. In the last afterglow, he signaled me to advance. He had found nothing, either of Valentin or Carbajal, except the ancient tracks of our northward journey.

We watered the horses and waded them cautiously eastward up the river.

"Of course it is quite possible," Ancón whispered, "that Carbajal has covered his tracks just as we are doing now."

He worried, sniffing the air like a hound. Every hundred paces we stopped while he listened, though the stream gushed with such a racket that I could not understand what he expected to hear. Before long I could no longer see Ancón in front of me, so dark it was. Over my left shoulder I saw, low in the west, the fingernail crescent of a new moon—the worst possible bad luck. I turned my horse around thrice, at the end of each circle defying the omen by wetting my right thumb with spittle and reciting an Ave Maria. One star, white as tinsel, hung under the moon.

To occupy my mind against fear, I reckoned the days that had passed since my flight from Lima. Aghast, I discovered that this was Saint Martha's day, exactly a year since my arrival in the new land. Not once this day had I even thought of my patroness or offered her praise. No wonder the new moon had spelled me. I made right the omission with prayers of greater urgency and more ring of truth than I had addressed to her in all the other saint's days of my life.

Ahead of me, Ancón stopped again. A fallen tree blocked the watercourse.

"This is luck," he whispered. "Fresh tracks would surely show where anyone has gone around. Stay here."

He dismounted in knee-deep icy water, handed me the reins of his horse, and began to prowl the left-hand bank on his knees, feeling for sign with his hands. Soon I could no longer see him, but heard his movements. He crossed over, walking the tree like some forest animal who could feel in the dark, and descended toward me by the other bank.

The horse tossed his head, almost freeing my hand of its rein, and whinnied.

Ancón was beside me in an instant, soaking wet. He mounted, holding The Red One's bridle at the bit to prevent my flight. We stood motionless. Above the gurgle of the river I thought I heard hard splashes, and once the strike of metal on a rock.

"He moves away," Ancón hissed. "Stand still."

Motionless we remained a long time. More stars burst into the sky, so that at last we could see a few paces dimly beyond us.

Now my mule flicked up his ears and chewed his bit.

Ancón did not wait to verify this new distress. Still leading The Red One, he cautiously mounted the bank and went straight upward into a thick of trees. In the soft mat underfoot we made no noise. We climbed until we could no longer hear the river.

Ancón reined, and drew my mule alongside him. He put his head down to my ear.

"Valentin is ahead of us. There is only one set of tracks at the tree. I think it was his horse we heard. But Carbajal is behind us. That's what the mule heard."

I prayed Saint Christopher's protection against night alarms, Saint Barbara's against capture, and that of Saint Martha to keep horse and mule quiet.

Thus we remained until my knees were numb and my body danced with cold as though I had been bit by an Italian tarantula. I put my blanket over my head like a cape and soon, despite best intentions, dozed away into fitful sleep. Thus the night passed.

At dawn, again fed a meal of dried corns, I held both horses while Ancón stalked afoot to the river. In the half-light of the birds' awakening, I jumped at every chirp, and my heart throbbed at every hiss of wind. Finally I could no longer remain mounted. I almost fell as I stepped down and lay against a tree, holding the reins of the horse and mule. Both were irritable, tugging against the restraint which prevented their foraging for food. After a few minutes rest I arose, walked the mounts to a patch of bunch grass, and let them graze. The sun had passed the meridian before Ancón returned.

Carbajal, he said, encouraged by three sets of shoe prints at the fallen tree, had continued upstream some distance, using the Indian trail on the right-hand bank. He had stopped, probably at the first light, to examine the river bed again for tracks. Either he had found only one set or none, for he was confused. Men on foot had explored both banks of the river, both up and downstream. Béatriz did not seem to be with the party. Quickly Ancón had returned to the fallen tree and obliterated there the marks of our uphill climb. He then had circled about, across the river, for evidence of Valentin, but had found none. He therefore concluded that Valentin, driven by Carbajal, had continued upstream. Ancón was delighted that I had fed the horse and The Red One.

Leading our mounts to the river for a drink, we took the trail, followed it for half a league, then swerved again into the forest. I let the beasts graze while Ancón spied the land. He returned much puzzled.

"I find what I thought was Valentin's mark, but it is not he. There are distinctly two separate hoofprints, one horse having no right front shoe. Traders, probably. Carbajal has continued on."

"Then where is Valentin?"

He shrugged.

"He may have doubled back on foot to find you. But in that case either we or Carbajal should find his horse. We must go on, anyway. Valentin can catch up with us at the silver mine."

All afternoon we followed Carbajal. Toward sundown he sent men ahead to examine the river, and far up the hills to right and left. None, however, were dispatched toward the rear. Lest our mounts give us away, we climbed the slope until we were well out of earshot. The horse and mule were tethered and I went to sleep at once.

Ancón woke me, his face a wrinkled smile. Carbajal had returned down the valley.

"He will surely see our tracks where we used the trail, and double back. We must get away."

We saddled for another night's hard riding.

To my surprise, Ancón led us to the river, and turned boldly upstream. After only a few minutes, he resumed the trail. We stepped forward at a fast walk, rapidly climbing.

Cold shadows reminded my guide of hunger. Without stopping, he offered me the monotonous cakes and parched maize.

"We have the advantage, now," he said cheerfully. "If Carbajal follows, he must continually confirm that we are still beyond him. That will be slow work in the dark."

The river ebbed to a brook and finally to patches of springs. Oftener now the trail, never much more than a footpath, crossed rocks. The timber stunted away, exposing our backs to a wind so bitter that soon my hands were numb and heavy, and I seemed to have no toes at all. My back became rigid, as though all my muscles were sheathed in ice. I remembered stories of the first Spanish women to arrive in the land, who crossed the high sierra toward Quito in winter and died of exposure along the way. Theirs was a longer and loftier climb, but I knew, as the hours passed, what death by cold must be like. Atop the mountain Ancón stopped, where a long spur of rock cut off the wind. The rest was for the horse and mule, not for us.

Ancón was just tightening his cinch, preparatory to moving on, when we heard a horseshoe scrape against rock on the trail behind us. Weary as we were, and feeling secure, we had not bothered about a lookout, even though the cliff cut off both sight and sound. We were still scrambling, clumsy cold, into our saddles when a single rider appeared: a huge, ponderous bulk in the night. The figure reined jerkily at sight of us, then groaned "God be praised."

It was Béatriz.

We helped her dismount and gave her a ration of corn. She in turn passed to us a *borracha* of *chicha*. In that sky-cold, the burning brew was a medicine to warm the blood. Both Ancón and I had a Carbajal-sized pull at the flask.

Béatriz had not seen Valentin. She was almost too exhausted and frozen to stand, and insisted on exercising circulation into her limbs instead of lying down. As she limped painfully back and forth, she told us of herself.

When Carbajal wrested himself from her grip as we fled, she hit him with the candlestick. In his wine, loaded also with many mugs of drugged coffee, he went down. She flayed him with an iron pot from the fire, but could not knock him insensible. His roars awoke his men. By the time they were saddled and he had discovered his mule was gone, and Ancón also, the sounds of flight had died away.

Carbajal sat down on the ground, held his head, wept like a child for his mule, then fell into a drunken torpor. There was no pursuit that night. Beátriz hid in a storage hut.

Shortly before dawn, two riders galloped toward Chancay. They returned after sunrise with word that no one had passed the river bridge. Blaspheming noisily, Carbajal mounted a gray mule and with his entire party rode toward the north. Béatriz recovered her horse, which, having thrown a shoe was of no use to Carbajal, and rode into Chancay. No one there had seen either Valentin or ourselves. Armed with a *borracha* against the mountains, Béatriz had set out upriver, as I had told Valentin I would do. She had encountered and followed a single set of horseshoes, thus misleading Ancón later into believing two mounted men rode together.

It was her horse that had neighed above us at the river. While we had scrambled up one bank, she had scaled the other, and hid in the wood. Thus Carbajal passed between us. Thence our movements were similar. She heard us proceed east, and concluded that Valentin and I had joine Not daring to shout in that echoing valley, she set out afte. us.

So now we were three again, but without Valentin.

Ancón was restless at all this talk. He cut it off finally,

helped fat Béatriz to her saddle, and set off briskly, his course now downward toward a valley we could sense rather than see. Béatriz followed.

But The Red One acted up. He refused to let me mount, side-stepping and pointing his nose back along the trail. I led him to a boulder to climb aboard, but again he stepped away. My companions now were out of earshot.

And then I knew why the mule was fretful. Distinctly behind me I heard the clop of horses. The Red One also heard them. As frantically I tried again to mount, he broke away and trotted rapidly toward his approaching master. I could not pursue him. I could not cry out.

XXX

On the mountaintop there was no cover but the night. I climbed to the summit of the rock above the trail, full in the paralyzing wind, and lay down. In a moment Carbajal and his men appeared below and drew up in the lee of the vicious gale.

"Well," I heard the old demon gloat as he patted his mule affectionately, "so you found your way back to me, Bermeja my love. You wouldn't be separated from old 'Sisco now, would you? Good boy, good boy."

A lamp was lit while the marshal examined his mule.

"He's been ridden hard and far, but in the last hour has cooled out. So they're still half a run of the glass ahead of us, but one horse carries double weight, the other has thrown a shoe. We'll catch them on the plain. Now that Bermeja is back, I can ride again. . . . Come, men, there's no use freezing on this summit. Let's go."

I followed afoot.

It is one thing to ride a trail at night on a sure-footed beast, another to walk it, turning the ankles over every loose stone, snagging numb toes in every exposed rock and hole. The mountain funneled at last into a rapidly descending canyon. Here the wind broke, and soon the deadness left my limbs. Again I heard the whisper of running water, and saw above me by faint starlight the steep jut of rock walls. By the time the timber again appeared, I could not go on. I fell into a thicket as into a warm blanket.

Obviously, in this canyon, Ancón and Béatriz could not return. Even when they missed me, which in the dark might be a long time, they would hear Cabajal and run. Eventually, if they were not caught, they would circle back. I must continue to meet them. But not now. I could scarcely move.

I drank from the brook, which alone gave voice to the lonely rocks above. Here there was not even a puff of wind, for which, in my chills, I thanked merciful heaven. I must even have slept a little.

Wide awake suddenly, I heard hoofs coming down the gully from above. A solitary horseman this time, proceeding cautiously. It could be only one person in all the world.

With a cry I scrambled to the trail. The horse stopped, then came on quickly. Its rider vaulted down and took me in his warm arms.

"Valentin! Oh, Valentin!" I murmured, trembling.

"Lisa, Lisa!" he responded. "Thank God and Our Holy Mother."

We stood there, arms about each other in the dark, while the little stream gurgled and the horse, its warmth penetrating my body, waited wearily beside us. When I did not stop shaking, Valentin unrolled his poncho and put it over my head. He did not try to kiss me.

Somewhat vexed, I described rapidly the situation in front of us, concluding that it was safe for us to follow. He agreed, but cautioned that Carbajal might pause for sleep, and we must not blunder into him. Little of the night remained. If only to keep warm, we should go on.

Up behind his saddle, a poncho for shelter and Valentin's strong body for reassurance, my confidence returned like a surge of surf. My arms around Valentin's waist, perhaps more tightly than the uncertain trail required, I asked him about himself.

At his escape, he had ridden immediately to the stone bridge, not daring to enter Chancay lest he be arrested by Pizarro's commander of the town. He hoped to find travelers who might help him, but none appeared. Shortly after dawn, seeing two of Carbajal's men, he withdrew up the river. From the vantage by the fallen tree, he had watched for two days. He had just decided to ride back to Chancay and inquire, if possible, of Carbajal's movements, when he heard horses whinny. He walked his horse far up the slope to await the dawn. The next day he had followed Carbajal upriver, downriver, and back up again, and had found me. Now he urged me to quiet, lest our chatter prevent us from hearing danger ahead.

At dawn we saw that the road led across a small plain, then steeply upward to a summit. We dared not emerge from the trees, for riders hours ahead of us on the slope opposite could see every moving head below. Valentin's horse, patient under its double burden, required rest and food. We camped off the trail, snugly out of sight, by a pool of water and deep green grass.

Ancón had anticipated Valentin's need with a small pouch of corns, but these were now exhausted. We had nothing to eat. But I did not particularly feel the edge of hunger. Valentin's calm face was food enough. Solicitously, Valentin bedded me down warmly. Again I thought he would kiss me as I lay before him. Again, impassive, he did not. He looked down long into my eyes, read and considered my invitation. His hand clumsily caressed my cheek, and that was all.

"God rest you well," he whispered, and rolled up in his own blanket.

At dusk, crossing the plain, we bought parched corn,

boiled eggs and a strip of cured meat from an Indian farmer who evidently lived there alone. He spoke no Spanish. By signs we discovered than Ancón and Béatriz had passed during the night, riding hard across the open land. Carbajal had looted the Indian's granary, taken most of his hay and all his *chicha,* while encamped upon him for half a day. Just before the sunset, Carbajal had moved on.

Valentin tried to buy the old man's mule, but the Indian would not part with it. We went on, wordlessly riding together. As the slope steepened and dark came down, Valentin dismounted and led the horse. Again the timber surrendered to wind-swept rock. After dawn we reached a summit from which, to the east and far below, greened a long, wide valley patched with oval tillage. To the north a far-off church spire reminded me of my morning prayers.

Valentin pointed toward the house of God.

"Jumin, probably," he said, his first words in many thousands of frigid steps.

Nowhere below was there visible movement to warn of Carbajal.

"I don't think he knows about my mine," Valentin said. "He will ride hard to the south, to overtake us before we reach Aldana and Mexía at Juaja."

We descended the mountain. In two hours we reached the easy plain. After a rest, Valentin mounted, I behind him, and we turned north, weaving through timber at the base of the slope.

I thought us secure now, and began to talk, but Valentin shook his head. Provoked, for he did not need to be that reticent, I maintained a piqued silence all the way to Jumin. Carbajal had not been there. Even his name drew fear, the men casting frightened glances as though wondering where to hide.

Valentin did not inquire for his partner, Griego. We went to a tambo and had our first meal in many days, with bitter red wine natively grown. To all who inquired, Valentin said we proceeded to Juaja and thence to Lima. At a store I was able to buy a ridiculous Indian blouse and skirt of coarse red and blue wool, my first change in eight days. The hooded costume I never wanted to see again, and gave to the wife of the shopkeeper.

Valentin smiled his familiar boyish tenderness when he saw me dressed like an Indian. My skirt was scandalous, not covering my ankles. By now Valentin had made cautious inquiry, and had located Griego. The mine was well off the Inca road, a league and a half northeast in the mountain.

We rode, however, southward out of town. After many minutes, Valentin veered toward the hills, skirted Jumin and bore northwest, carefully avoiding habitations which now were frequent. We located a horse track, followed it, and broke into a clearing in which last summer's maize stalks leaned brown and wind-blown. Half a dozen huts, livened by running children, were dirty and uninviting. Griego emerged from one of them, pulling on his harness.

Despite the filth of his lodgings, I tumbled to a pallet and slept like the blessed dead.

That night I heard the wondrous news that Gasca had indeed arrived in Peru. The word was all over the north country, and Griego even had details. Father Gasca had left Panama, as we had known, on Easter Day with four hundred soldiers and the fleet. But the devil himself had stirred such a storm in the waters that three weeks later eleven of the ships, torn and leaking, refuged on the Island of Gorgona. From there Gasca took a galley to Galo, one of the numerous islands in the Bay of Guayaquil, while Admiral Hinojosa reunited and repaired his forces. During his month's wait for Hinojosa, Gasca luckily encountered the northbound Paniagua and from him received Pizarro's defiance. His duty now clear, Gasca with all his forces struck the mainland at Tumbez and, after weeks of organization, was ready to journey down the great Inca highway, liberating the towns, then uniting with Aldana and Mexía at Juaja.

"Then he will pass by here!" I exclaimed.

"Yes," Valentin answered, "and we must meet him with much powder. We have work, Friend Griego, you and I, and little time. We will start tomorrow."

Over a good dinner, our first in eight days, Griego directed many questions toward Andrea Cepeda, and finally asked Valentin bluntly whether he had any chance with her. He knew, he said, that her eyes were on Valentin, but was equally sure that her hopes there were futile. He thought she would make him an excellent partner in settling the highlands.

To my surprise, Valentin did not encourage him and finally, sensing resistance, Griego left us by the embrous fire. I chastised Valentin's coldness toward his friend and partner, saying I thought Andrea a perfect mate to so wise and learned a young man as Griego. In the new Peru, I exclaimed, Griego, who was scientist of gunpowder, engineer of irrigation and farming, would become a great colonist, well worthy of Andrea; while she, with her respect for the old ways of Castile, would be right for him. Valentin did not respond. Indeed, he was indifferent to my words.

"Am I ugly that you disfavor me?" I said at last.

He shook his head sadly. He had decided, after much time for thought that, now he was surely Carbajal's son, I was forever out of his reach. He was what he had feared, a bastard, and worse than that, the son of a traitor. The best that awaited him, therefore, was someone as unfortunate as himself, someone like Andrea, whose father must surely hang. If he could not aspire to me, then Andrea at least was wonderful and beautiful, and further, loved him.

"She will need a strong arm now more than ever," he said, "whereas your need of me lessens by the day. With her I always feel like a man; with you, like a boy."

So long as this mood was on him, he was right. I wanted no baby for a mate, nor one unsure of himself. But I did not say so.

Since we were discussing Andrea, I thought this a good time to inquire why he had chosen her as queen of the tournament instead of myself. I confessed that I had worn my ribbons and had sought him in the paddock.

"You did?" he asked, eyes wide.

"Yes, Valentin, I did. Is she so much better for you than I?"

He weighed my boldness thoughtfully.

"At that time, my lady, no," he answered. "I wanted very much for you to be my queen. But Pizarro courted you. I dared not affront him. Before the tournament he suggested that his niece Francisca, as the leading lady of Peru, should have the honor. Cepeda warned me that Pizarro meant to wed us, for the people were starved—as well you know—for some manifestation of love."

I giggled, but said nothing.

Listlessly, Valentin shrugged.

"So when Cepeda suggested his daughter as an easy compromise, I agreed, although I did my best to dissuade Andrea from attending, not wanting to hurt her. . . . Now, perhaps, I have not hurt her so badly after all."

He arose heavily, adjured me to sleep, and went to his own lodging.

Next day he and Griego left early for Jumin to persuade the Indians, despite the curse on the mine, to return and help to manufacture powder. I sat lazily in the cold sun

291

after they were gone, still fatigued by my flight from Lima, grateful for the prospect of several months of rest, and then the joy of reunion with Father Gasca.

About mid-morning I heard the stamp of many hoofs on the trail below the camp. Valentin and Griego had, indeed, been fortunate to find their helpers so soon.

With a rush, many men spurred at a gallop into the clearing and surrounded me.

Carbajal leered down at me from his red mule.

"The lark should rightly rise from the thicket," he said, mocking me. "It is not sporting to take one on the ground."

He signed to two of his men, who dismounted and seized me. Desperately I looked about for help. Carbajal shook his great head. "Nobody," he said drily. "Nobody to help the lark. You did not think I would time my visit to encounter my son again? No, no; then I would be obliged to hang him. This way is better."

I was mounted on a mule and carried off.

Carbajal rode swiftly south. He knew every hectare of the country, every concealing boulder, every spring of water. His pace was incredible, as much as twenty leagues a day; yet I was not as fatigued as on my flight from Lima, for Carbajal knew how to space his energies and those of everyone with him. Now I saw the genius of his mule train, for riding in a wool-padded wooden cradle on the back of a steady, sure-footed beast which shied at nothing and never stumbled, was luxury itself. I even began to respect the Andalusians, for whose mule affection I had always shared Estremaduran contempt; in this respect, the southerners were more canny than ourselves. Carbajal was sensitive to the needs of his stock as well as his men, his eye quick to detect fatigue or hunger. With his troop he was gentle, not bullying; quiet, not blustering; another nature altogether. Likewise he was solicitous of me, hiring an Indian girl at the first village to serve me, and without show securing my comfort and privacy at every stop. I could not have asked more gallant or thoughtful escort, though his speech was of the brothel and his manner coarse and vulgar.

For three weeks, ignoring the Transfiguration and the Feast of the Assumption, never pausing at church or shrine, heeding priests only to search and insult those he encountered on the march, Carbajal pressed southerly. I had no chance to escape him. The first night from the mine of Jumin, we skirted Juaja, where the training ground of Aldana's men glowed in many campfires. Thereafter we rode boldly through every town except Cuzco, where Centeño was. In all that time I detected no hint from any passer-by that Valentin might be following.

Our ride seemed to take us across the roof of the world, except that even taller crags, snow-stern and cruel, threatened over us. Carbajal used every lee and windbreak, yet I almost froze my face, hands and feet, my nose a lump icicle, while the wind burned my eyes to constant tears. Once we crossed a swift river on a suspension bridge built of reeds, which swayed and rolled like a seasick ship as we passed.

We were never hungry. Carbajal took what he needed from anyone unlucky enough to have a hen or pig or basket of corn, and none disputed him. He was not afraid to be seen, for he moved too swiftly for pursuit by any band large enough to oppose him.

Often he rode beside me, amusing me with ribald stories of his days in Italy, during which he had participated in every battle, and had forgotten no trick learned in any of them. His manner was not boastful, for he made no effort to claim distinction for himself, even when describing, blow for blow, his encounter with the great French Chevalier Bayard when they dueled at the Battle of Garigliano and neither could best the other. He had seen the French King Francis captured at Pavia. He had been an ensign under the sapper Navarro at Ravenna, the worst blood-letting of the century. He had been in the party of the Constable of Bourbon which captured the Pope during the great sack of Rome. In all these engagements he had not overlooked his own fortunes. For example, he told me that at the sack of Rome, he knew better than to line up with the other captains for a share of the spoil, for he had too often been bilked by the greedy generals. Craftily, he had stolen a notary's seal for himself; then the next day sold it back to its rightful owner for sufficient funds to finance his passage to the New World. And he had brawled and wenched, cozened and deceived, raped and looted, wassailed and debauched, in almost every city I had ever heard of, remembering each detail too convincingly to be doubted.

Often, too, he spoke of the future of Peru. For all his barbarity, he knew that the day of the conquerors had ended, and that the colony must soon enjoy a long period of peaceful settlement. He was disturbed that Pizarro was determined to marry me, when the Inca Coya would so much better calm the Indians and put them to work for their Spanish masters. One day, listening to this, I interrupted that surely he could not still believe Pizarro would again rule Peru, now that Gasca had arrived.

He had not heard this news, and compelled me to prove that it was true. Convinced, he sat his red mule thoughtfully for some time.

"Then I am glad," he said gruffly, "that my son eluded me. I am too old a dog to scratch much longer these dangerous Peruvian fleas, and in any case I have but one talent, to make war. Perhaps my son has also the sense to make peace. If I thought so, I would hang, when my time comes, in good spirits."

Again I begged him to turn back, and join Friar Gasca, but he only became angry. He would fight until he died, he said, and good would come of it. Either Pizarro would win and consolidate the country, or he would go down so bloodily that no one again would rise in Peru with any heart for rebellion. In either event, peaceful days lay ahead.

"I am not such a mad old man that I do not see this," he insisted. "One way or another, I serve my generation, in the only way I know how. But I still think I shall live to see the crown of Peru upon your head. Remember, young lady, that in my years I have lost many battles, but never a war. I do not propose to do so now, even though in winning I must kill the only son I am proud to own as mine."

Assumption Day was a week passed, and August almost ended; the harsh wintry mountains had yielded to a dry warm desert of red sandstone and iron rock pocked bleak with gullies and roiled by dust storms when, late one morning, trailing a ribald river, we came upon the outriders of Pizarro's army. The governor had left Arequipa a fortnight before, to graze his way slowly toward the uplands.

The lord of Peru descended from his horse to greet me.

XXXI

I did not know what to expect at this new meeting with
Gonzalo Pizarro, and I was some days finding out. On the
march, his lordship was altogether different from the man
who, in Lima, had ruled Peru. Indeed, he was much more
exciting, for he was concerned only with what he knew
best. Where he had vacillated, violently enraged at his
administrative frustrations, impotent to check the unseen
scheming at his back, incapable of instinctive love for hu-
manity which is the purple of kingship, and in tense idleness dissipating his substance for lack of martial exercise,
he was now a clear-eyed decisive general. The leadership of
500 men, most of whom he knew intimately and over
whom he could exert discipline, was the zenith of his
talent. Pizarro was as well-gifted to lead a half a thousand
as he was inept at governing half a million. A small group
he understood and could control; indeed with such success
that to a man, if the Judge Cepeda be excepted, his followers were as tenaciously loyal to him as he demanded they
be. He fed them well, promised them fantasies of wealth,
occupied them as much with sport as with toil, and allowed
their women to follow his camp. So confident was he of his
own might, so active in the display of it, that every man
swaggered as did he. What he promised was a kingdom
rich enough to satiate any greed, free from the oppression
of Spanish rule and Castilian justice, a Church subservient,

the law a compendium of license. Castile, he swore, never would reach Peru. To his cohorts this was an extension forever of the morals of war, a denial of civilization, and they found it good.

We moved slowly, climbing again into the nude hills. A litter carried me by day; a tapestried tent sheltered me at night. I knew no hardship except the cold. So sure had Pizarro been that Carbajal would capture me that he had brought rich garments with which to adorn me.

With hound and hawk Pizarro hunted every morning from dawn until noon to provide food for his men, while the camp, which included a rabble of women both Castilian and Indian, a hundred children and thirty priests, proceeded leisurely northeastward. Fifty or more of the distinguished knights traveled with fine tents, heavy furniture, costly rugs, and retinue, so our progress was never more than three leagues a day. At sundown, his lordship's dinner was well-tabled; even on the march he journeyed as a king, with splended canopies and a rush of servants.

For some days I was a favored prisoner in this babel. Except for the moment of extravagant welcome, Pizarro was too burdened of command to attend me. I saw him, riding or strutting, and received his greeting but nothing more. He was a man who trusted no one with even the minutest detail, so he was furiously busy. But one evening he rode to my litter as camp was pitched and told me I was expected to dine each evening at his table.

So that night, in a rich Venetian gown, I presented myself at the governor's tent. Cepeda greeted me. Even in armor distinguished by the great blue cross of Saint Jago on his black satin cloak, he groveled. Seeing my distaste, Carbajal stepped quickly between us and offered me his arm, leering at the judge as we walked away. When Pizarro entered, ripe with the odor of horse sweat, we sat at once to table.

Pizarro was buoyant. A spy had returned from Lima with news he eagerly relayed to me. Lorenzo de Aldana was enraged that Valentin had not defended the capital against Carbajal's raid. Loudly he accused Valentin of using Carbajal's foray as an excuse to carry me off and deflower me, thus rendering me unworthy of Aldana's prize. So he would kill Valentin on sight. But of Valentin himself the spy brought no word. Carbajal and I riposted glances across the table.

Delighted at this proof of rift within Father Gasca's forces, Pizarro courted me with elaborate kisses of the hand, attention to my words as though each was a gold ducat, and flamboyant flattery in the manner of my countrymen who, where women are concerned, must be the best liars in the world.

Immediately after dinner, as though at a signal, all the men withdrew, leaving Pizarro alone with me. Fondly he surveyed me over his brandy glass, telling me that he could even think more clearly when I was present. He wanted my judgment on a matter uppermost in his mind. He was learning, I thought sharply, how best to handle me.

His problem was an open friction between Carbajal and Cepeda which had become so dangerous that one of them was apt to be killed. Cepeda had begun the campaign months earlier, his reprisal to Carbajal's insult to Hipólita Cepeda in the cathedral at Lima. He had insinuated that Carbajal was too old and too drunken for supreme military command. He had accused him of cowardice in not dislodging Centeño from Cuzco. Now his attack was more subtle; he asserted that the ancient had grown soft. He had of course discovered that Valentin's escape from Carbajal could have been arranged only with the campmaster's connivance, and had convinced Pizarro that Carbajal could no longer be trusted and might even be planning to defect to Father Gasca at a crucial moment. What did I think?

I told him that I had twice begged Carbajal to join Gasca's enterprise and had been forthrightly repulsed. Further, Valentin had tried to persuade his father to desert Pizarro, promising to support his old age, an importunity Carbajal likewise had spurned. Thus to my mind Carbajal had been proved by fire, and the treachery Cepeda implied sounded to me like a scheme the snaky judge might himself employ.

My argument displeased Pizarro. He pondered my appraisal, rejected it, and decided to send Carbajal once again from the camp on a bridge-cutting diversion designed to pin down Centeño in Cuzco.

Weary of Pizarro's problems, I turned to my own, and asked what he planned for me. He brightened, and told me that he had been unable to fling me from his mind. Until Cepeda had suggested kidnapping me, he had been more restless than ever before in his life. Then when Cepeda had read him a letter from his wife giving oblique encouragement to his suit, he had sent Carbajal to fetch me.

"I really did not want Valentin," he said, "I just wanted him out of the way, and I was curious whether the old hawk could be trusted to bring down his own young."

He searched my face a moment.

"I know you favor Valentin," he went on. I sought to speak but he cut me off. "He fooled me for a while by courting the Cepeda child; but he would not have rejected my niece Francisca unless you had encouraged him, and when he carried you off, he showed his cards. But he plays a very bad hand. Lorenzo de Aldana is a mighty hater, as I know, and will dispose of your suitor without help from me. So I have the field to myself. Not—" he hurried on, "that I had any anxiety about him except as it concerned your own mind. I want you to love me."

"My conditions have not changed," I said. "It is not

enough for you to love me; you must have a different love than any you have shown me, my lord."

"You will change," he replied casually, and refilled his glass. "You told Señora Cepeda that you must see Gasca dead before I may claim you. You shall have that wish as a wedding gift."

"I'm afraid," I said, "that my student studied his lessons very badly."

"I am the teacher now," he replied at once, as though he had thought the matter through. "Unfortunately, our instruction must be delayed for a time. Meanwhile you are my hostage, and my guest. You will forgive me if I personally guard this treasure so many would take from me. You have sagacity and courage, two excellent qualities to breed into a dynasty of Peruvian kings, I think."

Father Gasca's movements were reported almost daily by Pizarro's spies. The friar journeyed down the highlands as slowly as the governor climbed northeastward. Many men had joined Gasca, until his army was the equal of Centeño's. At this last intelligence, received on Michaelmas, we pushed more rapidly forward, so that by the time Gasca had reached Juaja, we had crossed the snow-inundated summits. So high were we that the clouds lay below our vision, obliterating the valleys and all sense of altitude. Stormy hurricanes and ice pellets drove against us. The air was thin, with little breath in it, so that each step was a labor. Frostbitten and dizzy, light-headed, stomach-ill of what the natives called the mountain sickness, we came, on the eve of Saint Luke's Feast, to a brown plateau sheltered on all sides by snow-capped volcanoes. The plain was 12,000 feet above the ocean level. Distantly we saw the inland sea of Lake Titicaca, whose farther waters fused with the horizon. This was the valley of Huarina.

But Centeño, by forced marches, had beaten us there,

and camped with his entire army between Pizarro and the gold of Charcas. Nothing served the governor except attack.

Carbajal, his mission ended, rejoined us with reports that Centeño, a man of seventy, suffered so of pleurisy in the windy open space, that he was borne on a litter. Further, the campmaster said, Centeño had just received a messenger from Gasca commanding him not to fight, but to detain Pizarro until Gasca arrived to squeeze the governor in a pincer between two mighty armies.

Next day, therefore, the 25th of October, Pizarro sent Cepeda to Centeño's camp under a flag of truce. All the governor wanted, he was to say, was peace, and he was to beg his old comrade the boon of unmolested passage eastward.

Centeño, however, did not fall into this trap. He replied that he served his former commander best by refusing the request. He urged Pizarro to accept Father Gasca's clemency while there was yet time, and pledged his own honor that Pizarro and his followers, if they surrendered at once, would be given full amnesty. To prove the folly of force, Centeño said, he had moved his army to a new and stronger position, flanking the lake with his right hand, pivoting on the other wing around the foothills of a peak which wore a white cape of snow.

Cepeda brought other intelligence which his men had picked up in the enemy camp. With Centeño was all the treasure he had intercepted in many months of blockade between Pizarro and his mines, a cache of 1,400,000 pesos in gold and silver.

Carbajal, called to council, begged Pizarro to accept Centeño's advice. "This chaplain Gasca has already proved himself fool enough to keep his word," he argued. "See how he gave the captains back their ships in Panama. See how he treats Aldana, Mexía, and even Benito Suárez, the assassin of Nuñez Vela; he pays them deference and enriches them at our expense. If I have learned nothing else in the wars, it is that there is always a time for submission. That time is now, my lord."

But Pizarro was too greedy for the fortune Centeño bore, a sum making unnecessary a long encampment in the far hills of Potosí, to listen to his wise campmaster. Instead, he summoned the army, and told them of the treasure, promising them all their past dues and much spoil besides by sundown of the morrow. Eyes avid, the soldiers raised a cheer to the mountains.

That night Pizarro's men sharpened their swords and carefully tested bowstrings, arquebuses and pistols. Carbajal was everywhere, superintending everything. But he paid most attention to the arquebusiers, and again I saw his cruel genius. He assigned a man to each gunner, to stand and reload. Each artilleryman was allotted three firing pieces, so he would always have one ready to fire. Thus Centeño's infantry would be unable to time its charge after a volley, to grapple hand to hand before the weapons could be repowdered, for every rush would be met by deadly shot. But even more vicious than this was the shot itself. It was not the usual pellet of lead, but a bullet split carefully down the middle into two halves, to each of which was forged a short length of sharp chain. When fired, the two halves would spread taut the chain and send among the enemy a scythe of sufficient force to shatter lances, de-hoof horses, and decapitate men. Truly, Carbajal had no chivalry whatever, and I prayed that Valentin was safely with Father Gasca, and not with Centeño.

Before dawn the priests confessed the 480 warriors and gave them the wafer. Attentive was every man to these devotions, knowing that Centeño outnumbered Pizarro two to one, and five to one in cavalry. On Carbajal's arquebus and pike rested the decision.

Striking his camp, Pizarro summoned me. Along with the other women, he said, I would be permitted to watch the battle from a knoll. But eight men would guard me, lest I succumb to so foolish a notion as flight to the enemy camp. He begged for a favor from me, saying he would wear it proudly. But I lied, and said I had none of the green and amber colors of Canillejas with me.

The day, Friday 26 October, had all the quality of fiesta. On a low mountain spur to the southwest, 10,000 Indians assembled for the agreeable sport of seeing Spaniards murder each other. Nearby, dressed in their best and with pennants flying, gathered the wives, mistresses and children of both armies, the noncombatant merchants, the other followers of the camps and priests, in all probably twice outnumbering the 1,500 adversaries. To give the scene an even more gala touch, Centeño erected a tent from which to command the battle, for he was still litter-borne. Surrounded by a special force to defend the rich treasure, he might well have been the alcalde of Seville witnessing the season's first bullfight from the highest rank of the arena.

The sun rose cold and red, spurred aloft by a driving wind. My guards escorted me, grumbling at missing the fight, to a place among the women on the ridge. Below and to my left, I easily identified Carbajal in the center of the field, astride his mule, over his armor a green-embroidered vest, on his head a steel bonnet with barred visor. He placed his pikes with care to defend four small field pieces. Pizarro was below me, his entire cavalry troop beside him, a meager showing of seventy-five in which, prominent, was Cepeda's Cross of Saint Jago and the lawyer himself, a huge mace at his belt. Pizarro, as always, was a glitter

303

of knighthood, unmistakeable. His mail glistened from the silver that was in it. His overvest was of crimson velvet edged in gold. His black stallion was covered to the knees with a tapestried blanket. He sat quietly, lance at rest.

Across the ground, Centeño's infantry, a maize field of pikes, occupied the center, backed by eight formidable falconets and flanked by two companies of arquebus. On each wing were at least a hundred cavalry, perhaps more. Suddenly from the nearer cavalry a bold figure loomed higher than any other. I recognized neither horse nor armor, but the man needed no identity but size. It could only be Valentin.

I was still staring at him, his every familiar gesture speaking to me and tearing my heart, as Centeño's foot soldiers advanced until they were within cannon range. There the line paused, reluctant to begin the carnage, and Carbajal stood motionless, facing the fray on his red mule. Centeño's men walked forward another hundred paces and stopped again. Along the wing, among the restless cavalry, Valentin sat quietly.

Carbajal motioned tauntingly for the attackers to come on. They did not oblige him. Quickly the marshal sent a score of his own men forward to test Centeño's line. They were repulsed.

Now in Centeño's camp I saw Gasca's spy, Fray Barahona. After his labors from the very beginning of this adventure, I did not blame him for taking the battlefield, unarmed though he was. But I could not approve his folly. He rushed toward Carbajal, shouting, "Now is the time," unaware that a reckless charge was Carbajal's only hope for victory. Barahona went down, his head razored by an arquebus scythe. But his fatal impetuosity had done its work. With a surge, Centeño's infantry advanced to avenge him.

Unmoved, Carbajal awaited the charge, one hand high

in the air. Below me, Valentin's wing held its place, awaiting the outcome of the contest in the center. When the attack had closed to fifty paces, the Demon of the Andes brought down his hand. A volley exploded. Before the victims could rally, Carbajal's men had each seized another loaded weapon, and fired again. Two hundred men fell like cut wheatstalks.

Diagonally across the field behind this disaster, Centeño's cavalry from the right wing smashed into Pizarro's little troop, shattering it. Men and horses littered the ground. Valentin moved forward into this melee.

Pizarro, his lance broken, slashed with an axe, fighting three men at once. One managed to seize his bridle, and was brained by a great blow. Valentin pressed toward him, and I began to pray. I knew what I had never known before. I loved him. I did not want him to die.

But another figure intervened. It was Cepeda.

I could well understand Cepeda's deliberate bid for a hand encounter with Valentin, the most formidable of the opposition, before the eyes of his leader. He who so often had been called a coward, now in the elation of battle must prove himself a hero. His great blue cross a beacon, Valentin swerved toward it, leveling his lance. But someone besides Cepeda also met the rush, and two lances struck Valentin's shield. He went over. So, too, did Cepeda.

In a moment I saw the two again. They were afoot, Cepeda, head bare of helmet, his mace overhead, and Valentin before him, sword high. For an instant Valentin hesitated, as though recognizing his foe and wishing to spare him. But Cepeda granted no such chivalry. He surged. Valentin's sword bore down, and Cepeda, a bloodstreak from brow to chin, buckled to his knees. Valentin turned away. Cepeda was helped to a horse and fled, following Pizarro who had galloped to the protection of Carbajal's center.

As Pizarro ran, Centeño's bugler pealed the ecstatic trumpet of victory. But the boast was premature. Hearing it, Carbajal stormed the infantry center, scattering it like chaff in a mill, and bore down on a phalanx of pikes which protected Centeño's cannon. At this, Pizarro rallied the remainder of his cavalry and overrode the phalanx. Seeing the carnage, I thanked Our Holy Mother that Valentin was elsewhere on the field.

Carbajal, leaping from his mule, turned the cannons around and settled his murder on the foot soldiery. Many fell. As the rest wavered, I saw Valentin again. He had shed off his heavy plate, and in chain mail had taken command of the arquebusiers, whom he led along the exposed flank toward the critical center. Carbajal's next blast caught this force at close quarters, but Valentin did not fall. He disappeared, leaping, into the smoke.

Now the battlefield was exactly reversed. Centeño's cavalry were in Pizarro's rear, and his guns, turned by Carbajal, were directed at himself. Unmounted, bolting horses whinnied through the chaos. On the spectators' hill there was not a sound.

Centeño's cavalry charged into death from its own cannon in the hands of Carbajal. The marshal had formed his pike and spearmen into an abatis. What few mounted men escaped the cannonade were impaled on the abatis, hauled down and daggered. The attack recoiled, veered, and struck from the other side, only to find it, too, impregnable. In this forest of spears, Centeño's army melted away.

Again I saw Valentin. He lay prostrate, aiming his arquebus. The shot killed a pikeman an arm's length from Carbajal.

Before Valentin could reload, the battle was ended. Those of Centeño's men still afoot or ahorse scattered to north and south. Centeño, lashed to a charger, joined the rout. At this, my guards raced to share the looting.

Pizarro, pursuing Centeño, came upon the fortune in gold and silver, and prudently stopped. Indians from the opposite hill began rushing to the battlefield to murder the wounded and loot the dead. The spectators also flooded down, until I was alone on the promontory.

But Valentin had seen me. He staggered erect, staring in unbelief at the defeated field. A riderless horse trotted past him. Valentin seized the rein, stumbled to a boulder from which he could mount, firmed himself in the saddle, and dashed toward me. Veering, he captured another horse. I ran down the slope to meet him.

"In God's name," he greeted me, "mount and ride."

We fled, unmolested, toward the north. No one paid the least attention to the movements of anyone else. Every man was intent on his private business.

The horses seemed as eager to flee as ourselves. For an hour they cantered, nostrils distended, across the icy plain. Neither snow patches nor boulders deterred them. They slowed only when the route began a crooked descent with a sheer cliff on our left hand. Over this they walked warily. As soon as the danger was passed, they resumed their former gait. Once when I was small, I rode out from Cáceres on a pony to the olive groves. On the way home, the pony began to run. No check of mine bothered him by so much as a stride until, at the stable door, he stopped violently and pitched me over his head. Our ride reminded me of that day.

At last, of their own accord, the horses fagged into a beaten walk. Valentin turned to me.

"What happened?" he asked, stunned.

"I don't know," I said.

"I thought we had won."

"You had, but Carbajal refused to believe it. Either God or Satan fights with him, and it could not have been God."

He thought that over, reviewing the battle in his mind.

"Yes," he agreed at last. "The old monster refused to believe it. Satan fought with him. Gasca can never beat him."

"Why were you there?" I demanded.

He was too weary to rein his emotions longer. Tears cut the smoke-dirt and dust on his high cheekbones.

"I brought Centeño a message," he groaned, "commanding him not to fight. But Centeño would have glory, and so we have lost everything."

XXXII

For eight days we forced our way to the northwest, trading our news of the incredible defeat for food and lodgings. We had only one desire, to join Father Gasca. We even bypassed Cuzco, having no heart to acquaint that city with the tragedy that had overtaken the best of its men. Two days before the Feast of Saint Michael the Archangel, we arrived at last at Juaja, stunned and exhausted.

Gasca did not at once recognize the tattered girl and the ragged cavalier who were taken to him by the camp guards. He had heard nothing of the tragedy among the clouds.

His joy at seeing us was crushed by the destruction of Centeño's army. Destroyed was his dream of achieving peace without bloodshed. For fifteen months he had labored craftily, whittling away Pizarro's strength by razor-edged letters. His corps of diligent "missionaries" organized by hero-dead Fray Barahona, had flowed through Peru like subterranean rivers, undermining the foundations of Pizarro's citadels to bring them down one by one, more surely than a frontal assault by a military host. His example of truth and love had been more devastating than any cannon. Now 500 men lay dead on the plains of Huarina. Brute force had conquered love.

Disappointment plain upon his homely face, he listened

to our description of the battle. During the recital familiar faces appeared: Paniagua, the ambassador; Hernán Mexía of the stringy beard; Admiral Hinojosa; the bishop of Lima, Geronimo Loaysa. When our story ended, Friar Gasca closed his eyes for a moment in prayer. Then calmly he asked the bishop to arrange a *Missa Solemnis* for the battle dead, followed by a *Deum Laudamus* in gratitude for the safety of Valentin and me. After that, he would address the assembled army.

This done, he smiled wanly, held out his arms, embraced me and kissed my forehead.

"I would grieve for your tortures, little sister," he remarked drily, "did I not know that you had enjoyed every moment of them. . . . I have a surprise for you, one that will be most welcome to you."

He handed me over to Paniagua, who led me along a camp street to a comfortable tent. I stepped inside, into the arms of Béatriz. With her were all my trunks, from both Panama and Lima.

I embraced her as though I had met one of my own sisters. As she sponged and scoured me and dressed my hair, we exchanged adventures. She and Ancón, on missing me, had turned back, then fled before Carbajal. After crossing the valley where lived the old Indian, they had swung north, awaited Carbajal's passing, then returned up the canyon in search of me. Concluding finally that I had been captured, they continued east, eventually reaching Lima, where Ancón had left her with Mexía, who in turn had taken her to Gasca.

"So you saw Lota?" I asked.

Béatriz nodded unenthusiastically. She did not approve of Lota, that was evident. My maid had moved to a splendid house with her baby. There she had a maid, a cook, and a nurse for the child. Mexía had accompanied her to Mass, and called on her every afternoon. Béatriz had been settled into this establishment, but after a few days had moved to Doña Matilde's house in Callao. Lota sent two servants to fetch her, but Béatriz had refused to go, on the valid contention that she belonged to Father Gasca, not to Lota. Mexía had not married Lota, that was certain.

Dressed for the two Masses in black satin and lace, and a manta I had not worn since leaving Spain, I began to live again, though I was bruised, creaking of bone, and weak from the long flight. I longed to sleep a night and a day together, and knew that once I went to bed, I probably would be unable to rise for several days.

After the Masses, Father Gasca addressed the camp from a rocky knoll. I was amazed to see at least a thousand men in the company. Gasca told them as much as he knew of Centeño's defeat, and warned them against fear or dejection. He emphasized the right of his own cause, but did not minimize the reality that Pizarro, after such a fantastic victory, would be acclaimed as unbeatable and thus gain prestige throughout the country. Undoubtedly the governor would occupy Cuzco, and from there recruit a large army. Gasca still believed, however, that Pizarro's house must fall of its own rottenness. Therefore he was content to wait.

He said he had been given, by a soldier recently arrived in camp, a letter written during the previous civil war by a crown judge in Cuzco, one Gáspar de Espinosa, to the late rebel Diego Almagro. He begged attention while he quoted from it.

"If all the men who were ever in the world," he read, "with those who are now alive and those who are yet to come, would give their attention solely to serving God and to guiding affairs by the light of reason, remaining content with what is justly theirs and belongs to them, there would not be so many wars and so many great battles. But as it is the inclination of the human mind to wish to command and dominate, in following this ambition not only have many great lords and kings perished, but their souls also have been put in danger of perdition.

"What suffer most are the miserable countries, which are wasted and ruined, and most of their people killed, the buildings in their cities left in ruins. If now you become the author of war, what benefit is it? After deaths on both sides you will become your own murderer, and there will come a judge by royal order, and you will lose the government and your own life."

Calmly Gasca looked about the camp.

"So it must be with Pizarro," he said. "We shall move our camp to the valley of Andeguaylas, where there is food enough for the winter. In the spring, if he has not already submitted, Pizarro shall, in truth, lose both his government and his life."

Valentin joined me immediately after this discourse. He, too, was bathed and well-adorned, and Mexía was with him. The little captain warned us that Aldana, fearful that in faraway Lima he would be overlooked for important command, had arrived in camp that morning and immediately had usurped control over the artillery. Mexía begged Valentin to shun Aldana, who was still hot with jealousy and anger. Aldana's claims credited himself with everything Mexía and Valentin had done jointly, thus greatly ennobling his position so that even Hinojosa deferred to him, but even this must not provoke Valentin to challenge the vain conqueror, who would welcome the opportunity to kill him.

Mexía then turned jauntily to me. "I am still in this competition," he said, "though after your gallant rescue from Pizarro my standing diminishes."

The men escorted me through a camp street crowded with tents, men, horses and garbage. Almost at my door we saw a man, arms bound and well-guarded, conducted by two soldiers commanded by Aldana. Ignoring Mexía's warning, Valentin and I both ran to the captive, for he was Joge Griego.

"What means this?" Valentin demanded angrily, gripping his sword hilt and facing Aldana.

"I am hanging a man for treason," Aldana gritted, "and unless you wish the same fate, stand off."

Valentin stood his ground. Bitingly, Aldana said God must have directed him to the camp that day, for the Greek had given Gasca a great deal of very bad powder, evidently hoping it would be used in battle against Pizarro, thus causing Gasca's defeat.

"Then hang me, too," Valentin said evenly, placing his arm about his partner, "for Griego and I are in this together."

Aldana's beautiful teeth flashed. "I have no doubt of it," he said, and bared his sword.

Valentin met him calmly. He was no longer the inexperienced blade who had been buffeted by Mexía in Panama a year before.

"This gives me great pleasure," Aldana said, and braced his feet. Mexía rushed away. Valentin waited. When Aldana saw that he could not taunt Valentin into a rash attack, he began to feel Valentin's defense with agile flicks of his sword, while soldiers rushed about proposing wagers on the outcome. The crush was so tight that there was scarcely room for the adversaries to parry and thrust.

But no harm was done. Mexía returned with a strong guard, knocked up the swords, and hauled Aldana and Valentin, and Griego too, to Gasca's tent.

The friar was provoked at the disturbance, which interrupted a council with Hinojosa and Paniagua. But he was even angrier to discover that any man had been condemned to death without his knowledge. Valentin boldly demanded that Griego be released. Aldana as persistently

313

proclaimed that Valentin be arrested for perfidies both in Lima and in collusion with the Greek. The friar said he had taken Valentin's word for the merits of the powder, knowing nothing himself of such matters.

"The claims are ridiculous," Aldana shouted. "I have looked at the compound. It is pale and inferior. You have only to run your hands through it."

Gasca asked him if he had tested it. Aldana insisted that there was no need; if he knew anything, it was powder. The friar ignored this arrogance. Placidly declining to hang any man without a defense, he proposed that two cannons be set up and fired, one with the old powder, one with the new.

Aldana was wrathful at this challenge to his knowledge, but Gasca insisted, stating that he, not Aldana, required the enlightenment.

Griego's bonds were cut. Valentin and Griego carefully loaded a lombard under Gasca's moody eye, while Aldana supervised a crew in the tamping of another gun, and Admiral Hinojosa, as supreme army commander, stood by attentively. There was a great difference between the powders. Griego's was a pale yellow rather than a greyish black.

Aldana fired first, toward a huge boulder, to set up a mark. His ball lodged in the earth halfway to the rock, a fine score of two arquebus-shot lengths.

Smilingly, Griego lit his fuse. His projectile soared to the boulder and splintered shale from it, as a cry of unbelief surged from the onlookers.

Aldana was not convinced until ten rounds had been loosed from each gun. All of Griego's raced true to his target, punishing the rock with their force. Three of Aldana's tries fizzled and scarcely left the muzzle.

Griego explained to Gasca that the standard powder, in

use since the days of Navarro in Italy, was compounded of ten parts saltpeter to two of carbon and one and a half of sulphur. But Griego had discovered that the saltpeter of Peru was so much stronger than that of Spain that very little carbon and sulphur, finely ground, produced twice as strong a detonation without bursting the cannon, whether falconet or lombard, and produced identical effect also in muskets and arquebuses.

Gasca insisted on experiments with all types of weapons. Hinojosa became enthusiastic. Ignoring Aldana's defiance, the admiral gave Valentin the rank of captain, placing all the arsenals under his command. He ordered Griego to concentrate on manufacture of the new formula, and the soldiers to practice with it exclusively.

Gasca was elated. "One shot with the new powder should convince Pizarro," he said, "that we can stand back and cut him to pieces."

Aldana, however, was dark. Seeing this, Gasca placed his long, awkward arm around Aldana's shoulders, and pressed him into the privacy of a tent. In a few moments Aldana reappeared, red of face but outwardly calm, and ordered his guard to prepare for immediate return to Lima.

Now indeed I sought my bed. As I had anticipated, a fever struck me, and I did not rise for a week.

By the beginning of the Nativity season we were encamped in Huamanga, astride the Inca road some leagues north of Juaja. Into camp late one afternoon, beaten and begrimed, staggered Bishop Solano of Cuzco without escort. For a time he was unable to speak. Then he recited a story which, if hatred of Pizarro was needed to fuse our camp, provided the forge for it.

After the battle of Huarina, where he had attended Centeño, the bishop had returned to Cuzco. A month later,

Carbajal struck, late in an afternoon. Two score of the most distinguished men, including Prince Paullu, were seized and hanged.

"Not the prince!" I cried, remembering his part in the women's rebellion.

"He was the least of them," the bishop went on. Next morning Pizarro had entered the town on foot, humbly clasping his silver Madonna. He had walked to the cathedral, demanding a *Deum Laudamus* for his victory. The bishop was in the act of celebrating a Requiem for Carbajal's victims of the previous night. When he refused to halt it abruptly in favor of Pizarro's request, the governor in a fury commanded Carbajal to find a convenient tree for the bishop's neck. Solano fled through the vestry and treasury and only by a miracle escaped to Gasca.

He also had other news. Centeño had reached Lima, almost dead. And in the awful battle 350 of Centeño's men had been slain, another hundred of the wounded daggered by looting Indians. Fifty more were overtaken by Marshal Carbajal and garroted, since there were no trees on the high plain. Pizarro had lost only a hundred men.

Naturally, I inquired of Cepeda, since I had seen Valentin wound him. The judge was in Cuzco, the bishop said, horribly disfigured. So bad was the scar from brow to lip that his nose was split in half, and Cepeda wore a black mask over his face.

The season in the sierra is the reverse of that along the coast. It was midwinter, with driving snow, bitter winds, and sleety rain. I was housed, fortunately, in the town. The main camp was frostbitten and dreary. Yet every day new arrivals bulged the complement of fighting men. Valentin made powder by day and night, surging with joy at military command, importance and usefulness. I, too, asked Father Gasca for work.

316

He was composing a new letter to Pizarro.

"You still think to win him over?" I exclaimed in unbelief.

"I may still try, little sister," he said. "I cannot destroy even such a villain without giving him every chance."

The new communication, however, was not conciliatory. It accused Pizarro baldly of treason, on the basis of an intercepted letter from Pizarro to the king which accused Gasca of causing such war and chaos that the governor proposed to kill him in His Majesty's service. Despite this, the friar opened the door of mercy, ending, "Insignificant as I am, Your Excellency would have little cause to fear me if I had not on my side God and the king, justice and fidelity, and all the good vassals who serve His Majesty. But fighting against all these, Your Excellency has good reason to quail, and if you do not repent and return to the service of both majesties, divine and human, you will lose both body and soul, as you will shortly see."

I now resumed my old task, as in Panama, of sorting, preserving and copying Gasca's documents. He saved everything that fell into his hands, as evidence against Pizarro.

In a few days an answer arrived to Gasca's final offer of mercy. But it was not from Pizarro. It was from Carbajal, in his own hand. The defiant old demon was in a fury.

"Where in Holy Writ," he asked, "do you find it permissible to proclaim with your fox's conscience that the king has given you secret instructions to do battle against the governor?" He defiled Hinojosa and Aldana as "the Panama turncoats who sold their lord as did Judas for private gain," for which they, and Gasca, "would perish by fire, for I expect justice from God."

He said it was a waste of time to send further offers of pardon, "for on receiving your last letter by knavish

317

priests, I hanged the two of them. Perchance you and the devil will understand why we need to be pardoned for placing our lives at the service of the king."

As I read this to Gasca, he smiled. "My offers of the king's clemency to Carbajal's men are undermining him, else he would not be so outraged. Proceed."

"I will leave soon," the letter continued, "for where Your Reverence is. We are so few and you are so crookedly valiant. When you meet us you will curse him who sent you here, and even the day you were born. May the Lord preserve your reverend personality by permitting, through His most holy clemency, that your sins should bring you into our hands, that you may once and for all cease to do so much harm in the world."

Gasca heaved with amusement.

"We prick his skin," he chuckled. "You must admire the old devil. Even his iniquity is heroic."

In January, Governor Andagoya of Panama arrived with 200 men; early in February Governor Benalcázar from New Granada with twenty knights. Two weeks later, on Ash Wednesday, Centeño, fully recovered, led Aldana's army of 500 from Lima. Eight days after this, from Chile came the explorer Valdivia with all his men. All that army of "missionaries" who so astutely had prepared the populace for Gasca's arrival, now were in camp for the Lenten observances, their political work ended. Where to lodge them became a problem, and how to feed them another, headed as they were by three distinguished personalities, the bishops of Lima, Quito and Cuzco. All of them had risked their lives; Gasca could not decently send them home. He appreciated their desire to witness the degradation of Pizarro and Carbajal.

At last, the day before the second Sunday in Lent, Aldana arrived with eleven heavy guns which he had stripped from the fleet. The army now numbered more than 2,000 men. It must move, for supplies were exhausted from twenty leagues distant.

I went out on horseback to greet Aldana, hoping to placate him. But he only upbraided me, before all his staff, for being so unseemly. I belonged, he said, in Lima with the other women. To snub him, I returned to town ahead of him.

Next day Father Gasca called together his council, as famous and brave a band as ever gathered under a single banner. The friar recognized the talent that stood before him. Bowing meekly, he said that he did not propose, with such brilliant counsel, to take any military decision himself. The time now had come for him to follow, rather than to lead. He asked Admiral Hinojosa to take command.

The admiral sought advice concerning the best route to Cuzco, since he wished to cross the perilous Apurimac River before he was discovered. This eliminated the easy Inca highway. An alternative was to cross a 14,000 foot summit and thence proceed by the Urubamba River from the northeast. But this, he pointed out, would exhaust the men, laden as they were with cannon and equipment. Aldana pointed out another way, midway between the two, wooded, marked with sheer precipices and deep ravines, perilous but perfect for concealment. Two rivers must be crossed, though Carbajal long since had cut the bridges. If such a passage were possible, the army would emerge upon the plain at the gates of Cuzco. Aldana and Benalcázar were ordered forward with a detachment to sound this route, the entire camp following the next day, a Saturday.

As the main camp broke up, Friar Gasca appeared suddenly in the door of my lodgings. Béatriz and I were packing a single light trunk for the journey.

"I was afraid to find you so occupied," his excellency said. "I regret that you cannot go."

At first I thought he was teasing me. Then I realized that, busy as he was, he would not have wasted time on a playful errand. He explained that he and the council had agreed to abandon the Peru-honored custom of taking women to the wars. He could make no exceptions.

"You have done well, little sister," he said, "better than I dreamed possible for any woman. From the very beginning of this enterprise you have been in it boldly. Almost every step of the way shows your footprint. And your little strategy to liberate Lima was—I must admit—something a priest never would have contrived."

"You know that, too?"

He rolled his awkward head merrily, and spread his hands.

"There is a place in these wars for friars and women," he laughed. Then he became firm again.

"But now for a time, your work and mine are done. As I have surrendered the command to my generals, so you must yield the fighting to the soldiers. I have arranged an escort to take you to Lima."

"Do you ride with us, Excellency?"

He shook his head.

"I see what you mean; but it is impossible. Please do not argue with me about it, child. When the battle is won, I shall send for you."

"No," I said. "I have risked as much as any man in this war, and every man but yourself, and your infantry commander Aldana, recognizes me as a soldier. Do not force me to disobey you by commanding me thus, for I would be grieved to defy you. But when you fight Pizarro, I have as much right to be there as yourself."

He stared at me, angry. Then he smiled. "Find someone to protect you, then," he said, "for I will not have you on my mind."

320

Naturally, I went first to Valentin, but he refused me curtly. He did not say so, but I thought him pleased that for once he would have no responsibility for me. I then sought out Aldana, which proved my desperation. He was pompous, as I knew he would be. Was I out of my wits? Could I not imagine what would happen to me among 2,000 men? When this business was finished he would claim me, as he had every right, for who among the suitors had done as much as he? On the day of his claim, he wanted no further taint on me. Bad enough that I had wandered through the mountains with Valentin, who one day would answer to him. Now I would mind my place and be off, as he was busy.

There remained only one hope. I went to Paniagua. Surprisingly, he agreed to take me. He was infirm, and I could wait on him. This meant, of course, being at the tail of everything, among the priests; but it was better than nothing. Béatriz found me a practical Indian wool dress and shawl; I put them on. I packed in a saddlebag one black and one brocade dress, with accessories and my best jewels, except for my Aunt Sortella's greatest gift to me, the long rope of brown pearls. These I gave, with a kiss, to Béatriz, reminding her of my promise.

She knew the value of the offering. Tearful, she tried to refuse. So I put them over her head, and bade her look in my hand glass. The pearls, so complimentary to her skin texture, so handsome an adornment to her ample bosom, ended the argument. I told her that if she would guard my trunks in my absence, I would never again ask of her any service. Indeed, I said, I knew in my heart that her master would set her free. Then I asked her about Ancón.

She tittered coyly. He was at Lima, in charge of the messenger service between the capital, the fleet and Gasca.

For a moment all her front teeth gleamed. I wondered what had happened to her in the mountains. At least more, I reminded myself, than between Valentin and me.

The bugles echoed to the mountains. The supply trains rolled. A day ahead, Aldana's track disappeared in dust. A mighty parade set out toward the south: Admiral Hinojosa leading a line of knights in armor, caparisoned horses, banners sacred and royal, the standards of a score of captains, and afoot 1,500 infantry and a host of chanting priests. Ahorse, waiting to protect the rear and goad the stragglers, was Hernán Mexía with a company of lancers armed for battle. He waved to me as I passed.

XXXIII

We moved with exasperating slowness, covering only two leagues a day through thicket, bramble and dense forest, skirting gorges, risking precipices, following an ancient, abandoned Indian trail. Occasionally a small green valley, an emerald set in a ring of mountains, broke the peril and provided camping ground. Even in flight before Carbajal, and racing from the heights of Huarina, I had not encountered a landscape colder or wilder. Now I understood why the women had been left behind. Many marches were so precipitous that the knights dismounted and led their horses, while thirty mules strained to bring up a cannon. A misstep in these icy perils meant death in a gorge a thousand feet below.

Passion Sunday found us at the River Abancay, a deep, swift, spring-swollen torrent. As we approached the main camp, Aldana and Benalcázar threw a suspension bridge across. An entire day from sun to sun was spent crossing the bridge.

During the lull, Paniagua sought out Gasca, and returned with news. Spies from Cuzco reported Pizarro in the Inca capital, fighting desertions and dissensions. Carbajal, for insisting that Pizarro advance boldly and capture Lima, had been deposed of his marshalship. He now served as an infantry lieutenant under Cepeda, Pizarro himself assuming supreme command. Remembering the campmaster's wily preparations for Huarina, his canny instinct for victory, his indomitable indestructibility, I prayed that Pizarro would make other equally grave mistakes before ever the armies collided.

Paniagua, twinkling, had word for me, too. Pizarro had taken heavily my flight from Huarina, hanging all of my erstwhile guards. But he had proclaimed loudly that he would have me back. Next time, however, I would be a spoil of conquest. He would marry the Coya after all, but keep me in his household to humiliate me. Every man of his army had orders to bring me to him unharmed after the battle, with double share in the spoil to him who delivered me.

On Good Friday, the army reached the Apurimac, only twenty leagues from Cuzco. The river was a cannon-shot wide and impassable. An effort to float a raft lost five men in the bold current.

Gasca ordered a halt until after Easter Day. Meanwhile everyone, even the priests, scavenged the woods for materials to build a bridge. The ring of axes was muffled, lest Pizarro scouts, foraging for food, be alerted to our presence. Not until after the Easter Mass, an awesome ceremony graced by three bishops and 200 priests, was construction of the bridge begun. By sundown two liana cables had been stretched across the gorge and anchored to the cliff.

Hinojosa was worried by a mountain height on the opposite bank, reached through a narrow defile which ten men might hold against an army. While engineers frantically built rafts on which arquebusiers might be ferried to protect this peak, a fire was seen late at night across the water. Pizarro scouts had discovered and burned the bridge cables—and, more serious, discovered the presence of an army.

With the desperation of ambush, Valdivia stretched a pontoon bridge, at the cost of eleven lives. Two hundred marksmen under the hero of Chile scaled the height, just in time to meet and repulse a force of 100 Pizarro cavalry which rode madly toward the same objective. A suspension bridge was at last reared by sundown of Easter Monday. Gasca's host, which had taken the day around to cross the little Abancay, surged over the more hazardous Apurimac in a night, though sixty horses slipped from the swaying structure and were drowned. Four more days were required to bring the cannon up the mountain, but Pizarro had lost his chance. Proof, I thought, that Carbajal was no longer in command. The old demon would never have made so fatal a mistake.

Next day Valdivia's scouts observed Pizarro's army arrayed on an ancient Inca parade ground five leagues from Cuzco, called by the Indians Sacsahuamán and by the Spaniards Xáquixaguana. By evening we all could see it from our mountaintop. Hills stretched in a horseshoe around a level plain less than a league long and somewhat narrower, at the far end of which a ditch drained a swamp. On the hills the Incas had built summer palaces in years past, from which to review their troops. Pizarro's camp lay below us, one flank against the swamp, the other invincibly keyed to a precipice. The only approach to him was straight across the level ground, into the death of Carbajal's cannon.

Since the day was Saturday, Gasca did not hurry to the plain. He would not put upon his conscience a battle on the Lord's day. Shortly after midnight, however, in the first hour of Sunday, Valdivia led the advance guard into a descent of the mountain, hidden by a thick mist.

Off to the left, a vulnerable hillock commanded an excellent site for cannon of either army. Incredibly, Pizarro had not occupied it. At dawn, Hinojosa saw a detachment set out from Pizarro's camp to remedy the error. He dispatched Valentin and a troop of arquebus to seize it themselves. They reached it barely ahead of the enemy who, finding it occupied, cautiously withdrew. Valentin called for his cannon, and set four lombards on the ridge. He was still too far away, with ordinary powder, to lob a ball into Pizarro's camp; but with the new compound, he and Griego thought they might reach it.

Meanwhile Hinojosa arrayed his army on the flat. Obeying Gasca's request to avoid battle on the Sabbath unless attacked, he secured his dispositions, while the priests, I among them, remained upon the mountain. There, carrying food to Paniagua who was exhausted from the long march, I encountered Father Gasca.

"Our little sister has in truth become a nun," he said, seeing me surrounded by priests.

Responsibility now in other hands, Gasca had nothing to do, and seemed reluctant to leave me. I gave Paniagua's gruel to a passing priest to deliver for me, and walked on with Gasca. Soon we overlooked the fateful plain.

"There is yet a night in which to pray that no more lives be lost," he said quietly. "I know God hears me, and I still have hope. I do not believe there will be a battle tomorrow."

"It is impossible to stop it," I murmured, scanning the calm valley in which 3,000 antagonists stood alertly at arms.

"All things are possible to God," the friar said, making the sign of the Cross over the battlefield. His cassock whipped by a gentle breeze, his tall body tense as he spread wide his arms in prayer, he looked like a Cross himself upon the mountain.

The rising mist of Monday, 9 April 1548, revealed Pizarro's thousand men drawn up as at Huarina, with Carbajal's guns and Cepeda's infantry in the center, arquebusiers beyond on each hand. But now the governor had sufficient cavalry to place a squadron on either wing. In our line, much the same order prevailed, except that far to the left on the strategic knoll stood Valentin with his lombards.

My eyes were on Valentin, when I saw Father Gasca approach him across the ridge. I hurried to them both. Valentin showed no surprise; perhaps because where I was concerned nothing any longer could upset him. From this vantage we plainly saw Pizarro, in silver mail and a gold-encrusted helmet, walk toward his stallion, which was held by Burgos, the page.

"Now is the time, I think," said Gasca, "to let them know that we have the new powder. Aim for Pizarro, and fire one lombard."

Valentin measured his angle of fire, and struck a fuse. The ball soared through the morning sky, squarely striking the page not two steps from Pizarro's head.

The governor could not believe, for a moment, that the shot could have come from so far away. He looked about uncertainly. Many of the infantry, drawing into the battle line under urging from a tall horseman who wore a black bandage across his face, paused in consternation at the unbelievable distance the ball had carried.

Gasca nodded.

"Fire no more. Let them think about the one." He walked rapidly away.

I remained with Valentin. He motioned me to follow his excellency.

"No," I said, "I remain with you."

His young face set in a hard cast. Without another word he strode to me and slapped my face with each hand.

"You will do as I say," he commanded sharply.

"But Valentin," I protested, "I want to stay with you."

"No," he said.

I sat down on a rock.

And then, oh, the mortification of it. He swept me to my feet, measured the distance carefully, and smote me on the cheek with his clenched fist.

I reeled, then went after him with my fingernails, my fists and my voice. He parried my attack for a moment, then lost patience with me utterly. Looping me off my feet, he set me firmly across his knee, and laid on with a bitter hand. Even when I screamed and kicked he did not leave off, but belayed me the harder, until my hips and legs were numb. I beat his thighs with my fists, and bit him. He laughed.

Not until I was quiet except for my sobbing, did he relax, and throw me to the ground. I ran back to the mountain as rapidly as my weak legs permitted, accompanied by the laughter of all the soldiers who had seen my disgrace. Still weeping, I reached the height where Gasca and the three bishops stood.

"What ails our little sister?" his excellency asked, comforting my shoulder with his strong arm. I told him that Valentin had beaten me.

He smiled broadly.

"It is indeed a day of victories!" he exclaimed. "Now sit down and thank God, who has blessed you, and pray that this battle may not take place."

I did not feel blessed at all. Yet, looking across the ridge to Valentin's knoll, I knew that if he died that day, I would die, too. He loved me. He had put aside his pride to prove it to me.

"Merciful Mother," I prayed, "do not let him die. Bring him back to me, and I will be a good wife to him, and never again give him cause to beat me."

A gentle sun scattered the last lazy mist on the field below. In Pizarro's center, the man with the black-patched face rode slowly forward, leading out the infantry. Hinojosa's center likewise moved forward a hundred paces, but did not fire.

Pizarro's foot soldiers, mortally afraid of the new powder, also halted. But not their leader. He spurred his horse to a gallop and rode madly to Gasca's lines, where he surrendered. It was Cepeda.

In both armies, every eye turned to the knoll to see what the friar would do.

He leaned down, drew the cowardly judge to his feet, and put his arm around him, within sight of 3,000 pairs of eyes.

Even as the soldiers stared, another knight galloped from Pizarro's lines to seek Gasca's vividly demonstrated mercy. A dozen arquebusiers stumbled forward, as though to overtake him. Then it became evident that they were only following his example.

Admiral Hinojosa, his eyes hawking greedily, shouted to his men to stand firm and hold their fire.

In the opposite camp, Pizarro appeared dumbfounded. He reined his horse nervously in a circle as though uncertain what to do. Another group of infantry detached itself from Pizarro's front and ratted across the field.

Pizarro spurred, sounding trumpets for a charge. Even as he did so, a hundred of his soldiers deserted him. Pizarro motioned for the cavalry on the opposite wing to head them off. They passed the recalcitrants without pause, and themselves surrendered.

Still not a shot had been fired on either side, except Valentin's long cast which had brought down Pizarro's page.

Now a host of soldiers, evidently they who, defeated at Huarina, had been impressed into Pizarro's service, ran with shouts toward Centeño's beckoning ensign.

Seeing himself alone, Pizarro reined and dashed back to the safety of Carbajal's center. Thus disencumbered of their leader, his entire cavalry from the left flank hurled their lances to the ground and crossed the field to the shelter of Benalcázar's forces. In another moment the battleground was alive with men, all running, unarmed and in surrender, toward the promontory on which Gasca, again with arms outstretched, stood like a Cross.

Only twenty horsemen surrounding Pizarro, and a dozen artillerymen on foot near mule-mounted Carbajal, remained of what fifteen minutes before had been a mighty array of a thousand lances, swords and gunners.

Pizarro lowered his lance and charged, his faithful score beside him. Just before entering the royal lines, they raised their shafts in submission. Only Carbajal now held the field, with the feeble few who served his guns. But the Demon of the Andes would not submit. Kicking his mount, he made off across the swamp toward Cuzco, his helmet lost, his gray beard swirling. Three of his soldiers mounted and followed him.

So desperately Carbajal rode that at the creek bank The Red One stumbled. The giant went down, his mule on top of him. His companions seized him and rode him in triumph to Gasca's summit.

Still not a shot had been fired. Not a man remained on Pizarro's side of the battlefield.

Father Gasca closed his eyes, his face lifted to the sky.

"Jesu!" he murmured. "We thank Thee."

As Carbajal approached the friar, Centeño ran to intercept him, fearful that even in his extremity the ancient marshal might do Gasca violence.

"Who are you?" Carbajal roared.

"I am Centeño," said the victim of two-score flights from the monster's noose.

Carbajal paused, bellying a great laugh.

"I crave your pardon," he said. "It is so long since I have seen anything but your back, I had forgotten your face."

Gasca went quickly to the marshal, for a crowd of angry soldiers gathered, demanding that he be hanged at once to the nearest tree. Carbajal would not speak to the friar. He was led away, defiant, under the guard of Centeño.

Pizarro, who had surrendered his sword to the first knight he encountered, was not even presented to the victor. Gasca refused to see him, and certainly would not touch his sword.

As though a dam had broken, Gasca's army drove across the plain to loot the enemy camp. Great treasure was there, for the soldiers of Peru carried their gold with them, trusting it to no one. Soon the ground was a swarm of men, who ransacked luggage, fought for precious armor, and captured horses and supplies. On the mountain, the priests began a *Te Deum* with one exultant voice.

Suddenly I was seized by the wrist and flung about. Valentin dragged me in a rush of steps to Father Gasca.

"What means this?" the friar asked.

"My share of the spoil," said Valentin. "There will be many who claim her later. I have guarded her, I have fought for her, and she is mine."

Solemnly Gasca turned to me, but did not speak. He searched my face.

"I acknowledge the claim," he agreed. "It is a very rich prize, and you deserve it."

Valentin lifted me from my feet and started to carry me off, but Gasca stopped him.

"My son," he said calmly, "you have waited this long; surely you can delay a little longer. I charge you to publish the banns, and I myself will marry you in the cathedral in Lima."

"It's well with me," I said, snuggling into Valentin's strong arms.

"But not with me," Gasca roared. "Put her down."

331

XXXIV

✝

That night the war council met to decide the fate of Pizarro and Carbajal. Gasca pleaded that they be returned to Spain for His Majesty's disposition; but the others would not consent. They pointed out that Pizarro had ordered the death sentence for 340 men during the rebellion, their only sin being that they had refused to join him, and that the trees of Peru were peopled with corpses from Carbajal's hangings. Even the Bishop of Lima demanded that they be executed the next day, on the battlefield. Reluctantly Gasca yielded, but insisted that Cepeda, who also was marked for death, be sent to Spain for trial, since his bold desertion had started the rout and prevented a carnage.

Valentin, who stood with me during this sentence, turned sadly away. I followed him to the tent where Carbajal lay in chains.

"What do you want, young champion?" the old man asked.

"I am sorry to tell you, sir," Valentin answered, "that tomorrow you are to die."

"Of course I am to die," Carbajal exploded. "They are not idiots enough to let me go."

"Is there anything I can do for you?" Valentin continued.

Carbajal's voice softened, though his words remained belligerent.

"What service can you do me, lad?" he inquired. "Can you set me free? If not, there is nothing."

A priest entered, and Carbajal railed at him.

"I come only so that you may unburden your conscience before you leave this world," the priest said.

"Basta matar!" Carbajal barked. "I die, so what?"

"Recall the Father, confess your many sins, and receive absolution."

"Sins? I have no such burden except the debt of a half reale which I owe the keeper of a grog shop in Seville."

"At least," the priest persisted, "repeat a Pater Noster and an Ave Maria."

"Pater Noster, Ave Maria, get out of here," the ancient demon spat. He looked at Valentin more calmly, then turned to me. "I see that it took a young hawk to bring down the lark. It is well."

Valentin tried to mumble thanks to his father for permitting his escape from the tambo at Guara. But the old one would not even tolerate this.

"It was for myself," he said, "not for you." He asked whether Valentin still proposed to colonize the highlands and restore the ancient farmlands of Jumin to their former greatness. Valentin assured him that this was his intent.

"And you," he turned to me, "will be with him?"

"I will be with him."

He nodded again. For a moment I thought he might touch me. But he would not give way to softness, and suddenly he roared in all his old fury. "Get out, both of you. You give me a headache, a fine thing when this is the last night my head will meet my shoulders."

In the morning the entire camp, victors and vanquished, assembled on the plain. Carbajal was led out in a basket drawn by two mules, his arms tied. As he passed Gasca he shouted, "Cradles are for infants and also, it seems, for old men." Those were his last words. At the scaffold he refused,

333

by shaking his head, the ministrations of a priest. He put his neck on the block for the broadaxe.

There was not a sound over the great crowd, no cheer, only grim silence, when he died. Valentin, beside me, crushed my hand in a bruising grip as the corpulent old man's head dropped.

Now was Pizarro led out. As always, he glittered with splendor. Over a gold-embroidered blue velvet doublet he wore a yellow cloak heavy with gold ornament, and a cap to match. But his degradation was complete, for the proud Estremaduran was subjected to the basest possible insult for a cavalier of his province. He was mounted on a mule. He had spent the night with his confessor, and held in his unbound arms the silver image of the Madonna which had been his pocket companion since the early conquest.

He saw me, and stayed his guards. He observed my hand in Valentin's, and the tears on Valentin's unashamed face for the father he had found and lost. The governor's mien was composed, his hand steady. He smiled down at me from his humiliation, removed my jeweled poniard from his belt, and presented it to me.

"What was it you said when you lost this," he asked solemnly, "about a dinner of herbs?"

" 'Better a dinner of herbs where love is, than a roasted ox and hatred within,' " I answered.

"Yes. And you said love was necessary to rule either a woman or an empire."

He looked toward Gasca, and abased his head. Then he returned me his gaze.

"I only want you to know," he said, "that now I understand. I should have taken your advice. Adios, and may God attend thee, little lark, in all your flights."

At the scaffold, he walked alone up the steps, kissed his Madonna, and faced the crowd. "Of all my riches," he said in a strong voice, "I have nothing, not even these garments, for with them I must pay my executioner. I implore those of you who have grown rich from my bounty to purchase a Mass for the welfare of my soul. This I beg, that it may be well with you in the hour of your own death."

He knelt, prayed for a moment, then asked the executioner to employ a steady hand. The axe struck off his head.

The next morning, Gasca assembled his closest companions and gave them their rewards. Three of the *cartas blancas* he had brought from Spain were now filled in above the king's signature. One made Bishop Loaysa an archbishop. Another proclaimed Admiral Hinojosa permanent Captain General of Peru, with a handsome life income. The third he put temporarily aside as he gave absent Béatriz her freedom; Hernán Mexía one of Pizarro's estates in Arequipa; Aldana and Centeño each rich farm and mining lands. He conferred Spanish citizenship on Joge Griego, also.

He looked finally at Valentin, the other king's parchment in his hand.

"Captain Guerrero I confirm in his silver mine near Jumin," he said, "and give him this."

The parchment removed forever the cloud on his parentage by making him a knight of Santiago, the recognized heir to the arms of the Guerrero family of Arévalo.

Now he looked toward me.

"To Captain Guerrero and our little sister, Doña Eloisa, I give each other, for God in His wisdom has drawn them together, and who am I to run contrary to His wishes in any matter."

Aldana, somewhat haughtily, wished Valentin and me well. Then came Mexía, as shy as ever.

"It is just as well that I did not win the prize," he said, "though I was first in line."

"You have married Lota!" I exclaimed.

"Not yet," he said. "But she says I had better, before next feast day of Saint Jago, or she will have another sin upon her conscience. I hope you wish us well."

"I do," I said, "with all my heart."

Joge Griego was next. He said he kissed my feet in his happiness that I would be with Valentin in the highlands, and revealed that he would accompany us, and Father Gasca, to Lima, and thus be on hand for the wedding.

"I have been writing to Andrea Cepeda," he said. "Perhaps you will not be the only lady in the mountain country."

Father Gasca interrupted us.

"It is time we started," he said. "Are you coming?"

Valentin turned to me.

"You told me in Panama to choose well the next time I asked you to love me. Do you remember?"

"I remember it well, my lord," I replied.

"Come, then," he said. "This time I give you no choice in the matter whatsoever."

He took me quite firmly by the hand, as Father Gasca smiled.

ABOUT THE AUTHOR

HARTZELL SPENCE was born in Clarion, Iowa, the son of a Methodist minister. During his early years, he lived in Fort Dodge, Sioux City, Burlington and Mason City, Iowa, in Omaha, Nebraska, and Denver, Colorado. He attended the University of Iowa, graduating in 1930 with a Phi Beta Kappa key. On the side, he gave lessons on the flute, worked for the college paper and wrote "true confessions" for the magazines under a wide variety of female pseudonyms.

Mr. Spence then went to work for United Press in Des Moines and in 1935 was assigned to New York. His first success, *One Foot in Heaven,* was published in 1940, and he shifted to Hollywood to work on the screen treatment of this best seller. From there he set off for South America with his bride; they wandered around Peru, Ecuador and the Amazon jungles, where he acquired material for a novel *Vain Shadow,* published in 1948, as well as gray hair and amoebic dysentery.

During the war Mr. Spence was editor of *Yank* and later became a colonel in the Air Corps. At this time his wife and children moved to a 718-acre Virginia farm, which was immortalized in *Happily Ever After* (1949). When the war ended he turned to writing full time, and contributed articles and stories to such magazines as *The Saturday Evening Post, Collier's, Look,* etc.

Among his other successful books were *Get Thee Behind Me* (1942) and *The Big Top* (written with Fred Bradna). Mr. Spence and his family moved a few years ago to Essex, Connecticut, where they live today in an old house overlooking the Connecticut River. "My trouble with a historical novel," says Mr. Spence, "is that I love the research too much, and respect it too much. In planning *Bride of the Conqueror,* I indulged myself by studying every scrap of available evidence relating to the period."

P E R U

· 1 5 4 6 — 4 8 A.D. ·

Locating only places important
to "BRIDE OF THE CONQUEROR"

———— Royal Inca Highway
———— Roads

G